BAY OF SIGHS

Mermaid Annika is proud to have been chosen for such an important quest. But now that her identity has been revealed, her time is running out. She knows that soon she must return to her people. But she also knows that she is in love with Sawyer King – the brave and loyal adventurer with secrets of his own.

BAY OF SIGHS

BAY OF SIGHS

by

Nora Roberts

Magna Large Print Books
Long Preston, North Yorkshire,
BD23 4ND, England.

British Library Cataloguing in Publication Data.

A catalogue record of this book is
available from the British Library

ISBN   978-0-7505-4453-5

First published in Great Britain in 2016 by Piatkus

Copyright © 2016 by Nora Roberts

Cover illustration © Allstar Picture Library by arrangement with
Alamy Stock Photo

The moral right of the author has been asserted

Published in Large Print 2017 by arrangement with
Little, Brown Book Group

Magna Large Print is an imprint of Library Magna Books Ltd.

Printed and bound in Great Britain by
T.J. (International) Ltd., Cornwall, PL28 8RW

For my grandchildren,
my magick and miracles

My heart is like a singing bird
Whose nest is in a water'd shoot;
My heart is like an apple-tree
Whose boughs are bent with thick-set fruit.

CHRISTINA ROSSETTI

Fortune favors the brave.

TERENCE

PROLOGUE

The story was told, generation by generation, in song and in story, until time misted it into myth and legend. But some believed, as legends brought comfort.

And some knew the story as truth.

That in another time, in a realm as old as the sea, three goddesses created three stars to honor and celebrate a new queen. A star of fire, a star of water, a star of ice, meant to shine over all the worlds, they forged and brightened with wishes for a strong heart, strong mind, strong spirit.

These, the moon goddesses, stood as guardians over the worlds, as watchers of gods, demigods, mortals, and immortals. Though of the light, they understood war and death, blood and battle.

There was another, of the dark, whose great thirst, whose unquenchable greed blighted her heart to black. Nerezza, the mother of lies, cursed the stars even as she coveted them. On the night of their creation, she winged her power to them as they flew to the sky, enspelling them. One day, by her curse, they would fall from their shining curve around the moon.

When she possessed them, all three, when she held their power, the moon would die, the light would cease, and she would rule over the dark.

So it was that the moon goddesses – Celene the seer, Luna the kind, Arianrhod the warrior –

13

gathered their magicks to protect the stars.

But such things require sacrifice and courage, and eons of hope.

The stars would fall; they could not stop this fate, but they would fall in secret, and remain in hiding until a time, in another realm, when those who came of them united in the quest to find and secure those stars.

Six guardians who would risk all to keep the stars from Nerezza's evil hands.

To save the light, and all the worlds, the six would unite, would offer all they were to the quest, and the battle.

Now the six, from lands far-flung, had come together, had forged their bonds, their loyalties, had shed blood and given their own to find the first star, so the goddesses met again.

On the white beach where they had birthed the stars in joy and hope, they gathered under a moon full and ice white in the dark sky.

'They have bested Nerezza.' Luna took the hand of each of her sisters. 'They found the Fire Star, and have put it beyond her reach.'

'Hidden it,' Arianrhod corrected. 'And cleverly done, but none of the stars is beyond her until they are home again.'

'They defeated her,' Luna insisted.

'Yes, for now, yes. They fought bravely, risked all in battle, gave all for this quest. And yet...'

She looked to Celene, who nodded. 'I see more blood, more battle, more fear. Strife and dark to face where terrible pain, terrible death can come in an instant and last for eternity.'

'They will not yield,' Luna said. 'They will not.'

'They have proven their courage. Courage is truer when there is fear under it. I do not doubt them, sister.' Arianrhod gazed up to the moon and the place where for so long three sparkling stars had curved. 'But neither do I doubt Nerezza's hunger or her fury. She will hunt them, and she will strike again and again.'

'And will enlist another, a mortal.' Celene stared into the sea, its black glass, and saw the shadows of what might be. 'Whose hunger is a mate to hers. He has and will kill for prizes less vaunted than the Stars of Fortune. He is poison in the wine, a blade in an offered hand, snapping teeth behind a smile. And in Nerezza's hands, a weapon, keen and swift.'

'We must help them. They have proven themselves, we agree,' Luna reasoned. 'We must be allowed to help.'

'You know we cannot,' Celene reminded her. 'Every choice made must be made without our interference. We have done all we can, for now.'

'Aegle is not their queen.'

'Without Aegle, without this place, without the moon and we who honor it, they have no world. Their fate, our fate, all fate, is in their hands.'

'They are of us.' In comfort Arianrhod tightened her grip on Luna's hand. 'They are not gods, yet more than mortals, each one with their own gift. They will fight.'

'And as important as battle, they will think, and they will feel.' Celene let out a sigh. 'And they will love. Mind, heart, spirit, as much as sword and fang and even magicks. They are well armed.'

'So we trust.' Flanked by her sisters, Luna lifted

15

her face to the moon. 'Let our trust be their shield. As we are guardians of the worlds, they are guardians of the stars. They are hope.'

'And valor,' Arianrhod added.

'And they are canny. There.' Smiling, Celene lifted a hand, gesturing to the swirl of color streaking over the sky. 'They pass by us, through our world, hurtling toward the next. To another land, to the second star.'

'And all the gods of light go with them,' Luna murmured, and sent her own.

CHAPTER ONE

For an instant, like a single beat of wings, Annika scented the sea, heard the voices lifted in song. Here then gone, a blur within the blur of color and speed, but it swelled in her heart like love.

Then came a sigh, and the echoes of sighs, another kind of music. Bittersweet. And this washed through her like tears.

So with joy and sorrow mated in her heart, she fell. Tumbling, spiraling, spinning in a breathless rush that added a reckless thrill and a quick panic.

A thousand wings beat now, a thousand and a thousand more, with whipping wind, a wall of sound. And color flicked away into the dark as she landed abruptly enough to lose her breath.

For a moment she feared they'd landed in some deep, dark cave where spiders would crawl, and worse, much worse, where Nerezza waited to strike.

Then her vision cleared. She made out shadows, what she knew as moonlight, and felt the firm body beneath hers, the arms wrapped right around her. She knew that shape, that scent, wanted to snuggle right in, Nerezza or not.

It was a wonder, a star-struck sea of wonder, to feel his heart beat, so fast and strong, against hers.

Then he shifted a little, and one hand slid up, then down her hair. The other skimmed wonderfully over her bottom.

She snuggled right in.

'Um.' Both hands came to her shoulders now, but his voice spoke close enough to her heart that his breath tickled it. 'Are you okay? Are you hurt? Everybody okay?'

She remembered her friends – not that she'd forgotten them, not ever. But she'd never lain so intimately on a man before – on Sawyer – and she liked it very, very much.

She heard grunts, short groans, some cursing. Doyle's voice, close by and annoyed, clearly said, 'Fuck me,' which she knew wasn't an invitation to mate, but an oath.

She didn't worry about Doyle. After all, he was an immortal.

'Sound off.' That was Bran, somewhere a few feet away. 'Did everybody make it? I've got Sasha. Riley?'

'What a ride!'

'One you finished with your knee in my balls,' Doyle added.

17

Annika heard a thump, which she interpreted as Doyle shoving Riley and her knee aside – as balls, she'd learned, weren't just the round toy that bounced, but a man's sensitive area.

'I'm here,' she called out, and experimented by wiggling a little on Sawyer's sensitive area. 'Did we fall out of the sky?'

'Not far from it.' Sawyer cleared his throat and, to Annika's disappointment, shifted again and sat up. 'I couldn't slow it down. I've never taken six people this far. I misjudged, I guess.'

'We're here, the six of us, and that's first on the list,' Bran stated. 'Now, are we where we aimed to be?'

'We're inside,' Sasha commented. 'I can see windows, and moonlight through them. Wherever we are, it's still night.'

'Let's hope Sawyer and his time and space-bending compass got us where and when we want. So let's find out.'

Riley pushed to her feet. The scientist – archaeologist. Annika rolled the word in her mind as her people, the merpeople, had nothing to compare. They had no lycans either, she thought, so nothing and no one quite like Riley existed in Annika's world.

Dr. Riley Gwin – tough, compact body, wide-brimmed hat that had somehow stayed on her head – strode to the window.

'I can see water, but not the view from the villa on Corfu – we're higher up. A road, steep, narrow. We've got steps leading down to it. I'm pretty sure this is Capri, and this is the villa. Bull's-eye, Sawyer. Kudos to the traveler and his

18

magic compass.'

'I'll take them.' He stood, hesitated, then held out a hand to help Annika up. Though her legs were strong and agile, she let him.

'Let me see if I can find the lights,' Riley began.

'I can help with that.'

Bran, on his feet, an arm around Sasha, held out his hand. The ball of light hovering over his palm illuminated the room.

Seeing her friends lifted her heart as the song had. Sasha, the seer, with her hair like the sun and her eyes of the sky, and Bran, the sorcerer, so handsome with his magick lighting him. And Riley, one hand on the butt of the gun on her hip – at the ready – her dark gold eyes looking everywhere at once as Doyle, a warrior through and through, stood with his sword already drawn.

And Sawyer, always Sawyer, with the compass of the traveler in his hand.

They might be bruised and bloodied from the last battle, but they were safe and together.

'Is this our home now?' she wondered. 'It's very pretty.'

'Unless Sawyer dropped us at the wrong address, I say this is the new HQ.' Though her hand stayed on her gun, Riley moved from the window.

The room had colorful cushions on a long bed – no, Annika reminded herself, a sofa. And chairs and tables with pretty lamps. The floor – they all had reason to know – was hard, with large tiles the color of sun-beaten sand.

Riley moved to one of the lamps, turned the switch and, with the magic of electricity, it lit.

'Let me get my bearings, make sure we're in the

19

right place. We don't want a visit from the *polizia*.'

Riley moved out of the room through a wide, arched opening. In seconds, more light poured through. Sheathing his sword, Doyle moved out after her.

'Here's all our stuff, at least it looks like all of it. And it looks like it had a softer landing than we did.'

Annika peeked out. She didn't know what to call the space with its big door facing the sea, and the archways leading to other spaces. But their bags and boxes sat in a pile in the center of it.

And with a muttered curse, Doyle heaved his motorcycle upright.

'I had to drop the stuff first so we didn't end up landing on it,' Sawyer said. 'Bull's-eye or not, Riley?'

'It fits the description I got,' Riley went on. 'And the location. There's supposed to be a large living area with glass doors leading to a... And here we go.'

More lights, and as Riley said, a large room with more of the sofas and chairs and pretty little things. But best, oh, best of all, the wide, wide glass to bring in the sky and sea.

When Annika rushed forward to open the glass, Riley stayed her hand.

'Don't. Not yet. There's an alarm system. I have the code. We need to turn it off before we open this, or anything else.'

'Panel's right here,' Sawyer told her, and tapped it.

'Give me a sec.' Riley dug a piece of paper out of her pocket. 'Didn't want to trust my memory in case the trip scrambled my brains.'

'Shifting doesn't scramble brains.' Grinning, Sawyer knocked his knuckles on Riley's head as she keyed in the code.

'Go ahead and open it, Annika.'

When she did, she twirled out onto a wide terrace, where there was night and moon, sea and the scent of it all, all perfumed with lemons and flowers.

'It's beautiful! I've never seen it from so high.'

'But you've seen it before?' Sawyer asked her. 'Capri?'

'From the sea. And beneath, where there are blue caves and deep water and the bones of ships that sailed long ago. There are flowers!' She reached out to touch the petals of flowers spilling out of hefty pots in bright colors. 'I can water and tend them. It can be my job.'

'Deal. This is the place.' With a satisfied nod, Riley set her hands on her hips. 'Kudos again, Sawyer.'

'We should check through it in any case.' Bran stood at the opening, dark, intense eyes scanning the sky.

Nerezza often came from the sky.

'I'll be adding protection over the more usual alarm system,' he continued. 'We caused her pain, and harm, so it's unlikely she'll gather herself enough to come at us again tonight, if indeed she can find us. But we'll sleep better with a layer of magick over all.'

'Split up.' With his sword sheathed, his dark hair tumbled around his hard, handsome face, Doyle nodded agreement. 'Go through the place, make certain it's clear and secured.'

'Should be two bedrooms down here, four more upstairs, and another common space. It's not big and plush like the villa, and we won't have all that outdoor space.'

'Or Apollo,' Annika put in.

'Yeah.' Riley smiled. 'I'm going to miss that dog. But there's room, and it's well located. I'll take the upstairs.'

'You just want first call on the bedrooms.'

Riley grinned at Sasha, then frowned. 'You okay, Sash? You're pale.'

'Just a headache. A regular headache,' she said when all eyes turned to her. 'I don't try to fight the visions anymore. It's just been a very long day.'

'And so it has.' Bran drew her close to his side, whispered something in her ear that made her smile and nod. 'We'll take upstairs as well,' he said, and with Sasha, vanished.

'Oh, cheat! No fair using magick!' Riley charged toward the steps and up.

'Three up, so three down to clear this floor. I'd sooner bunk down here,' Doyle said with a look around, 'closer to the outside access.'

'You and me down here then,' Sawyer decided – to Annika's disappointment. 'Closer to the kitchen and the food. Let's see what we've got.'

The two bedrooms stood side by side. Not as big as the ones they'd left behind on Corfu, but with nice beds and pretty views from the windows.

'Works,' Doyle stated.

'Works,' Sawyer agreed after opening another door to a bathroom with a shower.

The door slid in and out of the wall, delighting

Annika so she had to push it in, pull it out a few times before Sawyer grabbed her hand and pulled her away.

They found another room with what Sawyer called a bar, a big television on the wall (she *loved* television), and a large table where colorful balls stood in a triangle on a green top.

Annika stroked her hand over the top. 'It isn't grass.'

'Felt,' Sawyer told her. 'It's a pool table – a game. You play?' he asked Doyle.

'What man who's lived a few centuries hasn't played pool?'

'I've only lived a few decades, but I've played my share. We'll have to have a game.'

There was a powder room – though no one powdered anything in them that Annika had seen – and then the kitchen and eating area. She knew immediately Sawyer was pleased.

He wandered through it. A tall, lean body that moved, she thought, as if never hurried. Her fingers wanted to brush through all the dark gold hair the sun had streaked, shaggy and windblown from the traveling. And eyes, gray like the sea in the first silver light of dawn, that made her want to sigh.

'The Italians understand cooking – and eating. This is excellent.'

She knew something about cooking now, had even learned to make a few dishes, so she recognized the big stove with its many burners, and the ovens for baking and roasting. A center island held its own sink, which charmed her, and another sink – wider – stood under a window.

Sawyer opened the box that kept things cold –

23

the refrigerator, she remembered. 'Already stocked. Riley doesn't miss a trick. Beer?'

'Oh, absolutely,' Doyle said.

'Anni?'

'I don't like the beer very much. Is there something else?'

'Got your soft drinks, some fruit juice. And wait.' He pointed up to a rack holding bottles. 'Wine.'

'I like the wine.'

'Got you covered then.' He chose a bottle, passed a beer to Doyle, took one for himself, then wandered to a door. 'Pantry, also stocked. We're in business.'

He opened drawers until he found the tool to open the wine. Corkscrew – such a funny word.

'I don't know about anybody else, but I'm starved. Shifting that many that far, it hulls you out.'

'I could eat,' Doyle decided.

'I'm going to throw something together. Riley was right, Sasha looks pale. We'll eat, drink, decompress.'

'Have at it then. I'm going to check outside.' With his sword still sheathed on his back, Doyle went through another wide glass door.

'I can help you make the food.'

'Don't you want to grab up a bedroom?'

'I like to help make the food.' With you, most of all, she thought.

'Okay, let's keep it simple. Quick pasta, tossed with butter and herbs. And we've got ... yeah, we've got tomatoes, mozzarella.' He pulled the cheese from the refrigerator, handed her a tomato from the bowl on the counter. 'You remember how to slice these up?'

'Yes, I can slice very well.'

'You slice them up, then find a plate or tray or platter.' He spread his hands to show her size.

He had strong hands, but was gentle with them. Annika thought gentleness was its own kind of strength.

'And you lay them out with the cheese on top of the tomato,' he continued, so she knew to pay attention. 'Drizzle this olive oil over them.' He set a container on the counter.

'Drizzle is like rain, but only a little.'

'You got it. Then you're going to take this.' He walked over to the windowsill, where some pots sat, and broke off a stem with leaves. 'It's basil.'

'I remember. It adds flavor.'

'Yeah. Chop it up some, sprinkle it over everything, grind a little pepper on there, too, and that's a wrap.'

'It's a wrap.'

'It's finished,' he explained.

'I will wrap it for you.'

Pleased, she braided her waist-length black hair back and away. She got to work while he put a pot of water on the stove, poured her wine, drank his beer.

She liked the quiet times with him, and had learned to savor them. There would be more fighting; she knew, accepted. There would be more pain. She would accept that, too. But she had been given a gift. The legs that allowed her to walk out of the sea and onto land, if only for a short time. The friends who were more precious than gold.

25

The purpose that was her legacy and her duty.

And most of all, Sawyer, whom she'd loved before he even knew she existed.

'Do you dream, Sawyer?'

'What?' Distracted, he glanced back at her as he found a colander. 'Sure. Sure, most everybody does.'

'Do you dream of when we've done our duty, when we have all three stars? When the Stars of Fortune are safe from Nerezza? When there is no more fighting?'

'It's hard to see that far when we're in the middle of it. But yeah, I think about it.'

'What do you wish for most, when this is done?'

'I don't know. It's been part of my life for so long – the quest if not the battle.'

But he paused in what he was doing, considered. She thought that – the paying attention – was also strength.

'I guess, maybe, it would be enough for the six of us, knowing we've done everything we had to do, to sit on a warm beach and look up and see them. See the three stars where they're meant to be. Knowing we did that. That's a pretty big dream.'

'Not for wealth or long life?' Her gaze slid toward him. 'Or a woman?'

'If I could rub a lamp, I'd be an idiot not to take all that.' He paused a moment, shoved his fingers through his shaggy blond hair. 'But the friends who fought with me, that warm beach? That would do just fine. Add a cold beer and it sounds perfect.'

She started to speak again, but Doyle came back through the doors.

Though a tall man, and well muscled, he moved lightly on his feet.

'We don't have the outdoor training space we had in Greece, but we've got a lemon grove we could use, and more privacy than I figured on. Though Bran could add to that anyway. There's a garden – smaller scale than the one at the villa. And pots of herbs and tomatoes out on the terrace. Big table out there for eating, and that portion's covered by a grape arbor. Shady, but the bees may be an issue. We've got a pool.'

'Yeah?'

'Again, smaller scale than Corfu. It's right off the patio deal, which is probably why they planted trees on either side of the grounds. They'd want some privacy. Do you care which bedroom?'

'Nope. Take your pick.'

'I will. I'm going to stow my gear.'

As he went out, Riley came in.

'You guys read my mind.' She walked over, slung an arm around Annika's waist. 'Starving. What are we having?'

'Sawyer is making pasta, and I'm making tomatoes and cheese with the oil and herbs. We're going to eat, drink, and decompress.'

'I'm for it.'

'Your friend of a friend stocked the kitchen,' Sawyer told Riley.

'Yeah, we owe for that. Beer or wine?' To help her decide, she took a swig from Sawyer's bottle, a sip from Annika's glass. 'Tough choice. It's pasta, so I'm going for the wine. Bran and Sasha beat me to the master – but there's two of them in there, so that's fair.'

'Doyle and I are bunking down here. Two rooms and a full bath. It works.'

'Good enough. Annika, you get your choice of what's left up there. Sasha and Bran will use whatever's left over to set up her studio and the magick-works. Terraces up there, too. We won't be able to walk to the beach from here, but we can take the funicular.'

'What is the funicular?' Annika asked.

'It's like a train, but in the air. You pay, and you can ride it down to town, or closer to the beach, or—'

'I want to ride it! Can we ride it tomorrow?'

'Maybe. It's a strong walk down to the shops in Anacapri and a steep hike back. And to get down to Capri town means a bus or cab or a serious hike. No cars in Anacapri. If we need one, I'll find us a ride, and we'll park it in Capri, but mostly we're on foot or public trans. I'm going to do a quick check outside on security.'

'Doyle just did.' Sawyer slid spaghetti into the pot of boiling water.

Riley hesitated, glanced toward the door. Then shrugged. 'No point in me walking in his footsteps.'

'We have a pool,' Annika told her.

'Yeah, I got that. And I might just try it out before I turn in. Table out there, right? Why don't we eat outside?'

'I'm for it. Set us up.'

Riley poured herself some wine, lifted it to Sawyer. 'I'm all over it.' She got another glass when Sasha came in with Bran. 'Wine – it'll put some color in your cheeks.'

'I'd love some wine. And food. Sawyer, Annika, you're the best.'

'Italian beer? I'll be happy for that.' Bran opened the refrigerator, got his own. 'Doyle?'

'Our immortal's stowing his gear.' Sawyer stirred the pasta as steam puffed. 'We're taking the two bedrooms down here.'

'That leaves you a choice upstairs, Annika.'

'Riley said you need a room for your painting and for Bran's magicks. You should choose it. I'm happy with whatever is left.'

'If you really don't mind, we could take the room across from ours. It's the smaller of the two left, and big enough for what we'd need. And yours would face the sea. You'd rather wake and sleep with the sea.'

Touched, Annika moved to hug Sasha. 'Thank you.'

'I'm across from you,' Riley told her. 'I love me a sea view as much as the next guy – or mermaid – but there's something to be said about looking out over a lemon grove.'

'And guarding the rear flank,' Bran added.

'And that. We're eating outside. As soon as I find plates.'

She found them, as colorful as the cushions. With Sasha helping to set up, they went out as Annika meticulously added the herbs to her dish.

'Is this right? Did I do it the way I should?'

Sawyer glanced at her tray. 'Looks perfect. I just need a few minutes to put the rest together.'

'But we need candles! And flowers.' Annika dashed out to hunt up what she considered a properly set table.

Sawyer tested the pasta, turned off the burner. 'Sasha okay?'

'A little more shaken, apparently, than the rest of us. Food and rest should do the trick.' He looked over as Doyle came back in. 'I've done a basic protection spell on the house and grounds, but will want to layer over that before we turn in for the night. She'll find us, sooner or later, and she'll be right pissed.'

'She'll find us,' Sawyer agreed as he drained pasta. 'It'll be a lot tougher for her to find the Fire Star where and how you've hidden it.'

'Which says to me she'll come harder for the next.' Doyle lifted his beer, drained it. 'In her place? I'd decide I'd underestimated my enemy in the first round of things. Her pride would lead her to that conclusion. She'll go harder, bloodier.'

'And it may be cannier,' Bran added. 'Much of what she did was rage and violence. Whatever it cost us, it cost her more. She may, if wise, consider more strategy than force. We'll need to prepare for that.'

'We need to eat.' Sawyer dumped the pasta into a bowl, tossed it with the butter and herbs he'd prepped. 'And we need to sleep.'

'You're not wrong. And we need to celebrate, however briefly, the fact that we're safe, whole, and together.'

'And ready to search for the next star.'

Bran nodded at Doyle. 'For the next. Water or ice, we can't know, not yet. But the fates sent us here, where the inestimable Riley has again secured us a roof and beds, food. Tomorrow's soon enough, isn't it, to plot our own strategies?'

30

'It'll have to be, because this is ready. Grab that tray, will you? And the wine. And I could use another beer.'

Sawyer stepped out into the lemon-scented night where a slice of moon shot soft blue light over land and sea.

Annika, being Annika, had fashioned a bouquet of flowers out of napkins, and gathered candles from around the house.

'I couldn't find the...' When the word escaped her, she mimed striking a match.

'Matches,' Sawyer supplied.

'I'll take care of that.' Bran simply flicked his fingers, and the tea lights and tapers glowed.

With a laugh, Annika clapped her hands. Then rushed over to hug Bran.

'I hugged Sasha and Riley. We're all together, in this new place.' She turned to wrap her arms around Doyle, coaxed a smile out of him. 'We have good food and good friends.'

Last, she turned to Sawyer, embraced him, indulged herself by breathing in the scent that was only his. 'Nerezza is not with friends, and can't have what we have.'

'She doesn't want what we have.'

Sasha swayed once, then straightened. Her eyes were dark and deep, and saw more than the sea and the slice of moon.

'She has no wish for friends or love or affection. She is lies and greed and ambition, all dark. She is the dark. Now she rages, and she knows pain. But soon she'll seek, and plot, and come. She thirsts, and the thirst is for blood. Our blood, for nothing else can slake that thirst. She will come,

31

however we curtain our world. The Globe of All will find us. And she will find another, one to join in the hunt. Greed blinds, greed binds. The god takes the man; the man takes the god in a bargain sealed in blood. On this island, in these waters, in the songs, in the sighs, there will be battles new. Blood runs, pain strikes. And betrayal comes with smiles.

'On this island, in these waters, in the songs, in the sighs, the star waits, blue and pure, for the innocent and the valiant. It is not tears that form the Water Star, but tears will be shed before it is found.'

She swayed again, white as a ghost. Bran caught her to him, held her. 'Just breathe, *fáidh*.'

'I didn't fight it. I swear I didn't try to block it. I just... Everything just felt a little off.'

'The shift. I've never traveled with a seer before, not anything like this,' Sawyer added.

'Scrambled brains?'

Sawyer slanted a look at Riley. 'Not exactly, but maybe the vision just needed to, you know, catch up. You want some water? I'll get you some water.'

'No, no, I'm all right. Better.' Sasha breathed out. 'Actually better. It was like I couldn't quite get my balance. Now I can. So maybe, yes, maybe it was the shift. And God, it's been a day, hasn't it? I'm just going to sit down.'

'And eat.' Moving quickly, Annika filled a plate with pasta, scooped out the tomato and mozzarella. 'You need to eat the food.'

'And I will. We all will. It came on so fast. It was, yes, like it caught up and slammed into me. And so much of it's brutal. Just the feeling inside it all. Her fury and need to destroy us. Not just hurt or kill now. Destroy.'

'You said she'd find someone,' Riley reminded her. 'A man.'

'Yes, but I don't know if it means male or just human. But she'll find someone, and this person will join forces with her.'

'After battling a god?' Doyle heaped food on his plate. 'I've no worry about dealing with a mortal.'

'Says the man who can't die,' Riley put in. 'Humans are canny, cagey, and dangerous. If Nerezza makes a deal with one, it's because he – or she – is useful to her. Don't get cocky.'

Sawyer passed the bowl to Annika. 'Well, now we know which star we're looking for in and around Capri. The Water Star. We can take that off the list of what we need to figure out.'

'It's blue, and beautiful. Unearthly blue. I don't know if I can capture the tones of it with paint. The Fire Star, it flashed and burned. And this...' Sasha closed her eyes a moment. 'It glowed and seemed to ... ripple. Water? Maybe that's why.'

After she'd wound pasta around her fork, sampled, Sasha closed her eyes again. 'Oh, this is good, Sawyer. This is just exactly right. I'll take the breakfast shift.'

'No, I've got it. You get the morning off.'

'I can help again.'

'And see.' He gestured to Annika. 'I've got my top sous chef, willing and able.'

'I made this.' Annika carefully cut a bite of the salad. 'And it's good.'

'Damn good,' Riley concurred, and took a second helping. 'I'll hit research mode tomorrow.

33

Maybe it's knee-jerk to figure the Water Star's in the water, but the first was – or under it. I know some of the caves around here, water and land. I'll find out more.'

'You spoke of both land and sea,' Bran pointed out. 'Of songs and sighs.'

'Like when we were flying.'

'What?'

'Not flying,' Annika said to Sawyer. 'What it feels like to fly, or what I think it would feel like to fly. The traveling. The songs and the sighs when you brought us here.'

'What songs and sighs, Annika?' Bran's dark gaze arrowed to her.

'You didn't hear them?'

'No.' He glanced around the table. 'I don't think the rest of us heard anything.'

'All I heard was the tornado.' Though she watched Annika, Riley continued to eat. 'I've been through a few, and that's what traveling Sawyer's way sounds like to me. But you heard singing and sighing.'

'Only for a moment. It was so beautiful. It–' She pressed a hand to her heart, then cupped it out. 'It made my heart big. There was the wind, and the colors and light. It's very exciting. Then the songs, just music with words I couldn't hear all the way. And sighs, but not sad ones – or not all sad. Sweet, but with some sadness. A little sorrow with the joy. Is that right?'

'Mermaid ears, maybe?' Riley speculated. 'Water Star, mermaid. Interesting.' She took another bite of pasta, smiled. 'We're going to need another boat. I'll get on that.'

Later, when the house was quiet, when all her friends slept, Annika stepped out on the terrace outside her new room. The sea drew her – she was of it, from it. She wished she could fly down to it, wished she could swim inside its heart for a little while.

But the sea must wait.

She had the legs, and she prized them, though now that she'd told the others what she was – she'd had no choice – her time with them was a ticking clock.

So she wished on the moon-slice over the sea that she might sing and sigh inside Sawyer's heart, in the time she had left. She wished he might feel what she felt, if only for a single day.

Duty came first, and she would never shirk it. But she could hope inside her heart that she would do her duty, fulfill her legacy.

And know love before she returned to the sea forever.

CHAPTER TWO

In the morning, Annika woke early. She chose one of her pretty dresses that swirled around her legs – a lovely reminder she had them – and hurried straight down to the kitchen.

She wanted to make the coffee. She'd learned how in the villa on Corfu, and liked doing things ordinary people did. But this new house had a different machine, and would take some time to figure out.

She liked figuring things out, too.

Today she wanted real flowers for the table, so she wandered outside and down toward the garden. And saw the pool. The pale blue water under the first soft beams of sunlight.

The sea was too far for a morning swim, she thought, but this. Well, it was right here. Trees flanked the yard, making a kind of green wall. In any case, she didn't understand the human fuss about bodies. They were as natural as hair and eyes, as fingers and toes, and no one made a fuss about hiding them.

Besides, she longed for the water, and saw no reason to go back to her room and find the suit to swim in. Instead, she pulled off the dress, tossed it onto a chair. And dived in.

The water embraced her, gentle as a mother, sweet as a lover. She skimmed along the bottom, her sea-green eyes open and lit with pleasure. Delighted, she swam the length of the pool, back again, then, pushing off the bottom, let her legs spear up into the air and sun.

And slice down into the water again as a tail.

Sawyer, a cup of coffee in his hand, stopped dead on the skirt of the pool.

He'd come out to see who was up, who'd put the coffee on. He'd known it was Annika the instant her legs had come up and out of the water – long, dusky gold, and perfect.

Then color had swirled around those legs, winking, flashing like precious gems, gems that went to shimmering liquid before they'd become the mermaid's tail.

It took his breath. Knowing her for a mermaid and seeing her transform were two different things. And it simply took his breath. Even before he caught it again, she flew up, long black hair streaming, arms outstretched, tail sparkling, her face bright and beautiful.

She arched in midair – and Jesus, she wore nothing *but* the tail – then slid backward into the water again.

His body reacted, and it didn't matter he reminded himself he was a man, and what man wouldn't go hard watching a gorgeous, naked mermaid. He tried to think of her as a sister, got nowhere. Did better listing her firmly as a teammate.

Most of all he had to stop her from swishing that amazing tail around. They had neighbors here.

She came up again, laughing, flipped back to float. He ordered himself not to look at her breasts – too late – but managed to shift his gaze to her face. She had her eyes closed, a quiet smile on her face as she floated, with the only movement the gentle flick of her tail fin.

'Annika.'

Her eyes opened; she smiled over at him. 'Sawyer, good morning. Do you want to swim with me?'

Oh, yeah. Oh boy, yeah.

Couldn't, shouldn't, wouldn't.

'Ah, not right now. And you can't, ah, you know, be right out here with the tail. Without the legs. And naked. Somebody could spot you.'

'There are the trees, and it's so early.'

'Windows over the trees – if somebody happened to look out just the right way at the right
time.'

'Oh.' With a little sigh, she lowered the tail into
the water. And now he saw her legs lightly kicking. 'I didn't mean to, but it felt so good I forgot.'

'It's okay, just don't... No, don't get out.'

He actually felt panic as she glided toward the
shallow end, stood. That body – willowy and
perfect and ... wet. Water sparkled on her skin,
diamonds on gold dust.

She was killing him.

'I – I'm going to get you a towel. Don't get out
without any... Just wait.'

He hurried back inside. Coffee wasn't going to
do much for a throat that had gone bone dry at
the way her hair slicked over those really, really
pretty breasts.

He tried counting backward by threes from a
thousand, and still had to take a minute, adjust
himself – only human – when he grabbed a pool
towel from the utility room off the kitchen.

When he came out again, she'd stayed obedi-
ently as she was.

'You need to...' He wound a finger in the air.
'Around. Then the dress.'

He didn't see anything but the dress, which
meant she wouldn't be wearing anything under
the dress. And it wasn't smart to think about that
either.

He stared at the lemon trees as he held the
towel over the pool. 'Why do women always
cover their top half, and men don't always?'

'Because we don't have ... and you have.'

'The breasts,' she said as she stepped out of the pool, wrapped the towel around herself. 'Sometimes the maids wear shells over the breasts. But this is for fashion.'

He risked a glance, relieved she'd covered everything. 'Mermaid fashion?'

'Yes. We like adornments, too. I made coffee.'

'Yeah, good. Thanks.' He picked it up from the table, took a sip. She'd made it strong enough to fight the champ, but he had no problem with that. 'If you're going to swim, you really need to wear a suit and keep your legs on.'

'I apology.'

'No. No, don't be sorry.' He risked another look. Now she stood in the dress, long hair wet and sleek as a seal. 'It's amazing. It's beautiful. It must feel weird for you to swim without it.'

'I like the legs.'

'Yeah, they're pretty great. Once we score a boat, we should be able to go out far enough, or you deep enough to tail it out when you want. But in the pool, broad daylight, it's better if you don't.'

'For a few moments it was just morning, with the little pool of water in the sun, and the smell of the trees.'

'One day it will be just morning.'

She looked at him then, into his eyes. 'You believe?'

'Yeah. I believe.'

'Then I can't be sad. I'll help you fix the breakfast, and I can set the table. What will you make?'

'The way we're supplied right now? Pretty much anything. What do you want?'

'I can pick?'

'Sure.'

'Can you make – it's not the pancakes because you...' She made a rolling motion with her fingers. 'And put something delicious inside.'

'Crepes.'

'Yes! Can you make those?'

'You got it.'

She liked working in the kitchen. So many smells and colors and tastes. Sawyer said they'd make eggs and bacon, too, and the crepes would have peaches in them and honey over them so they'd be sweet.

She helped him mix, and he showed her how to make the crepe, let her try one all by herself. As she did, Sasha came in.

'Good timing. Everyone's stirring around. God, it smells good in here.'

'I'm making a crepe.'

'Fancy.' Sasha walked over, put an arm around Annika's waist, watched a moment. 'And you're doing a good job of it.'

Sasha reached for a coffee cup. 'Should I set the table?'

'The table! I forgot to get the flowers. We need the plates and the glasses and the napkins, and–'

'Why don't I take out the plates,' Sasha said.

With her bottom lip caught between her teeth, Annika nodded as she carefully slid the crepe onto a plate. 'Did I do it the right way?'

'Looks perfect,' Sawyer told her.

'I need to get the flowers now.'

As she dashed out, Sasha leaned back against the counter. 'Never a boring tablescape with Annika.'

'Maybe you can sort of explain to her about

swimming naked, at least in the daylight.'

'Was she?'

'Unless you count the tail.'

'Uh-oh.'

'No harm I could see, and she just got caught up. I think she got what I was telling her about it, but maybe, you know, another woman. I think, on Corfu, she went down to the beach early every morning, swam out, and under, way under, to give herself that ... ritual, I guess it is. But here...'

'I'll make sure she understands. Do you need any help here?'

'No, I've got it.'

'Coffee, coffee, coffee,' Riley mumbled as she staggered in. She poured a mug, inhaled the scent, took a gulp. 'Bang!' she said. 'That's coffee.'

'It'll put hair on your chest,' Sawyer said. 'Oh, right, you just need the moon for that.'

'You're a riot.' She grabbed Annika's crepe, folded it into her mouth, said, 'Good,' around it.

'Give me fifteen minutes, you'll get better than good.'

Sasha took plates outside, came back in for glass-ware, got caught up in a kiss as Bran came in. By the time she went back out, Annika was at work.

She had the plates in a semicircle around a little tower of empty flower pots. From the top one spilled napkins in bright colors with folds and ripples. At the base of the flower blossoms and leaves, a few pretty stones formed a pool.

'It's a rainbow waterfall,' Sasha guessed.

'Yes! And its water feeds the little garden. It's water that blooms, so you can swim in the flowers.'

41

'That's a beautiful thought.'

'It's a happy place. The dark can't go there. There should be a place, I think, where the dark can't go.' She looked down at the bracelets circling her wrists – the magick Bran had fashioned for her. 'A place where no one has to fight.'

'We'll push the dark back, Anni. It may be all we can do, but it matters.'

'Yes, it matters. Friends matter. We friends will have a pretty breakfast on our first day of our quest for the Water Star.'

With a rainbow waterfall.

They spoke of practical things over the meal. Getting the lay of the land – and the sea. Divvying up the household chores.

'We're not as isolated here,' Bran pointed out. 'We could use a basic cover story. Friends on holiday?'

'Say a working holiday for me.' Riley scooped up eggs. 'Sticking close to the truth always helps. I'm an archaeologist, doing a paper, some research. So questions I might ask are covered there. I've got more Italian than Greek, and can talk the talk. Anybody else?'

'*Io parlo italiano molto bene.*' Doyle cut into a crepe.

Riley's eyebrows arched. 'Oh, yeah?'

'*Si*. I've had considerable time for languages.'

'That'll be handy if we need another interpreter. I'm going to make some calls, tug some lines. We're going to need a boat and diving gear.'

'You wheel that deal,' Sawyer told her. 'You're good at it.'

42

'One of my specialities.'

'It wouldn't hurt to have a car or van on tap,' Bran pointed out. 'We may need to go farther afield.'

'I'll see what I can do.'

'Might as well leave my bike inside where it is, unless we need it. I'll set up a training area in the grove. We can use the trees for cover,' Doyle speculated. 'Plenty of hills for hiking.'

'I like hiking.' Annika ate the last of a honey-drizzled bite of peach. 'Can we hike down to the beach?'

'Maybe later,' Bran told her. 'I have some work if Sawyer can help Doyle set up the training area.'

'I'm on it.'

'Annika, you could help me while Sasha and Riley deal with the cleanup here. We want to re-plenish the medicines. You'll make your calls,' Bran said to Riley, 'work your own brand of magic.'

'We need to go over the maps for this area,' Doyle pointed out. 'And work out some strategy.'

'Agreed. Could you do another assignment chart, Sasha?'

'Right after KP.'

'Okay, go team.' Riley clapped her hands to-gether. 'Let's get started.'

She liked working with Bran, not only because of his patience, but the delight of his magicks. She had no skill as a witch, but he'd shown her during their time on Corfu how to crush leaves or petals, how to measure.

He could and did make weapons, like the

43

potions of light and power that had defeated Nerezza and her beasts on Corfu. He could call the lightning and use it as skillfully as the others used gun or bow or sword. She had witnessed what he could do, and believed his power greater than any witch she'd known. Even greater than the sea witch or sorcerer.

But he would spend much time on the healing arts as well. Though she understood some felt fear or illness at the sight of wounds and blood, Annika saw a need. And felt pride when Bran told her she had a skill for healing.

She had no wish to be a warrior, though she accepted the war. Her weapons were her speed and agility – in and out of the water. And the bracelets that shot power or blocked it.

When Sasha joined them, Annika made an excuse to leave them. Because they were in love, and time between lovers was precious. She wandered the house, familiarizing herself with its chambers – rooms, she corrected.

Following Riley's voice, she stepped into one flooded with light, where Riley paced and talked very fast on the phone in a mix of English and Italian.

'*Che cazzo, Fabio!* What kind of deal is that? Two weeks minimum, and likely four or six weeks. *Stronzate.* Don't try to hose me. I could go to a stranger and get a better rate. Okay, that's what I'll do. Oh, and I'll be contacting your mother while I'm here. She and I really need to have a nice chat because I find my memory about that night in Naples is coming back. Same to you, *amico.*'

She listened, listened, her smile going sharp

44

and satisfied. *'Quanto?* Better, some better, but...
I really miss talking to your mother. Oh, that's for
two weeks? Now you're talking. That works, you
keep the deposit either way. What's that?'

Riley threw back her head and laughed. 'Baby,
you *wish* I was squeezing your balls. Four-week
minimum's a deal. We'll pick it up tomorrow.
She'd better be seaworthy, Fabio, or remember
how I pulled your ass out of the fire in Naples?
I'll be shoving it right back in. *Ciao.*'

She swiped off the call, swaggered over to
Annika. 'High-five.'

When Annika looked toward the ceiling, Riley
laughed again. 'No, no, slap my hand. It's a high
five. It's a fucking A. We've got a boat, and I
wrangled the cost down.' She rolled her shoulders. 'I did squeeze the little asshole's balls.'

'What kind of balls?'

Riley pointed at her crotch. 'Those kind.'

'Oh, yes. I know those kind. But how did you
squeeze his balls when... It's an expression.'

'You're catching on. The diving equipment was
easy. Fabio's cousin Anna Maria's in charge of
that, and she's giving us rock-bottom rate. I'd
have taken Fabio's next-to-the-last rate if he
hadn't tried to squeeze my balls first. Anyway.'
She shoved the phone in her pocket, dusted her
palms together. 'Done. And I've got the sister of
a friend's boyfriend who'll lend us his van for gas
and beer if we need it.

'So, where's everyone else?'

'Sasha and Bran are up the stairs making
magicks. I think Sawyer and Doyle are still in the
grove for the training part.'

'All right then. You need to put on pants.'

'Pants.'

'Yeah, those ones that hit about here?' Riley tapped the flat of her hand just above her knee. 'The ones with all the pockets. And the tank you can tuck into them. I want to work on some of my moves, and you've got the best. And we'll work on your hand-to-hand. But you can't go doing flips in that dress, especially since there's nothing under it.'

'I like dresses better than pants.'

'Maybe so, but when you go commando and do handsprings and flips, you're flashing.'

'Flashing?'

'The girl parts, Anni. The parts we tend – right or wrong – to think of as private. Maybe we'll get you some bike shorts. You could wear them under a dress.'

'Bike shorts.'

'We'll look into it. But for now, go ahead and change. I'll see if Bran can spare Sasha. She needs the work.'

'She does better.'

'Yeah, she does,' Riley agreed as they started upstairs. 'You're a good coach.'

'Thank you. I like to help.'

Pleased, even if she had to wear pants, Annika went to her room to change, and wound her hair into a long, thick braid.

She left her windows open, and though she would go outside, took a moment to lean out, drink in the air, the fragrance, her view of the sea.

On the narrow road below, she saw people walking up the steep, steep hill in boots and shorts. Maybe they were bike shorts, but she knew what a bike was, and they didn't have one.

She saw bushes and trees full of blooms, and, farther out, people on the sickle of beach, boats plying the blue water.

Sometimes she liked to swim beneath boats, look up at their shadows and try to guess where they would go.

But today she saw a woman walking slowly up the steep road and pushing a fat-cheeked baby in a ... walker, runner... Stroller! A stroller. Plastic bags hung heavily off the sides of the stroller, and another bag crowded into its little basket.

The baby laughed and clapped her chubby hands as the woman sang.

Annika wished she could paint like Sasha. She would have painted the woman and the baby, laughing with the long, high road still ahead of them.

The woman looked up, caught Annika's eye. So Annika waved.

'*Buongiorno,*' the woman called out.

She had bits of languages, because she liked to listen and learn. '*Buongiorno,*' she called back. Not sure how to make the sentence, she mixed her languages together. 'You and your *bambina* are *bella.*' Annika held out her hands. '*Bella.*'

The woman laughed, angled her head. '*Grazie, signorina. Grazie mille.*'

And singing again, the woman and her baby continued the steep climb.

Her mood buoyed by them, Annika danced downstairs and outside to train for war.

She saw Sasha and Riley on the strip of lawn

47

between the pool and the lemon grove. Pretty plants and bushes added color at the edges, and the tall, slim trees formed a green wall.

Not so much room, so they'd have to … practice smaller.

Still she enjoyed watching Riley work with Sasha on the hand-to-hand. A punch, a pivot, a kick. Like a dance.

After a short run, Annika executed a double handspring, landed soft, and mimed punching both of her friends with the backs of her fists.

'Show-off.' Sasha grumbled it.

'There's not so much grass, but it's very nice. You can practice your rolls, Sasha.' Annika rolled her hands to demonstrate. 'Then the jump up.'

'Double roll,' Riley decided. 'Come up, side kick, backhand.'

'Seriously?'

'You need to start combining the flips and tumbles with the rest. You're wicked good with a crossbow, pal, but we all know you can't always fight at a distance. Agility, mobility, power. Right, Anni?'

'This is right.'

'Make her do it first.' Sasha jabbed a finger at Riley.

'You want me to do it first? I'm first.'

Riley slapped her hands together, rolled her shoulders, flexed her knees a few times. Then she sprang forward, landing on her hands, tucked into a roll, a second roll, then pushed up, kicking one leg out to the right, her arm with its fisted hand to the left.

Annika applauded.

'Don't encourage her,' Sasha mumbled.

'You can do it, Sasha. Remember. Tight, tight.' Annika tapped a hand on Sasha's belly. 'Power there, power in your legs.'

'Okay.' Shaking her arms, Sasha blew out a breath. 'Okay. Tight, tight, power, spring, roll, kick. Oh, God.'

She gave herself a short, running start, threw her body over for the handspring.

Annika nodded, then winced, because while the spring was very good, the roll went off-center, the second roll more off-center. So when Sasha tried to heave herself to her feet, she landed on her face.

'Damn it!'

'Ten out of ten for the face-plant,' Riley decided.

Sasha rolled over, gave Riley the beady eye.

'You did the handspring very well.' Annika crouched down, rubbed Sasha's shoulders.

'Right.'

'No, I think left. This is left, yes?' Holding up her left hand, Annika wiggled her fingers. 'You did the handspring, but then you tipped to the left on the roll, and more left on the next. You had no center, so no balance. I'll show you, slower than Riley.'

She stood, didn't bother with the running start but seemed to fold over like water from a pitcher.

'Tight, tight in the center,' she said as she tucked, rolled. 'Keep tight, knees go loose to push up.' Fluidly, she flowed up to her feet, shot one leg out, one arm. Held the pose like a statue.

'Can I just throw rocks at the bad guys?'

'Sometimes.' Annika smiled. 'But you can do this. I'll help you. Tight, tight,' she repeated. 'Like

49

squeezing. Try.'

This time, though she stayed on her feet, Annika moved with her – gave Sasha a tiny nudge on the roll. 'Squeeze! Tight! Tight, tight, and push!'

Sasha landed – wobbled, but landed. Regained her balance, executed the kick and backhand.

'Good! So good.' Annika applauded again.

'I tipped left again. I could feel it.'

'But not so much as before.'

'You pulled it off,' Riley told her. 'Do it again.'

'Okay. Okay. Don't help me this time. If I fall on my face, I fall on my face. But I'm going to get this bastard.'

'That's the spirit.' Riley slapped her on the shoulder.

She did it again, wobbled again, nearly overbalanced, but pulled back.

'Together,' Annika decided. 'All three.'

'Oh boy, okay.'

'Tight. A fist in the belly.'

Riley nodded. 'On three. One, two, three!'

Sawyer stopped at the edge of the lemon grove. 'Check it out.'

With Doyle, he watched the three women spring, roll, spear up. 'The brunette's got speed and form,' Doyle commented. 'The blonde's got game, and she's coming along. But the mer-girl? Makes it look like a stroll on the beach.'

'You'd think there'd be an adjustment for her – moving in water, on land. But either way, she just flows.'

'Great legs.'

Doyle started forward again as the three

women discussed something with Annika gesturing with her hands. And stopped to watch when Riley shook her head, but backed up. And laced her hands into a basket.

Annika ran toward her, jumped to hit one foot in that basket, and as Riley pushed up, flew into a perfect backflip to land in what Sawyer thought of as the Superhero Lunge. Low, one knee bent, the other leg cocked out, one hand resting on the ground.

'I should be taking videos,' Sawyer added.

Then Annika spotted them, leaped up to run forward.

'Come practice with us!'

'I could practice the rest of my life and not pull that off.'

'I can teach you.'

'Bet you could,' Doyle put in, 'but we need to take a hike, get a better sense of where we are, our position, our weak spots.'

'Agreed.' Riley nodded, then looked up at the wide blue sky. 'But that's a big weak spot.'

'We'll need to be ready for it.'

'Bran's working on it, and could probably use a break from that. I'll go tell him we're heading out. Ten minutes?' Sasha asked.

'Works for me.' Sawyer smiled at Annika. 'You'll need shoes.'

They set out with light packs, taking the narrow road up its steep incline first. The day, already warm, offered a baking sun over their bird's-eye view of sea and sand, of houses jogging down the long slope in their soft roses and whites and umbers.

51

As they walked, Sawyer drew maps in his head. He was good at maps – had learned at his grandfather's knee. The compass – a gift, a charge, a legacy – required knowledge of place and time. The hand that held it, the traveler, needed more than luck and magicks.

They passed groves of olives, of lemons, and he added them to his mental guide. The gardens, the houses with shuttered windows, the ones with windows open to the air.

From their high view, Riley pointed toward the mainland.

'Capri used to be part of the mainland, and was peopled during the Neolithic age. Colonized by the Teleboi, then the Greeks of Cumae. The Romans took it over in 328 BC.

'But Augustus – ninth century – developed it. Temples, gardens, villas, the aqueducts. Tiberius, who came after him, built more. And the remains of his villa are on top of Monte Tiberio. We're heading that way, though it's a hike yet.'

'Have you been there?' Sasha asked her.

'Yeah, it's been a while. I came with my parents. Hell of a place, Villa Jovis, even now, and more than worth exploring if that's what we're after.'

'A god might enjoy having her own HQ in what remains of a Roman emperor's villa,' Bran speculated.

'Yeah.' Riley thought of it while they continued the steep climb. 'It's got some grandeur left, but it's a long way from private. You see people going up, like us, people coming down? That's likely the destination. It's a big draw on the island.'

'The island's potholed with caves,' Doyle

pointed out.

'It is.' As she walked, Riley sent him a curious glance. 'Have you been here before?'

'I have. Longer ago than you. Petty wars. The English and French wanted Capri, fought over it.'

'In 1806 – French occupation overthrown by the English. In 1807, French take it back. Which side were you on?'

'Both.' He shrugged. 'It was something to do. It's changed in two hundred years. The roads, the houses, the funicular. But the land takes longer to change. I know some of the caves, the grottos.'

'The Grotta Azzurra.' Annika beamed. 'It's so beautiful. I, too, visited with my family to bathe in the water and the light.'

'The Blue Grotto seems like a slam dunk for a Water Star,' Sawyer imagined. 'Which is probably why it won't be.'

'Its light burns blue only after it's lifted. Now it waits, cold and quiet.'

They stopped, turned to Sasha. Bran laid a hand on her arm. 'What else do you see?'

'Her. I see her, through the smoke and broken mirrors. Nerezza, the mother of lies. She'll make her palace in the dark, of the dark, and there forge a new weapon against us. Promises of power seeded on thirsty ground. She waters with blood. A new dog for a new day.'

Sasha fumbled for Bran's hand. 'How did I do?'

'You did well. Headache?'

'No. No, I'm fine. I let it come. I can't bring it, but I can let it come.'

'Your face is pale.' Digging in her pack, Annika took out a water bottle. 'Water helps.'

53

'It does.'

'So does food, and there's some up ahead. I smell pizza,' Riley said.

'Wolf nose,' Sawyer commented.

'That's exactly right. I vote lunch.'

Riley's nose proved accurate. In under a quarter mile they sat outside a little roadside trattoria.

'Have you got your sketch pad?' Sawyer asked Sasha.

'Never leave home without it.'

'Can I borrow it a minute? I want to get something down while it's fresh.'

Intrigued, Sasha pulled out her pad, a case of pencils. 'You never said you drew.'

'Not like you.'

As the vote for pizza rounded the table, as beer and wine were served, he sketched out his map from memory. The curve of the land, the sweep of sea and beach, the rise of hills. He added the road they'd traveled, positions of houses, groves, fields.

Riley leaned over to study the work. 'That's pretty damn good, cowboy.'

'You gotta know where you are. Which is here – or the house is here. We came up this way, over, and now we're here.'

He drew a compass rose at the bottom of the page.

'What do we have if we go back and down?'

'You'd end up at the Piazzetta – or as it's known by locals, *chiazz*. The square – little, as the name indicates – is the social center and tourist haunt. Cafes, bars, and, fanning out from it, the narrow streets, the shops–'

'Shopping?' Annika interrupted Riley's explan-

54

ation. 'We can shop?'

'We'll need to eventually. Supplies, ammo. You'll get trinkets,' Riley assured her. 'Up here, that's the Marina Grande.'

'Got it.' Sawyer penciled the name in.

'We'll pick up the boat – another RIB – our equipment there in the morning. We have a van on tap if we need it, but I don't recommend driving here – van or bike – unless we have to. Public transpo's good, plus we have Sawyer if we need to get somewhere fast. The funicular goes from Capri town to the marina if we need that. It's just getting there. Bus is probably the best way to get to the marina from the house.'

'Just how do we get weapons on a bus?' Doyle demanded.

'I'll come up with something,' Bran assured him.

Since the pizza came out then, hot and bubbly, it blocked an immediate argument. But sensing one coming, Sawyer took a stab.

'We could hike it. Public transpo when and if, legs otherwise.'

'A reasonable compromise,' Bran declared. 'We can see how it goes. I'll deal with the weapons either way, and we can consider the hike to the marina part of our morning calisthenics.'

'I like calisthenics,' Annika said. 'I like pizza, and this wine is very nice. I can hike to shop.' She gave Sawyer an under-the-lashes smile. 'You could go with me.'

'Ah–'

'We should walk off lunch,' Doyle put in, 'and get in an hour's weapons training. I bet there are shops around the marina, Gorgeous. You'll get your chance.'

'I like my weapons.' She studied her bracelets, smiled at Bran and Sasha. 'They're pretty. It's nice to have a day together. To practice, yes, to train and to plan. But just to walk in the sun with all the flowers and trees. To eat pizza. To just...'

'Just be?' Bran suggested, and plucked a starry little flower out of the air.

With a laugh, Annika tucked the flower behind her ear. 'Yes. To just be together. Here, where Sasha said to come. Where Sawyer brought us. Where here' – she laid a hand on her heart – 'I know we are meant to be.'

'Seventh daughter of seventh daughter knowing?' Riley asked.

'Yes, it may be. But I know. And I feel, I feel so strong that we'll find the Water Star, that whatever weapon is forged against us, it will never be enough. The dark cannot win, so the light must.'

'You're a light, Anni,' Sawyer told her, and made her heart swell.

'One of six. It's good to be one of six. Can I have more pizza?'

Sawyer took a slice, slid it onto her plate. 'All you want.'

They hiked back for weapons training. Annika liked using her magic bracelets, and liked even more practicing with them in the lemon grove. The floating balls Bran conjured for her could slide and bob behind trees, try to hide, so she had to be quick and clever to deflect.

And careful not to destroy so he didn't have to stop his own training to make her more.

56

She didn't mind sharing the grove – it smelled so nice! – while the others practiced with bows. But when the time came for the guns, she couldn't pretend not to hear that awful sound.

Bran said he blocked it so it couldn't reach outside the grove, but inside, the sharp, brutal sound boomed and echoed until she slipped away.

She would practice more, alone, but she wanted to be away from that sound, from the stink the guns made.

Because they excused her from using guns, she'd make up for it, be useful somewhere else.

She missed the dog, and the chickens they had in Greece – for the company and for the tending. But though the garden here wasn't as big, it still required weeding. The house still needed order.

Sawyer had shown her how to make the sun tea, so she searched the kitchen for what she needed. She learned well, she reminded herself, and could do this small task alone. She was here to learn as well as to fight and to find.

She was here to help. She knew the water in the pot had to boil, and this took time. While she waited, she gathered laundry. Some clothes had the blood and gore from the last battle on Corfu. She would make them clean again.

This also took time, considering the machine that washed clothes wasn't the same as the machine in the villa. She did what she thought was right, put the big glass jar in the hot water. She forgot the word Sawyer used, annoying herself. But this step was to make sure no bad things got into the tea or jar.

Because Bran had taught her about herbs, she

went outside, cut some as she'd seen Sasha do.

She cleaned them, put them in the big glass jar. Once she'd added the water, put on the lid, she carried the jar out into the sun.

Now the sun would do the work.

And she could weed the vegetables and harvest the ripe ones, as she'd been taught.

It would be so pretty, she thought, to live this way, without the training, the fighting. To tend a house, a garden, to make tea with the sun. To find a dog who liked to play. A house by the sea, so the water was always close. A place she could live with her friends, where she could share Sawyer's bed.

Oh, how she wanted to learn what it was to mate with him.

She could dream, she told herself. It hurt no one to dream. To dream of a house by the sea where she lived with her one true love and her friends, and all the worlds were safe from the dark.

She knew most of it could never be. She had only three turns of the moon before the legs were no longer hers, and the sea once again her only home.

But she could dream, and do all she could to beat the dark.

She straightened when Sasha crossed the lawn, put the basket of tomatoes and peppers on her hip.

'These were ready.'

Sasha took a look, nodded. 'They sure are. You've kept busy.'

'The sun's making the tea. I used the mint and the plant that smells like lemons, and the chamomile.'

'Very nice combination.'

'It looks pretty already, but it needs more sun time.'

'Maybe, but when the rest come, they might not give it more. It's thirsty work. I think they plan a pool break. Gardening's thirsty work, too. I bet you'd like a swim.'

'Always. Um ... I have laundry in the machine, but it's not the same machine. Can you make sure it's right?'

'I'll look on my way up.'

'For your suit.'

'No, actually, I'm taking a different break. I need to paint.'

'A vision?'

'No, I just need to paint. The way you need to swim.'

Her smile soft, Annika nodded. 'Because it's what you are.'

'Exactly. But you know, I may bring my easel down here. I don't need alone as much as I did.'

'Then I'll bring out the glasses and the ice.'

Sasha led the way inside, turned into the small laundry.

'I did the soak with the salt for the blood. And the little bottle Bran made to help purify.'

She went through the steps she'd taken as she pulled clothes out for Sasha's inspection.

'You did everything just right.'

'When they're dry, I can fold them like you showed me. After the break. I can get my suit and swim.'

'And after the break, Bran wants everyone to help, the way you did at the villa, with protection. Drawing the curtain, and security.'

'There are brooms.'

'Good. This time you can help teach me, as I slept through the last round. And after that, when we're curtained and protected, we'll hold our first war council on Capri.'

'The men and Riley.'

'They're the most experienced, but you and I, too, Annika. We've fought, we've bled. We all sit on the council now.'

She set the table with glasses, a big bucket of ice, clipped the mint as Sawyer showed her and made it into a bouquet in a little vase. She formed slices of lemon into a flower on a small plate. And because someone was always hungry, created a display of fruit and cheese and crackers.

Pleased, she ran upstairs to change into the suit for swimming. She'd only asked for one before she'd started this quest. It made so little sense to swim in clothes she had only thought to need one. Now she decided she would take some of her shopping money and buy another. Or perhaps two more.

Clothes were fun and pretty, and one of the best things about having legs. She stepped out of her room as Riley opened the door to hers.

'Pool time,' Riley announced. 'Sawyer and Doyle are already down there.'

'Oh! Can I see?'

Riley shrugged, gestured to the terrace doors. 'Go ahead.'

She dashed over, saw Sawyer and Doyle sitting by the pool, facing each other in talk. On the lawn, Bran stood with Sasha as she set up her easel.

Simple joy radiated in her voice as she called

out. 'Hello!'

Sawyer looked up, smiled – she loved his smile, so quick, so bright – and waved at her.

Leading with that joy, she leaped onto the rail, dived.

She heard Sawyer shout something, did an easy, happy roll, and slid blissfully into the pool. *'Merda!'* He jumped in, ready to drag out her unconscious body when she surfaced, laughing. 'Christ, Anni, you could've broken your neck.'

After sucking back her hair, she blinked in curiosity. 'How?'

'It's not that deep, and from that height, you could've hit your head on the bottom.'

'Why would I do that? My head knows where the bottom is.'

'Looked like fun.' Riley leaned on the rail above.

'It is fun.'

'Humans might know where the bottom is,' Sawyer told her, 'but they can't slow their descent or pull up when they hit the water the way you can.'

Annika looked up at Riley. 'You shouldn't dive from there.'

'Got it.'

Annika took Sawyer's hand, tugged him in a little deeper. 'We can have a race. Racing is fun.'

'Yeah, like any of us has a shot against you.'

'I would swim backward.'

'And still,' Sawyer said as Doyle let out a snort. 'But okay, challenge accepted.'

He went back to the end, waited for her to roll onto her back. 'Ready? Go!'

He gave it some power, counting off seconds in

61

his head. And when he slapped the other end, she was already sitting on the side of the pool, casually squeezing water out of her braid.

'Show-off.'

'Showing off is fun.'

He thrilled her by pulling her back into the pool.

Mmmm, bare skin. His hands, for just a brush, on her hips. His eyes laughing into hers, then not. Like the brush of hands, only a moment, not laughing, but looking deep.

And his face close, close enough for lips to meet.

Then he let her go, let the water separate them.

'Leg race next time – on land.'

'My legs are very strong, and very fast.'

'Yeah, we'll check that out, Aqua-Girl.'

When he sank below the surface, she swam over him, then down to skim along the bottom until she could quiet the longing. When she surfaced, she stretched out to float.

She heard the voices, the splash of Riley diving in.

It was like her dream, she thought. All her friends together with the sun and the water. And that was enough for the day.

Even the work was like the dream. All her friends together with Bran's magick. His magick was so pretty, so bright and strong. They swept away all the dark, laid light with the powdered crystals and bespelled water. Then, with a shield from human eyes beyond the wall of trees, he rose up to spread the protection from the top of the house to the ground below.

'I didn't know it would be beautiful,' Sasha murmured, gazing up at him.

'Irish has style.' Riley draped an arm around her shoulders. 'We did all this in Corfu, but I've got to say, it doesn't get old. Okay, inside or out for war council?'

'We're as protected out here as in there, and it's too nice to sit inside, even for war.'

'Agreed.'

'I need to finish the new chart – for chores. I'll do that tonight. But I'll take dinner. It would be nice to have war talk over, as much as it ever is, before we eat.'

'I've got some maps upstairs.'

'I can fold the laundry now,' Annika said. 'Should there be wine?'

'Baby.' Riley swung her arm away from Sasha, over Annika. 'There should always be wine. Let's get started.'

Annika sat while the others pored over the maps. Riley pointed out caves she knew, or had researched. Doyle showed them others he remembered from long ago.

'Do you know any underwater caves, Annika?' Sawyer asked. 'Any we don't have marked?'

'We only came here.' She reached out to touch a spot on the north of the island. 'The Grotta Azzurra. It's tradition to bathe in the blue light. But we didn't stay or seek other places. So many people, you see. There are other places not so ... inhabited?'

'Did you hear the sighs or the songs when you came with your family?' Sasha wondered.

'No, but I didn't listen. I was young, and it was

beautiful and exciting. I had no purpose. I could look, from the sea.'

'Not alone.' Reaching over, Bran touched her hand. 'No one ventures alone. We know she'll come, and send her dogs. The attacks will come on land, from the air, in the water, as they did before. We have to prepare for that. No one ventures alone.'

'We're more closed in here than we were at the villa.' Doyle looked around, scanning trees, roof-lines. 'Advantage and disadvantage. We have less area to defend, but less room to maneuver. The light bombs took out swarms of the dogs. Actually, calling them dogs is an insult to dogs.'

'I like Sasha's minions.'

'Minions then,' he said with a nod to Riley. 'She'll send them again. Losing them means nothing to her. She'll just send more. Can you use the light bombs on the bolts, on the bullets and blades?'

Bran sat back, arched his eyebrows. 'That's interesting. I can work on that. Sure, I can work on that.'

'You wounded the– Was it a Cerberus, Riley?'

'Three-headed hound of hell. Sure looked like one.'

'You wounded it,' Sasha continued. 'And hurt and frightened her. Aged her. I can't see what weapon she'll forge, but she needs something to combat what you can do at full force.'

'What *we* could do,' Bran reminded her. 'I wouldn't have been strong enough without you.'

'It's a good thing you don't have to do without me. Still, it took all we had to hold her off.'

'And kick her ass,' Sawyer added. 'She ran. You beat a god. We beat a god and her minions. And it's not cocky to say we're going to do the same thing here, whatever she brings. But I wouldn't say no to a load of magick bullets.'

'There's good cover in the grove,' Doyle pointed out. 'We make our stands there rather than out in the open.'

'Add some surprises in the open. Take some of them out,' Riley calculated.

'She spread that mist on the ground. It bit.' Now Sasha judged the distance to the grove. 'We can set off the light bombs from there – bolt, bullet, blade, magick.'

'I can do this with my bracelets,' Annika pointed out.

'It's a plan.' Riley reached for her wine. 'Covers land and air. Now water.'

'Harpoons, knives – a magick assist?' Sawyer added. 'And mermaid.'

Annika smiled. 'My bracelets also work well in the water, and I'm faster there than anywhere else.'

'We've never asked,' Sasha began. 'How do you communicate with your family? With others like you?'

'Oh. It's...' Annika touched her head, her heart. 'You think. You feel.'

'We can speak, but it's often without voice.'

'I see where you're going.' Riley leaned toward Annika. 'How about other sea life? Fish, whale, that sort of thing?'

'We have understandings. They don't think as we do, though the whale can be wise, and the

65

dolphin is smart and clever. But fish? They forget quickly.'

'Dory.' When Annika looked blank, Sawyer explained. 'From a movie. We'll stream it sometime. They're wondering if you can maybe sense the bad guys – underwater?'

'Oh. I don't know. They are not fish, not mammal, not people. They're other. But I can try. I will try.' She set her jaw. 'It would help.'

'An early-warning system. Otherwise, we do what we've done?' Sawyer glanced around the table. 'Buddy system, stick together, do the work. If things get too dicey, I can shift us. We should have a secondary location. If we have to travel from the water, we'd come here, but if we have to travel from here?'

'How about Monte Tiberio?' Riley suggested. 'High ground.'

'If that works, I'll get the coordinates. Meanwhile.'

Sawyer took out the compass, opened the bronze case.

When he set it on the map, it glowed, shimmered in place on Capri. But didn't move.

'Gotta work for it,' he said, and pocketed it again.

'I'll start just that.' Bran rose. 'Bullets, bolts, and blades. And bracelets. Interesting.'

'I'll dig into research. See if I can find out anything about sighs, songs, more underwater caves.' Riley pushed to her feet. 'Do you want the map?' she asked Doyle.

'Maybe later.'

'I'll get dinner started.' Sasha pushed a loose pin

66

back into her bundled-up hair. 'Can you help, Annika?'

'Yes, I like to help.'

When Sasha and Annika went inside, Doyle leaned back with his beer, looked at Sawyer. 'Happiest siren I've ever seen. Nobody would blame you for moving on that.'

'She doesn't... I don't think she gets that. It. It's like hitting on somebody's little sister. From Venus.'

'Looks all grown-up to me, but your call. How about we take a walk, past the grove. See what, if anything, we might want to fortify.'

'Good thought.'

While they ate under the stars, Andre Malmon adjusted his formal tie. He expected the evening ahead to be a tedious bore, but duty called. He rarely answered when duty called, already regretting doing so now.

Still, there was a potential for new contacts at this dull charity affair. Contacts were never boring. He wanted something new, something exciting.

So little excited him these days.

What hadn't he done, after all? What hadn't he seen? What couldn't he have simply by flicking his fingers?

His last two adventures – he never called them jobs, though he charged exorbitant fees for his services – had barely amused him. So little challenge.

The woman he was currently seeing had begun to annoy him just by existing, as did the whore he used for more inventive play. He expected he'd dispose of them both very soon.

He had offers pending, of course, but none stirred his juices. Murder? Easily done, but he no longer killed for a fee – unless the kill offered him personal pleasure.

Theft? Sometimes intriguing, but again why steal for someone else? He'd rather steal for himself – and couldn't, at the moment, think of a single thing worth the effort.

Kidnappings, brainwashings, mutilations. Ho-hum.

Of course there was the standing offer of fifty million for a unicorn, or its horn.

Money couldn't buy sanity.

If he got bored enough, he might take the time and effort to have a fake horn fabricated. But that was scraping the barrel clean.

He passed a hand over his hair – gilded blond, perfect waves around a handsome face with a sharply sculpted mouth, a thin nose, and deceptively quiet blue eyes.

Perhaps he'd kill Magda – his current *amore*. Not the whore, whores weren't worth the killing. But Magda, the heiress with the hint of royal blood. Magda, the beautiful and serene.

He could stage a murder/mutilation, add touches of the occult and sexual perversion. Such a scandal!

It might perk him right up.

He scowled at the knock on his bedroom door, turned when it opened.

'I'm sorry, Mr. Malmon.'

'You'll be sorrier.' His voice, cold and British,

carried a whip of temper. 'I expressly told you not to disturb me.'

'Yes, sir. There's a woman here to see you.'

He stepped forward. 'What does 'not to disturb' mean to you, Nigel?'

'She's waiting in the drawing room.'

Nigel, stoic and discreet, offered a card. Incensed, Malmon started to strike it away, but the look in his butler's eyes stopped him.

Blank. Next to dead. He merely stood, staring, the card held out.

Malmon snatched the card, the glossy black rectangle with the bold red lettering of a single name.

Nerezza

'What does she want?'

'To speak with you, sir.'

'She got past the gate, past Lucien, past you?'

'Yes, sir. Shall I serve refreshments?'

'No, you bloody well won't serve refreshments. Go hang yourself, Nigel.'

And pushing past the butler, Malmon started down to the parlor. He felt annoyed, certainly. But he was also curious. He hadn't been curious for *days*.

He checked the derringer up his right sleeve. He never went anywhere, not even inside his own homes, unarmed. And since Lucien appeared to be as useless as Nigel, walked into the parlor.

She turned. She smiled.

She was a vision. He couldn't have said her beautiful, but beauty blinded him. Dark hair

69

swept in coils over her shoulders, made all the more striking by a streak of white bolting through the black.

And black were her eyes, black and wide and mesmerizing against pale white skin. Lips red as blood curved knowingly.

She wore black as well, a dress that molded her tall, stately form.

'Monsieur Malmon.' She walked toward him, glided without a sound – and her voice, faintly exotic, caused his heart to trip. *'Je m'appelle Nerezza.'*

'Mademoiselle.' He took the offered hand, touched his lips to her knuckles, and felt a thrill like no other.

'Do we speak English? We are in England, after all.'

'As you wish. Please, sit, mademoiselle.'

'Nerezza, please.' With a slither of skirts, she sat. 'We will be good friends, you and I.'

'Will we?' He struggled for aplomb, but his heart raced, his blood pounded. 'Then we should begin our friendship with a drink.'

'Of course.'

He walked to the bar, poured whiskey for two. Taking charge, taking control – he thought – by not asking what she'd prefer.

He came back, sat across from her. They touched glasses.

'And what brings you to me, Nerezza?'

'Your reputation, of course. You're the man I need, Andre.' She sipped, watching him. 'You will be the one I need. And for my needs, when fulfilled, I can offer you more than anything you've had. Dreamed of having.'

'I have much, have dreamed of more.'

'If it's money, I have all you require. But there are things worth more than gold and silver.'

'Such as?'

'We'll speak of that, but tonight we'll speak of stars. What do you know of the Stars of Fortune?'

'A myth. Three stars, fire, water, ice, created by three goddesses to honor a young queen. And cursed by another.'

Her lips curved into a smile sharp enough to slice bone. 'What do you think of myths?'

'That many are uncommonly real.'

'As these are real, these stars, I assure you. I want them. You will find them and bring them to me.'

Her eyes were bottomless, lured him into the black. But pride demanded he resist. 'Will I?'

'You will. Six stand in your way.'

'No one stands in my way for long.'

'So I have seen, or I would not waste my time, or yours. If you accept the challenge, if you wish to know what I will give you in return, come to the address on my card, tomorrow at midnight.'

'There's no address on the card.'

She smiled, rose. 'Come there, and know your own fortune. Until then.'

She glided out before he had the wit to stand. But when he strode to the doorway, she was gone. As if she'd vanished.

He pulled the card out of his pocket, saw he'd been wrong.

An address was clearly printed on the card.

Fascinated, baffled, more than a little un-nerved, he pressed the house intercom. 'Lucien.'

'Sir?'

'Where did she go?'

'I'm sorry, sir, where did who go?'

'The woman, the woman in black, you idiot. Who else? Why did you let her in without permission?'

'Sir, no one has come to the house tonight. I let no one inside.'

Furious, he strode away, calling for Nigel. His anger grew until he stormed downstairs, following temper into the butler's apartment.

When he saw Nigel hanging from his parlor chandelier, he stopped dead.

And laughed.

He was no longer bored.

CHAPTER THREE

With dawn came the soft, shimmering light and the diamond drops of dew on the grass.

And with dawn came calisthenics.

Annika liked calisthenics. She liked dropping down and giving Doyle twenty. The squats and lunges, the shuffles and the jumping jacks were like dancing – the moans and grunts and pants (especially from Sasha) always made her laugh.

Sawyer called Doyle a fucking drill sergeant, and that made her laugh, too. She understood the fuck word was a curse – so versatile! – and used a lot during calisthenics. She understood drill was a tool. But the only sergeants she knew were the sergeant majors, the name land people gave the little striped fish who liked swimming in the reef.

Imagining big, handsome Doyle as a little fish boring into coral made her laugh through her pull-ups.

'What's so funny?' Sweaty, face pink from exertion, Sasha scowled as she braced for her own pull-ups.

'Doyle is a drill sergeant major. Sawyer said.'

'A...' Sasha sneered over at Doyle, who stood signaling her to start. 'You're now a fish,' she called out to him, then mumbled, 'God, help me.'

She did one cleanly, a second reasonably well, and a third very shakily, her face going toward red with effort, wet with fresh sweat. Her arms visibly trembled.

Annika started to applaud, and Sasha hissed.

'I've got one more. Goddamn it.'

Annika held her breath because Sasha made a sound of awful pain, almost a scream, but her friend pulled up on her trembling arms, managed the fourth before she dropped to the ground in a panting heap.

'Good job,' Doyle told her. 'Sloppy form, but gutsy. Shoot for five tomorrow.'

'Shoot for five, my butt. I might shoot you tomorrow.'

'That's the spirit.' Reaching down, he hauled her to her feet and out of the way. 'You're up, Gwin.'

Riley set, did a smooth dozen in the time it had taken Sasha to strain out four.

'I might shoot you, too,' Sasha said darkly. 'I might just be in the mood for a double homicide.'

'You did four,' Annika reminded her. 'The first time, you couldn't do even one, but today, you did four.'

'Yeah, yeah.' Then Sasha blew out a long breath. 'Yeah,' she said in a stronger tone. 'And tomorrow I'll shoot for five.'

They had breakfast, and did the morning chores Sasha had listed on the new chart. Then it was time to hike to the marina.

Annika wanted to run. She could barely wait to dive into the sea. But she liked watching how Bran and Sasha held hands, or how Doyle and Riley argued over who would drive the boat.

The air smelled beautiful, with the breeze bringing scents of sea and flowers, of the lemons, of the grass. The walk provided gardens to admire, the flight of birds. And time with Sawyer.

'Will you take pictures in the water?'

'Yeah, I'm set for it.'

'If you taught me how to use the camera, I could take pictures of you. When you take them, you aren't in the picture.'

'I got a couple selfies.' He demonstrated by holding his arm out, pretended to click a camera.

'Oh! That's clever.'

'But I can teach you. Never hurts to have a backup for documenting.'

'Then I can help you take pictures in the water, and out of the water. I hope we can walk in the hills.' She gestured toward the mountains. 'I know we might find her there, have to fight her there, and the quest is the most important. But the walk would be exciting and new. All the things to see we haven't seen before.'

He gave her a shoulder bump she knew was a sign of affection. 'Gotta have the bright side.'

'The bright side helps us face the dark.'

'Can't argue.'

'In the last battle, I was afraid. I believe we'll win, we'll do what we're meant to do, but I was afraid.'

In a gesture she knew was affection and comfort, he brushed her arm with his hand. It made her want to sigh.

'We're all afraid, Anni.'

Surprised, she looked up at him. 'No one seemed afraid but me.'

'Every last one of us,' he corrected. 'If we weren't afraid, we'd be crazy. You know what courage is.' He said it, didn't ask it, but she nodded.

'It's bravery. It's facing the dark.'

'That's right. It's facing the dark, even when you're afraid. That's every one of us, too.'

She tipped her head toward his shoulder, knowing since he thought her brave, she could be braver still.

'Why don't you have a mate?'

'A... Well, um, I've had to move around a lot. Getting to this point, it's taken some doing.'

'But there was sex?'

He took off his hat, swiped his fingers through the thick, streaky blond hair she wanted to swipe hers through. After he settled the hat again, he pushed his hands into his pockets.

'You know, if you want to know about that kind of thing, you should talk to Riley or Sasha.'

'Oh, I know about sex. It's not so different in my world. We can have sex as we like. It's a bright side.'

He had to laugh. 'Definitely qualifies.'

'But when we find our mate, when we pledge, there's no other after. Like Bran and Sasha, there is only one.'

'That's nice. It's what most people hope for.'

'So there has been sex for you, but no mate.'

'There you go.'

The way went narrow, with buildings closing in. He distracted her from talk of sex by pointing to a shop window.

'Oh, we can come back to shop! I have the itch.'

'Tell me. You've always got a shopping itch.'

'No, no, the payment. The ... *scratch!*'

Though he grinned, he draped an arm over her shoulders to steer her away from a shop window. 'Right.'

'Look at the pretty food.'

Pastries and little cakes, pretty as jewels, tempted behind the glass.

'We should definitely grab some pastries to take home. And down there? Gelato.'

'What is it?'

'Outstanding.'

'Outstanding,' she repeated as they navigated the steep, narrow street.

Sawyer took her hand. The retail shops might not be open yet, but he'd had the experience of shopping with her in Corfu, and knew she could run off impulsively, like a terrier after a squirrel.

'I'll buy you a gelato on the way back,' he promised.

'Thank you.'

'But we've got to head straight to the boat now.'

'This village? It's all very big, and very small.

They have vegetables and fruit there–' She pointed to a stand. 'Look at the colors, the shapes. I don't know what some of them are. Are they all for eating?'

'Yeah. Some as they are. Some you want to cook first.'

She looked at everything, absorbed everything. He found it part of her charm. She ran her fingers over the walls of buildings to test the texture, would surely have run after a stray cat if he hadn't had a good grip on her. But he managed to steer her along, keep up with the others as they passed people sitting at tables outside cafes with their little breakfast cakes and strong coffee, through a cluster of colorful homes, beyond the hotels with their awnings and umbrellas, and toward the boats and piers and docks.

'There.' Riley pointed toward a boat, much like they'd used in Corfu.

The ... Annika had to dig for the name, but found it. The rigid-hulled inflatable.

Then Riley nodded toward a skinny man with a lot of teeth who walked toward them. The many teeth in a wide, wide smile made Annika think of a shark.

'I've got this.'

Riley strode forward, began an animated conversation in Italian. Annika recognized some of the words, and some of them were rude ones.

Sasha took out her sketchbook, and started to draw the world around the marina – the spread of awnings, tables, buildings, the stack of buildings climbing up to the tall, tall hills.

'He wants more money,' Doyle told them.

77

'She's telling him, in various ways, to stick it.'

Obviously confident in Riley winning the day, Doyle swung onto the boat.

'She said—' Annika struggled for the words. 'Something about his ass and a hole.'

On a laugh, Sawyer tugged her toward the boat. 'She called him an asshole. It's an insult.'

'An asshole makes a bargain then tries not to keep it.'

'Among other asshole behavior.'

Riley came back, and the skinny man didn't show as many teeth. 'Fabio, my team. Team, Fabio. The dive club's just down there. Fabio's graciously agreed to give me a hand with the equipment, but we could use a couple more.'

'I'll go with you. *Come va,* Fabio?'

Fabio showed Sawyer more teeth. *'Bene.'*

'I'll go with them.' Bran kissed Sasha on the forehead, strolled away with Sawyer.

It didn't take long. They wheeled back the tanks and the wet suits and the equipment the others needed to survive under the water. And a cooler full of ice and water, and even some of the fruit juices she liked, and the Cokes – she liked them, too.

While they loaded it, secured it, there was a lot of talk in Italian, but without the rude words now.

And at last – at *last* – they were all on board, and skinny Fabio released the ropes that held them to the dock.

Riley tapped two fingers to the brim of her hat. *'Ciao,* Fabio. You fuckhead,' she added in a mutter.

'A fuckhead is an asshole?'

78

Riley tipped down her shady glasses so her tawny eyes laughed into Annika's. 'A fuckhead is a really big asshole. My friend Anna Maria, who is neither asshole nor fuckhead, says we can moor the RIB at the dive club while we're here. It'll make loading and unloading easier.'

Riley walked forward to what they called a wheelhouse, where Doyle worked the controls. 'I pilot today, remember?'

'Just getting us away from the fuckhead.' But he stepped aside, gave her the wheel.

Then they were skimming over the water, nearly as good as being in its heart. Doyle stepped out of the wheelhouse to go over the equipment.

'I don't need the tank,' Annika began.

'Better if you gear up, like the rest of us.'

'We could run into other divers,' Sawyer explained. 'People would notice if you're diving without equipment.'

'So I just pretend.'

'That's right.'

'I can do that.'

'We stick together,' Bran reminded them as Annika stripped down to her bathing suit. And as Sawyer tried not to watch her strip down. 'However unlikely Nerezza's found us this quickly, we can't take chances. Everybody stays in sight.' He glanced toward Sasha.

'I don't feel anything. But I appreciate everyone keeping me in sight, in case I start any underwater dream-walking.'

'I'll look out for you,' Annika told her.

'I know you will.'

'We'll say, as it worked before, Sawyer and

Annika at point, Sasha and I behind, and Doyle and Riley at flank. All right?'

'Works for me.' Sawyer zipped up his wet suit. 'First time I've started a dive knowing I'm swimming with a mermaid.' He grinned at Annika. 'Adds to it.'

'But keep the legs, Gorgeous,' Doyle warned as Riley turned inland toward high cliffs.

'I promise. Unless there is an attack.'

'Speaking of, any luck on the bolts, bullets, and blades?' Doyle asked as he hefted a harpoon.

'Considerable, but it needs work yet. A few more days, then we'll see. For now, should we say one harpoon to each set of buddies? With Sasha's skills with a crossbow, I'd say she's the one in ours.'

Doyle passed her the harpoon. 'Can you handle it?'

Sasha frowned at it, tested its weight. 'Yes. I can do this.'

'I don't want one,' Annika said immediately.

'It's okay, I've got it.'

'Sawyer, Sasha.' Doyle looked toward the wheelhouse and Riley. 'You want to argue over who mans the harpoon?'

'We'll switch off. I pilot, you take the harpoon. You pilot, I take it.'

'Fair enough.'

Riley stopped the boat, pointed. 'First cave on today's list is at about two o'clock, and about twelve feet under to the entrance. A narrow channel opens up into a canyon after about forty feet. It's a tricky dive for a novice.'

'I'll be fine,' Sasha stated, pulling on her wet suit.

'You passed novice stage in Corfu.' After stripping down, Riley reached for her own wet suit. 'The mouth's small, we have to go in single file – and it's easy to miss.'

'I can find it.' Geared up, Annika sat on the side of the boat. Then doing what she wanted most at that moment, she rolled backward into the sea.

Though the pull was to go down and down, she surfaced immediately. It was enough, for now, just to feel the sea around her. She waved to the others.

'You've got to give us a minute here.' On deck, Riley hauled on her tanks.

Content, Annika swam around the boat, under it, careful to keep in sight, to stay aware, but basking in the feel of home.

When she circled again, she saw Sawyer. He pointed to his camera, so she posed, turning upside down as if doing a handstand.

She felt Sasha enter the water, then Bran. Moments later, Riley and Doyle. At Bran's signal, she flipped around, swam ahead.

But not fast, she reminded herself, pacing herself with Sawyer, tuning herself to the others as she would to a school of fish or others like her. A knowing.

Fish swam by without a thought for them. She felt the slow pulse of a starfish that slept on a rock, heard the quiet fanning of sea grasses.

She felt Sawyer's heartbeat – not so slow as the starfish, but steady and calm. His movements, and the others, came to her like whispers.

Deeper yet, she saw the mouth, gestured, but realized the others couldn't see it as she did. So she gestured again, continued to go down. She waited until the others were ready before sliding into the opening.

Fearless, Sawyer thought. In the water, she was fearless. And impossibly graceful. She moved through the narrow channel like the water itself, in a flow. The walls narrowed, barely wide enough for a man to pass, and the light went murky. In that narrow space, in that murky light, she turned, swimming backward. Though he couldn't see her face, he knew she smiled, probably counted heads before she turned again, continued on.

He saw an eel curled along a crevice in the rock, and hoped it stayed where it was. He wasn't fond of anything resembling snakes.

The walls widened, then opened into the canyon. There the light shifted, just enough. He could see, high above, openings in the cliff that let the light leak through.

They spread out, two by two, to search. More, he thought, hoping Sasha might sense something, as she had with the Fire Star. He looked for anything unusual: a formation of rock, a change in the water, a flicker of light.

He nearly panicked when he lost sight of Annika, circled fast. He pulled out his knife, started to rap the hilt against rock to draw the attention of the others. Then saw her rising up from the dark below.

She took his hands quickly, squeezed them, released them to rub hers on his cheeks.

Doyle signaled time. Annika took Sawyer's hand again, tugged him toward the channel, then slipped into it ahead of him.

By the time he hauled himself onto the boat, she'd pulled off her mask. 'Your heart beat so fast!'

'What?'

'In the canyon, at the end, it beat.' She slapped her hand rapidly on her own heart. 'Why?'

'I couldn't find you.'

'I was right under you. Just deeper, to look. I could always see you.'

'I couldn't see you. We couldn't see you,' he added.

'Oh.' She unhooked her tank. 'I forgot. I forgot you can't see the way I do in the water. I'm sorry.'

'Sorry for what?' Riley pulled herself on board.

'I went deeper, and didn't stay in sight. I'm sorry. I won't do it again. I could see all of you, but went beyond what you can see in the water. I made Sawyer's heart beat fast.'

Riley smiled over Annika's shoulder as she helped Annika take off the tanks. 'I bet it's not the first time.'

'Funny. How do you know my heart beat fast when you were deeper and out of sight?'

'I can feel it. In the water, I can... It's not feel like I can feel your hand,' she said, taking his. 'But I can feel it.'

'Interesting.' Glancing at her, Bran threw open the cooler. 'You can feel heartbeats of living things when you're in the water?'

'Yes. Or is *sense* the better word? Know?'

'And you can see much farther than we can,' Bran continued.

'I forgot that. I could feel – sense? – Sasha's heart on that day in Corfu, and know where to

83

look. And see her. The legs weren't fast enough, so I needed to change them.'

'But even with the legs, you can feel and see?' Riley grabbed a Coke, tossed Sasha juice.

'In the water. Are you angry?' she asked Sawyer.

'No. No, I'm not mad. You just gave me a jolt. Remember, we're buddies down there.'

She sat beside him, tipped her head to his shoulder. 'I'll be a better buddy.'

'Good enough. How'd you do, Sasha?'

'I was fine – I can't say I much like those tight openings, but I did fine. But I didn't feel any-thing, unlike Annika.'

'Let's cross it off.' Sucking her cap of hair back, Riley guzzled water. 'And hit the next. We should be able to do three today. All of them in this general area. We've got others to try on the east coast, and down to the south. But we can finish up this section today.'

Sawyer figured Annika could have dived all day and half the night, but the rest of them put in a solid five hours under the water, on the boat, with a short break for a quick lunch.

They found nothing but the appeal of sea life, rock formations, and in one cave a crude carving on rock with the names Greta and Franz inside a heart with the date 15/8/05.

He liked to think Greta and Franz stayed together, maybe living in a little farmhouse along the Rhine.

He hadn't expected to stumble across the star the first day out – didn't think any of the team expected that kind of luck. A quest required time, effort, sweat, and risk.

And when gods were involved, blood.

But steps had to be taken, and they'd taken them for the day. Best of all, they hadn't encountered any of Nerezza's minions. Any day no one had to shed that blood was, in his book, a good day.

Once they'd docked the boat, turned in the tanks, he shouldered his pack. The hike home loomed, but there'd be beer at the end of it.

'Now we can go shopping.'

As one, the other five stared at her.

'There are many shops, and pretty things, and all the people. And Sawyer said we could have the outstanding.'

'A beer sounds outstanding,' Doyle commented.

'She means gelato.' Reluctantly charmed again, Sawyer shifted his pack. 'She doesn't forget anything.'

'I could go for gelato,' Riley considered.

'And I need another suit for swimming. I only have one.'

Now Riley arched her eyebrows. 'What you have is a fraction of one.'

'Worn brilliantly,' Doyle put in, and made Annika smile.

'I think gelato's an excellent plan.' With her damp hair drawn back in a tail, Sasha scanned the marina. 'I bet it's an easy find, too, and on the way.'

'Let's find out.' Bran took her hand.

Within five minutes, after tugging Annika away from window displays of shiny objects, they met rock-hard determination.

'This shop has suits for swimming. I need this.'

85

'Take her in, Sawyer.'

'Oh, no.' His determination just as rock-hard, he shook his head at Riley. 'That's a girl thing. That's absolutely a girl thing.'

'I'm going with Sawyer on that.' In solidarity Bran slapped a hand on his shoulder. 'I say the females deal with this, and the rest of us head right up there.' He gestured. 'We can pick up more beer.'

'I'm going with them.' Riley stepped over to the male side.

'Wait a minute,' Sasha began.

'I'm going to find what we need to make Bellinis. We definitely need Bellinis.'

'Bellinis.' Sasha sighed, looked at the shop, weighed shopping chaos against Bellinis. 'All right, you've sold me. Annika, I'll go in with you, but you can't try on everything. You have to stay focused.'

'I won't. I will. Then we'll get outstanding gelato.' She dashed straight inside.

'They better be exceptional Bellinis,' Sasha muttered, and followed Annika inside.

She found such a pretty suit with red flowers, and another in bright, bright green, and what Sasha called a wrap almost as thin as air, and shoes with pretty seashells that left most of the foot bare. With Sasha's help, she bought them all, and another wrap with blue waves over white for Sasha.

'For you.' She offered the little bag. 'For helping me.'

'Oh, no, Anni, you don't have to buy me something for helping you.'

'But it's for you.' Firmly, Annika pushed the bag

into Sasha's hands. 'The blue is like your eyes. It's a gift for you, and makes me happy to give.'

'Thank you. It's beautiful. We really have to go now. Remember, we have to carry all of this.'

'Pretty things never weigh too much.'

To Sasha's mind, a couple of bikinis that barely covered the essentials weighed virtually nothing, but she steered Annika out of the shop.

'There they are.' Wary, Sasha kept a solid grip on Annika's arm as they walked up to where the rest redistributed bottles into packs.

'You're exempt,' Riley told Sasha as she hefted her heavier pack. 'Fair's fair.'

'I can carry more.' Annika turned around, offered her pack. 'It's not heavy.'

Doyle zipped a couple bottles of Italian beer inside her pack. 'That'll do it. We've got the rest.'

'There's gelato!' Annika dashed up the steep street as if her new sandals had wings.

She'd struck up an animated conversation with a couple of American tourists by the time the others caught up.

'Jessica likes the chocolate, but Mark likes the pistachio. It's a nut.'

'Right. How ya doing?' Riley signaled Sawyer to ease Annika away, distracted the couple with small talk until they wandered off.

'They were very nice, but I don't know whether to listen to Jessica or to Mark. And oh, there are so many pretty colors.'

'Pick two,' Sawyer suggested, and her eyes went wide.

'I can have two?'

'Two scoops in a cone.'

'Two scoops in a cone,' she repeated. 'Which do you pick?'

'You pick first. You're not going to go wrong.'

'I think ... the pink, and this green? They'll look nice together. Like a flower.'

'Strawberry and mint. Nice combo. It's on me,' he told the rest. When, even after he'd paid, Annika just admired her cone, he demonstrated on his own. 'You want to eat it.'

She took one delicate lick, then another. 'Oh! It's like eating joy!'

Weird, Sawyer thought as they hiked with packs, bags, and cones, but she made him feel like a hero for giving her her first taste of eating joy.

Because of it, the hike back went easy.

They scattered on the return, and as Sawyer moved faster, he snagged the shower ahead of Doyle. He washed off the salt, the sea, the sweat, felt fully human again as he drank half his first beer in the shower.

When he got out, he heard laughter from the kitchen. Female laughter. And though it appealed, he thought it wise to take a little time, a little distance from Annika.

His lust quotient there kept rising, no matter how studiously he tried to suppress it.

He took the rest of his beer outside, pulled a lounge chair into a patch of shade, and settled in with his tablet. He needed to email home, update his family. Maybe he'd read a chapter or two of one of the books he'd downloaded.

He dashed off the emails, promised pictures to follow. Told himself he could take an hour off, to read, or doze, or whatever the hell, then he'd do some research.

Riley was the queen there, but he had lines to tug as well.

Then she walked out, the mermaid in one of her floaty, filmy dresses, her hair loose, waving a little from its time in a braid. She carried a tray of flutes filled with frothy peach-colored liquid.

'Riley says it's Bellini time.' She set the tray on the table, picked up two flutes. 'She made them, and we had sips – Sasha and I.' She handed him a flute, sat on the grass with those incredible legs folded. 'The gelato was eating joy, and this is drinking it.'

He sampled to please her. 'Fancy. Good. Good and fancy.'

'Sasha said a monk found – discovered – champagne, and said it was drinking stars.'

'I've heard that.'

'Stars are meant to be for beauty and light, and for all the worlds. Nerezza won't drink them.'

'Damn right, she won't.' Sawyer shifted, tapped his glass to hers.

'Damn right.'

Sasha and Bran came out, chose another patch of shade with their drinks, Sasha's sketch pad. Riley settled in the sun with a Bellini and, like Sawyer, a tablet. Doyle came last, gave the Bellinis a look of suspicion, then shrugged, took one. He, too, chose the sun.

'I like when we're all together,' Annika murmured. 'Even apart, like this a little bit, but together. I'll miss it, miss everyone, once we return the stars to the Island of Glass.'

'We'll have a reunion.'

'I don't know that word.'

'It's like when people who've been together, then go separate ways, come back together again to celebrate. For a night, or a couple of days.'

'A reunion.' She thought it would be a new favorite word. 'You'd come?'

'Sure. I bet Bran could fix it up, somewhere private, by the sea. We'll have gelato and Bellinis.'

'And pizza.'

'Pizza goes without saying.' He couldn't help himself, and stroked his hand down her hair. 'We'll end Nerezza, but that won't end us.'

CHAPTER FOUR

At midnight, far too intrigued to resist, Malmon studied the house matching the address on the card Nerezza had given him. He'd already had one of his men take photos of it earlier in the day, and had assigned another to find out everything there was to find on the woman.

It both angered and intrigued him when everything to be found was nothing at all.

But the house suited her, to his mind. Even as he studied it now, from the smoked glass of the limo, he could imagine her inside. It held an eerie grace with its old stone, shielding trees, the gargoyles perched on the eaves.

As his did, it stood back from the road, behind a gate. He appreciated the desire for privacy, the power it took to command it.

What would she offer him? He had to know.

When he ordered the driver to pull up to the gate, he found himself unsurprised it opened immediately. Once the driver opened his door, he stepped out, a confident man in a bespoke suit, who believed he'd already seen and done all there was to see and do.

The wide, arched door opened as he approached. A man, pale of face, dark of eye, stood silently.

Malmon stepped into a foyer lit with dozens of candles. In the shifting, shimmering light, the pale man closed the heavy door. And Malmon's heart beat quickly.

'My mistress waits.'

The man's voice scraped rough, like a lizard's tongue over flesh. Malmon followed him up the stairs – more candles, and urns full of lilies so red they looked nearly black in the candlelight. Lilies so strongly scented they swam in his head.

He entered a large drawing room where Nerezza sat in an ornate chair, almost a throne, that glimmered gold. Its back rose up behind her with a carving of intertwined snakes at its peak.

She wore the same red as the flowers, so deep it showed black, with rubies like fat drops of blood dripping around her throat, from her ears.

An odd bird – not a crow, not an owl, but some odd combination – perched, like the gargoyles, on the wide arm of the chair.

Her beauty struck him like a bolt – both fierce and terrible. And so, in that moment, was his desire for her.

She smiled, as if she knew.

91

'I'm pleased you came. Leave us,' she told the servant while her dark eyes stayed on Malmon's face. She rose, her gown rustling like papery wings, and glided to a decanter. Poured deep red into glasses. 'A drink, to new friendships.'

How dry his throat; how fast his pulse. He struggled to keep his voice even, casual.

'Will we be friends?'

'We have so much in common already, and more to come.' She watched him over the rim as she sipped. 'You came because you wonder, and your life has few wonders now. You'll stay because you'll know, and you'll want.'

Her scent seemed to twine around him, made him think of everything dark and forbidden.

'What will I know? What will I want?'

'You'll know what I tell you. You'll then tell me what you want. Your choice to make.' But her eyes told him she knew that choice already. 'Shall we sit?'

She didn't sit on the throne chair, but moved to a curved settee, waited for him. And said, 'The Stars of Fortune.'

'You believe they exist.'

'I know they exist. The first, the Fire Star, was found only days ago, in an underwater cave in Corfu.'

His interest piqued, and some irritation with it. His network should have picked up that information. If true.

'You have it?'

Something dark, and far more terrible than beauty, slid in and out of her eyes. 'If I did, I'd have no need for you. I told you there are six who

92

stand in the way. They found the star, they have it, and – for now – it's beyond my reach. Now they hunt for the next, and I hunt for them. I ... underestimated their inventiveness. I won't do so a second time.'

Now he smiled, believing he held the advantage. 'You want my help.'

'Your skills, your thirst, combined with mine. Force alone proved inadequate. I require guile, and human ambitions.'

'Human?'

She said nothing to that, only sipped again of the wine that swam in his head like the heady scent of lilies.

'You know two of the six.'

'Do I?'

'Riley Gwin.'

'Ah, yes.' Even the sound of her name made his mouth thin. 'I know Dr. Gwin. A bright, resourceful woman.'

'She's more than that. Sawyer King. And I see you have no love for this one.'

'He has something I want, and haven't yet managed to take.'

'The compass. It can be yours. I have no use for it.'

Fascinated, Malmon leaned toward her. 'You know of it, what it's reputed to do?'

'He is the traveler, for now, able to shift through time, through space as long as he possesses the compass. You want that power.'

'I'll have it. It's simply a matter of time. One way or the other, I take what I want.'

'As do I. With these two are four others. None

of the six are only what they seem. If you choose to do what I ask of you, I'll show you what they are, what they have. And what they are, what they have can be yours. I only want the stars.'

The compass. He coveted the compass, and only more since he'd failed to ... acquire it.

But she clearly coveted the stars, so a bargain must be struck. 'If, as you say, the stars exist, nothing six people are or have can compare to their worth.'

'The guardians – these six – are not all I'd give you. The offer of money is too usual for you and me, Andre, though I can give you more than any man can hold. You can choose more wealth, but I think you'll make another choice.'

'What else is there?'

She lifted a hand, and in it rested a clear ball of glass.

'Parlor tricks?'

'Look and see.' Her voice whispered over his skin like ice. 'Look into the Globe of All, and see.'

'Something in the wine,' he murmured as clouds and water stirred and stirred inside the glass.

'Of course. Only to help you forget all of this should you choose to refuse me.' And, she thought, to make him – like his servant – susceptible to suggestion.

Hers, should he disappoint her, would be for him to return home, take the weapon he now had at the small of his back, put it into his mouth, and pull the trigger.

If he refused, he was of no use to her.

'Look and see,' she said again. 'See the six. Guardians of the stars. Enemies of Nerezza. See them, and what they are.'

He saw Riley standing under the light of a full moon, saw her transform into a wolf that threw back its head to howl before running into shadows.

He watched Sawyer, holding the compass, vanish in a golden light and reappear in another.

He saw a man hold lightning in his hands, a woman who spoke of visions and things yet to come. Another man run through with a sword who rose again, healed and whole.

And the woman, the beauty who dived into a night sea and rose up with a jeweled tail.

'You see the truth.' Nerezza spoke quietly, watching the dazed and dazzled look in his eyes. 'What they have, all and each, you can possess. Do with what you will. Think of hunting the she-wolf, the thrill of it. She has a pack, more hunting. Think of possessing the mermaid. Of owning the compass. Of harnessing the magician, the seer for your own purposes.

'Or destroying them. How it would thrill to destroy such creatures. Your choice. Enslave or destroy. And the immortal?'

She smiled when he looked at her again, when she saw what she'd known she would on his face. The greed for life.

'This could be yours.'

'Immortality.'

'A payment, if you choose. I can give this to you.'

'How? How can you give me immortality?'

'I am Nerezza.'

'Named for the goddess who cursed the three stars.'

She rose, lifted her arms. The candlelight swirled into walls of fire. Her voice was a thunder that dropped him to his knees.

'I am Nerezza. Goddess of the dark.'

The strange bird gave a cry, almost human, then swooped. Malmon felt a quick sting at his throat, but made no sound. He trembled with awe, with lust.

'Refuse me and leave, never to see again the wonders. Accept my task, and choose your payment. Wealth, power? Life eternal?'

'Life! Give me immortality.'

'Give me the stars, and it's yours.'

The fire died to candlelight; she sat. She held out a paper, and a silver quill. 'A contract, between us.'

His hands shook – fear, excitement – he'd forgotten what it was to *feel* so much. To calm himself, he drained the wine in the glass, then accepted the quill.

'It's written in Latin.'

'Yes. A dead language for immortality.'

He read Latin, as well as Greek, Arabic, Aramaic. But his heart thudded as he translated. He wanted more time. A night to think, to settle his nerves.

She rose, skimmed her hands down, and the gown spilled away, leaving her naked, magnificent.

Nerves smothered under lust.

'Once signed, we'll seal. It's been too long since I've had a man in my bed. A man worthy of it.'

He could take a goddess, have immortality, possess all the powers he'd seen inside the ball of glass.

96

He signed his name, and she hers. He watched those names bleed and burn into the parchment.

Then she took his hand. 'Come with me, and we will do all there is to do to each other, until the light comes.'

She took her fill of him, took with a voracious hunger he nearly matched. Because he pleased her, well enough, in bed, she knew she would use him there again.

When he slept, she smiled into the dark.

Men, of all worlds, of all natures, all species, were to her mind the simplest of creatures. They might spring to act, to violence more fiercely, more quickly than the female, but the female remained cannier and more clever.

And the male? Sex would always rule them. The offer of it, the act, the need.

She'd had only to offer this when he hesitated, and he had signed the contract, in his own blood. That blood now burned and bound him.

He belonged to her now. And when he helped her take the stars, when she granted him his choice of immortality, he would belong to her – as ever she wished – for eternity.

When Annika couldn't sleep, she crept downstairs. She saw the light under the door of the room where Sawyer slept, and yearned to go in. Just to sit and talk to him, or better, to lie with him in the bed, quiet and warm.

But she understood when doors were closed, those inside usually wanted alone.

She slipped outside to stand and look out over the flowers, the steep road where the singing

97

woman had pushed her baby in the stroller, and out to the sea.

Here and there on the slope down, and along the land below, lights twinkled against the dark. Faintly, very faintly, she heard music and wondered if someone danced.

Overhead, over the indigo sea, the moon turned toward its dark time. When she'd been a child, her mother had told her how the sky faeries nibbled away at the light of the moon until they were full, then breathed the light back. And so the moon turned.

A pretty story, she thought now, for a young one, to ease fears. She thought of her family – did they sleep? She knew she'd brought them pride when she'd been chosen for the quest. They believed in her, trusted her to succeed.

So she could not, would not fail.

Her mother would understand the dreaming part, the longing part, the loving, and would offer comfort when Annika returned home. But she wouldn't weep long, Annika promised herself. She would have done what she was meant to do, preserve the stars, return them to the Island of Glass. And she would have had this time with her friends who were her family in this world.

She would have her memories of them, of Sawyer, who was and would be her only love.

But she could wish – wishes that caused no harm were never wrong. So she picked out the brightest star, and made one.

Before her duty was done, before she returned home forever, she would know Sawyer's love, and he would know hers. And from love would come joy for both.

The wish slipped quietly into her heart and eased it. When it eased, she heard the sighs. Far-off, like the music. Hardly more than a breath on the air, yet it tingled along her skin.

She stepped forward, as if to move toward that whisper of sound. And heard another.

A footstep, a rustle in the shadows. She pivoted toward the sound, braced to fight.

'Relax, Gorgeous. It's Doyle.'

'Oh.' She straightened from her crouch, loosened her fists. 'I thought you slept.'

'Just taking a last circuit around the place.'

She heard the sharp slither of his sword homing itself in its sheath before he stepped into the light.

'Can't sleep?' he asked as he walked up the steps toward her.

'Not yet. Did you hear? Did you hear the sighs?'

'No.' His eyes sharpened like his sword on her face. 'When?'

'Just now, just a moment ago. Like when a breeze stirs leaves, but not. Not that. From the water, but ... I don't know.'

'Everything means something.' He laid a hand on her shoulder. 'I'd wager you'll hear them again.'

Then he looked up as a door opened above. Annika looked up with him when she heard voices – Sasha and Bran.

'I just need some air.'

Concerned, Annika stepped forward until she saw Sasha leaning on the rail of the terrace, Bran's hands on her shoulders.

'Sasha. You're sick?'

'No. No, I'm not sick.'

'She had a dream,' Bran said. 'A hard one. And one everyone should hear. Since most of us are up, you should wake the others. We'll come down when she's steady.'

'I'll get Sawyer.'

She ran inside, straight to his bedroom door. In her haste she forgot to knock, but burst straight in.

He sat in the middle of the bed, legs folded, maps spread out, and books, with the compass in his hand.

'What!' In one fast move, he rolled off the bed, grabbing the gun on the table as he sprang to his feet. 'Nerezza.'

'No, no. Sasha. She had a dream. Bran says we need to hear.'

'Christ.' He rubbed his free hand over his face, carefully set the gun down. 'Okay.'

'Were you swimming? I would swim with you.'

'Swimming? No, I've been working on something.'

'Why are you wearing the suit for swimming?'

He looked down at his boxers, had a moment of ridiculous and acute embarrassment. 'They're not – they're something else. Give me a minute, and I'll come out. Ah, remember how to make tea?'

'The sun tea. But it's night.'

'No, the hot tea.'

'Yes! With the water boiled in the kettle.'

'Why don't you go make tea? I bet Sasha could use some.'

'I'll make it right now.'

She hurried away, leaving his door open. He shut

100

it, heaved out a breath. First she'd shoved his heart into his throat, running in so he'd thought Nerezza and her hounds of hell had attacked.

Then she'd plopped his heart at his feet, the way she stood in the filtered moonlight in filmy, flowing white.

He should've told her to put on something else, he thought as he grabbed jeans. Like four or five layers of anything else. But he doubted anything she wore would stop what she stirred inside him.

Just too late now, he decided, pulled on a shirt, and went to make sure she didn't burn the house down making tea.

She had it under control, and Doyle leaned against the end of the table watching her.

It irked him – an itch under the skin – the way Doyle watched her.

It irked to be called away from work, especially since he'd just decided to call it a night and get some sleep. Now they'd have another powwow, with Annika walking around in that white thing that showed every line and curve.

Then Riley came in, looking several degrees more irked than he was. For some twisted reason, that smoothed him out again.

'I was asleep for exactly three minutes before the Black Knight beats on my door. Where's the coffee?'

'I'm making tea,' Annika said, ever cheerful.

'Tea's for sickbeds and your aunt's parlor. Black coffee or booze is for meetings after midnight.'

'I'll have coffee,' Doyle said.

'I guess neither of you wants to sleep once we're done.'

Riley flicked Sawyer a glance as she grabbed two mugs. 'If coffee keeps you awake, you don't know how to sleep.'

The annoyance on her face faded as Sasha came in with Bran. 'Hey. You okay?'

'Yes, yes. I'm sorry to drag everybody up, but I – we – think it's important.'

'Only Riley was sleeping.' Annika carefully poured the boiling water into the teapot. 'Sawyer was working, and Doyle and I were outside.'

'You and Doyle. What were you doing?' Sawyer demanded before he could stop himself.

'Having a conversation,' Doyle said easily, then pulled out a chair at the table.

'You should sit down,' he told Sasha.

'I think I will, thanks. It was intense.'

'If you dreamed about diving without tanks again, I'm putting a tether on you.' Riley walked over. Slapped a mug in front of Doyle, sat with her own.

'Nothing like that.'

Annika brought cups, the pot, the little strainer for the leaves. 'It has to... It's not step.'

'Steep,' Sawyer supplied.

'Steep. Then I'll pour it for you.'

'Thanks, Anni. All right.' Sasha took a breath. 'There was a room, lit by what seemed like hundreds of candles. The furniture struck me as antiques, wealthy, and European. Except for the chair. Nerezza's chair – that thronelike chair I saw her sitting in, in the cave.'

'But it wasn't the cave,' Riley prompted.

'No. No, I'm sure it wasn't. There were windows – elaborate window treatments – I could see some

102

sort of garden, mostly in shadows, outside the windows. Trees. She sat in the chair, and a strange blackbird perched on the arm. Not like one of the things that attacked us. Smaller, but something lethal about it. Eyes more like a lizard than a bird. And there was a man – he seemed human. Late thirties, early forties, I'd guess. Attractive, in a dark suit.'

Pausing, she pushed back her hair, tumbled from sleep. 'She got up, poured something into wineglasses, but I know it wasn't wine. Even in the dream I could smell it – blood and smoke, and something cloying. But he drank.'

She shuddered. Annika jumped up immediately, poured the water through the little strainer. 'You need tea.'

'I'm still cold. I can still smell whatever she gave him.' Grateful, Sasha picked up the cup, warmed her hands. 'I couldn't hear what they said – it was like insects buzzing. But she showed him the Globe of All, and I could see each of us in it, as clearly as I see all of you now. Riley turning into the wolf under the full moon, Annika with the mermaid tail sparkling in the sun. Bran, lightning in his hands, Doyle coming back from the dead, Sawyer with the compass. Myself, dream-walking. She knows all of it, and now he knows. Fear was like a hand squeezing my throat. Flames rose up, everywhere around them. I could see through the fire, see them, but there was no heat from it. It burned so cold. I wanted to get out, away. I couldn't get out. The bird screamed, and flew across to them. It raked its beak over the man's throat.'

103

Sasha lifted her fingers, traced a line down the side of her throat.

'He barely blinked. He just stared at her, at Nerezza. I could feel his lust, his greed. Even when she took a snake, a silver snake, and held it to the wound, he didn't move.'

'Entranced,' Bran said.

'It seemed so. It drank the blood. Hissing, coiling around her finger, it drank the blood. He took it from her, used it like a pen, pressing its head, its fangs onto a kind of parchment.'

To steady herself, she drank tea. 'She stood up, and her clothes fell away. His lust was huge. I know he signed his name – I couldn't see what he wrote, but I know. And what he signed burned into the parchment, oozed blood, spewed smoke. The blood went black like the smoke; the smoke red like the blood. Then...'

She closed her eyes a moment, carefully drank tea. 'Then, the smoke coiled up like the snake, and it slid, slithered into the wound on his throat. He made a horrible sound, and his body convulsed and twisted – impossibly – and the room shook, so violently that I fell. But he only sat there.

'She leaned toward him, licked the blood from his throat. The wound closed – left a scar, but closed. And closed in whatever had gone into him. She has a mark here.' Sasha laid a hand on her heart. 'A symbol in dark red. A bat with the head of a snake. I swear it moved when she led him out of the room, spreading its wings. The bird swooped over me, screamed my name, dived down. And I woke up.'

Riley reached over to grip her hand. 'I'd say you

could use something stronger than tea.'

'No, this is working. She didn't know I could see – I'm sure of that. She was so intent on him, on what she wanted from him, on what she intended to do to him, she didn't sense me at all. And the man, he was completely in thrall – exactly as the term means.'

'Why a man?' Sawyer wondered. 'A human?'

Once again Sasha shuddered. 'I don't think he was just a man when she'd finished with him.'

'There's that.' Sawyer nodded. 'Obviously they made some sort of deal. Contract?'

'She showed him who and what we are,' Doyle pointed out. 'A man, whatever else he might be, can travel unremarked. A spy?'

'Or another kind of weapon.' Bran ran a hand down Sasha's arm, added more tea to her cup. 'As Sasha predicted.'

'She did evil to him,' Annika murmured. 'If he's innocent, we have to help him. Can you find a way to undo what she did to him?'

'I can't say,' Bran told her. 'I can't be sure what she used on him.'

'First thing would be to try to figure out who he is. You'd recognize him if you saw him again,' Sawyer said to Sasha.

'Absolutely.'

'Can you draw him?' Riley asked. 'If you can do a solid sketch, I can tug some lines. I've got a contact or two who could run face recognition. We could get lucky.'

'I can draw him, the bird, the room, all of it. Believe me, it's imprinted.'

'I'll get your sketchbook.'

When Sawyer started to get up, Bran waved a hand. Sasha's sketchbook and pencils appeared on the table.

'Saves time.'

'Yeah, it does.' Sawyer sat again.

'He looked successful, sophisticated.' Steadier now, Sasha began to sketch. '*Innocent* isn't the word that comes to mind, though Annika has a strong point. About six feet, I'd say, athletic build. Not like Doyle, but fit. Even before he drank, there was an edge about him, a calculation, a hard look in his eyes.'

Strong cheekbones, straight jaw, a narrow blade of nose, a sharply defined mouth. A rich wave of hair.

Even before she'd finished, Riley looked up from the sketch, met Sawyer's eyes. Saw the same recognition.

'Fucking Malmon,' she said.

'Andre fucking Malmon, and he's no innocent bystander.' Sawyer pushed to his feet.

He remembered, too well, the near miss in Morocco. If he hadn't been quick enough, he'd be dead, his throat slit ear to ear.

'How the hell did she hit on him? On Malmon?'

Though Riley shrugged, her gaze went hard. 'Like calls to like.'

'You're sure?' Doyle demanded.

'Dead sure. Screw coffee. Get us a beer, Sawyer. Malmon hooked up with the queen of the damned. Yeah, she forged a weapon, as prophesied.'

'Whatever she made him, I don't see how it can be much worse than the original.' Sawyer set beers on the table.

'But he was human–' Annika began.

'Depends on your definition.' Riley grabbed a beer. 'He's cold-blooded as a snake, kills for sport and profit, steals for the hell of it. And he hunts any kind of game there is. Including human.'

'I thought that was urban legend.'

Riley shook her head at Sawyer. 'Don't count on it. My intel is, every three years he holds a tournament. His own Most Dangerous Game. People cruel enough, bored enough, rich enough, pay him five mil to hunt for a week on some island he has off the coast of Africa. A dozen people as prey. At the end of the week, the one with the most kills gets a trophy. A freaking trophy.'

'But this isn't ... human.'

'That's right.' In agreement, Riley lifted her beer toward Annika. 'So let's not worry about helping him out of his contract. He'll come for us, and he's smart, he's skilled. He won't come alone.'

'He has his own team of mercenaries,' Sawyer confirmed. 'The kind who'd gut a baby for pay. Sorry,' he said immediately when Annika gasped. 'We all need to know what's coming.'

'He's got mercs. We've got more.' Doyle opted for a beer after all. 'We took out what she threw at us on Corfu. We'll take out what comes now.'

'But...' Sasha set down her pencil, picked it up again. 'It's different, isn't it? We killed creatures, things she'd created, unnatural things. We're talking about people.'

'You're going to have to get over that. An enemy's an enemy.'

'Doyle's right.' Bran laid a hand over Sasha's.

'We have no choice in this. He knows what Riley is, and Annika. He wouldn't kill them, not at first, it seems to me.'

'Sold to the highest bidder.' Voice sharp, Riley took a long drink. 'Same with Doyle, most likely. Think of the hours of fun he'd have with someone who can't die. That's a sadist's dream date.'

'I don't understand,' Annika began, but Sasha stood.

'Dark called to dark, and it answered. Promises given, taken, in blood. What she made him gives him more, and gives her more. He is her creature now, the man and the beast. The hunt begins and ends with human blood. Black magicks drink, white magicks burn. Between, the star waits to gather and light in the hands of the pure. Through the battle and the pain, through the water, of the water. Courage, sons and daughters, though the snake strikes. Risk all for all, and prevail.'

Sasha sat again, caught her breath. 'Wow.'

'I'll say. Want that something stronger now?' Riley asked her.

'No, that was strong enough.'

'Seems like the seer has spoken.' Riley lifted her beer again. 'Buck up, team. Bran's going to make us some fire, and we're going to burn Nerezza's ass again, and that bastard Malmon's while we're at it.'

'Then I'd suggest everyone get some sleep.' Doyle stood up. 'We start combat training at dawn. It may take him a few days to select his own team, to get here and set up, to come at us. We'll bloody well be ready.'

CHAPTER FIVE

Annika didn't like the new training. It held a meanness, like the guns. Striking each other, throwing each other to the ground. How to slash or stab someone with a knife.

She wanted to say no, as she had with the gun, no, she would not.

But she knew she must. Bran couldn't make her a magick weapon for this.

She didn't like seeing Doyle sweep Sasha's legs out from under her so she fell, or Riley kicking so hard toward Bran's belly. Her friends slashed at each other with knives, and though Bran had charmed them so they couldn't harm flesh, it made her hurt inside.

To avoid most of it, she danced, tumbled, flipped out of the way rather than on the attack. When she couldn't avoid, she held back, afraid to hurt those she loved.

'Come on, Annika. You're faster than that.' Feet planted, Doyle tapped a fist on his hard chest. 'Come at me, come hard.'

Hoping to satisfy him, she started forward, did a handspring, started a flip, but he caught her foot, used momentum to push her up and back. She barely had time to adjust and land on her feet.

'Hey, take it easy.' Sawyer broke off sparring with Riley, took a punch in the belly for his trouble. 'Hey, you, too.'

'Love tap,' she claimed.

'Good thing we're not in love.' He started toward Doyle. 'Ease up a little.'

'Easing up gets you hurt. She's easing up, and that's the problem. You're holding back, Gorgeous. Truth.'

On a pleading look, she lifted her hands. 'I don't want to hurt my friends.'

'Holding back's what's going to hurt your friends. Go with me,' he murmured to Sawyer. Fast, smooth, he had Sawyer in a grip, and a knife to his throat. 'How do you keep me from cutting his throat?'

'The knife can't hurt him.' Though she didn't like it there. 'Bran fixed it.'

'Got you there, friend.'

Unamused, Doyle grunted, flipped the knife point-first into the grass. In an instant he had Sawyer in a choke hold.

'Hey!'

'Play along.'

'Play my– Fuck,' he managed as his windpipe seemed to narrow.

'What if I just snap his neck?' The muscles in Doyle's arms rippled as he applied pressure. 'The right grip, the right pressure, it's done. Quick and quiet. What do you do?'

'You won't hurt him.'

'Just a little more pressure.'

When Sawyer began to wheeze and struggle, Annika's eyes widened. 'Stop.'

'Make me. Stop me. He could be dead any second.'

'I said stop!' Lifting a fist, Annika shot out light,

110

struck Doyle's choking arm, his throat. She sprang forward an instant before Doyle released Sawyer.

Sawyer coughed out a couple breaths, bent over to rest his hands on his thighs.

'It didn't hurt you because you're not evil.'

'Gave me a buzz,' Doyle told her. 'And if I'd have been a bad guy, I'd be down for the count. That's how it's done. You okay, kid?'

Sawyer gulped in another breath, nodded. Then straightening, came back hard with an elbow into Doyle's gut.

Now Doyle coughed out a breath. 'Good one.'

'You earned it, old man.'

'We're hurting each other.' When tears trembled in Annika's eyes, Doyle stepped back.

'All yours.'

'Okay, listen.' Sawyer swung an arm around Annika's shoulders, turned her around. 'Let's walk a little.'

'Doyle hurt you. You hurt Doyle. Sasha said Riley broke her butt.'

Not the time to laugh, Sawyer warned himself. 'It's an expression. But yeah, we're going to hurt each other a little. Some bumps and bruises, and some bruises on the pride, too. But, Anni, what comes at us won't have knives that won't cut, won't pull punches. They could be worse than what she sent before because they're human. They can think and plan instead of just act. They'll kill me – I'm expendable. I don't have value.'

'No, no, you–'

'To them, I am. Probably Sasha, too. Bran if they can manage it. And they'll take you and Doyle and Riley. That's worse, what they'll do to you is worse.'

She stopped, turned to face him, to read his eyes. 'They'll kill you?'

'They'll try.'

'And Sasha?'

'Odds are – kill or capture. And for us, one's the same as the other. We have to survive.'

'It's our duty.'

'That's right, and we have to protect each other. That's more than duty. I'll take the bumps and bruises now. Doyle's tough, but he's right.'

'Do you want to kill people? To take their lives?'

'Absolutely not. But to save you, us, myself, the stars? I won't hesitate.'

'Then I'll hurt you.'

On a laugh, he cupped her face in his hands, pressed his lips to her forehead.

She simply flowed toward him, all but melted against him, surrounding him with her scent – both sweet and mysterious at once. He had only to shift, only to change the angle of his head for his mouth to meet hers.

And that shift, that change of angle would change everything else.

'Okay. Well.' He gave her a quick rub on the arms, stepped back. Tried not to look too long into those dreamy sea-green eyes. 'Let's see if you can hurt me before Doyle calls it for breakfast.'

They spent another day on and in the water, found nothing that pointed them toward the star. But there was gelato on the way home, and Annika considered that the happiest part of the day.

When they reached the house, the men wan-

112

dered off into the grove. Annika thought nothing of it as she set out another jug of sun tea, but Riley, apparently, thought plenty.

Wearing her orange Chucks, a Grateful Dead T-shirt over baggy cargoes – and a suspicious expression – she stood, hands on hips. 'Man talk.'

'I think they went to shoot the targets.'

'I don't think so.' Riley turned as Sasha stepped out with her sketchbook and a large pitcher of sparkling pink.

'I tried my hand at this juice drink – raspberry and lemon with sparkling water. I think it's pretty good.'

'We'll be the judge.'

'Where's everyone else?' Sasha asked as Riley poured the juice over a tall glass of ice.

'Exactly. The everybody else with a penis went off into the grove. I smell man meeting.'

'They can have it. I'm hot, tired, and parched.' But as she sat under the pergola, Sasha frowned toward the grove. 'What could they be meeting about?'

'Strategy. Protecting the womenfolk from the Nerezza-Malmon duo.'

'That's insulting.'

'You bet. This is pretty good.'

'I like it very much,' Annika added as she sampled her own glass. 'We can have a woman meeting. We protect, too.'

'Damn skippy.'

'Who is Skippy? Why are you mad at him?'

'It's an expression. Like bet your ass.'

'People are always betting their asses. Language is fun.' Because of the shade, Annika took off the glasses that dimmed the glare of the sun. 'But I think the men worry because I won't use the gun, and Sasha has to practice fighting.'

'I call bullshit.' Scowling now, Riley aimed her displeasure toward the grove. 'You've both proven yourselves, and more than once.'

'I agree with that,' Sasha said, 'but Annika's right, too. I'm not as quick or as strong as the rest of you. I'm better, and I'll get better yet. And, Annika, you're plenty quick and strong. The bracelets more than make up for a gun.'

'Damn skippy.' Annika grinned as she tried out the expression. 'In the water, I'm the best, and we can use that. Riley shoots the gun very, very well, and she's fast in a fight. Sasha is better with the crossbow than even Doyle, and she sees so much of what we need to know. We've been chosen because of what we are, what we can do. What we will do.'

'We're not a team if we're in two camps,' Sasha pointed out. 'The men, the women.'

'It's natural for men to worry about the women in their family. We're family.'

Riley drummed her fingers on the table. 'Go ahead, Anni, be logical.'

'We worry, too,' Annika added. 'I would do all I could to protect them, and you, and so I have to hurt you when we practice. When we were attacked in the water in Corfu, the first time, I wasn't ready. I was too happy to be in the sea. But since I listen, I watch. I protect.'

Sasha reached out, laid a hand on Annika's. 'You saved me.'

'In the last battle, you went to the high cliff with

114

Bran, because you knew he would need you. We all needed you. And in the full moon, when Riley changed, she came to fight with us as the wolf. With no weapons but fang and claw. They know this, all this. But men will worry about their women.'

'You're more tolerant than me.' But Riley shrugged. 'I'll give them space until they take too much of it.'

'We have more. You're the smartest.'

'You're starting to improve my mood, Anni.'

'Sawyer is so clever, and Doyle has lived so long, has much experience. Bran is smart, and he has magick. But your brain is the biggest. You find things out. Dig them out.'

'I haven't dug up anything on the sighs and songs yet, but I'm working on it.'

'You will find it, or Sasha will dream it. And we'll know.' It wasn't simplicity or innocence in Annika's words, her tone. It was faith.

'Knowledge is a power and a weapon, and you give us knowledge. The men understand all of this. Still ... Sawyer protected me when I wouldn't learn how to shoot the gun. Doyle didn't try to force me, and Bran made me these.'

She lifted her hands so the copper gleamed in the dappled sunlight. 'He knew I would fight better, be stronger with these. When you were the wolf, Sawyer made you a fire on a rainy night. This is kindness and care. Doyle knocks Sasha down so she'll get up again, but he doesn't knock her down as hard as he knocks Riley. Because Riley's stronger.'

'And meaner.'

'In a fight?'

Again Riley shrugged, but she grinned with it. 'I can be all-around mean when I need to.' Then sat back with her sparkling juice. 'I never thought to have a mermaid explain men to me.'

'Is it wrong?'

'No. You hit all the right spots. Like I said, you're more tolerant, but I can't argue any of your points. Especially since I have the biggest brain.'

'And maybe I was wrong,' Sasha considered. 'Maybe it's good to separate now and then. We get the female perspective, they get the male. Then we bring both to the team.'

'Can I ask a question about men, but not about battle?'

'Of course.'

'How did you get Bran to kiss you, the first time?'

'Unintentionally, I guess. We were both a little angry.'

'So to get Sawyer to kiss me, we should be angry.'

Out of the corner of her eye, Sasha saw Riley's eyebrows lift into her long fringe of bangs. 'Not necessarily. Everyone's different. You have feelings for Sawyer.'

'He fills me with feelings.'

'So make your move,' Riley said. 'Can't the female make the first move in your world? Kiss first?' she added for clarity.

'Oh, yes. It would be silly not to be able to kiss the male you want, if he's willing.'

'If I'm any judge, Sawyer would be willing.'

'But I can't. I'm not permitted to kiss a land

116

person the first time. He must want me, show me. He must choose.'

'Why is that?'

'Our females have the power to lure men – humans. To seduce so the choice isn't a choice for them. Long ago, and not so long ago, some of my kind lured men, sailors and explorers.'

'Sirens.'

'Yes. The song of the siren is beautiful and powerful, but it can be dangerous to the human she calls. We take an oath not to use the song, and never to first kiss a man if we're granted legs. An oath is sacred. I wouldn't be worthy of this quest if I broke the quest because I want to kiss Sawyer.'

With her heart in her eyes, she looked toward the lemon grove. 'But I do, very much.'

'Hamstrung.' Riley looked at Sasha. 'Personally I don't think he's going to be able to hold out for much longer.'

'I think it's honor holding him back. He doesn't want to take advantage of you, Annika.'

'How could he take advantage? If I didn't want him to kiss me, I would say no.'

'It's not always that black-and-white for ... land people,' Sasha told her. 'It doesn't take a seer to know he'd very much like to kiss you.'

'You believe that?' Annika's eyes sparkled like the drink as she looked at Riley. 'Do you?'

'Damn skippy.'

On a laugh, Annika pressed her hands together. 'I'm so happy I talked to you. This is hopeful.'

'You can't ask him to kiss you?' Riley said.

'No. It's forbidden until after the first time.

117

After the choice.'

'Can you ask why he doesn't kiss you?'

Annika started to speak, then frowned. 'It's different to ask why not. It's … conversation, and seeking answers. Not asking for an act. No one told me it's not permitted to ask a human why not. Only not to ask them to.'

Laughing again, she grabbed Riley's hands. 'This is so smart!'

'Big brain, and some experience with human males.'

'I should go ask right now.'

'I wouldn't.' Quickly Sasha reached over, joined her hands with Annika's and Riley's. 'I think it's best to wait until it's just the two of you. Until you're alone. Asking him in front of the men? He'd feel awkward.'

'Oh. I'll do as you say. You've helped so much.'

'Girl power. The other part of that,' Riley continued, 'is you tell us what happens after you ask why not.'

'It's good to talk to females. Males must feel it's good to talk to males.'

'You won that argument. And here they come now.'

Riley thought Sasha had been right. You didn't need the sight to know Sawyer had a case for their mermaid. Sunglasses didn't disguise the fact that his gaze went straight to Annika, lingered there before he put on his affable smile, sauntered across the lawn to the table.

'That looks good.'

'Then it's lucky I made a large pitcher – and brought enough glasses out for everyone. Before

I knew you three were having a summit in the grove.'

Bran walked behind Sasha's chair, ran a hand down her hair. 'We did some calculations on the best positions for the light potion when it's fully cured. The first of it should be ready after sundown.'

He sat beside her, lifted the pitcher. 'What have we here?'

'A kind of raspberry lemonade.'

'I'll get a beer.' Noting the glint in Sasha's eyes, Doyle hesitated. 'Or not. You pissed, Blondie?'

'I might have been. Riley would have been. But fortunately all around Annika made some salient points about the male of this species and many others – and their instincts to protect their women. Even when the women are capable. And that men sometimes require or desire the company of men. Otherwise, we wouldn't be in such amiable moods.'

'Appreciate it, Gorgeous.' Doyle dumped some of the sparkling juice into a glass.

'I said what I did because I believe you respect us. If I believed you didn't respect us, I would be angry.'

'Not only respect. Depend on. And love.' Bran took Sasha's hand, brought it to his lips. When he lowered it, Sasha held a rose, yellow as sunlight. Bran smiled at Annika's audible sigh. 'With love comes concern.'

'I don't see you kissing our hands, Irish.'

Now Bran laughed, gestured to Riley. 'Give it over.'

'Maybe later.'

'Meanwhile, I think I've worked out how to fulfill Doyle's suggestion for the weapons. For that, I could use your help, *fáidh.*'

'Then you'll have it.'

'Once it's ready to test, I'll need everyone.'

'For magicks?' Annika asked.

'For magicks.'

With a flick of his fingers, Bran produced a rose as pink as candy, another as white as ice. Offered the pink to Annika, who beamed over it. The white to Riley.

'And while we scouted out the grove, and the areas beyond for placing the light bombs, Sawyer had a thought.'

'You had a thought?' Riley smirked at him.

'It happens once or twice a year. We're talking defense, offense, strategy, holding our ground against attacks. And I figure we're going to be dealing with Malmon now, too, and his mercs. The human element. As a fellow human, if I wanted to storm the castle, I wouldn't come at it from below. I'd... Can I?'

When he reached for the sketch pad, Sasha nudged it toward him.

'So we're here. Grove here, road there,' he said as he drew a rough map. 'Closest neighbors here, here. Bad strategy to send troops up from the road. Maybe a few as a distraction, but it's wasting men and effort. You come from the flanks, but the real vulnerability is west and above. The ground keeps rising. Rough terrain, mountainous. They couldn't come fast, but–'

'Long-range weaponry,' Riley put in, got a nod. She rose, walked back from the pergola, looked up. 'Some pretty decent cover. We'd have our own cover in the grove, and with the house itself to some extent, but a good sniper – and he only uses good – could pick us off.'

'He doesn't want us dead,' Sasha began. 'Or not all of us.'

'Tranquilizers.' With her hands in her pockets, Riley continued to scan. 'He knows what we are, knows he can't kill Doyle anyway. And he'd want me and Annika alive. We're worth a lot more to him alive and captured. Bran, Sasha, maybe he'd be curious enough to want them alive and incapacitated, but Sawyer? All he wants is the compass. Shooting you in the head's the easy path there.'

'Don't say it,' Annika murmured.

'Sorry, but he's already tried to kill Sawyer once. He'll try again.'

'For all the good it'd do him. He kills me, he still won't have the compass. You can't just take it,' Sawyer explained. 'It has to be given. You know, presented. Otherwise, it'll just go back to my grandfather.'

'Hmm.' Riley walked back to the table. 'Does he know that?'

'He should, but he was pissed off enough in Morocco to send an assassin. Could be he hasn't dug deep enough to know how it all works.'

'Yeah, Malmon and his anger issues. What's the plan?'

'We'll need to scout out the area before Malmon gets here. I don't guess your contact's gotten back to you on that.'

'Not yet, but she will,' Riley assured Sawyer.

121

'Doyle knows the terrain.'

Riley raised her brows at Doyle. 'It's been a couple hundred years. Is your memory that good?'

'It's good enough. Since it is, we'll be heading up tomorrow instead of out to sea. We can't find the star if we're dead or in a cage.'

'Can't argue. And once we're up there – more climbing than hiking – and figure out what would be their best vantage points?'

'We set traps.'

Riley shot a finger at Sawyer. 'Now you're talking.'

'We can't use the light bombs,' Bran pointed out. 'We can't risk an adventurous tourist or a local setting one off, being burned.'

'My bracelets wouldn't hurt them.'

Bran nodded at Annika. 'Exactly so. So I have to conjure something similar, something that will harm only evil or one with evil intent. I've some ideas on it.'

'Then you should be relieved of household chores this evening.'

'I'll do Bran's tasks,' Annika said.

'Thanks for that. I'll need Sasha's help, and I believe she's down for head chef tonight.'

'I'll cover it.' Sawyer shrugged. 'No big.'

'Then we'll get started.'

'The rest of us will get in some training in the grove,' Doyle said as Bran and Sasha rose.

'I was afraid you'd say that.'

Doyle glanced at Sawyer. 'An hour, then there'll be beer.'

Though Annika didn't like beer, she trained for

the hour. She didn't like the bruises Doyle gave her when he showed her how to defend against what he called holds and grips.

He reminded her she'd like a cage much less.

She liked wine and helping Sawyer make dinner, so enjoyed both. She got to make something he called bruschetta – cutting the long bread in half, toasting it – while he cooked chicken for the dish he called alfredo.

'Remember how to mince?'

'Cut up, very, very small.'

'Very small, those Roma tomatoes and that garlic.'

She applied herself to it, imagining how nice it would be to cook with him like this without the bruises from training or the thoughts of fighting ahead.

'The chicken smells so good.'

'It'll taste even better with the fettuccini alfredo. Good job. Now the basil I cut from the herb garden? You need to slice that, really thin, but slice, not chop. Right?'

'I know what's slice, what's chop. If I lived on the land, I'd have a garden of flowers and herbs and the vegetables, too. I'd sit in it every day and drink wine.'

'Sweet deal.'

He showed her what else to do, with a little wine, the oil, the vinegar, with cheese and with pepper and salt.

'That's just going to sit awhile,' he told her while he made a sauce in a pan. 'So the flavors mix together.'

She liked the way he looked as he stirred things

– his body relaxed, his hair catching light from the sun as it came through the windows.

'In the house on land, I'd have a big kitchen like this, with the windows for sun, the big, shiny box for cold things, and all the pretty dishes.'

'A big-ass pantry.'

'Big-ass pantry,' she repeated.

'A long, wide peninsula, doubles as a breakfast counter.'

'A peninsula is a land mass with three sides in the water.'

'Points for you.' Playfully, he shot a finger at her. 'In the kitchen it's a kind of counter. For food prep, and for people to sit, eat casual, or keep you company while you cook.'

'So you're not lonely. Do you have this kitchen?'

'Me? No. My folks have a nice kitchen, and my grandparents? It's a mix of old-fashioned and practical updates. But we're building a dream kitchen here, from scratch.'

The idea of dreaming with him sang in her heart. 'What color is it?'

'What's your favorite?'

'Oh, there are too many for one to be the best.'

'Then we'll go with green, like your eyes. Stainless steel appliances, commercial-grade six-burner gas range. Maybe dark gray for the cabinets.'

'Your eyes are gray. I like gray.'

'A lot of open or glass fronts on them – for those pretty dishes of yours. Walk-in pantry, farm sink, big windows. South facing so you can have your herbs in pots through the winter. Good start,' he said as he filled a pot with water.

'Can it be near the sea?'

124

'Hey, dream kitchen, remember? The world's your oyster.'

'Oysters are very small,' she began, then understood. 'An expression.'

'You got it. It means you can have anything you want.'

'I'd want the dream kitchen in a house near the sea. And we would cook in it together every night.'

He looked over then, and she *felt* him start to speak. But Riley came rushing in.

'Malmon's in London.' She grabbed a glass, poured wine. 'My contact says he's been seen going and coming from this house in Hyde Park, one that belongs to this rich dude and his third wife. And they haven't been seen for a couple days. More? Malmon's butler hanged himself. Police investigated – no foul play, straight suicide.'

'Why the butler?' Sawyer wondered.

'Can't say, but no signs of drugs, struggle, force. Word is, Malmon's making arrangements to rent a villa in Capri, and tapping some of his mercs for the trip.'

'They know where we are, but with him still in London, putting it together, we've got some time yet.'

'Nerezza knows,' Annika pointed out. 'She must know if this Malmon does. She could come sooner.'

'We'll be ready,' Sawyer assured her. 'And as far as ready, dinner nearly is.'

'Riley is to set the table.'

'What? Oh, right.'

'I'm making brush-etta.'

'Bruschetta,' Sawyer corrected.

125

Annika mouthed the correct pronunciation as Riley grabbed dishes.

As they ate together, all six, and planned, Annika kept an eye on the sky. Nerezza would send her creatures through the sky.

Later, she stepped out front and watched the sea. When Sawyer came out, she let herself lean against him.

'You should try to get some sleep. I really think we've got a couple days yet.'

'Why do you think that?'

'I think she'll use Malmon first, see what he can do, if he can cause some damage. We hurt her last time, and she won't forget that. And she failed, so it figures she'll try something else. Malmon's the something else.'

'You can't let him hurt you.'

'Don't intend to. What else?'

'I like to hike. Tomorrow we'll walk in the hills, but ... we won't go into the sea. In Corfu, I could go down to it late at night or very early in the day. Now it's too far.'

'I can take you down.' He drew out his compass.

'You would?'

'Sure. You can get in a quick swim, then you need to sleep. Tomorrow's going to be a hot, hard climb. The pool's going to have to do after that. Go ahead, get your suit.'

When she smiled, sliding her gaze up to him under her lashes, he nodded.

'Okay, I get it. That kind of swim. Well, it should be late enough for it.'

'I don't change the legs until I'm in the water

126

and away from the shore.'

'All right. Ready?' he asked and took her hand.

'Oh, yes.'

She held tight as they flew.

CHAPTER SIX

With her hand still in Sawyer's, Annika found herself on a little pebbled beach. Sheltered by rocks and cliff walls and lit by only the light of the waning moon, it struck her as both romantic and beautiful.

'Oh! This is so nice. It's like closing the door to the room. Private.'

'I scouted around a little, in case you needed a spot.'

How could she not love him? How could she not give her heart to such a heart?

'You're kind. Kindness is a strength, so you're very strong. You'll swim with me.'

'I'll keep watch.'

'You said we had time before they come.'

'Yeah.'

'So you can swim.' She took his hands, drew him closer to the water. She would never use the siren's song to lure him, but her eyes seduced. 'It will help you sleep, too.'

'I don't have any trunks.'

'You have the something else? Under your pants. If you're shy.'

If that didn't make him feel like an idiot, nothing would. 'Yeah, I've got them.' He pulled a chain out of the compass, locked it around his neck before he pulled off his T-shirt.

Annika simply slithered out of the dress, stood naked in the silvered light.

'*Blin!* You could warn a guy.'

'What is that word? *Blin?*' she asked, and picked up the dress, tossed it over a rock.

'It's...' Where did he look? Where did he look? Well, Jesus, he was a man. He looked at her. 'Russian, something you say when you're surprised.'

'I like being *blin.*' She ran into the sea, vanished under the dark, frothing waves.

He'd just stay on shore – that was smarter, safer. But her head rose up, above the waves. 'Come swim with me! It's wonderful.'

He hoped it was cool, he decided as he pulled off his jeans, toed off his sneakers. He could use cool after that long hot look at her, pale and perfect gold in the moonlight.

He waded in, nearly to his waist, got a jolt when he felt something wrap around his legs. When she tugged – he realized quickly she'd coiled her tail around him – he went under.

He couldn't resist stroking a hand over the sleek curl of it. Then she used it to propel him to the surface, rose up beside him.

'Now you're wet all over.'

'You, too.'

She did a slow roll so that gorgeous, glimmering tail shimmered up into the light, slid under the surface again.

'We can swim as far as you like,' she told him. 'I can bring you back to the land.' When he tapped the compass, she nodded. 'Yes. You can bring us back, too.'

Facing him still, she glided away.

'Not for too long,' he reminded her, and kicked to keep pace.

She went under, then speared up to do a playful dive over him. Maybe he let her lead him out farther than he'd intended, but he had to rank swimming with a beautiful mermaid in the moonlight of the island of Capri top of his personal list.

'Hold your breath,' she told him, and taking his hands, pulled him under, then took him speeding through the dark water.

She pulled him up, into the night, into the air and moonlight, a foot away from the rock.

'Seriously cool.'

'It was fun?'

'E-ticket. Yes. Best fun ever.'

'You swim very well. You're strong in the water, but still tire. We can sit on the rocks until you're ready.'

She laid her hands on the rock, boosted up as smoothly as a gymnast, and smiled down at him as she squeezed water from her hair.

Maybe he was a little winded, he decided as he hoisted up beside her. Besides, if he sat beside her, he wouldn't face those bare and beautiful breasts.

'So mermaids really do like sitting on rocks, watching the sea, the ships, the shore?'

'Yes. We're of the water and the air. We need time in both to be happy. Humans can have the land, the air, the water. Long ago, there were some jealous of this who lured the men in ships to the rocks, or pulled them into the deep to

129

drown. This is shameful. We take oaths never to harm our own or people of the land.'

'Like Riley's pack takes an oath.'

'Yes.' She lifted her face to moon and stars. 'I have a question.'

'Okay.'

'Why don't you want to kiss me?'

'What?'

'Today you kissed me here.' She touched a finger to her forehead. 'But this doesn't count. I'm allowed to ask why you don't want to kiss me.'

'We're teammates.'

'Yes. Bran and Sasha are teammates. I don't think that's the why.'

'It's part of the why,' he insisted. 'And look, you haven't been on – in... You haven't been in this world very long. You're still learning how things work.'

Her chin jutted up; her shoulders shot straight. 'I know how kissing works! Have you stopped learning how things work? I think it's never okay to stop learning.'

'Okay, that's true. Even profound. But we've got a lot going on, and ... priorities. And it's like Sasha said once, there's this purity to you, so I don't want to change, you know, the balance of things.'

'None of these are real answers. And I've made you awkward,' she said, stiffly now. 'I'm apology – I'm *sorry*. You were kind to bring me to the sea. We should go back now.'

'Look, look, look. I don't want to hurt your feelings.'

'Not giving true answers is hurtful.'

Frustrated, he shoved his fingers through his

130

hair. What was he supposed to say to a hurt, pissed-off mermaid? 'I'm trying to give you true answers. And I'm trying *not* to hurt your feelings, or anything else. I didn't expect the question.'

'So you couldn't think of better answers that aren't real?'

And sometimes she got things entirely too well. 'Not exactly. It's not that I don't want to kiss you, it's–'

'How do I understand that?' she demanded, and faced him with eyes of stormy green. 'Does "not-that-I-don't-want" mean "I want?"'

'No. Maybe. Yes. Hell.'

He grabbed her shoulders, managed to rein himself in enough to touch his lips very lightly to hers.

The storm died out of her eyes as she nodded. 'You want to kiss me like the brother of my father. This is an answer. Thank you. We should go back now.'

Before she could slide off the rock, he tightened his grip on her shoulders. 'It's an answer. It's not the truth.'

'You can't tell me the truth?' Distress moved over her face as she touched a hand to his heart. 'It's an oath? I would never ask you to break an oath.'

'No. No, it's not an oath. It's a...' Hang-up, a situation, a... 'Mistake, maybe a mistake. Or maybe this is. I guess we both need to find out.'

His hands glided up from her shoulders to cup her face. She drew in a breath, held it with her heart drumming as for a moment, forever, he just looked into her eyes.

131

And he looked into her eyes still as his lips touched hers, lightly as before. But not as before. Soft, so soft, light as the butterfly on the flower.

She wondered if the flower felt this stirring, this yearning.

Then his lips rubbed hers, pressed. And worlds opened.

Her breath released; her eyes closed as he took her so slowly, so gently into those worlds. Worlds of sweet pleasure, of new tastes, of quiet wonders.

Her lips parted, answered his, and it was like sliding deep and deeper into the warm and the lovely.

He'd known, somehow known, he'd be lost if he ever took this step. No compass could ever guide him back to solid ground again. She gave, absolutely, her hand pressed to his heart as if to hold it, her mouth, her tongue gliding with his as if created for him.

The scent of the sea, her scent, mixed together, enchanted him. And always would. The sound of water against rock – that constant mating – the sound of her sighs, blended like one. Bewitched him, and always would.

Everything good and right and worth fighting for coalesced in that single kiss. And still, he wanted more.

But he remembered what he could never allow himself to forget. Honor. And so he eased back.

'Annika.' He kept his hands on her face because, oh boy, how they wanted to wander down. While he struggled for the right thing, the honorable thing to say, to do, she smiled. All but blinded him with the light of it.

'Now I can kiss you.'

'You just did.'

'No, no – first. Before I couldn't, but now–'

Her arms came hard around him. Her mouth took his in an explosion of passion that blew the sheer concept of honor all to hell.

She burned against him, a torch on the water, impossibly hot and bright. He dived into the fire, letting himself take, be taken. Her skin, soft as velvet. Her breasts, firm and perfect and finally filling his hands. The miracle of her tail, sleek and wet and fascinating as the texture changed.

He knew he should slow things down, knew he should stop, but she coiled and curled around him while her upper body arched to offer until all he heard was the beat of his own blood.

Desperate now, driven to taste those perfect breasts, he shifted to lie her back on the rock. She turned with him, just as eager, and they slid off the rock, into the water.

Dazed with lust, he went under, started to push to the surface. She pulled him straight up, laughing.

'I got too happy.'

Once more she curled around him, and with her arm circling his neck, kept him afloat without appearing to move at all.

It struck him he was in over his head, in more ways than one.

She laid her head on his shoulder, nuzzled there.

Lust didn't cool so much as melded with affection so he found some balance.

'Can't be too happy,' he said, stroking her hair.

'I feel so full of it, I think I could stay like this and never run out.'

But they couldn't stay, he reminded himself. They'd already been away from the house, from the others, longer than was wise.

'I know we can't,' she said before he could. 'But one minute more. Here, now, the darkness is precious and good. Soon it won't be.'

'One minute more.' He let himself enjoy the minute, floating on a moonlit sea, buoyed by a mermaid.

She didn't press for more. He felt the way her tail moved the water as she leaned back, drew him along.

'What did you mean, you couldn't kiss me before, but now you could?'

'We're not allowed.'

'To kiss?'

'No, that would be sad, wouldn't it?' Her hair flowed over the water, black silk against indigo. 'We're not allowed to kiss a land person first. To ask for the kiss, to take it. It has to be given, by choice. Then we can give back.'

'What, like an Ariel thing?'

Puzzled, she frowned. 'Ariel is ... of the air?'

'Maybe. It's a character – a mermaid in a story.'

'Oh! I don't know the story of Ariel. Will you tell me?'

'I'll do better. I'll show you. We'll see if there's a way to get the DVD or stream it – it's a movie. A Disney movie. Anyway, she had to wait for the prince to kiss her in the story.'

'You're a King. Sawyer King.' Laughing, she lifted her head, kissed him again. Her tail swirled back and forth. Then her legs kicked before they both stood in thigh-high water.

'Will you kiss me when I have legs? I can ask now.'

Amused, allured, he cupped her face again, kissed her.

'We've got to get back – and you need that dress. Small chance of the *polizia* coming along, but we could get arrested.'

'For kissing?'

'For public nudity.'

'There are strange laws and rules here.'

But she waded back to the rock, slipped the dress over her head. He grabbed his jeans, his shirt, tugged the jeans over the wet boxers.

Instead of taking her hand, he wrapped his arms around her waist. 'Ready?'

She circled his waist with hers. 'Yes.'

When they stood in front of the villa again, still entwined, she hugged harder.

'It's different to travel when you hold me. Everything is different when you hold me. If you came to my room, we could lie together and you could hold me.'

He asked any god listening for strength. 'Long, hard day tomorrow. You need to go up, get some sleep.'

'It's hard to do what needs, but you need sleep, too.'

'Yeah. You go on in. I'll be in, in a minute.'

To please them both, he kissed her, then again, and once more until her eyes were dreamy when she turned to go.

'Good night.'

'Night,' he said as the door closed behind her, then sat on the step until he could settle down.

An instant later he was on his feet, the knife out of the sheath on his belt and in his hand.

Doyle stepped out of the shadows. 'Stand down, soldier. Just taking a last pass before turning in.'

As Sawyer slid the knife home again, Doyle sauntered forward. 'Hell of an offer you just turned down. I don't know whether to admire or pity your willpower.'

'Neither do I.'

'I'd tell you to try a cold shower, but you're already dripping. Taking a chance shifting down to the sea. Then again,' Doyle added when Sawyer remained silent, 'even admirable or pitiable will-power only goes so far.'

'I think I liked you better when you didn't say much of anything.'

'Can't blame you.' As he passed to go inside, Doyle gave Sawyer a friendly punch on the arm.

For himself, Sawyer decided to stay outside, and drip, a few minutes longer.

At least he didn't have breakfast duty, and considering the hike ahead of them, no calisthenics at dawn. He made up an hour of the sleep he'd lost in the night trying not to dream of a naked Annika. He figured coffee would do the rest.

In the kitchen, Bran cooked his one and only breakfast specialty – a full fry. Since Sawyer had no complaints, he grunted a greeting, grabbed a mug for coffee.

'Ready here in ten minutes,' Bran told him. 'Doyle wants to be off as soon as we've cleaned our plates.'

'I'm ready.' Literally, as he'd spent some of the restless night ordering his pack. 'Need help here?'

'Under control.'

'Then I'm taking this outside.'

He stepped out, and there was Annika, dressed for the day in cargo pants and boots and a tie-dyed tee she'd wanted because she'd thought it looked like rainbows. She sang under her breath as she created one of her tablescapes. A pyramid of juice glasses had chains of little flowers and clover spilling out of them and into a pool at the base.

At the base stood what he thought were figures she'd fashioned out of toothpicks, leaves, more clover.

As he started over, she looked up.

'Good morning!' She ran to him, jumped into his arms. The kiss managed to be as bright as a May morning and dark as midnight.

'Wow.' Riley came out with her own coffee. 'What did I miss?'

'Sawyer kissed me.'

'Yeah, got that. Congrats. Slow and steady wins the race, huh, cutie?' she said to Sawyer.

He wasn't feeling slow or steady at the moment, so just sat down. Natural, he decided. Everybody should just act natural.

'Flowerfall?'

'Yes! And we're all having a holiday. See, the mirror it sits on is the Island of Glass, and we can have one perfect day after we find the stars, take them back.'

'I could do with a perfect day,' Riley decided.

'It will be. I wanted to make a garden, but we

137

don't have time.'

'A flowerfall's its own garden.'

Pleased with Sawyer's comment, Annika lifted her face to the sun. 'Maybe this will be a perfect day.'

If perfect days included hard, sweaty climbs, this one qualified.

'The Phoenician Steps.'

As Sasha stared up, and up, Riley grinned. 'Named so because they once thought the Phoenicians built them. Now we know they're courtesy of the ancient Greeks. And,' she continued as they started the climb, 'were once the only way to access Anacapri. Remember, when you start to huff and puff, when your quads start to whimper, the women who used to have to go up and down them, nearly a thousand steps each way, to get water, carried that filled jug on their head all the way up again.'

'Did you say a thousand?' Sasha demanded.

'Nine hundred and twenty-one, to be exact.'

'There are times I wish you didn't know so damn much.'

'But it's pretty.' Looking everywhere, Annika practically danced her way up. 'All the flowers and the green.'

'And easier going up than coming down. Steep, uneven,' Riley qualified.

'We nearly lost two men in a rock fall the last time I climbed these steps,' Doyle remembered.

'That's what the nets are for now.'

Up they went, past houses and fields of wild-flowers and yellow broom. Up beyond chestnut trees and a tiny vineyard with grapes still young and green.

When they reached the top, Riley checked her watch. 'Thirty-six minutes. Solid.'

'There won't be stairs for the rest.' So saying Doyle continued on, and Riley rolled her eyes behind his back.

The sun beat down, relentless, and at times even the excuse for a track Doyle chose gave way to huddles of rock. Annika clambered over and around them, as hardy, it seemed, as the tiny wildflowers that pushed their way through crevices to find the sun.

Birds winged overhead, and now and then one might dart by, in absolute silence. The occasional lizard baked itself or scrambled into its own crevice as boot struck rock.

Sawyer gave a passing thought to snakes, of which he was distinctly unfond.

When Annika let out a gasp, he gave snakes a more direct thought. One hand grabbed hers, the other his gun.

'What is it?'

She pointed toward a tall stand of rocks and the scrub that clung to it. Sawyer's hand relaxed on his gun. 'A goat. A mountain goat.'

'A goat.' She stared up at the goat as the goat stared down at her.

'It doesn't look like the cheese. We ate the cheese. The goat cheese.'

'Right. They make the cheese from milk. Goat's milk. They milk the goat.' He began to see the hole he was currently sliding into. 'Ask Riley. She's the smart one. She'll explain it.'

'All right.' Annika scrambled up ahead, nimble as the damn mountain goat, to ask Riley.

'One way to avoid explaining teats.' Bran hauled himself up, reached back, helped haul up Sasha.

'In this case, I didn't know where to begin.'

'I could begin by stopping for ten minutes.' Sasha swiped her forehead, pointed. 'There's some stingy shade over there. God knows when we might get another chance.'

'There's a thought. Doyle!' After the call, Bran signaled the group ahead. 'Ten-minute break, in this bit of shade. I swear the man could march from here to Naples if there was a bridge.'

They sat on the ground, on rock, angled into the shade from a shrub arching out of rock. Overhead, the goat let out a derisive call.

'Easy for him to say,' Sasha muttered, and sipped from her water bottle. 'I suppose the three spots you've marked for the bombs aren't enough.'

'It's a fine start.' Bran patted her knee.

'Hell of a view.'

Sasha might have scowled at Riley, but she looked back down, and could only sigh. 'Yes, it's a hell of a view, and I'd love to paint it sometime. But I swear I thought we'd climbed as high as Mount Vesuvius by now, and it's still a good half mile to the cave Doyle's aiming for.'

'What cave?' Doyle demanded.

'The one you remember from when you soldiered here. The one we're heading to.'

'I never said anything about that cave.'

She looked back into his cool, steady gaze. 'But... No, you didn't. You didn't say anything. But that's where you're leading us.'

'Reading minds now?'

'No. No. I just–' She shook her head, rose. 'Give me a minute.' She got up, walked out on the goat track, stared northwest. 'I can see it. I don't know if what I see is your memory of it or something to come. I don't know if she'll use it, but she's not there, not now. Bats, spiders, dung in the cool and dry. But she's not there.'

She re-angled herself, southwest. 'Inside the great mountain she'll make her palace. Those who climb on it, bask in its views, drink and dine around it are but ants to her. Less than nothing. She'll be there, soon enough. But it isn't the time, it isn't the place to strike the final blow. Her weapon's forged, but ours isn't. We won't end her here, but lives will end.'

Suddenly, she clutched her head in her hand.

'She feels me. Bran.'

He rushed to her, laid his hands on her head. 'Block her out. You know what to do.'

'She claws at my mind. She's so strong.'

'So are you, *fáidh*. Look at me, look here.'

Her eyes, full of pain, lifted to his.

'Stronger together. Pull from me.'

She nodded, drew from him, shuddered once, then just dropped her head on his shoulder. 'She came in so fast. I wasn't prepared.'

'But you blocked her, and quickly. You get better, stronger every day.' He took her back to the shade, then skimmed his hands over her water bottle to cool it. 'She'll have the time she needs to rest.'

'Just until my head clears all the way.'

'You should have water.' Annika nudged Sasha's water bottle back on her. 'Bran made it

141

cool to drink. And this – this is the energy bar. But they don't taste so nice.'

'No, they really don't, but I can use the boost.'

'You were talking about Monte Solaro,' Riley said.

'If you say so.'

'That direction, great mountain. In Anacapri.'

'We're on the Anacapri side of the island now,' Doyle told her. 'But we're one hell of a hike from Solaro.'

'Malmon won't base there, or base any of his troops.' Clearer now, Sasha drew in a breath. 'It's for her. She'll deck it out, probably bring Malmon there, but your cave, I think. He may use that. I might see more when we get there.'

'I can get us there.' Sawyer rubbed her knee. 'It's been a hard climb already.'

'I'm okay, really. I think I was having such a hard time because this was building up, and she was ... scratching at me and I didn't know what it was. I'll make it fine.'

'If you change your mind, I'll get you there.'

To prove she could handle it, Sasha got to her feet. 'About half a mile, right?'

'About,' Doyle agreed. 'You'll make it, Blondie, or it's double the squats tomorrow morning.'

'Hell with that.' Swinging her pack back on, she headed up the rocky track.

Annika dashed forward to walk with her. 'We're mountain goats.'

'You move like one. Nimbly.'

'I was given very good legs. You were born with yours, and they're also very good.'

'They have muscles I didn't know legs could

have – which is something. But right now every one of them is crying, and that's something else.'

'We should sing.'

'Sing?'

'To take your mind away from the crying muscles. I heard this from a boat when I was a little girl, and it's fun to sing. 'Buddy, you're a boy make a big noise–''

'Queen?' Sasha said with a quick laugh.

'What queen?'

'No, Queen's the band who sang it. The name of the band.'

'But the voices I heard were men, not queens.'

'Hard to explain. Anyway, good, classic rock choice, but I don't know all the words.'

'I do.' As Riley sang the next line, Annika laughed, joined in.

'Freddie Mercury would be proud,' Sawyer decided when they hit the chorus – words Sasha knew, and all three rocked it out.

'The sea queen had a good point. There's a reason soldiers sing or chant on a long march.' Doyle glanced back at Bran. 'She'll make it.'

'Oh, I never doubted it.' Pride and love simply swarmed through him. 'Her strength of will would carry her even when her legs tire. She's more courage than the lot of us as she came into this with more fear and less knowledge.'

'She's more knowledge now, because if my memory serves, she's headed straight for the cave I've chosen.'

'You'll let her keep point then, and see if she leads us to it.'

'I don't mind bringing up the rear,' Sawyer put

in. 'Singing's not the only way to distract the mind on a march.'

'It's a fact they're not hard on a man's eyes on the walking away.'

'Hard to comment,' Doyle decided. 'I make one on the blonde's ass, I risk a jolt from the sorcerer. Make one on the sea nymph's, the traveler may take a swing at me.'

'There's one more besides,' Bran pointed out.

'The she-wolf?' Doyle shrugged. 'Not bad.'

'We should sing another!' Annika swung up on a pile of rock – yes, as nimble as that mountain goat.

'Do you know another one?' Maybe she had to catch her breath, but Sasha was game.

'Oh, yes. I love listening to music from the boats or from the places on the shore. I know this one, but I don't understand most of the words.'

She shut her eyes, ticked her hands in the air a moment as if reaching for the beat. Then to the astonishment of everyone on the hillside, lifted her voice into a soaring aria.

'*Tvoyu mat,*' Sawyer said, reverently. 'She's... Is that opera?'

'It certainly sounds like opera. And beautifully rendered,' Bran added, as with her voice still winging through the air, Annika jumped down to continue the climb.

'*La Traviata*. She's gone from Queen to Verdi.'

'You know opera?'

Doyle shrugged off Sawyer's surprise as the men moved forward. 'Live a few centuries, you know a lot of things. Just as I know a siren's voice when I hear it. Mind yourself, brother, or she'll have you wrapped up like a trout.'

'Already wrapped, I'd say.' Bran gave Sawyer's shoulder a slap. When the last note echoed off, and her companions applauded, Annika took a laughing bow.

'First, wow, major kudos on the pipes. Where'd you learn that?' Riley wondered.

'There is a big theater by the sea, far from here. For three nights they told this story with songs. It's not happy because the woman who sang that song dies.'

'That's opera for you,' Riley told her.

'But the songs and voices? So beautiful, so I went to listen every night they sang. I can teach you the song.'

'You couldn't teach me to sing like that if we had a couple decades.'

'And we don't.' Sasha stopped. 'It's there. The cave, it's there.'

The mouth opened, tall and narrow, in the rock. Spindly brush clung to the top, drooping down like a sagging awning. And over that a black snake slithered.

'Wall lizard,' Riley said.

'That's no damn lizard.' Sawyer's fingers itched for the gun tucked at his back under his shirt.

'Just a whip snake – not poisonous.' Smirking, Riley took out her water bottle. 'But they do like to bite.'

She took a quick swig, replaced her bottle, started forward toward the cave. Muttering about snakes, Sawyer stepped behind her.

'Wait! Stop!'

Leaping after him, Sasha grabbed his hand. Nearly at the mouth, Doyle and Riley turned.

'Don't go in. Don't...' Her eyes went darker, deeper. 'Don't go in. Don't go near.' She turned to Sawyer. 'Pain, fear, the shadows of death. Blood and rage. Water and traps. I don't know. I can't see clearly. You. Annika.'

'Annika?'

'It's not safe for you. For either of you. Don't go in. Stay away, Anni.'

'I'm here. Don't worry.' Her voice pitched to soothe, Annika took Sasha's other hand. 'We won't go inside.'

'He'll use it. Use you. One to the other. Don't believe him.'

'Malmon.'

'Malmon. Not what he was, not what he will be. But hers. You can't go inside.'

'Okay. We'll stay out. We'll stay right here,' Sawyer assured her. 'What about the others?'

'What?'

'Is it safe for us?' Bran nudged Sawyer aside. 'Do the rest of us go in?'

She let out a long breath. 'I don't feel anything for the rest of us. Just Annika and Sawyer. It's life and death for them inside. For us? It's a cave.'

'All right then. They'll stay out here, and we'll go in, see what we have.'

Sasha nodded. 'Please.' She took Sawyer's hand again, gripped Annika's. 'Promise.'

'You got it. We're out here.'

But when the others went in, he stared at the mouth.

'Promise me.'

'What?'

'Promise me,' Annika repeated. 'You won't go

in. You won't use the compass, and come back to go in and see.'

Since he'd toyed with just that, he hesitated.

'You promise me. I promise you. Because we believe in Sasha.'

Damn it. 'You're right. Okay. I promise, I won't go in – unless there's no choice. Unless one of us is in trouble inside. Good enough?'

'Yes. I promise the same.'

She took his face, kissed him. 'Now it's an oath, and can't be broken.'

He thought of Doyle's words – *wrapped up like a trout* – but didn't see where he had much choice.

CHAPTER SEVEN

The cave, they reported as they took time to rest, eat, drink before starting the hike back, was simply a cave.

Wide and deep and dry.

Sasha sketched it, added the dimensions Doyle estimated, as well as the narrow tunnel that forked off into a second chamber, wider, deeper than the entrance.

Using the sketch, Doyle marked the best places to lay their traps.

'Not too close to the entrance.' Bran, too, studied the sketch. 'We'd want as many of them inside as possible when, and if, I set them off.'

'Why the hell would they use a cave way the hell up here?' Riley wondered. 'He's after a villa – and that suits Malmon. A cave, that suits Nerezza.'

'It's not hers,' Sasha insisted.

'Whatever reason, he has something planned, or why see danger inside for two of us?' With a nod, Bran approved Doyle's marked positions. 'I can work with this. What I've made can cure in the cave as easily as it can in the workshop. What do you say, Sawyer? You and I take a quick trip down, gather what's needed, bring it back again?'

'Sure.' Instinctively Sawyer reached for his compass, then angled his head. 'You can get us down there, right? Like you took Sasha to the promontory in Corfu.'

'Here to there? I can, yes. Easy as a Sunday drive.'

'I've never traveled your way.'

'Well then, I'll give you a ride.' Bran rose, reached down. The men gripped forearms. 'We'll be back shortly.'

And they winked away.

'I miss driving,' Riley commented.

Doyle polished off a sandwich. 'Tell me about it.' He shoved to his feet, wandered off, then stood staring out at the sweeping view of blue water, white rock, and the green with the tumble of houses below.

'Looking for possible snipers' nests,' Riley concluded. 'Even though he knows this is too far up. They may HQ here, but they'll come down a ways, the snipers. When we get back, I'll see if I can find out if Malmon's bagged a villa. And he's going to want a boat. He has his own, so maybe he'll just bring that, or have it brought. The *Escapade* – his yacht. As if what he does is charming.'

148

'I hope we search for the star tomorrow. I like the scent of the land here.' To prove it, Annika drew in a long breath. 'And the way the sun strikes the water, the land. But if we find the star before he comes, we could be gone.'

'We face him first. On the land, on the sea. In the dark, in the light. Our lightning against his. He hurts you.' Again, Sasha gripped Annika's hand. 'It's your blood in the water. And Sawyer's on the ground.'

She dropped her head. 'They're coming too fast. I can't keep up.'

'You're pushing too hard.' Riley scooted around, knelt on the rocky ground to dig knots out of Sasha's shoulders.

'I just can't see it clearly.'

'You've blocked her. Stands to reason she's doing what she can to block you. Don't push it, Sash.'

Then Bran and Sawyer were back, nearly at the exact spot. Now both of them carried satchels.

'Supercool trip.'

'Another?' Bran demanded after a single glance at Sasha.

'Just in flashes. They're just flashes today.'

'Let it go for a bit.'

'See?' Riley rubbed Sasha's shoulders, then rose. 'Let's get started.'

'Won't they see what you put inside the cave?' Annika asked.

'I'll sink them into the ground, at Doyle's strategic points. This time they'll work in a chain reaction, at my command. The first goes, then all follow.'

'Will it kill?'

'It's war,' Doyle said as he strode back. 'And none of us can afford to be delicate about it.'

'Ease up,' Sawyer ordered.

'There's no easing up once they come, once they come at us. Munitions, and plenty of them. Room for cages for any of us they capture. That's what I'd use the cave for. And the prep area for sending men down from the west, for securing snipers' nests. Men,' he said flatly, 'who'll have guns with long-range capabilities. Men who kill for a living and who'll be trained to put a bullet in your brain in the middle of one of your cartwheels.'

Sawyer stepped in front of Annika. 'Back the fuck off.'

'No, don't shield me. Thank you, but don't.' Her hand wanted to tremble, but she willed it steady as she laid it on Sawyer's tensed arm. 'I know what must be. I took my oath.' She stepped clear, faced Doyle. 'You've killed men before, and you will again. I don't need Sasha's gift to know this. Land people kill what they are, and it's your greatest weakness, your deepest shame. I know those who come will kill, so we do what we must do. But it brings no peace or pleasure.'

'No. Neither. Ever.'

'Do you see them, the ones who've fallen for you?'

'Every one.'

She looked into his eyes a long moment, then took his hands. 'It's a heavy burden to carry. After this, we'll all carry it. I can't place the weapons in the cave. Show us where else they're needed. Sawyer and I will do our part.'

150

They took the second satchel and, using the map, hiked to the nearest location marked.

'You shouldn't be angry with Doyle for being harsh with me.'

'Can't help it.'

'You can,' she corrected. 'Because, as I do, you know he's harsh because he worries I will hesitate, and be hurt, or not protect another from harm.' To soothe them both, she leaned against him. 'You worry, too.'

'Sure, a little.'

'More than a little, I think, and I don't like to give you worry. Sometimes I need Doyle to be harsh, and make me remember.'

'Okay, but remember this, too. I've got your back.' He tipped her face up. 'And everything else.'

'I will. We're teammates.'

'You got it. Now watch this,' Sawyer told her as he carefully lifted a vial from the satchel, set it on the stony ground.

It lay a moment, then sank out of sight as if into water.

Annika said, 'Ahh. Bran has such a gift. But is it safe for others? Innocents?'

Though she caught at his hand, Sawyer deliberately stepped on the spot where the vial had been. 'Evildoers only. Mr. Wizard strikes again. Okay, next about fifty paces southeast.'

He looked at her as they veered off the narrow track. 'I know this is hard for you. You have the sweetest heart. But you're right that Doyle's right. You need to look at it in a hard light, Anni. Nerezza chose to take this direction, and the men she's using as weapons against us? They have a choice, too. Those choices take ours off the table. They'll end us, and more, end any chance of keeping the stars out of Nerezza's hands.'

She said nothing as he placed the next vial.

'Once Malmon's on the hunt, he won't stop. And he's good. He has almost unlimited resources to keep looking. And maybe, at some point, even to find the Fire Star Bran's already secured.'

'He would kill you.'

'In a New York minute. Like that,' he said, snapped his fingers. 'He doesn't value life, unless it's his own. Me, I'd just be dead – not that I'd be happy about it. But you, especially you, Riley, and Doyle, it would be worse for you.'

'How for Doyle? He's an immortal.'

'That's just the point.' Sawyer gestured, and they headed toward the next spot. 'He can't die, but he can feel pain. Malmon could and would give him pain for years.'

'I know there is cruelty.'

'But you don't understand it.'

'I never want to. But I understand, even though it's hard, we have to stop these men just as we stopped her creatures. We protect each other, and the stars. It's our duty. You said you don't want to take a life, but would to protect others.'

'That's right.'

'And our others, I know, would do the same. I can't do less. Let me place the next vial.'

Slowly, they worked their way down, with the breathtaking view spread before them. The sun splashed onto the sea, shimmered on white rock, and baked the green.

At one point Sawyer crouched down, then lay

on his belly.

'Doyle had it right, this is the perfect sniper's nest.' When Annika lay beside him, he pointed. 'See? That's our villa.'

'Yes, yes, I see. It's still a very long way.'

'They'll have a scope, a high-powered rifle, and you can bet a lot of skill. Here.' He scooted back, squatted to take a pair of small field glasses out of his pack. 'Look through these.'

She studied them a moment, then put them up to her eyes. Gasped and jolted. 'Oh! Everything jumped close.' She lowered them. 'But nothing moved.'

'Binoculars – it's the lenses, the special glass. It– Easiest to say magnifies. A sniper would have something like this, something called a scope, attached to the rifle.'

'And it would bring us close,' she murmured as she looked through the glasses again. 'I see. A miraculous tool used for evil.'

'In this case, yeah.'

'Then we place a vial here.'

Once they had, she turned to him, rose up to kiss him. 'This is the good, to balance the bad.'

'Then let's make it even better.'

He drew her in, took the kiss slow, quiet, deep. And wondered how he managed to go even an hour without having her pressed against him.

'You two really need to get a room.' Riley stood above them, hands on her hips.

'We're weighing the scales on the good side,' Sawyer told her.

'Whatever. Did you cover it down to there?'

'Every mark. Take a look here.'

153

Quick, surefooted, she picked her way down, then crouched as Sawyer did.

'Well, shit.' Like he had, she stretched onto her belly. 'You've got to give it to Doyle. This is prime for a nest. Get yourself an M24 or an—'

'AS-50,' Doyle said and jumped lightly down beside them.

Riley looked over her shoulder. 'Next on my list.'

He got down, shoulder to shoulder with her, nodded. 'Yeah, cover, stability, scope, and range. It's all right here.'

'Good as a clock tower,' Riley agreed. 'We walk outside, bang and bang. Ducks in a pond, all six.'

'Well, five out of six.'

'Right. You'd quack again.'

'They would overpower him – one man against many.' Sick at the thought, Annika looked down at Doyle. 'And give him pain, endlessly. We can't allow it.'

'Won't,' Riley corrected. 'You got any left?'

Sawyer patted the satchel. 'Three.'

'And you?' She tapped Doyle with her elbow as she pushed up. 'Any more spots strike you as bomb-worthy?'

'One or two.'

'Then we'll cover it.' She wiggled her fingers for the bag. 'Here come Sash and Bran. The four of you go on. We'll finish this off and catch up. Then I believe it's margarita time.'

'Not Bellini?'

Riley shook her head at Annika. 'After a climb like this? It's got to be the margarita. You know what's good with margaritas after climbing up and in the hills for a few hours setting traps for bad guys? Salsa.'

'Got you covered,' Sawyer told her.

By the time they got back to the villa, Annika wanted the pool, the comfort of the water. Since Sasha and Sawyer had already started to chop and slice, she ran upstairs, changed into one of her new suits and the wrap that flowed over it.

When she came out, Doyle stood on the far side of the pool, looking up at the hills. He wore sunglasses and had a hand resting on the hilt of the knife in his belt.

He looked like a warrior, strong and fit and ready to face whatever came.

'You don't have the beer.'

'I'll get to it.'

'You look up where we've just been because you worry. Did you miss something important? Will all we did be for nothing? You worry we'll be killed, in spite of all the work and planning. We won't.'

'Optimism's part of your charm, Gorgeous.'

'We won't,' she repeated and walked over to him. 'But you've seen more death than anyone should. An immortal faces death every day, but never his own. The losses, like the men who fell before you, are always there.'

She'd pinned it like a flag on a map, he thought, and shifted to look at her. 'How long do you live?'

'We live longer than land people. Much longer. So I know when I go home, when I'm back in the sea, that one day my heart will still beat and Sawyer's won't. It's very hard to know.'

'He's lucky to have you now.'

'We're meant,' she said simply, 'at least for the

155

time we have. Just as we're all meant to be here together, to search for and find the stars. To take them back to the Island of Glass. Because we're meant, we'll face what comes, do what we must.'

Because it was her way, she slid an arm around his waist, leaned against him. 'You're a warrior. A warrior isn't a killer because a warrior, a true one, has honor. The men who'll come aren't warriors.'

'No, they're not.'

'And when they come, we'll win. Today is for a job well done, and now for the pleasure of having it done. You should get the beer.'

'I should get the beer.'

It was rare for him to allow himself to feel or show true affection, but he found himself cupping her chin, kissing her lightly on the lips.

He walked toward the kitchen where Sawyer stood holding a tray of fresh salsa and chips.

'Do I have to kick your ass?'

Doyle glanced back. Annika stood a moment, arms and face lifted to the sky, then dived sleekly into the pool.

'Brother, if things were different, one whole hell of a lot different, you'd sure as hell have to try. But they're not, so we can save each other the bruises. You for beer or that Slurpee Riley makes?'

'I like the Slurpee.'

'Suit yourself,' Doyle said, and went in for beer.

Sawyer took the tray to the table, set it down, then walked over to look into the pool.

Annika lay on the bottom, eyes closed, lips gently curved, as if she dreamed some sweet dream.

Riley came out carting a pitcher of margaritas

nestled in a big bowl of ice. 'Sasha's bringing the rest.'

She set down the pitcher, rolled her shoulders. 'Boy, am I ready to dive into that pool.'

'Annika's in there.'

'So?'

'I think she's taking a nap.'

Riley walked over to the edge, looked down. 'Huh. Well, it'll have to be a ... catfish nap. Get it? That gives me time for some liquid refreshment.'

Back at the table, she dipped a chip into Sawyer's salsa, sampled. 'Oh, baby, you *know* what I like. I could eat a gallon of this stuff. Haul those glasses over, Sash,' she said when Sasha came out. 'Let's get this party started. Where's Bran?'

'He wanted to check on something in the workshop. He said he wouldn't be long. I think Doyle hit the shower. Where's Annika?'

'Taking a nap in the pool.' Riley poured three generous glasses.

'A nap in the pool.' Sasha took her sketchbook off the tray. 'Isn't it strange how quickly we get used to what we – or I, anyway – considered the impossible? Annika's asleep *in* the pool. Bran upstairs with his magick potions. One of us could get a wild hair and go pull a *Psycho* on Doyle while he showers.'

On a laugh Riley stabbed a fist in the air, made the high-pitched sound that went with the classic scene.

'I could ask Sawyer, hey, would you mind taking me back to France, say right about the turn of the twentieth century, because I'd really like to have a conversation with Monet.'

157

'Which one?' Riley wondered.

'Both, now that you mention it, but I'm thinking Claude first, a personal favorite.' Sasha sampled the margarita, found it perfect. 'So a little trip to Giverny.'

'I could do that.' Sawyer helped himself to salsa.

'Yes, you could. And in a couple weeks, when the moon's full, Riley goes wolf.'

Sawyer threw back his head and did a very effective imitation of a wolf howl.

'And me?' Sasha gestured with her drink. 'I never know when I might be having a conversation and start prophesying.' She drank, sighed. 'And after a few short weeks? It all seems absolutely normal.'

'Because it is, for us.' Riley lifted her glass in turn. 'So, here's to us – and fuck the rest.'

As they clinked glasses, Annika rose up, rested her arms on the skirt of the pool. 'Is it margarita time?'

'Come and get 'em.' Riley poured another glass.

When Doyle came out, a second cold beer in his hand, he saw Annika and Riley in the pool. Dr. Gwin might not be a mermaid, he thought, but the woman swam like a fish. Sasha stood at the side of the house, with easel and canvas, brushes and paint, and faced the sea.

Under the pergola, Sawyer and Bran had their heads together. He walked to them. Though he'd skipped the margaritas, he was a fan of Sawyer's salsa.

'What's the plan?'

'We were just kicking that around,' Sawyer told him.

'We're covered, as much as we can be, while we're here.' Bran looked over at Sasha, the arch of her back, the vulnerable nape of her neck as she'd bundled her hair up under her hat. Then up into the hills. 'But Annika tells us you're still worried.'

'Doesn't take much of a gap, does it? A bullet doesn't need much room.'

'Happy thought,' Sawyer muttered.

'We've laid traps, and I've added protection, but Doyle has the right of it. Some of it rests on Sasha. In Corfu, she knew when Nerezza would strike, so again, we were prepared. Added to that, we have the practicality of Riley's network of contacts. We should know when this Malmon sets out for Capri. Once he has, the fight for us is against two fronts. Men, and minions.'

'We're stronger than we were.' Again, he looked at Sasha. 'And more united. It will matter. I believe it will weigh on our side. Then there's a matter of the search.'

'No more clues from that quarter?' Doyle wagged a thumb toward Sasha.

'Not as yet. It's a great deal of pressure on her, so I'm asking if I'm not with her, someone else is. Always. She handles the visions well now, but the more open she is, the more Nerezza pushes to get in.'

'We've got her back.' Sawyer glanced toward the pool. 'Once it starts, nobody should split off alone, but we'll keep Sasha close.'

'Then we move on, do the work, which puts us out on the water. And in it.'

'Strategically, any serious attack should wait until we find the star. If having it were my goal,'

Doyle continued, 'I'd lie back, let the targets do the work, then go in, take them out, claim the prize.'

'But,' Bran said, and waited.

'It's not altogether about logic, is it, but about greed with some madness thrown in. Sasha prophesied Malmon wasn't what he was or would be. We have to assume, considering her visions, he's made a contract with Nerezza. We can't know what he is, what power she might have given him in exchange. Or how hell-bent he'll be on getting to us, as he knows what each of us has or is.'

'Hell-bent as fire and brimstone,' Sawyer said. 'Trust me.'

'That being the case, the odds favor he'll come at us, at least a testing run, an attempt to deplete our numbers, or take one or more of us captive. Or he may go full out, believing we have information here he could use to find the star himself.'

'He's a confident son of a bitch. I lean toward the full out. Not to kill, or not to kill certain ones of us. He'd rather capture, but he'd enjoy bloodying the ground while he's at it.'

'Or the water,' Bran put in. 'Which is where our search will focus.'

'And where we're most vulnerable.' Doyle slid his gaze toward Annika. 'Even with our advantage there.'

'I could arm the rest of you with the bombs, as we're calling them. They won't harm you as they will those who attack. But I'd have to do some work on underwater use there.

'And meanwhile we can't use guns under the water, and a harpoon is a single shot.'

160

'We handled underwater attacks before,' Sawyer pointed out.

'We have. But what I've been working on, with Sasha's help, is Doyle's idea about infusing blades and so on with something like the bombs. It's close to ready, or close to ready to be tested. It will help, considerably. But it may come to retreat, to Sawyer getting us out and away. Which is where we were, Doyle, when you joined us.'

'It takes proximity, that's the thing. That's why I brought us, boat and all, back to the villa in Corfu. I couldn't risk missing anybody, disconnecting.'

Well used to talk of war, Doyle helped himself to salsa. 'What happens if you disconnect?'

'Never happened, but I'm told if it does, it's a long fall into wherever and whenever for the passenger. On the boat, I know I can do it. Underwater, I could miss someone, and if we're into it, I'm likely to pull enemy back with us.'

'So what we need, if it comes to that, if getting to the boat isn't going to happen, is to do whatever we can to pull in around Sawyer, give him the chance for the full retreat.'

Slinging a towel around her waist, Riley stepped up. 'In the water,' she began and dumped more from pitcher to glass. 'We're two teams of three.'

'Is that so?' Doyle countered.

'It's so if you've got a brain. Annika, key advantage us. It's her element. She can hear and see farther than us or them. She can move faster than us or them. She gets her tail on? I wouldn't want to take a hit from it. Bran, advantage us. Nobody likes to get struck by lightning. He'd

161

take out more with a jolt than we will with diving knives. And he can get out on his own, take at least one of us with him? Right?'

'True, but I wouldn't leave any of you. That's not negotiable.'

'I don't mean that – and thanks. I mean, moving on to our next advantage, Sawyer. He's the escape route if and when. If Bran knows he'll get the rest of us, he can worry about getting himself out, if necessary.'

She sat down with her drink. 'The rest of us, we make sure everybody stays alive, no one gets separated.' Now she looked at Sawyer. 'Ever fired an underwater pistol?'

'Underwater pistol?' Bran's brows lifted.

'Yeah, it's specially designed to be used under water. Fires fléchettes, not bullets because the barrels aren't rifled, and they maintain their trajectory through hydrodynamics. They do the job.'

'I've heard of them – pistols, rifles. Frogmen, SEALs, right?'

She nodded at Sawyer. 'And so on. I might be able to score us a couple of them, and the ammo. It'll probably take a few days, but I have a source.'

'A couple of them doesn't arm all of us,' Doyle pointed out.

'It's going to take some wrangling to get two, and two's enough. You're a decent shot, but you're better with the bow or the sword. Bran? Pretty decent shot, but why waste the time when he's the lightning man? Sasha's getting better with a gun, but she's not there. With the crossbow? She's Robin Hood and all his Merry Men. And Annika's not going to use a gun, in the water or out. So two.

162

One for me, one for Sawyer. We're the better shots. And, in fact, if I can only score one, it goes to Sawyer. Dead-Eye's the best of us.'

'All right then.'

'One or two, I'm going to need to wire money.'

'Let us know how much,' Bran said, 'and we'll put it together. It's good to have, and if we can access this sort of weapon, we have to consider they'll be armed this way as well. Distractions,' he murmured. 'Something an enemy would be more inclined to shoot than us. I'll work on it. And it's good strategy, Riley. The two teams of three.'

'They'll have more.' Pale, Sasha stepped up to the table, set a canvas down.

On it she'd painted an underwater battle. The six of them, armed with knife, spear, pistol, surrounded by armed men. Twenty by Sawyer's count.

Blood spread in the water. And sharks came to feed.

Annika walked over, laid her hands on Sawyer's shoulders. 'The blood draws them, and they'll take all. The word you use is *frenzy*. It's truth.'

Riley blew out a breath. 'Does anybody else hear the theme from *Jaws?*'

She poured another drink.

CHAPTER EIGHT

Sawyer studied the painting. 'This is on my top five list. Of ways not to die.'

'Hey, me, too.' After a long, slow sip, Riley managed a smile. 'What's your number one?'

'Snake pit. You?'

'Drawn and quartered.'

'That's a good one.'

'What is drawn and quartered?' Annika asked.

Reaching up, Sawyer rubbed her hand. 'You don't ever want to find out.' He looked over at Sasha. 'You saw this?'

'Yes. Very clearly.'

'Us, surrounded by the bad guys, the sharks circling.'

'Yes!' Sasha snapped off the word as she shook her head at Riley's offer of a drink.

'Looks dire,' he commented. 'It also looks like we've got a wall between us and Bruce and pals.'

'Bruce?' Shaken, Sasha pressed her fingers to her eyes. 'Who the hell is Bruce?'

'Crew's name for the mechanical shark in *Jaws*,' Riley explained.

'Exactly so. Now sit.' Firmly, Bran nudged Sasha into a chair. 'We couldn't ask for a bigger distraction.'

Now Sasha just closed her eyes. 'A shark attack is a distraction? A distraction.'

'Damn good one. Odds are they'd go for the

prey in the outer circle first.' As he might a battle plan, Doyle stood, studied the painting. 'It's something I've missed in my extended life – a shark attack. And you, Gorgeous?'

'We can hear – feel? – them, and we stay away. But we can also make a sound they don't like, and warn others if they come to feed.'

'What sound?' Riley wondered.

Annika drew a breath, opened her mouth.

Though he heard nothing, Sawyer felt as if an ice pick had been jammed in his ear, and straight to his brain. In the distance, dogs began to bark.

'Wow. Okay.' Riley rubbed her ears.

'If they still come, you fight. Hit them here.' Annika tapped her nose. 'Hard.'

'Sometimes the shark go away; sometimes he wouldn't go away.'

'Quint,' Riley explained. 'Sawyer's still on *Jaws*.'

'The seas are filled with easier prey. Here, in the painting, the bad guys are easier prey than we are.'

'Annika's right.' Riley nodded. 'Plus, thanks to Sasha we're forewarned. How do we use it?'

'They're looking to capture, not kill,' Doyle pointed out. 'There's blood, some of us, some of them are wounded. But we're outnumbered more than three to one here, and we're all alive. If they wanted us dead, at least one of us would be. Or more seriously wounded than this.'

'And we're in a group,' Bran added. 'A fairly tight one. Tight enough?' he asked Sawyer.

'Yeah, tight enough. The trick's going to be getting to this point, letting them surround us, and holding it together.'

'We let them...' Calmer now, Sasha took the

165

drink she'd refused. 'Yes, I see.'

'Our instinct's going to be to fight, not surrender. But, we let this happen?' Riley tapped the painting. *'Their* instinct's going to be to take out the sharks, or try, or get the hell away.'

'We stay close enough to each other, I shift us back to the boat, and–'

'The sharks take the rest.' Riley lifted her glass toward him. 'To Quint.'

'Not the rest,' Doyle corrected. 'Odds are on a dive boat, and if I planned an attack like this, I'd have men stationed on the boat, and a couple, at least, on ours.'

'Buzzkill. Right,' Riley added. 'But still. Those teams won't be expecting us to pop out of nowhere. So, you or I get to the wheel, and fast. The others deal with the bad guys, if any, on our boat.'

'We'll deal with it. All of it,' Bran assured them. 'It's what we're meant to do.'

'What we're meant to do,' Sasha agreed, 'but we need to factor in one more thing. Abject panic. Those aren't mechanical sharks in a movie. And it only takes one of them to decide, hmm, look at the delicious chewy center.'

'Good one. We've got Anni's secret shark whistle as backup,' Riley reminded her.

'Even so, factor it in. Because I now have a list of my own – something I've lived my whole life without making. Being eaten by sharks is now number one.' Sasha gulped margarita. 'With a bullet.'

Prepared for an attack, resolved to do whatever needed to be done, they set out to search the next morning. And the day after, and the day after that. No attack came, nor did they find the star or any new path toward it.

Restless, Doyle prowled the yard during combat practice.

'Use your feet, Sasha!' He snapped the order out when she ended up on her ass, again. 'Stop going easy on her, Gwin, and go in for the kill.'

'She's holding her own,' Riley shot back.

'Bollocks. You've a knife in your hand, Sasha, use the damn thing.' When Sasha sliced out, missed the mark by a foot, he strode forward, grabbed her arm. 'Combat grip, downward stroke.'

He guided her arm, hard and fast enough to make the muscles still sore from the damn pull-ups twinge.

'It won't cut her, or don't you trust your man?'

'Yes, I trust him. I'm *trying*.'

'Try harder. She's not that good.'

Riley cocked a hip. 'Oh, really? Then bring it, big guy. Take me on.'

Obliging, in the mood for it, Doyle took the knife from Sasha, who muttered, 'I hope she kicks your ass.'

He glanced over. 'Put some of that pissed-off into your own practice next time.'

As he spoke, Riley hit him, dead center, with a flying kick, propelled him back a good three feet. She landed, set, smiled.

'Always be ready, always be alert. Isn't that what you hammer at us? Looks like you forgot, Sir Dick.'

'As you forgot to go in for the kill.'

They circled each other. She dodged the swipe with the knife, but not the fist in the belly. She

167

went down with it, jabbed the charmed knife at his thigh, rolled back and up.

'Missed the artery,' she said as they circled again. 'Won't next time.'

Jabs, feints, kicks, a punch.

Sawyer and Bran stopped their own practice battle to watch, and Annika lowered her arms as her practice balls hovered in the air.

Doyle swept Riley's legs out from under her, but she rolled again, backflipped up, kicked out as she did, aiming – a bit harder than practice called for – at the groin.

Doyle set his teeth, went over the pain – she'd hit her mark solidly – scored a point on her left arm.

'You'd be bleeding.'

'Wouldn't be the first time.'

They charged. Knives met, crossed. They held there, like pirates, eyes hot before Doyle shoved her back. She recovered, swung into a round-house kick, hit him chest high. He grabbed her foot, used momentum to thrust her into the air. She managed to flip, landed, but off-balance enough to have to reset.

He charged again, took her down, his knife to her throat. 'And you're done.'

'You, too, old man. My knife's in your gut.'

He lay on her a moment more, admitting only to himself he was winded and his balls ached like a bitch. Then he lifted enough to look down, and sure enough, her knife was hilt deep in his gut.

'Wouldn't kill me for long, but you'd still be dead.'

'Good thing I won't be fighting Lazarus. Get off me.'

'In a minute.' He looked around at the audience. 'I've got her down, and we'll say she's unarmed for these purposes. My knife's at her throat. What do you do? Annika?'

Without hesitation, she jerked up her arm. He felt a tingle in his knife hand. 'Perfect. Aim and reflexes. Bran.'

Bran flicked his hand, and the knife turned into a banana.

'A bit of humor,' Bran said. 'But effective.'

'Good enough. Sasha?'

She took Bran's knife, threw it. It hit Doyle in the back of the head.

'Impressive.'

'I was aiming for your back, center mass. But I'll take good luck where I find it.'

'Sawyer?'

With a hand in his pocket, he measured distance. In an instant he crouched beside Doyle and Riley, sliced his knife cleanly on Doyle's throat. And gripping Riley's shoulder, popped them both back to where he'd stood.

'Good enough.' Doyle got to his feet. 'Of course, this is saying any one of you has that split second to act.'

'We'll make the second,' Annika insisted. 'We're meant to protect each other. If we don't do all we must for each of us, we fail. If we find the stars but one of us falls, we fail. We thought you'd fallen that night in Corfu, and we grieved. Because we're family now. Family protects, always.'

'You used your second to shield Riley that night,' Sasha reminded him. 'Anni's right. It's the six of us who are meant to find the stars. If any of

169

us fall, we fail. We can't fail. I'll work harder.'

'You're better than you were. You've had the farthest to come.'

'I think that's supposed to be encouragement. You're angry,' Sasha added, studying Doyle. 'I can feel it. Angry and starting to doubt if we're on the right track, in the right place. If the vision I had that brought us here was just wrong.'

'You're still new at reading them.'

'She's yet to be wrong,' Bran reminded him. 'Impatience, while human enough, isn't productive.'

'The compass backs her up.' Sawyer took it out. 'It says here. I check it every night, and we're where we're supposed to be.'

'When you've lost something, it's always in the last place you look. Because when you find it,' Riley added, 'you stop looking. We haven't hit the last place yet.'

'Have you asked yourself why she's yet to come at us? We've been here nearly two weeks.'

'She has.' Bran slid an arm around Sasha.

'Not a day goes by she doesn't try to get inside me.' She reached up to the necklace Bran made for her, rubbed the protective stones. 'The gods have nothing but time, do they?'

'Gods and immortals,' Riley commented. 'But the rest of us? Not so much.'

'So we keep looking.' When Annika slipped her hand in his, Sawyer squeezed it as he spoke. 'Until we hit that last place. It's here, and I'm not going to complain about not having to fight to the freaking death for a week or two while we search.'

Couldn't they see five stood on one side, and Doyle alone on the other? Because she could and

170

did, Annika walked to him. Disarmed him by wrapping her arms around him in a hug.

'You're angry because you have no one but friends to fight with.'

'Maybe a little pissed off he has friends.' Riley smirked at him. 'And one of them kicked him in the balls.'

'Maybe. And maybe we haven't found the last place because we're looking in the wrong one. Not the island, I'll concede that. Seer and magic compass say Capri, it's Capri. But maybe it's not in the water, not in a cave. We haven't assessed other possibilities. You said in the water, of the water,' he said to Sasha. 'But what about fountains, wells, underground springs? Bays, coves, inlets?'

'The Bay of Sighs.' Sasha's eyes went deep. 'Lost between what is, what was, what will. There abides beauty without end, and regret. Are you worthy to pass between? The truest of hearts, the purest of spirits? Sighs for those accepted. Sighs for those turned away. Hope, never quenched for redemption. And the song sings from the star to guide you.'

Sasha let out her own sigh. 'They're waiting for us to find it.'

'Who?' Doyle demanded. 'Where?'

'I don't know. I can feel ... something waiting, hoping. But I don't have the answers, I'm sorry.'

'Neither do I,' Riley said. 'I've been digging on Bay of Sighs, but I haven't found anything yet. I'll keep looking, try different angles. A parallel world, maybe? A time shift – which would be Sawyer's deal. I'll try some other resources.'

'As will I,' Bran said. 'It may be someone in my

171

family knows something of it, or knows someone who might. Meanwhile, we search and eliminate.'

'We'd better toss some breakfast together and get down to the boat.' Riley paused, pulled out her phone when it signaled. 'Hold on. It's my Malmon contact.

'This is Gwin,' she said as she walked away.

'I can help you with breakfast because Riley is busy.'

Watching Riley, Sasha nodded. 'Let's get to it.' And headed inside with Annika.

By the time Riley came in for coffee, Sasha was flipping the last slice of French toast on a platter beside a heap of bacon.

'What did you find out?'

'I'll tell it all at once. Thanks for taking my KP, Anni.'

'I don't mind. I like to make the fruit bowl.'

'Looks good, smells good. I'll report while we eat.'

She didn't waste time filling her plate or filling the rest in.

'Malmon's still in London, but he's booked a villa – big-ass villa, overlooking Marina Grande. Degli Dei.'

'Villa of the gods,' Doyle translated.

'Fate's little wedgie, right? He took it for a month – doubling the asking price as incentive. His tenancy starts in three days. Word is he's enlisted John Trake.'

'I don't know that name,' Sawyer said.

'I do. Formerly Colonel Trake, United States Army, Special Forces. Black ops. Dishonorably discharged about seven years back, quietly, when he went way off the reservation. Got to like killing a little too much, and didn't worry about collateral damage, even when it included his own men, unarmed civilians, children. Trake's bringing along Eli Yadin.'

'That name I do know. Yadin was along for the ride in Morocco. Mossad – formerly, I think,' Sawyer added.

'You think correctly. He got a little too wild and crazy for them, and you have to be pretty wild and crazy to shock Mossad. He's an assassin, but he specializes in torture. One more name. Franz Berger. Hunter, tracker, sniper – of both the four- and two-legged variety of mammals.'

'How confident are you in your source?' Doyle asked her.

'Completely. She's with Interpol, and believe me, Malmon and the others on that list are very much on Interpol's radar. They're as interested in what he's putting together as we are.'

'We could do without blipping on Interpol's radar ourselves,' Bran pointed out.

'Then we'll have to be careful. We've got a few days. I'm thinking why don't we check out Malmon's digs here on Capri? Say tonight, when everything's nice and quiet.'

'A little B and E?' Sawyer forked a bite of French toast. 'Sounds like a good time. You know, if I could get my hands on a few things, I could put a few bugs together.'

'How do you put bugs together?' Annika asked. 'Why would you want to make bugs?'

'Listening devices,' he explained. 'We call them bugs. We go in, case the place, plant a few where it seems most logical. It could give us a leg up.'

'It could. First? You can make bugs?'

He smiled at Riley. 'I'm handy.'

'Okay, second. He's bound to sweep for them.'

'I could help there.' Bran considered. 'A spell to hide them from an electronic sweep. I could work that out.'

'More handy, and I'll make three.' Riley poured more coffee. 'Tell me what you need, Dead-Eye – and give me options. I'll tug some lines. But it may take a day.'

'I'll make you a list, we can break and enter tomorrow night. Three days,' Sawyer calculated. 'Maybe we'll get lucky, find the star before he gets here.'

'And if not?' Sasha looked around the table at the five people she'd come to trust above all others. 'We do whatever we have to do to protect the star and each other.'

Sawyer made his list; Riley tugged her lines. It made for a later start than planned, but Sawyer figured if he could put together a few bugs, give them some insight into Malmon's plans, it would be more than worth losing an hour in the water.

As he grabbed his gear, Annika stepped to the doorway of his room.

'I need to speak to you.'

'Sure.' But when she came in, closed the door behind her, he stopped what he was doing. 'Serious?'

'Important. In Sasha's painting, you're wounded.'

'We've all been wounded in this little adventure,

174

Anni. It looked like Doyle took a hit, too, so–'

'He can't die.'

'And I won't.' Reading the worry in her eyes, he went to her, took her hands. 'I'll get us out of there.'

'It's hard for you to travel with so many. Please, don't lie to soothe me. I won't be soothed with lies.'

'Not hard so much. It's tricky. But hey, I got us here, right?'

'It would be tricky – more tricky – when you're wounded?'

'Annika, there's no point worrying about that.' Now he ran his hands up her arms, held her by the shoulders. 'I'll get us out, and safe. You have to trust me.'

'I trust you. All that I am trusts what you are. But you'll be hurt. You and Doyle – he can't die but he feels pain. I'm not hurt in the painting, and I'm of the sea.'

'Okay.'

'I can get away from the men, from the sharks. I can – the word is *distract* – until you get away with the others, then–'

'Forget it.' A lick of temper had him tightening his grip on her.

'You must listen!' Temper slapped against temper. 'If the tricky is too hard, you can trust *me*. I can get away without the traveling. You take the others, leave me to–'

'I'm not going to leave you. I'd never leave you. No.' He snapped it out before she could speak again. 'If you think I would, if you think I'd even consider it, you don't know me.'

175

'Do you understand, I could get to the boat, my way, almost before you could, yours?'

'Doesn't matter. I'm not leaving you behind, not today, tomorrow, whenever the hell that painting becomes reality. Not anywhere, not anytime.' Because he read something in her eyes – she'd suck at poker – he released her shoulders to take her face in the same firm grip. 'And don't think you can pull away far enough so I can't connect. That's not happening either, and you'd just make it harder for me.'

'I don't want to make it hard. I want you safe.'

'I will be, and so will you.' He tipped her head back, just a little, laid his lips on hers. Quiet, soothing. At first.

Then she wrapped around him, surrounded him, and he lost himself in the warmth and wanting. He pressed her back against the wall, let himself take, let himself savor what she gave, let himself savor what she made him feel in his blood, in his bones.

The three rude bangs on the door barely registered.

'Sawyer! Get your hands off the girl,' Doyle ordered. 'We're moving.'

'We have to go.' Reluctantly, almost painfully, Sawyer took his hands off the girl.

'Why don't you have sex with me?'

'What?' He took a step back, as if from a live grenade. 'What?'

'Your sex part gets hard for sex, but you don't ask for sex. I don't know if I'm allowed to ask for sex. I don't know the rules of this.'

Because she gestured toward him – it – he had

176

to fight an urge to cross hands over his groin. 'I haven't... It's not that I– Rules.' He jumped on that concept. 'There are rules. Lots of complicated rules. We should talk about them. Later. We need to go.'

'You'll explain the rules?'

'I... Yes, probably. Later.' He grabbed his pack, opened the door. But oddly still couldn't suck in a full breath. 'But now, we have to go. Lost stars, worlds in peril, the evil mother of lies. You know, the usual.'

'When I know the rules, we can lie together in my room. My bed is larger.'

'Well, that's an idea all right.' Hastily, he slung the pack over his shoulder, and careful to keep one hand on the open door, grabbed hers with the other. 'Let's go.' He pulled her out of the room, kept going until they were outside where the rest waited.

He managed to separate himself enough to mutter to Sasha. 'Distract her. I need to talk to Doyle and Bran.'

'Well, I–'

Since Sawyer already moved ahead until he caught up with Doyle's faster pace, Sasha slowed a bit, pointed. 'Oh, look. A butterfly.'

The comment brought a puzzled look from Riley, but caused Annika to stop and admire long enough to give Sawyer some distance.

'Listen,' he said to Doyle, 'it wasn't all about hands.'

'I don't need to hear about the rest of your body parts.'

'Not what I mean. I need to talk to you and

177

Bran – and the other women – about this hare-brained idea Anni had about the painting, and how we need to watch her in case I didn't talk her out of it.'

He glanced back, casually, gauged he had enough room if he made it quick. And signaled to Bran.

Annika didn't mind walking with her two friends. She thought, perhaps, women would be less shy and nervous about sex.

'Can you tell me the rules of sex?'

'Rules?' Riley responded. 'What rules?'

'I don't know them, not here. Sawyer says there are many, and complicated rules. I don't see why they should be complicated, but I can learn them. I like to learn.'

'Complicated.' Riley snorted. 'I say simple. My top three? Both parties willing, available, and clean.'

'Those are very simple.' And very satisfying. 'Your rules mean Sawyer and I can have sex.'

'I'm still trying to work out why he hasn't jumped you yet.'

'Riley.' Sasha rolled her eyes. 'Different rules for different people. Or not rules so much as … sensibilities, and it's not always easy to explain.'

Riley ticked off on her fingers. 'Willing, available, clean.'

'An important foundation,' Sasha agreed. 'We really need a little more time and privacy,' she added as they passed people on the road.

'But you'll explain, so I'll learn.'

'We'll do that.'

'Thank you! Then Sawyer and I can have sex

178

like you and Bran. I'm sorry you can't have sex,' she said to Riley.

'You and me both, sister.'

CHAPTER NINE

They focused on the eastern side of the island, diving the inlets and deep caves. Annika heard no sighs, no songs. Only once did she feel something in the water large enough to be human or shark.

But it was only another pair of divers – a man and a woman – more interested in each other, it seemed to her, than in the sea life.

After the second dive, she led the way back to the boat. She would be vigilant now until they had passed through Sasha's painting, and all come out whole and safe again.

She pulled herself up, as always happy to take off the flippers, so awkward and odd, she had to wear when she had the legs.

Sasha came up behind her, then Sawyer. To be useful, Annika opened the chest with cold drinks. Sasha would want water, but Sawyer and Riley like the Cokes, and–

As she took out bottles, a bird swooped down to perch on the rail. She glanced over, smile ready.

Then carefully set the bottles down again, straightened.

'You aren't a bird.'

Sasha, busy unzipping her wet suit, looked over. 'Sorry, what?'

'This is her creature.'

The bird didn't stir, though it turned its deformed head, stared with glinting yellow eyes as Sawyer reached into his pack for his gun.

'Don't shoot it.' Sasha spoke in a whisper. 'Wait for Bran, wait for the others.'

As Riley pulled herself on board, a second bird dropped onto the rail. 'We've got company.' Riley pulled her knife from its sheath.

The birds were the size of pigeons, but with bodies sinewy, almost shriveled, and wide heads that turned front to back like owls'. The pair sat silently, and a third slid down to perch beside them. Their eyes, sickly yellow, stared unblinking. Oily black feathers remained tucked tight.

Bran dropped down on deck, angled his head as, behind him, Doyle pulled his knife.

'She sends this?' Dark amusement moved over Bran's face as he studied the birds. 'Her harbingers? To strike fear in us? This is what comes from her?'

Sasha turned, pressed a hand to her head, held the other out, a signal to wait. 'Come and see. So it says on the book of your god. And I looked, it's written, and behold a pale horse: And his name that sat on him was Death, and hell followed with him. So I send a pale horse and a rider. This is your death to come. This is your hell to follow. My birds will pick clean your bones, and my dogs will lap your blood.'

She shook her head fiercely as Bran started toward her. 'Wait. Wait.' Eyes shut, she breathed deep, and when she opened her eyes again, they burned like fired crystals. When she spoke, her

180

voice came strong to echo over the water.

'And we say, you will never hold the stars. Send your horse, your rider, send your worst, and we will bear it down, all down. And you with them until you age and whither and weaken. We are your death, your destruction. Come and see!' Sasha threw her head back, shot her arms down, fingers spread. 'Come and see!'

The birds screamed, spread wings, and flew toward Sasha. Annika threw up an arm, shielding Sasha's face, blasting out with her bracelet even as Bran threw bolts of hot blue at the remaining two. Their bodies went to fetid black smoke.

'I hurt her.' On a shaky, bewildered laugh, Sasha once again pressed her fingers to her temple. 'I hurt her. I felt her pain. I hurt her as much as, no, more, *more*, than she hurt me.'

'Your nose bleeds,' Annika murmured, and dabbed gently with a towel.

'It's okay. It's all right.' With eyes glittering with tears and triumph, Sasha looked at Bran. 'It's all right, so's hers. I did it.'

'*Fáidh.*' Overwhelmed, and not a little shaken, he pulled her to him, held her close. '*A ghrá*. Sit now, sit.' Even as he spoke, he drew her down to cradle her on his lap. 'She needs water.'

'I'm all right.' The laugh came again, a little steadier. 'Can't you see? I'm all right. I heard her scream in pain, in fury. And maybe, yes, I could use something for the headache, but I beat her. I beat her back, Bran. I was in *her* head.'

'Here now, let me take this.' Gently, he laid his fingers on her temples, ran his hands over her skull. 'Give me the pain, and it's gone.'

181

'Drink a little.' Kneeling, Annika urged water on Sasha, then took her hand, pressed it to her cheek. 'You were so strong, so brave.'

'I felt strong. I let her in. I knew it was time, knew I could do it.'

'Do you think I doubt you?' Bran kissed her. 'You took a few years off my life, but I don't doubt you.'

'She'll come harder now.'

Riley spared Doyle a look. 'And the buzzkill rides again.'

'She'll come harder,' he repeated, 'because now she knows the one she considered weak – and so did I – is so much stronger than she seems.'

'Damn skippy,' Annika said and made Riley laugh.

'You got that. So, she's throwing Revelation at us? Four horsemen, end-of-the-world shit? She can bring it. Bran, I say you cook us up more hellfire and fucking brimstone. We'll show her what hell is.'

'Malmon's no pale rider.' Sawyer pulled out a Coke, tossed one to Riley, took one for himself, offered a bottle of juice to Annika.

'You're Quick Draw today,' he told her. 'Anyway, Malmon's a psychopath, a thug with money.'

'He's more now,' Sasha reminded him.

'Whatever he is, you already said it. We'll bear them down.' He guzzled some Coke. 'Sasha Riggs, you just played mind games with a god, and won. Where are you going now?'

'I'm going to find the two remaining Stars of Fortune, then dance on a sunny beach. And we will.'

182

'To quote my girl here, damn skippy. But for now, I'd say diving's done for the day.'

'I'm fine, Sawyer. Honestly.'

'Fine or not, Sawyer's right. We're done today.' Doyle moved into the wheelhouse.

'Let's end it on a high note, Sash.' Dropping down beside her, Riley patted Sasha's shoulder. 'Besides, I want to get to shore, check and see if my contact's come through with what Sawyer's after.'

When she was sure Sasha was settled, Annika went over, sat beside Sawyer, took his hand. 'I understood.'

'Understood what?'

'I understood what you've told me, and what I knew in my head, but not my heart. When the bird that wasn't a bird flew at Sasha, and I destroyed it. I would have done the same had it been a man. I would have done the same.'

When she leaned into him, he put an arm around her, held her as Bran held Sasha as they rode the water back to land.

Once they reached the dock, Riley pulled out her phone. 'Give me five,' she said and walked away.

'Sasha should have gelato. A reward,' Annika insisted.

'Gelato's hard to turn down, but– That was fast,' Sasha said as Riley walked straight back.

'Fast and good. Got your list, Sawyer. I can pick it up in about an hour.'

'I've got me a project.'

'An hour. That's perfect. It'll give Annika, Riley, and me an hour to shop.'

'Shopping!' Beaming, Annika pressed her palms together.

'Shopping?' On a frown, Riley tipped down her sunglasses, blew at her bangs. 'For what?'

'Shopping needs no what.' All light and cheer, Sasha took Riley's hand, gave a warning squeeze. 'The three of us will do some shopping, pick up Sawyer's parts, and ... bring home pizza for dinner.'

'You've had a long day, and an experience,' Bran began. 'And as Nerezza's made this first move, we should all stay together.'

'She won't try for me again today, and I think I've proved I can handle myself. You're not going to try to tell us the three of us can't handle ourselves because we're women.'

'Don't go there, dude,' Sawyer warned. 'No way to win it. But we can hang while you–'

'Go.' Sasha pointed. 'All of you. If I get a reward it's a little girl-shopping time without men hovering.' To seal it, Sasha rose to her toes, kissed Bran lightly. 'We'll be home in two hours.'

'If you're not–'

'We will be.'

'Stay together.'

'Of course.' Sasha waved them off, waited until they were out of sight. 'All right.'

'I could shop for new earrings!'

'We're not going shopping.'

Annika's jaw dropped. 'But, you said–'

'Do you want to talk about sex?'

'Yes!' Annika grabbed Sasha's hand. 'It was a ploy!'

'That's right.'

184

'If we're going to talk about sex when I'm not having any, I want alcohol.' Riley scanned the marina. 'Let's find a place with a view and Bellinis.'

Within ten minutes – Riley moved fast – they sat on a shady terrace looking out at water and boats. Riley ordered in Italian, flirting with the waiter, who flirted right back.

Then she sighed, sat back. 'Just proving I could have sex if I opted for the one-nighter. So.' She gestured at Annika. 'The doctors are in. Proceed.'

'Are you a doctor, too?'

'She means we're here to listen,' Sasha explained.

'Oh. It's so nice to have friends who are female.'

'Truer words,' Sasha agreed.

'Sawyer says there are complicated rules about sex. If it's so hard and strict, how do people have sex?'

'Good question. I used to think there were so many complications it was better to just forget about sex. I really believed that was the right thing for me, until Bran.'

'Because you're mates.'

'Yes.' And wasn't that a wonder? 'I didn't know that he felt that way, the way I did. But the other part is, he accepted me, what I am, what I have. No one had before Bran. Before all of you.'

'And I didn't want to have sex with her.' Riley beamed at the waiter when he brought the Bellinis.

'But she's very beautiful, and kind and wise. You'd have pretty sex together.'

Intrigued, Riley angled her head. 'Are there gay merpeople?'

'Oh, yes. We're very happy.'

'No, I mean– Are you, or some of you, attracted to the same sex? Can you mate with someone of the same sex?'

'Of course – differently because of the body, and there will be no young created, but you want who you want, yes? Love who you love?'

'Cheers to that.' Riley picked up her Bellini.

'Is one of the rules you cannot?'

'We're eliminating that rule. Slower in some places, but we're working on it.'

Annika huffed out a breath, frowned at her drink. 'Are all the rules stupid?'

'Maybe some are, and the rules depend.'

Now Annika lifted a hand in frustration. 'How can rules depend if they are rules?'

'We're going to need more Bellinis,' Riley decided. 'And pastries.'

'I can get behind that. But the rules, Anni, depend on the people involved, the situation. For instance, if Bran had been married or promised to someone else.'

'That's the availability rule,' Riley added.

'I understand, and agree. I understand the willing. There must never be force. Clean – I'm not sure why this is important, at every sex.'

'It's not that kind of clean. It's more ... letting your partner know if you're healthy – sexually, that is.' Sasha shook her head. 'I don't see that as an issue for you or Sawyer, so we can table that complicated explanation for now. Other rules, the ones that depend? Some would come from the code or beliefs of who's involved.'

'I know code. Sawyer's honorable. Maybe too

much honor. I tried to explain to him that when the painting happens, I can get away. He can take all of you – because he's wounded, and leave me so–'

'Bullshit. That's never happening.'

Frustrated, Annika turned to Riley. 'But I can–'

'I don't give a rat's ass what you can. And if Sawyer had said different, I'd think less of him – and that's after I'd flattened him.'

'It's insulting, Annika,' Sasha said, more gently. 'It insults us for you to suggest that.'

'I don't mean to insult. I love you, all of you. I hurt his feelings?' Distress squeezed her heart, clouded her mind. 'Oh, I'm so apology. I will sorry to him.'

'Just put it away,' Riley advised. 'And remember, this is all for one, one for all.'

'All for one, one for all,' Annika repeated. 'This is a code. I won't forget it. I hurt his feelings, so he doesn't want to have sex with me.'

'I don't think that's it. Definitely more Bellinis.'

With a nod, Riley signaled the waiter, engaged in a long, flirty conversation.

Interested, Annika watched the waiter glance back at Riley. 'He would have sex with you.'

'Read that signal loud and clear. Sex with a stranger can be exciting, and the danger's part of the excitement. But I have enough excitement and danger going on right now. Plus, this is about you and Sawyer. I can promise you he's had sex with you a few hundred times in his head.'

'But I want him to have sex with his body.'

'Can't blame you.'

With a nod to Riley, Annika leaned in. 'He's

187

brave and strong and kind, and very handsome. But you don't have sex with him.'

'Huh. Okay, yeah, he's a cutie – a hot cutie, and nobody's wimp, but ... you want who you want, right?'

'Yes.' Pleased, Annika sat back. 'It's a mystery of the heart. I want Sawyer, and he wants me. His – your name for it – I can't remember.' She patted her lap.

'Lots of names for that.'

'We'll stick with penis.' On a laugh, Sasha poked Riley's arm.

'His penis gets hard – this is for sex – when we kiss, when he touches me. That's desire, and I see the desire in his eyes. But he doesn't put his penis inside me.'

'Is it just that simple in your world?' Sasha wondered.

'There can be a mating ritual – this is more serious. Or it can be for fun. For the needs.'

'Not so different. Look, this is a good balance here, I think. I'm probably looser about sex than Sasha.'

'Hey.'

'Before Bran,' Riley added.

'All right. Your point.'

'I'm saying Sawyer's code makes his rules – about you – complicated. He doesn't want to take advantage of you, or the situation. That doesn't mean he doesn't want to bang you, or imagine banging you.'

'Bang. Oh! Because the bodies...' Amused, Annika banged her hands together. 'I like it. It's a fun word. How do I make him, without force, stop imagining and start banging me?'

'Jump him.'

Riley blinked. 'Wow. You surprise me, Sash.'

'Called me a tight-ass.'

'Didn't, could have. Yeah, I'd go with jumping him.'

'As in combat?'

'No. You make the moves. You go to him, initiate the ... banging,' Sasha decided. 'You close the door, and you take off your clothes. Then, if necessary, you take off his.'

'Go, Sash.'

'Tight-ass no more,' Sasha said with a smirk. 'I wouldn't suggest this if I hadn't felt how much he wants you, Anni. It was so strong, I couldn't not feel it. I don't intrude, I promise.'

'It's a code, I know. But you felt his desire for me?'

'Yes. And his struggle to control it.'

'So I make it so he can stop the struggle.' Because her heart started to beat harder, Annika pressed a hand to it. 'This is allowed?'

'Even encouraged.' When the waiter came back, Riley sent him that hey-baby smile.

He showered flirtation on all three as he set down the next round, along with a little plate and a small platter heaped with cakes and pastries.

Belle donne.' He kissed his fingertips. 'It is my pleasure to give you service.'

Riley watched him walk away. 'Maybe I should rethink–'

'No,' Sasha said definitely.

'Easy for you to say; hate that you're right. But there's always pastries.'

'Can I help Sawyer with his struggle, jump him, so he bangs me tonight?'

'Your choice.' After a quick scan, Riley snagged a *zeppole* from the platter. 'But we need him to make the bugs.'

After some hard thought, Annika nodded. 'This is more important than banging. But if he finishes the bugs?'

'Jump away. What's that one?' Sasha pointed.

'If it looks good, what do you care what it's called? *Bombolone*. Think of it as a world-class donut. Here.' She picked up a pastry, a little frosted cake, set them on Annika's plate. 'You'll like them. Now it's a party.'

'I love parties. Thank you for helping me understand the rules and the codes of banging.'

'I don't think you'll need it, but–' Sasha took Annika's hand. 'Good luck.'

'Now eat and drink up, ladies. We've got a meet in about twenty minutes.'

'On the way to that, or to the house, we can shop?'

Before Riley could object, Sasha nodded. 'Actually, I think we have to. We can't go back without some evidence we did what we said we were doing.'

'Crap. But it's the lightning round of shopping. Fast,' Riley explained.

'Oh, I can be fast.'

'Yeah, yeah. I'll believe it when I see it.'

They came back loaded. Maybe Annika didn't hit Riley's goal of lightning round, but she managed to buy earrings – two pair – sandals – one with five-inch heels she navigated as if born in them – a tiny purse that would hold little more than air, but had a seashell clasp that charmed her, and three new dresses.

Together, they hiked the slope back carting shopping bags, Sawyer's parts, and three large pizzas.

'Where the hell are you going to wear those heels?' Riley demanded.

'She's going to wear them when she seduces Sawyer. She's going to walk in on them, take off her dress, and stand there wearing just the heels.'

'You may be new at this, Sasha, but you've got skills, and you've got strategies.'

'I had such fun! Your new earrings are so pretty on you, Riley.'

With a shrug, Riley accepted her own weakness. 'In a fight, all the opponent has to do is grab one and pull.'

'They look pretty. So do Sasha's, and Sasha will look beautiful in her new dress and the sandals. You should have bought the new dress I showed you, Riley.'

'I don't have a man to seduce.'

'You have a very good body. It's small and strong and agile, and your breasts are lovely.'

'Well, that doesn't get me laid, but thanks.'

'In my world both male and female would very much wish to bang you.'

So they walked into the house laughing, and drew Bran in from where he'd tried not to worry.

'Successful shopping, it seems.'

'Excellent shopping, and pizza as promised.' Sasha lifted her face for a kiss.

'I'll take the pizza into the kitchen. Doyle's in the grove, or was. Sawyer's outside, working on the plans for whatever you brought for him.'

'Riley can take that out.' Subtly Sasha gave Annika a nudge. 'We'll just go up, put away our shopping extravaganza.'

'This is strategy?' Annika asked as they started up.

'Give him a little time to miss you, to wonder where you are. Don't wear the heeled sandals yet. Save those for impact.'

'It's like a game.'

'A little bit, but one where you both get to win.'

At the door to her room, Annika put down her bags to hug Sasha tight. 'Thank you. You and Riley are my sisters in this world, and in mine.'

'I've learned what family is from you, from all of you. When this is done, I'm going to try to use everything I've learned with my own mother. I'll see you downstairs.'

'You should wear your new dress.'

At the door to her room, Sasha paused, smiled. 'You know, you're right. I'll put on my new dress.'

Annika understood games, and she understood rituals. She'd watched three of her sisters execute mating rituals. It involved flirtation, pretending disinterest, then flirtation.

Though she knew Sawyer couldn't be her life mate, she loved, would always love, so the ritual could be allowed on her part.

She changed – not into her new dress because Sasha should shine in hers. But she used the lip color and the brush with color on her lashes as

192

she knew women did to look even prettier.

After she went down, she made – as Sasha had taught her – a pitcher of sparkling fruit juice. On a tray she arranged the pitcher, glasses, and the bowl that held ice if needed.

Sawyer sat at the table under the pergola, with the things Riley found for him, a drawing he'd made, a kind of tool that reminded her a little of a gun.

Since Doyle sat across, watching Sawyer work, she smiled, carried the tray over.

'I made cold drinks because you'll want beer with the pizza in a little while. Bran will make it hot again for dinner. Is this the bug?' she asked while she poured the drinks.

'It will be. I need to attach this capacitor–'

'Is that a flux capacitor?' Riley called down from her terrace.

'Hah. Just need a DeLorean. Got enough here to build three room transmitters, so we'll need to figure out where they'll do the most good.'

'How did you learn to do this?' Doyle wondered.

'Curiosity, I guess. I took apart this old radio, then an old answering machine, one of my broken remote-control cars, stuff like that. Figured out how to work them together to play spy. This'll be a little more sophisticated. But it's pretty down and dirty.'

'You need dirt?'

'No, it's an...' Sawyer glanced up at Annika. 'Ah, you look good. I mean, you always look good, but–'

'Thank you.' She trailed a finger over his

193

shoulders as she walked behind him. Then sat on the edge of the table, her back to him as she faced Doyle.

Yes, she knew the ritual.

'You drive the boat very well.'

'Good thing.'

'It's a very good thing. Maybe you could teach me. I like to learn. And in return, I can teach you to do the handsprings.'

'I do handsprings, I can't hold a sword.'

'I can teach you to do it with one hand only. You're strong.' Deliberately, she reached over, tapped his biceps. 'You could spring with only one hand, so your sword sweeps at the legs, and your feet kick the face.'

'One hand?'

'Yes, I can teach you. And the running up a wall, both hands free, to flip back? It would be useful to you in combat. Would you like me to show you?'

'Sure. I'm up for something new.'

When he rose to go with her to the strip of lawn, he glanced back at a scowling Sawyer, then up at Riley. She grinned, then leaned on the rail to enjoy the show.

She heard Sawyer curse. 'Problem, cowboy?'

'Nothing. Just a little burn.'

She watched Annika, dress billowing down toward her head, gorgeous legs flashing up in the spring.

'I bet,' Riley said, and grinned again.

CHAPTER TEN

Sawyer worked through it. Riley had come through with what he needed, now he'd use it to make what they all wanted.

He did his best to concentrate, to ignore Annika's instructions to Doyle, Doyle's comments back.

And her laugh. Doyle – not much of a laugher – sure seemed to be having a hell of a fucking good time.

Cut it out, he warned himself when he felt annoyance and outright jealousy crawling over his skin. He had a job to do, worlds to save, and couldn't be worried about part of his team tumbling around on the stupid lawn.

Maybe he'd like to learn how to do a one-handed handspring. Doyle wasn't the only one with upper-body strength.

Maybe Doyle had the kind of upper-body strength that bench-pressed Toyotas, but still.

He tried to settle down. No point in singeing his fingers with the soldering gun again because he was watching them instead of what he was doing.

Then Sasha came out, sat beside him. 'We figured pizza in about an hour, if that works for you.'

Grunting, he finished wrapping enameled wire around a bolt, cutting off the ends. 'I want to keep at this,' he said, and stripped the ends of the wire. 'I can take it inside, grab a slice.'

'Anything I can do to help?'

He shook his head, picked up the soldering iron to solder the stripped ends to his new, tiny circuit board. 'Really a one-man job.'

'If you– Well, wow!'

'Wow, what?'

'Doyle just did a handspring, but with one hand.'

He looked up in time to see Annika give Doyle a congratulatory hug. 'Great.'

By the time he'd finished building two listening devices, on a table in the living area where he had room and some damn quiet, the moon was up, the stars out. And he needed a break.

He walked outside, and down, sat on the steps to look out at the sea.

'How did it go?'

He glanced back and up, saw Bran on the terrace. 'I got two done, and tested. I need–'

'Wait, I'll come down.'

When Bran came out, he sat on the steps, passed Sawyer a beer. 'Sasha said you stuck with water or caffeine during the build. I thought you could use this now.'

'Yeah, I can, thanks. Needed a break. It's not complicated so much as exacting, especially when it's makeshift. I could work on the last one tonight, but I think I'd start getting sloppy. We can wait until tomorrow night to plant them, or go with two.'

'We talked about it at dinner, already opted for tomorrow night. Don't push yourself tonight.'

'Appreciate it.' Content with the company, with

196

the beer, Sawyer turned his mind on the what's next. 'I can get us inside Malmon's villa, no problem. Since we won't have to deal with windows or doors to get in, we don't have to worry about an alarm system. But if they run to motion detectors, that's a problem.'

'Ah.' With a nod, Bran leaned back against the steps, looked up at the star-strewn sky and the waxing moon. 'And one none of us considered.'

Since the decision to check out Malmon's villa, Sawyer had considered a lot. 'Or internal cameras, that's another. If I knew, one, they had motion detector alarms or security cameras, and two, what type, and three, where the system's based, I could maybe bypass.'

Amusement had Bran's scarred eyebrow lifting. 'Is that the case then?'

On a quick laugh, Sawyer lifted the beer. 'I don't make breaking and entering a habit, but it's good to know things, and how things work. You can bank on Malmon installing that kind of security while he's in there. We don't know if it's already there. And if I'd thought of it before, maybe Riley could have found out.'

'She may still – we'll tap her on it. Otherwise, we take our chances, I think. If we set off any alarms, we can be out again before anyone checks.'

'I can probably make it look like a glitch. But the cameras–'

'I can find a way to deal with those, if there are any to deal with.'

'All right. If we're back around five like usual tomorrow, I'll have the third one done before sundown.'

'More than soon enough, as we think to wait until about midnight. Doyle wants a look at the grounds as well, and we'd want quiet and privacy for that.'

'Can't forget what Doyle wants.'

Bran took a contemplative sip of his own beer. 'Problem with Doyle, is there?'

'No. No... No problem.'

To Bran, three 'nos' in succession meant yes. 'I see he's learned some new moves from Annika.'

'What– Moves?' Sawyer's head swiveled so fast, Bran wondered it didn't twist off like a bottle cap. 'Oh, right, right. The famous one-handed handspring.'

'A forward one, yes. She claims she can teach him a backward one in no time. There's affection and admiration from him to her and back again. And, *mo chara*, if you think there's more than that on either side, you're, well, a git, that's all. She's yours, but for the asking. And now, since I've a mind to have my own woman, I'll say good night to you. And sleep well,' he added as he rose to go inside.

His for the asking, Sawyer thought and glugged down more beer. Not how it looked, not how it felt right at the moment. Besides, asking didn't seem right. She was new to this world. She still got words mixed up, had to have things explained to her. How could it be right to ask her to sleep with him?

Added to that, which was more than enough to his mind, she only had three months – less than two and a half now, he remembered – before she had to go back to the sea.

198

He was very much afraid if he asked, if he took, if he had her, he'd never in all his life – wherever and whenever he went – get over her.

He should never have touched her in the first place, given them both ideas. The simple solution? Don't touch her again. God knew they had enough to do, to risk without adding in sex and heartbreak.

He rose, took the beer with him to his room. Opened the door, and nearly dropped the bottle.

She sat on the side of his bed, got to her feet as he stood there.

'I waited for you.'

'Okay.' Carefully, he set the beer aside. 'Do you need something?'

'Yes. So do you, I think. And so I waited for you.'

Watching his face, she lifted her hands, nudged the two thin straps from her shoulders, and with a kind of shrug had the dress pooling at her feet.

The single thought that shot through his head was: I'm a dead man. In a fumbling rush, he shut the door.

'Annika, don't...'

Words slipped away as she stepped out of the discarded dress and stood, lithe and lean and lovely in shoes that were nothing but a few bright red straps and high, thin heels.

'You desire me.' She took a step toward him. 'I desire you. Will you take what I offer you? Will you offer me what I ask?'

He knew there were reasons, but he couldn't find and hold a single one. 'I'm supposed to–'

'Lie with me,' she said, and took another step. And her eyes, just her eyes, bewitching green, destroyed him. 'Mate with me.' And another step. 'Be with me.'

She wrapped her arms around his neck, pressed that long, beautiful body against his, and took his mouth.

Long, warm, slow, deep, she twisted him into knots, then set the knots on fire. Her fingers dived into his hair, gripped him there while his defenses crumbled to dust. Before he could find the will, the reason, to shore them up again, she slid her leg up his and breached the wall.

He surrendered to her, surrendered to his own spiraling lust. Screw the rules, he thought. Screw the risks. He pulled her closer, gripped her hair, all that wonderful hair.

They'd break them and they'd take them together.

When he backed her toward the bed, she lowered her hands to tug up his shirt.

'I want to see you, touch you. All of you. I need to take your clothes off.'

'Yeah, yeah, we'll do that. Just let me...' As they fell on the bed, his hands ran over her. Soft, smooth, sublime. 'Annika. Just let me.'

It was everything she'd imagined, everything she'd hoped for. This freedom he'd never given her before, the full passions in the way his hands took and touched, and the wild hunger of his mouth as it ... fed on hers with teeth, tongue, lips.

No one had ever kissed her just like this. With such appetite.

Eager to give him more, she pressed up against him where she felt the hardness, and he moaned against her breast as if in pain, but the kind of pain that spoke of need.

So she arched her hips against him again, felt a jolt in her own center, and a kind of lovely, lovely clutching.

The muscles in his back, his arms – all so different when lying on a bed – the softness under her, the hard over her, caused such *feelings* inside her.

Though she'd never undressed a man, it couldn't be so different from undressing herself – and she so much wanted to have his body, without the clothes, against hers. She reached for his belt, trying to stem her excitement so her fingers could work on the buckle.

'Maybe just hold on there,' he murmured, 'or it'll be over awfully quick.'

Her hands went still. 'Can it only be once?'

The sound he made, a mixture of laugh and groan, puzzled her.

'No. Not just once.'

'Then it can be quick this time.' Her need was now, now, now, so she pulled the belt free. 'I want to know. It's the first I've mated with legs.'

Breathless, next to desperate, he forced himself to stop. 'The first?' Of course it was the first, for Christ's sake. 'Does that mean, you're... Would it be like your first time? Ever?'

'Oh, you mean do I still have the shield?' She dragged him back again. 'No. This part is the same. But the legs, the bed, your legs. It's different. It's new. I want you between my legs. I want you inside me, between my legs. I want to know, Sawyer. With you.' Filled with those wants, with those jolts, she took his mouth again. 'Only you.'

She started to tug his jeans down.

'I've still got boots on. Wait.' He rolled, sat up. As he dragged violently at his boots, she reared up, circled him from behind, drove him closer, closer to madness with her mouth at his neck, her hands running over his chest.

Freed, finally, of boots, jeans, everything, he turned toward her. She stayed on her knees, her hair spilling like ink down her back, over one shoulder. Her gaze traveled down his chest, down. And she smiled.

'You're beautiful, and strong.' Reaching out, she trailed her fingers over his shaft, made his blood thrum. A thousand strings plucked at once.

'This is pleasure?'

'I don't think they've come up with a word for what I'm feeling.'

Still smiling, she lay back, her hair spread over the white sheets in long, rich rivers. A perfect gift, offered without guile or artifice.

'Mate with me, please. Put your pleasure inside me.'

She dazzled him, undid him, and in that moment owned him.

He lowered to her and, struggling to take care, to go slow in case she was wrong and it would be like her first time, began to enter the hot and wet.

'Oh. Oh.' Her fingers gripped his arm, nails digging in as she shuddered. And she cried out, with her eyes full of wonder. 'But this ... this comes at the end. It's the end?'

'No, it's not the end.' Every muscle trembled as he braced himself over her. 'Do you want to come again? Feel that again?'

'I can? Yes. Yes.'

She made a sound, low in her throat, when he went deeper.

He held there, strained to just hold there until her hips began to rise and fall.

'I need to... I need to.'

'That's right.' His lips skimmed light over hers. 'Do what you need.' Then he used his tongue, roughened the kiss when she came again, cried out against his mouth.

He thrust once, hard, deep, and she gasped, she arched.

'Yes. Again. Again.'

So he rode her, fast, hard. Just let himself take.

She felt that ending that wasn't an ending with him rise up in her again. As it flooded her, she threw her arms back, hooked her legs around his waist, moved with him, mated with him, flew along the wave, then the next.

Then what rose in her was more, more than pleasure and joy, more than all she'd ever known. She shuddered with it, and he shuddered with her.

When the true end came, it swept her into another world, one beyond beauty.

Even when he caught his breath, and that took a while, his heartbeat sang in his ears. When he rolled off her, she rolled with him, nuzzled up beside him.

And that felt exactly right.

'You're pleased with me?'

'Anni, there isn't a word big enough for what I am with you right now.'

'I'm the same for you. Making sex with legs is different. And with you, it's more. You have a very

203

good penis.'

He choked out a laugh. 'Thanks. I'm ... fond of it.'

'I am, too. Will you put it inside me again?'

No one like her, he thought, in this world. In any world. 'I'd say that's a sure bet after this.'

'And was this time awfully quick?'

He took her hand from his heart, kissed it. 'I guess the first part was – you know, the foreplay. The before the...' Jeez. 'Mating.'

'Ah, you mean the touching and kissing. I like that very much. It's better to have that longer?'

'Depends. But there's more stuff people like to do sometimes before the big guns.'

'More? What more?'

She wasn't innocent, he told himself. But she was unschooled in certain areas. 'You know, maybe you should talk about some of this with Sasha and Riley.'

'I did. That's how I knew to come here and take off my dress and wear just the shoes.'

'You... Really?'

'You liked the shoes. I'll tell them.'

He just closed his eyes. 'I bet you will.'

Slowly, she circled a finger over his heart, trailed it lightly down his chest. 'Will you do the more stuff to me? You'll teach me so I can do more stuff to you.'

'Annika, you kill me.'

'That's an expression. I would never hurt you.'

'I know.' As he turned his head to kiss her, a thought struck him like a bolt from a crossbow. 'I didn't protect you.'

'There was no danger.'

'No, I mean...' He pushed up, drawing her with him. 'Can you get pregnant?'

'Oh, no. I can't have young with you. We're from different worlds, not enough the same. I'm sorry.'

'No.' Relieved, he pressed his lips to her forehead. 'It's better that way. We've got a war going on for one thing. And you only have a couple more months–'

Quickly, she laid a finger over his lips. 'Don't speak of the end. Please. We have now.'

'You're right. If you worry too much about tomorrow, you miss appreciating what is. I appreciate what is, with you.'

She laid her head on his shoulder. 'I want to stay with you tonight.'

'I want you to stay. The bed's a little small, but we'll manage.'

'Yes.' She snuggled down with him again. 'Is it true it can be more than once?'

'Yeah. It's getting pretty close to being true right now.'

'Then before we sleep, you could show me one of the more stuff.'

'I could do that.' As he angled down to kiss her, he slid his hand down her body, between her legs.

'Oh! I like this stuff!'

He laughed, even as he made her come again.

In the morning, Sawyer headed outside for calisthenics feeling like a man who could run twenty miles – all uphill – without getting winded, then polish that off by eating the equivalent of a team of horses.

He found Doyle leaning against the outdoor

table, drinking coffee while the sky went pale and pink.

'The others should be right along,' Sawyer said.

'Mmm-hmm. You got lucky. It's all over you, brother,' Doyle added. 'And if it wasn't, I'm next door. Your mermaid's enthusiastically vocal.'

'Oh.' Sawyer studied his water bottle, then looked over at Doyle. 'Sorry?'

'No, you're not, and can't blame you. But you owe me.'

'How you figure?'

'She used me to get you worked up – classic strategy. She'd owe me, too, but she taught me a couple of solid moves, so she and I are even.'

Sawyer thought of the damn handsprings, and the jealousy crawling over his skin. 'Didn't see it coming.'

'They never do. So, payback? Take it up to her room, then I don't have to think about how I'm not getting laid.'

'Done. I was pissed at you.'

'Yeah.' With one of his rare smiles, Doyle lifted his coffee. 'Can't blame you there either. You're a lucky man, Sawyer. She's like no other.'

'I know it. It's why I pulled a muscle in my willpower not to go there with her.'

'Brother, when beauty falls into your hand, you hold on to it while you can. You could be dead tomorrow.'

'Well, that's ... inspiring.'

When the others came out, Annika walked straight to Sawyer, moved in for a kiss – the sort that made him wonder just how soon they could take it up to her room.

'Are you passing those out?' Doyle asked her.

On a quick laugh, she turned to him, laid her hands on his shoulders, kissed him lightly, sweetly on the lips. 'This is how you kiss family. Sawyer is family, too, but it's different. We have sex.'

'I heard.'

'I had stars in my head. It's very good sex that makes stars. And I learned about the more stuff. Did you know in the foreplay – such a good word – a man can–'

'Okay.' Hastily, Sawyer grabbed her hand. 'We should get started.'

After nearly an hour of squats, shuffles, push-ups, pull-ups, and whatever other torture Doyle could devise, Sawyer made a mountain of pan-cakes. His call as breakfast chef, and he was in the mood.

Halfway through the meal, and the discussion on how and when they'd case Malmon's rented villa, Riley's phone signaled. She took one glance at the readout, rose, and moved off, speaking rapidly in Italian.

When she came back, she picked up her plate, shoveled food in while she stood. 'Okay, I scored us three SPP-1Ms, with twenty-four cartridges. Best I could do for now, and the third's a bonus. We'll need to hit the kitty,' she told Bran.

'I'll take care of that part. Where do we pick them up?'

'We need to go out to his boat, so we'll have to get moving pretty soon. I'll need you to give me the cash, and some room. This guy doesn't like crowds.'

'How trustworthy is he?' Bran asked her.

207

'Well, he's a smuggler, a gunrunner, and a thief, so he's slippery. But he won't screw with me. He'll keep it straight – wouldn't want to damage his rep, or lose the sale if we want more ammo.'

'Are these guns stolen?'

Riley shrugged at Sasha. 'Don't ask, don't tell. We need them, we'll have them. Or three of them. Sawyer's the best shot, so I say he gets one. And me, and it should probably be Doyle for the third. Bran's good, but considering what he can already shoot, a gun's superfluous. And Sasha's a decent shot. Doyle's just better.'

'I'm fine with that, but I should learn how to use it. In case.'

'We can go over all that on the boat, once we have them.'

Though she didn't like the idea of more guns, Annika said nothing. She did her assigned chores, got her pack for the day, and with the others, walked to the marina.

As they eased out of the slip, Riley pointed. 'See that yacht out there? Ten o'clock?'

'Hard to miss,' Doyle answered. 'She's an easy two hundred fifty feet.'

'Yeah, Lester doesn't go for subtle.'

The smirk lit his gaze as he slid it toward her. 'Your smuggler's named Lester?'

'I used to know a rogue lycan named Sherman. Nice enough guy until he discovered the wonders of cocaine. After that, he really loved ripping out throats three nights a month. Anyway. Just head out, pull up on the port side. I'll take it from there.' She adjusted her sunglasses, took the bag of cash from Bran.

'Don't be alarmed if you see a couple of guys with automatic weapons. They're not going to shoot anybody.'

'Somehow that doesn't inspire confidence.' And because of it, Sawyer unclipped the holster from the small of his back, reset it on his hip.

'You're just as likely to see some bimbos sunning French style.'

'For that I need my camera.'

As they approached, Sawyer did see a couple of hard faces with rifles. And though he thought it unfair to assume bimbo, a trio of hot chicks wearing nothing but big sunglasses and tiny, tiny thongs.

'Riley Gwin,' Riley called out. 'Lester's expecting me. And this.' She held up the bag. 'Hey, Miguel, *¿qué pasa?*'

The burly guy with the AK-47 grinned. *'No mucho, chica.'*

When they lowered the boarding ladder, Doyle signaled Sawyer. 'Take the wheel. I'm going with her.'

'No, you're not.'

Ignoring her, Doyle stepped over, grabbed the ladder, and started up.

'Damn it. Got a friend with me, Miguel! I'll need some help getting the stock down the ladder.'

A moment later Doyle boarded, then Riley, and both moved out of sight.

'How long do we give them?' Sawyer kept his eyes on the men with guns.

'Ten minutes,' Bran decided. 'Can you read them, *fáidh?*'

'The one she called Miguel would like to see

Annika and me naked. The other one ... he feels a little unwell. Indigestion, I think.'

'Ten minutes,' Bran said again, 'unless Sasha feels a change.'

It took every bit of the ten, and as Sawyer worked out how best to protect his friends, get on the yacht, and save the others, he heard Riley laugh.

But he didn't relax until he saw her coming down the ladder, a leather satchel strapped cross-body and a metal case in one hand.

Doyle came after her, another satchel, another case, and some sort of box tucked under his arm.

'*Ciao*, Miguel.'

'*Hasta luego, chica.*' He blew her a sly kiss, but stood, armed, until Sawyer turned the boat out to sea.

'All good?' Sawyer asked.

'Five-by-five. Three Russian underwater pistols with cartridges, holsters, and cases. And a little gift for Doyle. Lester took to Doyle, which is fortunate, as Lester doesn't like alterations in agreements.'

'You couldn't have carried it all.' After taking off the satchel, Doyle passed it to Bran. 'Lester is barely taller than Gwin here, with a face like a rat after it's been squeezed in a door.'

'He's also worth about a couple hundred million, and is quite the bon vivant. He likes brainless, built women and hot, younger men, often at the same time. He'd have oiled you up and slithered all over you given half the chance,' she said to Doyle.

'Not my type. But I got a prime bottle of

tequila out of it.'

'Tres Cuatro y Cinco – that's not just prime tequila, it's the god of tequilas. It ain't for margaritas or Jell-O shots. It's for sipping and savoring. Anyway, Lester came through.'

She sat, opened a satchel. 'Let me show you our new toys.'

'First? Where am I going?'

'I'll take the wheel.' Doyle moved to the wheelhouse. 'I've seen the new toys.'

Because she didn't really want to see the guns, Annika rose. 'I'll go with Doyle. He's going to teach me to drive the boat.'

'Here, you take the wheel.'

As Sawyer moved aside, Doyle shifted Annika, put her hands on the wheel.

'I can?'

'I'm staying right here.'

Behind her the men exchanged a look that expressed appreciation on one end, acknowledgment on the other. With Annika occupied, Sawyer went back for a briefing on SPP-1Ms.

Once in the water, he didn't fire it – no safe target and no point in wasting ammunition. But he got the feel of it, the weight, the balance – a different sensation.

As they dove, with the search once again the focus, he kept Annika – and all the rest – in his eyeline.

Riley's intel could be wrong, or Malmon might have sent advance forces. But again they found nothing, and no one.

Still, he had a job to finish. When they got back to the villa, he focused on that. The others gave him room and quiet.

He glanced up when Annika came in.

'I'm sorry, but Sasha said you need to eat.'

'I'm nearly done.'

'She said she's making chicken parmigiana.'

And suddenly, he was hungry. 'Really?'

'And it would be time to eat it in thirty minutes.'

'That should work for me.'

'Sawyer? Will you lie with me in my bed tonight?'

'I was going to ask you the same.'

Her smile just brightened the room. 'Then I could put the laundry I folded – yours – in my room?'

'That'd be nice.'

But she should have more than just sex, he thought. Because however fatalistic, Doyle had it right. When beauty fell into your hand, you held on to it.

And in Sawyer's mind, you cherished it.

'Maybe we could take a walk around the gardens after dinner.'

'That would be nice, too. I like to walk with you, and have you hold my hand like Bran holds Sasha's.'

But over dinner, Riley suggested moving up the timetable.

'We head over to Malmon's villa, scope it out. We need to make sure it's empty. He could've sent staff or soldiers ahead, or arranged for locals to stock it up for him.'

'That's why we decided to go in after midnight,' Doyle reminded her.

'It's after eight now, and a good thirty-minute hike. We need to case it, find any exterior security, deal with it. After Sawyer pops us in, we may have more security to deal with. Then we have to find the three most logical locations for the bugs.'

'Why wait?' Sawyer had to side with her. 'Y'all mostly decided on the time to give me a chance to finish the bugs. They're done, so let's move it up.'

'And if there is someone in residence?' Sasha asked.

'We'll figure it out.' Considering that, Riley switched wine for water. 'It's a hell of a lot easier to figure out on-site than it is to speculate.'

'There's a point,' Bran agreed. 'So should we say we'll leave here at nine then?'

It wasn't the romantic garden walk Sawyer had envisioned, but he calculated every step took them closer to resolution. If they could eavesdrop on any of Malmon's plans, they could foil them, maybe turn them back on him.

And if they beat him badly enough, what use would he be to Nerezza? Whatever punishment she might mete out for failure, he'd earned.

'We're closer to the sea,' Annika told him. 'More above it, but closer.'

'He'd want a good view.'

They came to a wall.

'Other side of this,' Riley told them. 'The gate should be up ahead. It'll be locked. Smarter to go over the wall anyway.'

'Let me check it out.'

Sawyer moved ahead, came to the gate – iron,

elaborate, arched, and secured with an electronic lock. Behind it he made out a pebbled road wide enough for a vehicle, and shielding trees, bushes. But no cameras.

As he walked back, he scanned the area. More homes, but he saw no one on the road, no one in a window.

'I didn't see an alarm or cameras, but if we tried the gate, it might set something off. I can get us on the other side.'

'I've got mine.' Bran put an arm around Sasha's waist, floated up with her, over, and down.

'Never gets old,' Sawyer commented. 'Okay team, huddle up. Quick trip.'

He had them over the wall where the air was sweet with flowers and the night full of shadows.

'Stay together,' Bran said quietly. 'And keep out of the light.'

Keeping the pebbled road close, they passed through a lemon grove, circled around an area with stone benches and a small fountain, then through a garden lush with blooms and scent.

'Got our garden walk after all.' He gave Annika's hand a squeeze, then stopped. 'Wowzer.'

The villa loomed ahead, white as fresh snow with windows black and glittering in the starlight. The pebbled path split, one stream toward the house, banked with rose bushes, another toward an outbuilding.

The face boasted wide terraces held by carved columns.

It rose three stories, along with what he took as a rooftop terrace. The stream of moonlight turned it all into a charcoal sketch of indulgence.

'It makes our villa on Corfu look like the low-rent district.'

'I liked ours better. We had Apollo.'

Sawyer gave Annika's hand another squeeze. 'He's a great dog.'

'No lights on,' Riley pointed out. 'It's not even ten o'clock. If anyone was in there, we'd see lights.'

'Ones out here are probably motion-activated,' Sawyer said. 'You know, get home late, they come on as you get close to the house, so you don't fall on your face. Shouldn't matter. If anybody sees lights come on, they'll just figure someone's staying here.'

'Provided no one's in there, and just called it an early night,' Sasha pointed out.

'Let me check it out. I can be in and out, like the Flash.'

Before Sawyer could take out the compass, Riley gripped his arm. 'Not on your own, Barry Allen. Just like Doyle had to come with me this morning. I'll go with you.'

'Fine by me. Give us ten minutes.'

When they vanished, Annika frowned. 'Why did she call him that name? The Barry Allen name.'

'I have no idea,' Bran said.

'The Flash – his civilian name. Christ,' Doyle muttered. 'Hasn't anyone read a graphic novel?' With a shake of his head he moved into deeper shadows. 'I'll scout the grounds.'

'Keep close,' Bran warned.

'I'll be close enough.'

He vanished into the dark as Riley and Sawyer had vanished into the air.

215

CHAPTER ELEVEN

In just under ten minutes, Sawyer popped back, alone.

'The place is empty, and it's a simple exterior security system. We're fine inside.' He nodded as lights came on in the villa. 'Riley's scouting locations for the bugs. It's a hell of a place. I should've made a freaking dozen.'

'We'll work with what we have,' Bran said.

'We've got what we've got.' His hand went to his gun, then relaxed again when Doyle melted out of the shadows. 'Ready?'

Sawyer took Annika's hand, shifted them all inside.

Light splashed on smoke-gray tiles and dark wood in a soaring entranceway crowned by a double staircase.

'We did a quick sweep down here, another on the next two levels. Kitchen's stocked, and there's fresh flowers everywhere. There's an outdoor kitchen on this level, and another on the roof terrace. There's enough food for an army, but it wouldn't be like Malmon to have more than his personal security and key people in-house. He wouldn't house his grunts here.'

'And no word on how many he might have or where he'll house them.' Riley came down the grand staircase in scarred hiking boots. 'Eight bedrooms in this place, including two master suites. One's more masterful than the other, and you can take it to the bank Malmon would pick that. The bathtub's freestanding, natural stone, and big enough for a party. I want it for my own, but more to the point I vote for a bug in there.'

'I agree with that. He won't have meetings in there,' Sawyer added. 'But he's likely to use it – it's pretty princely – to make calls, send out orders, get sitreps.'

'I don't know that word.'

'Situation reports,' Doyle told Annika. 'Shorthand for it. Prime location would be where he'd meet with his team leaders.'

'Yeah, Sawyer and I talked about that. Main level – that's how we see it.'

'And you know him, we don't,' Bran put in.

'Yeah.' Still Sawyer looked around. 'We did, like I said, a quick sweep. We should spread out, do a more thorough one.'

They rejected the kitchen, the main-level bedrooms, a game room, and took it down to a spacious parlor with windows looking out over gardens and out to sea or an office and library combination with an elaborate antique desk, more dark, heavy wood, lots of rich Italian leather.

'What's your instinct?' Bran looked at Riley and Sawyer. 'Which strikes you?'

'He'd like lording that view over his underlings,' Riley began. 'And he might use the parlor deal, or the big terrace down here for a meet. But...'

'Office – that desk.' Sawyer nodded at her. 'It's command center. It's "I'm in fucking charge here." That's Malmon.'

'Do both.' Doyle scanned the office. 'You've

217

given us a clear sense of him, haven't you? He's not doing serious work above this level – not having his soldiers come into what he'd think of as more personal areas. Rooftop terrace, the pool, the setup? It's an ass-kicker, but main level, that's business.'

'Two down here, one in the bedroom. I should've made more bugs.'

'Whatever we might get is something we wouldn't have had,' Bran pointed out.

'Okay. Agreed? And done,' Sawyer said when he got nods. 'Bookcase is handy behind the desk. They will sweep.'

'I'll take care of that,' Bran assured him.

After studying the shelves, Sawyer picked up a small silver box, opened it. 'Pretty much tailor-made.'

As Sawyer slipped the device inside, Bran held a hand over it. For a moment it glowed clear, cold blue.

'A kind of shield,' Bran explained.

They repeated the process in the parlor, in the bedroom they believed Malmon would claim.

'I want to test it. I need one of you at each location. I'm going to shift back to our villa. Y'all give me, we'll say three minutes, then I need whoever's in the office to say something, a couple of sentences. Give it ten seconds, then same thing from the parlor, another ten, bedroom. If it works, I'll be back right after. If it doesn't, give me about two minutes for adjustments, go through the round again.'

It took two rounds before he was satisfied. Careful to leave everything as they found it,

Sawyer traveled them back to the villa.

'You look a little beat-up,' Riley observed.

'No, just used up some. A lot of traveling in a short span. It takes it out of you.'

'I'll make you a snack.'

He started to brush off Annika's offer, thought better of it. 'You know, that'd be great. I'm a little low on juice.'

As Annika hurried to the kitchen, with Sasha behind her to supervise, Sawyer sat under the pergola. 'Now we wait.'

'I'll keep trying to find out where he's housing his troops. If I get a hit, we might be able to screw something up for him. In fact, I'll—'

Riley broke off when Annika ran out. 'Sasha says they're coming. From the sky. They're coming.'

'Weapons,' Doyle snapped out.

Training paid off. In less than two minutes they stood together, fully armed, in the grove.

'Make them come to us,' Riley ordered. 'Make them maneuver. You up for this, Dead-Eye?'

'Count on it,' Sawyer replied, a gun in each hand.

They winged down from the sky, not the mutant batlike creatures from Corfu, but hundreds upon hundreds of the strange, vicious birds they'd dealt with on the boat.

Smaller, faster, more agile but no less lethal, they poured into the grove.

Sasha's bolt went through three at once, which burst into ash.

Sawyer fired, two-handed, while blades cleaved. Their wings, he discovered as one sliced through leaves, barely missed his throat, were as deadly as

219

talon and beak.

Out of the corner of his eye he saw Annika flip back, delivering two fierce kicks as her bracelets shot two more. And the wing that sliced through the sole of her shoe.

'Watch the wings!' he shouted. 'They're like razors.'

Dropping into a crouch, he fired right, left, then checked his timing. If he waited for a group he could, as Sasha did, take out multiples with one shot. One caught him as it fell, the keen wing grazing his shoulder before it went to ash. To avoid the next, he dropped, rolled, and took out a dozen more before he had to reload.

To his right, Bran blasted out streams to cover him. He caught sight of Riley falling flat on her back to avoid a low swoop, and Doyle's sword cutting through so she rolled away from falling ash, firing as she did.

He smelled the ash, the stink of it, and blood. The others', his own, as a trio he aimed for split apart. He took out the high two, but the one who went low caught him with talons at the ankle.

Mindful of his hands, he used the butt of his gun to smash at it, then put a bullet through it as it lay fluttering on the ground.

Then Annika lifted her arms, spun, spun, spun, bracelets flashing until ash fell like rain.

For a moment, the grove echoed with power, and with silence.

In a defiant gesture, Riley kicked at a pile of ash, then swiped at the blood trickling down her temple.

'Now I want a snack.'

Turning, Annika hugged her. 'I'll make you one.'

When he noticed her limping, Sawyer grabbed Annika around the waist. 'Did they get your feet?'

'A little. But they ruined my new shoes.'

As Sawyer felt the heat of battle fade into a laugh, Doyle sheathed his sword. 'Put a slice in my coat. Bet you can fix that,' he said to Bran.

'Seriously? You want him to use magick to fix your coat?'

Doyle only shrugged at Riley. 'It's a good coat.'

'Why don't we go inside?' Bran lifted one of Sasha's hands, bleeding, to his lips. 'Assess all the damage. I think we look at flesh first, then see what we can do about coats and shoes.'

'That was a hell of a move there.' Sawyer kept his arm around Annika as they walked. 'The last one – spinning?'

'I was very mad about the shoes. I had a lot of angry energy.'

'Looks good on you. You've got some nicks. Those little bastards are fast.'

'We kicked their ass. Don't say it,' Riley warned Doyle. 'I'm not an idiot. She just wanted to keep us busy, to see if we've got something new going – like her little lovebirds. Suicide squad, that's what they were.'

In the kitchen, Bran cleaned and dressed wounds with Sasha's help.

'Not too much damage, considering.'

Frowning, Doyle picked up his leather coat, poked a finger through the slice in the sleeve. 'I like this coat. It's only got about thirty years on it.'

'I'll have a look at it.' At the kitchen sink, Bran washed blood and balm from his hands. 'And

221

now that we're on the mend, I'll tell you we will have that something new. The bolts, bullets, blades – and the bracelets. I've nearly got what we'll want there. Another day, two at most.'

'Hot damn,' Riley said over a mouthful of salami and cheese.

'If it works as planned, we'll be able to take out a swarm of those bloody birds with one shot.'

'Even hotter damn.' As he ate, as he felt his energy level creep up from zero, Sawyer nodded at Riley. 'We're going to need to score more ammo anyway.'

'Got that covered.'

'Now you.' Sasha nudged Bran to sit so she could treat his wounds. 'It's the same as on Corfu. A nightmare like that comes out of the sky. We fight, bleed, kill, and no one notices. It doesn't happen for anyone else.'

'Best it doesn't, isn't it? Explanations only cause complications. I'm going out, make sure there aren't any stragglers.'

'Hell.' Riley stuffed another bite in her mouth, rose with Doyle. 'I'll go with you.'

Bran crooked a finger. 'Let's see the coat first.'

After Doyle tossed him the coat, Bran laid a hand over the gash in the sleeve as Sasha coated balm over one in his own arm.

Then he handed back the coat, battered as it had been, but undamaged.

'Thanks.'

When they went out, Bran smiled at Annika. 'You don't ask me to fix your shoes?'

'It's not important. Doyle's coat is like ... armor. I think it's a kind of armor for him. These

222

are only shoes.'

'Without them,' Sasha pointed out, 'your feet would have been cut more seriously.' She picked them up from the floor herself, handed them to Bran. 'So, they're a kind of armor, too.'

When Bran handed them back to her, whole, Annika hugged him. 'Thank you. I'm going to take Sawyer to bed now.'

Sawyer choked on a bite of salami; Annika offered him water.

'He doesn't say it, but he's very tired. The food helps, but now he needs to rest. Come to bed, Sawyer. You can sleep in my bed. Only sleep,' she added, offering a hand.

As she led him out, they heard her say, 'If you want to have sex, you should lie quiet and let me take you to the ending.'

With a half laugh, Bran tugged Sasha into his lap. 'What a woman she is.'

'But she's not.' Torn, Sasha stared after them. 'She's not of this world, and her time here is limited. It's limited because she saved my life.'

She pressed her cheek to Bran's, to the gift he was to her. 'I encouraged this between them. They both wanted, and I... But the love for him, Bran, it pours out of her. Deep and fierce and complete. Now, all I can think is, what will happen to her, to her heart, when she has to leave him?'

'Love is.' Treasuring his own, he stroked her hair. 'And sometimes the gods are kind to those who give it.'

'Not much evidence of that so far.'

'Right here.' He drew her into a kiss. 'How could I not believe in the kindness of the gods when I have you? Be glad for what they have now.'

'And have faith in tomorrow?'

'It's what we have. Now, you should rest as well.'

'And if I want sex?'

Laughing, he stood with her. 'I'll be happy to take you to the ending.'

The Andre Malmon who moved into the Degli Dei wasn't the same man who'd adjusted his black tie one fateful evening in London. He was no longer altogether a man.

And he liked it.

He liked the strength and the appetites that grew inside him. He'd even come to enjoy the pain that struck quick and fierce in his spine, as if two vicious hands wrung it like a wet rag.

If he'd developed a taste for blood and flesh, he had the means to indulge it. As he had with the whore he'd killed and drained on his last night in London.

He was becoming. Nerezza had given him this gift, and the promise of eternity and power – once he'd completed his tasks. And he could have and do with the six guardians whatever he liked, once he'd secured the stars.

Then he and Nerezza would rule all the worlds for all time. Together.

He'd considered just what he would do with the guardians. He wanted the compass – that was principle – just as he wanted to kill the annoying yokel who held it. Slowly, of course, and painfully.

He would hunt the inestimable Dr. Gwin, and force her to lead him to her pack. Just the thought of owning a pack of werewolves delighted him. Sell off some of the young, breed more, and have hunts for centuries.

The mermaid he intended to keep for his own. She would make a lovely display. The sorcerer – likely a quick death there. The seer he'd hoped to capture and keep, but they would see, as Nerezza wanted her destroyed.

And the immortal. Ah, once shackled and held, such a creature would provide decades of entertainment in the torture chamber even now being built for that purpose.

He would never be bored again.

Now, sipping a Bloody Mary mixed as a transforming demon preferred, he gazed out over the sunstruck view from the terrace. As the veins in his arms tended to bulge and pulse, he wore a long-sleeved shirt and dark glasses, as the brilliant sun irritated his eyes.

A small price to pay.

For tonight, Nerezza would come to him, and she would take him places with her body beyond pain, beyond pleasure.

But today, there was work to be done.

'Sir.'

His head turned, several degrees beyond the human, but the servant didn't blink or cringe. One who had, in London, had never been seen again.

'Commander Trake has arrived.'

'I'll see him in my office.' Malmon set the half-empty glass aside, walked away.

The servant allowed himself one small shudder as he picked up the glass to take to the kitchen.

John Trake, fit, forty, fiercely handsome with the

curved scar down his rugged right cheek only adding a dangerous appeal, walked briskly into Malmon's office on boots polished to a mirror shine.

He believed in discipline, in order, was quick to
mete out punishment to any under his command
who failed to maintain his standards.

Killing was simply a by-product of command,
and while he also believed, strongly, in profit for
work done well, he would – and had – killed for
free.

A contract with Malmon inevitably led to profit.
For this new work, so elaborate, so far-reaching,
so challenging, he'd already banked a million
euros. Each capture of the six targets would bring
another million, with a bonus of ten more upon
successful completion.

Six captures, and the three stars (he assumed
them jewels) Malmon wanted for his own.

He had sixty men under his command, and
twenty more civilian workers. In taking the
contract, he'd agreed to work with, coordinate
with Eli Yadin and Franz Berger, both specialists.

He considered Yadin a psychopath, and Berger
undisciplined, but had respect for their work and
the results of it.

Though nothing showed in his face, Malmon's
appearance surprised him. Pale as parchment,
thin enough that the shirt hung loose over his
torso, Malmon sat behind a large desk, eyes
shielded with dark glasses.

'Commander.'

'Mr. Malmon.'

'I trust everything is on schedule.'

'It is. The holding center will be completed tomorrow, on schedule. Yadin arrived yesterday, and is already supervising his own areas. We expect Berger by eighteen hundred hours.'

'Excellent. I expect you to put the holding center to good use, and quickly.'

'I look to report the first capture within thirty-six hours.'

'Alive, Commander. Alive is essential to my needs.'

'Understood.'

'And where are they now?'

Trake took a device from his pocket, consulted it. 'Their boat is anchored off the southeast coast. Do you want the coordinates?'

Once a man who gathered and examined all details, Malmon just flicked a hand. 'Not necesary at this time. As soon as their accommodations are ready, take them.'

'Within thirty-six, sir.'

'You've never disappointed me, Commander.' As Malmon stared, a dull yellow glow seemed to pulse behind the dark glasses. 'Don't let this be the exception to that rule.'

'I'll complete my mission.'

'I depend on it.' Malmon smiled, showing incisors longer, sharper, than they should have been. 'Contact me when the tank is ready. I'm particularly interested.'

After another long day in and on the water, Sawyer grabbed a shower, a beer, and headed straight to the radio and recorder he'd set up.

A few minutes later, Riley leaned over his shoulder, one hand braced on his back, listening as he did.

'Rewind. Doyle and Bran are winding down playing pool. I'll get them, and the others.'

When they all crowded in, Sawyer held up a hand. 'Nothing from the parlor yet, and no conversations from the bedroom – just moving around, probably staff unpacking for him. But we hit in the office. First came in about eleven fifteen. It's Malmon and Trake – I think Trake.'

'It's Trake,' Riley confirmed. 'I recognized his voice. And word is he's calling himself commander now. Gave himself a promotion. Play it back, Sawyer.'

The quality leaned toward tinny, but the words came through clearly.

'Capture, not kill.' Bran considered that when Sawyer stopped the recording. 'Sensible, controlled. Wipe us out, and it's more difficult to find the star we already have.'

'That's what Yadin's for. Torture.' Since it was handy, Riley took a swig from Sawyer's beer. 'We give up the location of the first, any information we have on the other two.'

'But we won't.' Annika looked from face to face. 'We swore an oath.'

'I'm not saying we'll wrap it up in a bow, but Yadin's really good in his chosen field. We don't want to be taken to wherever this holding center is. We don't want Yadin to start working on us. Within thirty-six,' Riley added. 'At least the wait for that's almost over.'

'He knew our coordinates,' Doyle pointed out. 'So they've got a GPS on the boat. It won't be hard to locate now that we know about it.' He looked at Bran. 'How far could you ... relocate it?'

'How's New Zealand?'

Doyle gave one of his quick, rare smiles. 'Should be far enough.'

'It won't stop them,' Sawyer said, 'but it's a finger in their eye, so I like it. Holding center. It could be anywhere, but I'm putting my money on the cave. Sasha got vibes there.'

'Maybe Bran should set off that chain reaction. Finger in the eye,' Riley commented, 'and a boot in the balls.'

'The boot's wasted if we're wrong,' Doyle pointed out.

'I can shift up there, take a quick look.'

'No.' Sasha cut off Sawyer's suggestion sharply. 'You need to stay away from there. And it's not time. I can't tell you why or how I know that. It's just not time.'

'Okay. We save the boot in the balls. And we listen.' Sawyer tapped the recorder. 'We keep listening.'

'A bit more,' Bran corrected. 'Tonight, all weapons, all ammunition. We'll be adding power there, and draw the light from the moon to seal it.'

The ritual, while simple enough, required all six, the potion Bran had brewed for days, and faith.

'You want us to put all our weapons into a big pot of goo.'

Bran arched his scarred eyebrow at Riley. 'It's a cauldron, and it's hardly goo.'

She leaned over the cauldron, studied the thick blue liquid. 'It looks like goo. A little like what my great-aunt Selma puts in her hair.'

229

'Hair, or fur?' Sawyer wondered, and got a sneer.

'It's pure,' Bran explained, 'and powerful. Not so very different from the light bombs, but in another form. This will coat blade, bullet, bolt – bracelet, and what is used to propel them, with that light and power.'

Annika laid her right hand on her left bracelet – only she could remove what Bran and Sasha had created for her. 'It takes trust.' She unclasped the left bracelet, then the other. Held them out.

'With your hand, your faith, put them in.'

Carefully, Annika laid the bracelets on the surface of the liquid, watched them sink beneath.

'Well, hell.' Sawyer took his combat knife, his dive knife, followed suit. And with some reservation, unholstered both his guns.

'You have to believe,' Annika commanded.

'Yeah. Yeah. Well, I've never believed in anybody the way I believe in the five of you. So...' He put his guns in the cauldron, added all his ammo.

Sasha put in her bolts. 'The crossbow won't fit all the way under.'

Bran brushed a hand over her hair. 'It will.'

With a nod, she set it in, bow first, and realized she shouldn't have been surprised when it simply slid in, vanished beneath the blue.

'Okay, here goes. You're one hell of a wizard, Irish. If I didn't believe that, I wouldn't be here.' Riley added knives – three – guns – two – ammo. Then pulled out her pocket knife. 'Might as well hit them all.'

'Didn't think of that.' Sawyer added his multi-tool. 'You never know.'

'I've had this sword longer than any of you have

been alive. Longer than your parents and grandparents have lived. So trust me, this is faith.' Doyle lowered his blade into the cauldron, then his bow and bolts, his knives, his gun, ammo.

Finally, they added the underwater weaponry.

'It's the clown car of cauldrons,' Sawyer decided, and made Riley hoot out a laugh.

'Here is trust,' Bran began. 'Here is unity. And here is power.' He pointed at the moon. 'The goddesses three created the stars. The goddesses three set us on this path. They guard, and now we guard against the dark, against all who would twist the pure into the profane.'

He lifted his other hand, began to draw it back slowly, as if pulling a great weight. As he pulled, white light spread over the blue. And now his voice reverberated, shook the air.

'In this place, in this hour, we call upon your light and power. Celene, Luna, Arianrhod, hear us, moon daughters, through air and earth and waters, and stir this brew with light, brilliant and bright. And with these weapons we employ, only evil to destroy. So pledge I, your son.'

He looked to Sasha, took her hand. 'So pledge I,' she said, 'your daughter.' And took Doyle's.

So they took their oath, one by one, in a circle around the cauldron, bubbling thick and slow.

And Bran raised both arms. 'As we will, so mote it be.'

Three sharp beams of light shot from the moon, arrowed into the cauldron. Sparks of it flew like stars, whirled above, dived below.

Then all went quiet.

'It's tough not to applaud,' Riley said after a

moment. 'You put on a hell of a show, Irish.'

'This one took the six of us, so well done, all.'

'Yeah, everybody take a bow. Now, what do we do?' Riley wondered. 'Just reach into the goo – magick goo,' she added, 'and take everything out?'

Bran simply turned his palms up, raised his hands. Guns, clips, knives, bows, swords floated up.

Without hesitation, Annika reached for her bracelets. 'They're still so pretty, and don't feel any different.'

'They will,' Bran told her, 'when you need them to.'

Sawyer plucked his guns out of the air, examined them, holstered them. 'That'll be in, what, under thirty-two hours now.'

'Less, I think – feel,' Sasha added as Doyle sheathed his sword. 'Less than that. They move in the dark tonight, the mother of lies and her pet. And tomorrow comes the blood. Blood in the water, and the death of men. And one of ours, one of ours, if the choice is wrong. I can't see who. I can't... It's murky. And so clouded with pain, and fear.'

'Easy now.' Bran drew her in. 'You reach too far.'

'What good is it if I can't *see*?'

'You've seen it's tomorrow.' Doyle hefted his crossbow. 'And we'll be ready for it.'

CHAPTER TWELVE

He woke with her curled around him, so he drew in the scent of her hair, her skin with every breath.

The coming day, and all it held, was now just a subtle lessening of the dark. So he indulged himself, let himself just be. Breathing her in while his fingers tangled in the dark silk ropes of her hair, while her heart beat, slow and steady at rest, against his.

He could imagine this, waking like this, morning after morning as his life spun out into weeks and months and years. He knew all about time, what it gave, what it took, what it offered. If he could, he would have used his gift, his legacy, for time and space to take them somewhere else, some time else, where they could have this together, as long as they lived.

But they'd both sworn an oath. He knew time, he knew distance. And he knew duty. The compass he carried wasn't a toy, it wasn't simply a tool. It was, would always be, a responsibility.

He accepted it, and all that went with it.

And she, he knew, accepted her own duty, the responsibility that came with her gift. When her time ended – it was always about time – she would have no choice but to go back to her world, her people, and live her life where he couldn't follow.

He didn't want to love her, didn't want to feel

233

as if he always had, always would. But she'd twined around his heart just as she did his body.

Would time, he wondered, ease the heartbreak he knew would come? He didn't need Sasha's sight to tell him he'd never forget Annika, would long for her and what might have been as long as he drew breath.

Yet what they worked for, fought for, what each one of them would die for, was so much more than one man's wounded heart.

They had time, he reminded himself. They had today, tomorrow, and the weeks to come. He shouldn't waste that precious time mourning the future.

He brushed his lips over her temple, drew her in a little closer. She moved against him, just a lazy slide of skin against skin. It simply lit him up, from his heart out.

Though the dawn had yet to break, the morning birds yet to sing, he saw her smile as she tipped her head back.

'Good morning. It's a very good morning when I wake with your arms around me. Did you rest well?'

'Yeah. You're restful, Anni.'

'I like to be quiet with you like this, before the sky wakes. Before Doyle wakes,' she said with a laugh in her voice, 'and everything is loud and fast. I can make you coffee.'

'No. You should stay right here.' Now he touched his lips lightly to hers, felt hers curve.

'You want to wake with sex.' Running a hand down his flank, she wiggled closer. 'Your penis is already awake.'

She made him love and laugh and long, so he found it impossible to separate one reaction from the other.

'I want you, Annika.' He kissed her again, soft and slow. 'Do you want?'

'When you kiss me, when I feel your body against mine, I'm filled with want. Take my want, Sawyer, and I'll take yours.'

So simple, he thought, and so complete. He sank them both into the kiss, felt that even dawn held its breath to give them this time. This precious time.

Gently, his hands moved over her gently, so he could savor every inch. The soft skin, the subtle curves, the long lines of torso and miraculous legs. Tenderly, his lips followed. Taking her want, he thought, giving her his.

She offered, accepted. Turning to him, melting against him as if everything she was had been waiting only for him.

Every move, every shift, every touch pulsed under his skin. Warmth and light and beauty that captured his heart like cupped hands.

Her breath merging with his in a soul-deep kiss. Her breast, perfect in his hand. Her hips rising up as he glided her over the first peak. In that moment, that hushed moment between the dark and the light, she was, would be, his only and his all.

'Annika.' Overwhelmed, he buried his face in the curve of her neck. 'I need you.'

His words shimmered through her. She knew poetry, and song and story. But no words she knew had ever moved her so deeply. To be needed by him lifted her heart, sent it soaring. Even as tears blurred her eyes, she laid her hands on his cheeks, lifted his face so she could look at him.

'I would give you all you need. Be one with me, before the sun comes. Before the sun,' she said again, and arched up in welcome.

And if she wept as they moved together, she could tell herself it was only from joy, only from beauty. Only from knowing he needed her.

She took the joy with her, through the push-ups and lunges, through breakfast.

She kept it clutched tight when Sawyer brought the recorder out to the table.

'It may not sit well after a meal, but everybody should hear this.'

'Another meet?'

'In a way,' he told Riley. 'From the bedroom recorder, just after midnight.'

'If we have to hear Malmon getting it on with some unfortunate working girl–'

'It's Nerezza.'

Sawyer waited a beat, pressed playback.

For a moment, there was a kind of living silence, like a throaty hum. Then what seemed to Annika like a crack in the air. Malmon's voice trembled, but Annika couldn't be certain if it came from excitement or fear.

I've waited.

When Nerezza spoke, it was somehow cloying, like honey dripping from a nest of bees. *And all is as I wish?*

All is as you wish.

No, my pet, all is not as I wish until the stars are

236

mine, and those who keep them from me are scream-ing.

All is in place so all will be as you wish. Please, my queen. I've waited.

The laugh made Annika shudder. *Will you not offer me refreshment first?*

Your cup.

But not yet sweetened. A moment later, Malmon hissed. *Ah, perfect. The pain only adds to the potency, and the flavor.*

'Blood,' Bran murmured. 'It would be his blood, freely given.'

Your room here is pleasing. I will stay here an hour with you.

An hour? But...You won't live with me here while I find the star for you?

In this place? One for mortals, for humans? *I make my own.*

The disgust in her voice rang clear, then turned to amusement.

Do not sulk, my pet. I'll give you paradise for an hour. Take off your clothes so I can see the progress of your transformation. And then you and I will sate our appetites.

'Transformation.' Riley nodded at Sasha. 'You said he wouldn't be what he was.'

'But I don't know, yet, what he's becoming.'

Ah, yes. You, too, are pleasing. Is there pain?

It comes sharply, then passes.

But you like the pain. It tells you you're becoming.

I'm stronger.

And will be stronger still.

I'll be invincible. Immortal. And together we'll rule all the worlds.

237

Of course.

'She lies,' Annika whispered. 'Can't he hear the lie?'

There was a sound, like a whistle of wind, a low growl.

Thudding, harsh grunting, hungry sucking, animal pants, and twice an agonized cry cut off as if sliced with a blade. Slaps sharp and ringing, moans like the damned begging.

Under the table Annika clasped her hands together. 'This is not what we do. This isn't sex. It's ... like the sharks. This is only feeding, without beauty or kindness. Or ... heart.'

'Sex isn't always kind, but yeah, this?' Riley shifted in her seat. 'Be grateful we don't have video.'

More! There was a guttural sound to Malmon's voice, something not completely human. *An hour. You said an hour.*

Did I? After a laugh, Nerezza said, *Sleep now. Yes, yes, sleep and dream, before you bore me. Soon, my pet, you'll bring me all I want, all that's mine. Fail, and your blood will more than sweeten my wine.*

Again, there was a kind of crack, then silence.

'That's it,' Sawyer told them.

'More than enough.' After grabbing her water glass, Sasha drank deep. 'She wanted to see him, so there has to be something physically transforming.'

'Don't look at me,' Riley said when Sasha did. 'I'm a hereditary, three-nights-a-month girl.'

'But you said there's pain, when you change.'

'Some. It's just part of it. She's not making him a lycan. That change is rapid, and the moon's not

238

full. My money's on demon.'

'And I agree,' Bran said.

'So we'll be fighting a god, a small army, and a demon.' Rising, Sawyer picked up the recorder. 'Awesome. I'll put this back.'

Though the recording had shaken her, Annika reached back for the joy of dawn. She held it close through talk of battle – for Sasha felt certain there would be a battle that day – and instead, slipped over the side of the boat to find what Sawyer called a tracker so Bran could send it far away.

She watched Sawyer strap on the special gun for in the water.

'Okay, this location officially takes us more than halfway around the island.' After zipping her wet suit, Riley picked up her gun. 'The gods can't accuse us of not being thorough or freaking tenacious.'

'I wish I could tell you I felt something, like I did the day we found the Fire Star.'

'It's not all on you.' Riley slapped Sasha's arm. 'Six of us in this. I forgot, with the triple-X Malmon audio, I think I've picked up something on the Bay of Sighs. Need to dig more when we get back, but I think I'm digging in the right spot. So if we don't hit today, maybe I'll come up with something that helps. Meanwhile? Ready to rock and roll?'

'The first cave's at two o'clock.' As he strapped on his tanks, Doyle raised his chin to indicate direction. 'About fifteen feet under.'

'Then let's hit it.' Sawyer sat on the side, rolled back into the water.

No matter how often they'd tried and failed in the search, swimming with her friends always brought Annika pleasure. Today dread clawed at that pleasure, at the joy of dawn.

She would fight if a fight came. She would never, never shirk her duty. But the image Sasha had painted kept floating into her mind.

Today, when she circled the others in the water, it wasn't in play, but to make certain everyone stayed close.

She saw the cave, and quickly, but didn't arrow toward it. Instead she kept pace with the others.

She went into the mouth with Sawyer, and though she didn't need it to see, found herself grateful for the light Bran made. There was a cleanness to it because it came from the good, and illuminated the fanning plants, the small fish that darted among them.

A broken shell, a shattered home, only increased the dread.

They didn't fan out until well inside. Even then Annika watched her friends more than searched. Riley swam up a wall, peering into crevices, small holes, while Doyle went deeper, and Sawyer pulled himself up on a narrow ledge. For a moment she nearly panicked that she wouldn't be able to keep them all in sight.

Then she saw a starfish, red as fire, sleeping on a rock. It soothed her, the peace of it, the prettiness. She swam closer, thinking to pet it, and realized it wasn't sleeping.

Charmed, she cupped it in her hands, felt a warmth from it, and when it swam away, toward the mouth of the cave, she smiled. It seemed as if lights had sparkled in its wake.

She wanted to swim after it, to swim in those sparkles of light. But her friends...

Ashamed that, even for a few seconds, she hadn't been vigilant, she turned in the water, saw Riley tap her watch.

So she did swim through the sparkles, though she lost sight of the starfish as Sawyer went first. But she felt that joy again, and wanted to go above, talk to Sawyer about swimming through the stars.

At the very moment it struck her, she heard the sighs, heard the song. Still distant, but closer than before. A guide, of course, a guide. And the sighs and songs calling them. Calling her.

Not this cave, but another. If she could catch the starfish, the guide, it would lead them. Excitement burst through her. She kicked her legs, reached out to touch Sawyer. He glanced back at her as he swam out of the cave.

And looking back at her, at the delight on her face, he didn't see the ambush.

The fléchette hit him high on the right shoulder.

Annika heard the terrible sound, saw the blood spill into the water. She burst out of the cave like fury, only to have Sawyer shove her back and behind him as he reached across his body to draw his own gun with his left hand.

She didn't think, but acted, punching out light from the bracelets, ripping it through the water to send men tumbling back. And Bran's lightning joined them. A spear sliced out and into a man's leg from Sasha's harpoon.

It was blood and madness. Sawyer's blood, the

241

blood of men.

And the sharks came to hunt, just as in the painting.

She knew what to do, to stay close. And though her stomach twisted when one of the sharks closed those jaws around a man, she told herself they were the enemy. As predicted, that enemy turned away, to fire at the sharks.

Sawyer signaled, closed the hand of his wounded arm around his compass. Prepared to travel, Annika shot out more light. And as she felt the pull, the swirl, something struck her hip.

Sharp, shocking. Her vision blurred, and she slipped away.

Blind with pain, Sawyer collapsed on the deck of the boat.

'Fuck, fuck, fuck. Get us out of here. I'm not sure I've got another one in me.'

'Let me see.' Face grim, Bran dropped down beside him as Doyle yanked off his fins.

'Anni.' Though her hands shook, Sasha reloaded the harpoon. 'She didn't come back with us. She's not with us.'

'What?' Shoving Bran aside, Sawyer lunged to his feet. 'I had her. I had her.'

'She dropped away. I could see it– I couldn't stop it. She – they – a dart in her hip. I couldn't–'

She got no further. Sawyer vanished.

'Christ. I'm going back in.'

'We've got company.' Doyle's statement stopped Riley from jumping back in the water.

'We're not leaving them down there.'

'We're not leaving anybody.' Doyle stepped out of the wheelhouse, grabbed his sword.

They swarmed out of the sky, swooping over the dive boat fifty yards away, diving toward theirs. Though blade and bullet were coated with Bran's potion and burst dozens into ash, the pitched and ugly battle took precious time. Enough for them to helplessly watch the other boat speed away as they fought.

'They've got them!' Weeping, Sasha grabbed Sawyer's gun, fired over and over. 'We have to go after them.'

'They've defenses of their own.' As they destroyed the last of the birds, a gray fog rolled over the sea, swallowed the other boat. Bran threw light at it, but it bounced off, like a ball striking a wall. 'Bitch.'

'We go after them anyway,' Riley insisted. 'They don't have that big a lead.'

'More than this boat can cover. And you're bleeding, Gwin.'

Doyle set down his sword, pulled the flap from the slice in her wet suit.

'Yeah, one grazed me. Just grazed.' She looked down at her side. 'Just a – ha-ha – flesh wound.'

'You wouldn't have that if you hadn't pushed me aside down there. Don't ever do that again.'

Riley raised her eyebrows at Sasha. 'You're welcome.'

'I mean it. Goddamn it. I can handle myself as well as you.'

'Settle down now,' Bran soothed. 'And you, sit down and let me have a look. Doyle, you'd best take us back to shore.'

'We can't. We can't go back. We can't leave them.'

243

'*Fáidh,* we need to deal with wounds, get more weapons. And we need to find them. On my life, we will find them. We'll bring them home.'

She dropped down, covered her face with her hands. 'I felt her go numb – a tranquilizer gun, I think. I felt her slipping away from us, but I couldn't reach her. It happened too fast. I couldn't get to her.'

'Then believe Sawyer did.'

'He's *shot.*'

'Believe,' Bran repeated. 'We'll bring them home safe.'

'Retreat isn't surrender.' Doyle turned the boat. 'We'll get them.'

She woke muddled, her head aching, her hip tender and sore. For a moment, a blessed moment, Annika thought she'd had a terrible dream. But as she tried to reach out for Sawyer, she felt the kiss and flow of water all around.

The sea, the men, the blood, the sharks.

As she struggled to clear her mind, make her body move, she saw yes, she was in the water. But the water had glass walls, and a closed glass top. Like a box.

And she had no clothes. Though she didn't have the ingrained modesty of land people, Annika understood that to have been stripped without knowledge and consent, to be trapped without covering in a box of water, was a deep and terrible violation.

She pressed her hands on the glass, looked out.

The cave. She believed it to be the cave, though there were changes. Lights and counters or tables, and machines. And men with guns. Her heart leaped, then froze when she saw Sawyer.

They had chained him, his arms over his head. Blood stained the bandage on his shoulder. They'd taken his wet suit so he wore only the trunks, and they'd chained him so his feet barely met the floor.

His head drooped, and she recognized he was still unconscious. Alive, she comforted herself. She could see his chest move with his breath. They were alive, and she had to get out, help him.

She lifted her arms to try to shoot light at the glass, hoping to break it, but saw the thick black covering over each cuff. Though she pulled, tried to tear, she couldn't remove it.

And when she shot light at the glass, it was weak, too weak.

So she beat her fists against it.

'There's our little mermaid.'

The words slithered through the water like eels, had Annika whirling, searching for the source.

He walked into the chamber, a small, thin man who made her think of a snake. He wore all black – a shirt with sleeves rolled to his elbows, pants with a thick black belt and silver buckle. His hair, black as well, slicked back from his face, leaving the cruel lines of it unframed. Sharp brows, a thinly smiling mouth, long, hard eyes of a shocking, nearly beautiful pale blue.

'We couldn't remove your bracelets – not without slicing off your hands. Let's hope it doesn't come to that.'

There was a singing quality to his voice. It might have been beautiful, like his eyes, but for

245

the coldness of it. He stepped up to the glass wall, studied her.

'How do you breathe? No gills that show. It's fascinating. But we have people who will figure all that out, one way or the other. But where are my manners? I am Eli Yadin, and I'll be working with you and your companion. The work can go easily, or not so easily. This will be your choice. Mr. Malmon will be here directly. He'll be very pleased to meet you.'

Yadin glanced at Sawyer. 'Both of you.'

She turned her back on him, curled up. A small defiance, but all she had.

'I can see you're a bit upset. I'll leave you to sulk for the moment. It's time to wake up your friend.'

She whirled back, her hands in fists, her fists pressed to the glass. Ignoring her, Yadin picked something out of a tray and broke it under Sawyer's nose.

Sawyer coughed, wheezed, jerked. Though the movement had the stain on his shoulder spreading, he tried to swing, tried to kick out.

Yadin only laughed. 'Ah, the defiance of youth! It's so much more entertaining to work with someone who has it. Yes, we have your lovely friend,' he added when Sawyer's gaze fixed on Annika. 'In a habitat created just for her. The others deserted you.' His voice softened, all but crooned. 'Ran away to save themselves. Left you and her to die. Or worse. It will be worse, so very much worse, unless you give me what I want.'

'Do I look like I give a fuck what you want?'

'Oh, so young, full of that defiance. And hand-

246

some.' He scraped a nail lightly down Sawyer's bare chest. 'For now.'

He went back to a counter, lifted a tray, tipping it to show Sawyer what it held. When he got no reaction, he turned the tray toward Annika.

She saw knives, so many knives, and things that gleamed silver and sharp and would clip like scissors. For a moment she went mad, beating against the glass, kicking against it, screaming so the sound came through the tank and its speakers in a high, thin wail.

'You don't want me to hurt him? How sweet. Perhaps I'll wait on these.' He set them down. 'But what will you give me for my patience? Mr. Malmon very much wants to see you in your true form. Be what you are, and perhaps I won't hurt him.'

'Don't. He's lying. Don't give him anything.'

Yadin turned, grabbed a weighted sap from the table, struck it viciously across Sawyer's face. As blood spurted, Annika shot up to the top of the tank, threw herself against the lid.

'Crude, but effective. Shall I do it again. Yes, why not?'

He struck the other side of Sawyer's face. When Sawyer went limp, Annika spun down, swirled out her tail.

'Ahhhh! Fascinating. And mesmerizing. You are a rare creature.'

The tank trembled when she whirled, fast, fast, then struck the glass with her tail. She whirled again, struck again. Prepared to strike a third time, but Yadin pressed some sort of stick against Sawyer's chest.

The scream came first, ripping her heart, then his body shook and shook, with his eyes rolled back white. And the sounds he made were worse than the scream.

Yadin turned again as Sawyer gasped, as his head fell on his chest. 'That was a light touch, do you understand? Do that again, and I'll fry his brains in his skull.'

She sank to the bottom, stared her fury through the glass. 'Better. Now, why don't we... Ah, Mr. Malmon. As you see, we're making some progress.'

Unlike Yadin, Malmon wore white, the shirt cuffed at his wrists. Though dark glasses shielded his eyes, Annika felt the burn of them as he stared at her.

'Glorious. She's glorious. I believe I'll keep her, at least for a time. Be sure not to damage her – at least in any way that shows.'

Dismissing Annika, Malmon turned to Sawyer. 'Not so cocky now, I see, but bleeding and beaten, chained like an animal. You might have had millions, but here you are.'

He stepped over, picked up the compass. 'And I have the prize after all.' As if amused, Malmon picked up the prod Yadin had set aside, turned it in his hand, then jabbed it viciously into Sawyer's belly.

Annika bowed her head, her tears sliding into the water as the terrible stick left small black burns on Sawyer's skin, as it made his body shake and shake.

Then Malmon plunged his fist into Sawyer's belly, and his body swung back so high, so violently, the shackles gouged his wrists bloody.

When Malmon lifted the stick as if to whip it across Sawyer's face, Yadin stepped forward. 'Mr. Malmon—'

Malmon whirled, his lips peeling back. Showing fangs.

Hastily, Yadin lifted his hands. Both fear and fascination flickered over his face, but he spoke in that same singing tone. 'You can, of course, do as you wish. But if you want information from him, it requires a certain ... delicacy, and patience.'

Malmon made a sound, like the hiss of a snake, but he lowered his arm. The hand holding the prod shook before he tossed it to the other man.

'Perhaps you're right. Do your job.'

'Of course. Now, Mr. King, Mr. Malmon is very interested in how this device operates. If you explain, there'll be no need for more pain. Then we can discuss the Stars of Fortune.'

His voice was hoarse, breathless, so he had to speak slowly. His left eye had swollen shut, but the right stared that defiance out of the blood and bruising.

'Sure. Boy Scout Manual. You can look up how to work a compass.'

'I like your style.' With a smile, Yadin shoved the prod into Sawyer's chest.

The oath was sacred. Never to use the siren's song on humans. But these men, Annika thought, as Sawyer's body convulsed again, these men weren't human. This was evil, and she would do what she could.

She drew it up from inside her, the song used to lure men, to enslave them. And lifting her head, gave it voice.

Yadin glanced back at her, the cruel smile curving his lips. 'She sings. Perhaps a dirge for her companion. It's...' Then his mouth softened, his eyes glazed. 'So beautiful. Can you hear it? It's so beautiful.'

The melody poured out of her, sweet, so sweet, so alluring. Through the water, her eyes glowed green.

The men at the entrance to the chamber put down their guns, walked forward as if in a trance. Though Sawyer's head lolled, his body relaxed. His lips curved. She heard him murmur her name, as if in a dream.

Malmon grabbed Yadin's arm, yanked. 'What the hell is wrong with you?'

'She is beyond compare. She must be free.'

'Have you lost your– A siren's song.'

Rushing to the tray, Malmon picked up a knife, spun behind Sawyer, held it to his throat.

'One note more, one more, and I slit his throat.'

She stopped, pressed a hand to her mouth to show silence. Before he withdrew the knife, Malmon slid the edge lightly over Sawyer's throat to draw blood.

'One note more,' he repeated. 'Snap out of it,' he ordered Yadin, and tossed the knife down.

'She... She ruled me.' On a laugh, Yadin moved closer to the tank. 'I was a puppet on her string. How did you resist?'

'Obviously I have a stronger will. Punish her.'

'Of course.'

Yadin went to one of the machines, turned a control.

The water filled with pain, snapped and burned. That high-pitched scream sounded through the speakers as Annika's body thrashed in the water.

'Stop, stop, stop! She's no good to you dead or damaged.' Sawyer twisted his bloody wrists in the shackles.

'That'll do,' Malmon said, and as if he'd merely paused for a drink, once again picked up the compass. 'I've only to think of a location – co-ordinates, as I understand it. And this will take me. And through time, as well.'

Malmon tapped the compass, tried to turn it, searched for a mechanism. 'Where is the watch?'

'It's not as simple as that.'

'Isn't it? We'll keep it simple for the maiden voyage. To the villa and back again.' Malmon closed his eyes, murmured the coordinates he'd memorized.

And stayed exactly where he was.

'It's not ruby slippers, you idiot.' He'd keep them focused on him, Sawyer thought, keep their attention away from Annika. If he could somehow disable Malmon, she could sing. She could escape.

Nothing mattered more.

It cost him another vicious shock. When he could breathe again, he hissed out a laugh. 'Yeah, that'll work. Keep that up, see where it gets you.'

'Convince him.'

With a nod, Yadin picked up a knife, set it down, a stiletto, laid it back. Settled on a scalpel. 'I can slice him, dice him, clip off his thumbs, put out his eyes. It will take some time, and I'll enjoy it. But there are some who take the pain. And

251

there is a quicker way.'

Yadin turned, gestured toward Annika.

'Convince him,' Malmon said again.

Yadin turned the controls, and Annika's world became agony. Through it, through her own screams, she heard Sawyer, shouting, cursing, begging. When the pain stopped, when she could only sink weakly to lie on the bottom of the tank, she looked through the glass at his bruised, bloody face, at the grief in his eyes. Could only shake her head.

Don't give them what they want, she thought, as hard as she could. Don't give them anything.

'I have to. Don't hurt her. Don't hurt her again. I can't tell you how it works. I can't tell you!' He all but screamed it when Yadin reached for the controls again. 'I have to show you. Don't hurt her. Leave her alone, and I'll show you.'

'It's love, you see.' Yadin lifted his hands. 'A man might suffer through unimagined pain for a cause, and die for it. But love? It defeats him.'

Malmon signed to one of the men. 'Let him down. If you try anything, anything, Yadin will turn up the current. She won't die, but she'll never be the same.'

'I said I'd show you.' Sawyer dropped to his knees when the chain unhooked.

CHAPTER THIRTEEN

When Sawyer reached out his cuffed hands for the compass, Malmon kicked him sharply in the ribs. In the tank, Annika slammed her tail into the glass.

Yadin turned, wagged a finger at her.

'Do you think I'll just hand it back to you?'

'I have to hold it. It's the only way to pass it to another. I...' He bought time, mind spinning, through a coughing fit. 'The first traveling has to be done with me. It's the only way to pass it, and give someone else the right to use it. Fuck it, Malmon, I don't make the rules.'

He looked up then, so far into the pain he'd moved beyond it. 'All I'm asking is you don't hurt her. You're going to kill me, once you've got the compass. That's the way it goes. But you've got no reason to hurt her. She's caught.'

Malmon leaned down, gripped Sawyer by the throat. Nails longer, sharper than they should have been pricked through the skin. 'Where is the Fire Star?'

'I don't–'

'Hit her again, Yadin.'

'No, no, no. Bran's hidden it with magick. I can take you to where it is, but I swear to God, I don't know if I can get to it, actually get to it. I can take you, show you. For fuck's sake, Malmon, I'm telling you the truth. I'll do anything you want.

253

Don't hurt her.'

'So it's the witch? Bring Berger in, and send for Commander Trake,' he ordered one of the men, and rose to walk to the tank. Staring at Annika, he spoke to Yadin. 'Put a hole in him – nonlethal, of course.'

Annika beat on the glass as Yadin chose a knife. Her eyes pleaded.

'Is he telling me the truth? If you lie...' Malmon watched her face as Sawyer choked off a scream. 'I'll have his thumbs removed next.'

She kept her eyes on Malmon's, on those dark glasses, pressed both hands to her heart as if swearing.

'That'll do.'

Malmon turned; Yadin slid the knife out from between Sawyer's ribs. And another man strode into the cave.

He stood tall, straight, with Viking blue eyes and close-cropped hair so blond it read nearly white.

He studied Annika. 'So it's true.' His voice was brisk, lightly accented. 'The world is full of mysteries. Will you fuck her?'

'No need to be crude, Franz.'

'Just curious. I would, just to see how it could be done.' He shifted, looked down at Sawyer. 'Messy business. A bullet in the brain's more efficient.'

'I prefer my way.'

After a shrug for Yadin, Berger gave Malmon his attention. 'The remaining targets just arrived back at their base.'

'Riggs, the seer. You have her description.'

'I do. The blonde. The quite fetching blonde.'

'You can put a bullet in her brain.' Malmon

watched Annika's reaction, pleased when she curled up to weep. 'And the sorcerer – wounded only.'

'Do you have a preference where?'

'You're the expert. Commander,' Malmon continued as Trake came in. 'Mr. Berger is about to do his work. Take a strike force, wait for Berger to complete his task, then move in, capture the survivors. I want Gwin and Killian alive. Damage this McCleary however you need, and see that he's well restrained.'

'Yes, sir.'

'And search their villa. I want whatever computers, notes, maps, all their papers, taken to my villa.'

Malmon dismissed them simply by turning his back and walking to Sawyer. 'Get up.'

Gritting his teeth, Sawyer managed to get to his feet.

'What are the coordinates for the Fire Star's location?'

Sawyer gave him longitude, latitude. Malmon walked to a computer, keyed it in. 'An island in the South Pacific? How ordinary.'

'It's uninhabited, and the star's hidden, shielded. He did a spell. I don't know how it works. I can take you, but I don't know if that breaks the spell. You don't have to kill Sasha. Listen, listen, she can be useful to you. Nerezza wants her gift. You can–'

Malmon hit him with a backhand that knocked Sawyer back ten feet. 'I know what Nerezza wants. You're not fit to speak her name. Speak it again, and I will give the mermaid more pain than any mind can survive.'

'I'll do what you want.'

'How long will it take, to go to the star, to come back?'

'The traveling itself? Two minutes.'

'You'll have ninety seconds. You.' He gestured to one of the men. 'You'll take him there, and back.'

'But–'

'Do you really think I'd allow you to take me? To attempt whatever plan you might have working in your fevered brain, with me? If you take more than ninety seconds, if you attempt to escape, to take the compass, she dies in agony.'

'Ninety seconds isn't–'

'It's what you have.' Malmon consulted his watch. 'Yadin.' Though something like disapproval crossed his face, Yadin sent the current into the tank.

'Again.'

'Stop! Goddamn it, I said I'd do what you want.'

'Now you know the price if you don't. Turn up the current for the tank, be prepared to switch it on. Draw your weapon, you moron, and I'd advise a sturdy headlock.'

The man stepped behind Sawyer, hooked a beefy arm around his scored throat, held the gun at Sawyer's ear.

'Excellent. Ninety seconds. Beginning now.' He put the compass in Sawyer's cuffed hands.

Sawyer kept his eyes on Annika, said her name. And vanished.

At the villa, Bran treated Riley's wound while the

others gathered weapons.

'Has to be the cave, right? It's where Sasha warned Sawyer and Annika. I know he could have them at the villa, but–'

'We can't be sure. It's more difficult to transport two wounded and unconscious prisoners into the hills. You have to be still until I've done this.'

'It's a fucking scratch. We need to move.'

'It's more than a fucking scratch, and we need to know where to move.'

'I said we'll get them back.' Doyle walked in, guns strapped at both hips, the sword on his back, a knife in his boot. 'I've been a soldier more than a couple of lifetimes. I don't leave fellow soldiers or friends behind.'

'We're not getting them back fussing over a little cut.'

'If not for Bran, you'd need a dozen stitches, at least, on that little cut.' Sasha walked in with a crossbow, a quiver of bolts, and the gun she'd only fired at targets holstered at her hip.

'Okay, all right. Then I say it's time for that chain reaction.'

'I'm with the doc on this.'

When Bran said nothing to Riley or Doyle, Sasha sat down. 'And if we're wrong, we'll have wasted the trap. I need to see. No one's said that, but everyone's thinking it. Do you think I can't *feel* it?'

'It'd help, sure, but, Sash, we all know you can't force it.'

'Why can't I?' she snapped back at Riley. 'Why can't I pull it in when it's needed? At a time like this, when two of us are– Why don't you tell me

257

what to do?' she demanded of Bran. 'Why don't you tell me?'

'Because it's yours, *a ghrá.*' He took her shoulders, kissed her brow. 'Because it's only you who can demand it.'

'Then I will, I do! Cast a circle, cast a spell. Help me.'

'With all I have, but there's no spell. It's your gift, your mind and heart. Only you can open it.'

'I need air. I need room. I need to *breathe.*' Desperate, she rushed outside, struggled to calm herself, to settle. When Bran followed, she pressed her fingers to her eyes.

He drew them away. 'Trust yourself, as I do.'

'As we do,' Riley corrected, and glanced behind her at Doyle.

'Yeah. We do.'

'Help me.'

Bran brought the hand he held to his heart. 'Feel me, open to me.'

'Love, trust, faith. Bran.'

'Open to yourself, *fáidh.* Let it come. You're so strong. Set the fear aside, for everyone. And just open.'

She felt his heart beat under her hand, steady. Steady. Closed her eyes and counted the beats. His. Hers. Theirs. Hers. Hers.

'Oh, they're hurt. The pain. It's horrible, and the fear is worse. She fears for him, tries to fight, but they hurt him. He fears for her, tries to fight. They hurt her. Trapped, she's trapped. Water surrounds her, but it's cruel. He enjoys hurting them. He knows how. And Malmon – he's not just a man. His eyes, his eyes, he hides them, but...'

'Where, Sasha? Where are Annika and Sawyer?'

'In the cave. Blood and death in the cave. Locked in a tank of water, hurt, losing heart. Weeping. Sawyer, so much blood. One chance, he feels one chance. I can't see it, not all. So many, and so much pain. Sawyer... Wait, wait. He's gone. He's gone.'

'Dead. No, no, no.'

She shook her head at Riley. 'Gone. Somewhere else. I don't–'

As she spoke, a light, bright as noon, burst in the hills, and the thunder followed.

'Sniper's nest.' Doyle grabbed Riley's arm. 'Inside, get inside.'

'Time for that chain reaction, Mr. Wizard.' Riley rushed inside, grabbed her weapons. 'And time for us to move.'

'They're coming.' Filled with her power, Sasha picked up her bow.

'Men, Malmon's men. They're coming here. They mean to take us.'

'They won't.' Bran lifted fisted hands, beat his fists together.

The hills above the villa bloomed with light.

One chance, Sawyer thought, and prayed he'd timed it right. He might not live through it, but he had one chance to save Annika. He felt the gun against his head, the arm tight at his throat. And did something he'd never done.

He let go.

The arm dropped away, and there was nothing. Not even a sound. He gripped the compass, brought Annika into his mind. He'd never tried a

259

shift within a shift, but he'd already counted off sixty precious seconds.

He had to make it back to her. If he couldn't get her away, at least she wouldn't be alone.

In the tank Annika lay still, eyes closed. She would fight again, beat and beat against the glass when she found the strength again. Now her body was weak, shaken. Only will kept her from simply drifting away.

She hoped they would kill her. They meant to kill Sawyer, she understood that. He would die if he came back, and he would come back.

He had too much honor to leave her behind.

She knew he hadn't told Malmon the whole truth – he still protected the star. She believed he had a plan, would try. But he was hurt, bleeding, all but broken.

With all her heart she wished he would travel on, be safe. Then she heard something like thunder. The water in the tank trembled.

When she pushed herself up, her vision went gray, but she saw Malmon rush out of the cave, shouting. Saw Yadin reach for the controls.

Then Sawyer was with her – like a dream – in the water. He lifted his bound hands up, put his arms around her.

Light flashed to blinding. The tank rocked and shook as if by a giant's hand. She heard screaming, such terrible screaming. Then they flew.

She wrapped her arms around him, felt his blood, wet and warm on her skin.

'I've got you,' he said in her ear.

'You came for me.' Before she could weep, they

260

tumbled to the floor.

She heard gunshots, shouting, saw more lights flash. Felt Sawyer go limp under her. She managed to lift her head, look at him. His face, white, bone white under the blood and the bruising. And from his shoulder, his side, more blood seeped.

She wanted to stand and fight, but had no strength left, not even to bring the gift of her legs. So she did all she could, and tried to shield his body with hers.

Now she did drift, for a moment, for an hour – she couldn't know. Dimly, she heard a voice. Riley.

'Fuckers won't try that again anytime soon. Now let's get this rescue party– Jesus, Jesus Christ. Bran!'

Hands on her, lifting her.

'No, no, Sawyer. He's hurt. They hurt him. Sawyer.'

'Bran's got him, Gorgeous. We've got him.'

'Doyle, take her out, into the pool. She needs the water. Riley, more towels. We need to stop this bleeding so Bran can work on him.' Sasha dropped beside Bran. 'How bad?'

'Very. He's lost a lot of blood. I think his cheek-bone's shattered, and his eye...'

'Let me help. I can take some of it.'

'It's too much, Sasha.'

'I can do it. I can help.' She laid a hand on Sawyer's cheek. Gave a shocked cry. 'Oh, God.'

'Stop. It's more than you can do.'

'It's not. Work through me.' Desperation, pity, love all tangled in her. 'You said you trusted me.

Trust me now.'

Riley hurried back, took one look at Sasha's pale, sweaty face, at Bran's utter focus. She dropped down, pressed a towel to the wound on Sawyer's side.

'Come on, Dead-Eye, come on. I'm damned if you're going to bleed out on this kitchen floor.' She looked up at Doyle. 'You shouldn't leave her alone.'

'She's doing better, and asked me to see Sawyer. She'll do better yet if I can tell her... Good Christ, the bastards worked on him.'

'That's enough there, Sasha.'

'A little more. I can do more. Doyle, tell her he's going to be all right, then get Bran's big kit. Riley?'

'Blood's slowed, but I can't stop it.'

'Bran will. He will. I see us, together. All of us. On a hill with a circle of stones, and the sea is blue. I see it, and we're six. Get the kit, Doyle, and tell Annika he'll be all right.'

'I'm here.' She came in, naked, legs shaky. 'I believe.'

'Here you go.' Doyle swung off his coat, wrapped her in it. 'You're cold.'

'He came for me. He tricked them, and he came for me. He risked all for me, for us, for the stars. He is courage.' Tears streamed as she knelt down. 'Let me help.'

Malmon crawled. The light, the terrible light, had blinded him.

All he saw was the dark. And the pain! Even now, with the screams and thundering dropped away into a brutal silence, his body burned.

He smelled his own smoking skin and hot blood.

But he lived, so he crawled over the scorched, stony ground. He craved water, cool, cool water, for his body, for his throat. He would have given half his wealth for a cup of water.

Then he heard her voice, and trembled.

'You failed me.'

'No, my queen. No. We were ambushed, tricked, but even now soldiers are taking them. You will have all six. Please, they hurt me.'

'Your soldiers failed, and are gone from this world as all the others you brought here.'

'Please, my love, my queen, the light burned me. My eyes. Help me.'

Full of pain, he crawled toward the sound of her voice, and was struck back.

'Why should I help one who failed me? I gave you a gift, and what have you given me?'

'All I am, all I have.' Blindly, he reached up.

'You are nothing. You have nothing but what I grant you. You had two tasks, my pet. The stars, the guardians. For these two tasks, I would have given you eternal life, eternal youth, and all you could wish for. You have none of them.'

'I will. I swear it, I won't fail.'

'You're blind. Weak. Nothing but a broken shell.'

'Help me.' Though every inch burned, he crawled again. 'Help me see, help me heal. I'll bring you the stars. I'll bring them bathed in the blood of the guardians.'

'You want to see?'

'Restore my eyes, I beg you. I can't find the

stars, can't kill those who stand against you if I can't see.'

'You want to see?' she repeated, and the laugh in her voice made him tremble. 'And if I grant you this, you will pledge yourself to my service?'

'I am your servant. I will be your servant. Have mercy.'

'Mercy is a weakness. I am strength. I'll give you sight again, my pet. I'll let you see.'

His eyes seemed to boil in his head. He screamed, screamed until his throat bled, covered his burning eyes as he tried to claw his way back from the pain.

The tears he wept were bloody.

Through the screams, through the agony, he heard her laugh.

And through the dark, he began to see.

Her hair flew around her face in coils, and on her face lived a mad satisfaction as he writhed and shrieked. Still, the man and what that man had nearly become held out its hands to her.

A supplicant.

'Never ask for mercy.' She smiled at him, almost kindly. 'And do not fail me again. There, crawl back in your hole.' She gestured toward the cave. 'And await my pleasure.'

'Don't leave me. Take me with you. Take me with you so I may serve you.'

'You wish to go with me?' As if considering, she circled him where he lay, her long black gown rustling like wings.

'I'll grow strong again. I'll bring you the stars. I'll bring you the heads of the guardians.'

'Words and promises mean nothing. Get me

what I want.' She leaned down toward him. 'Or the pain they gave you will be as nothing to my displeasure.'

'I will heal. I will give you all you want. Take me with you, my queen.'

'Very well. Take my hand.'

Shaking with gratitude, he reached out. The hand he put in hers was blackened, the skin peeling in sheets, and the nails an inch long, thickened, yellow, curved like claws.

'If you were not what I made you, what you're becoming, you would be gone like the rest of those you brought here, those who failed. Remember that. My pet.'

Pain came again, a shock of it, as if he'd been ripped out of fire into ice. The cold nearly shattered him. His bones seemed to crack and hiss. Then came the dark, complete.

When he blinked, he could see dimly. Some sort of room or chamber, with chains and shackles hanging from walls of stone.

The birds that weren't birds hunched on perches, eyes glinting yellow in the darkness.

'You will bide here. When you have become, I will have use for you.'

'The dark. The cold.'

'Ah, yes, there is still some of that in you, some that yearns for light, for heat. Very well.'

Candles and torches burst into flame. On their perches, the birds that weren't birds shrieked and fanned their wings. The walls, stone polished to a gleam, shot out dozens of reflections.

Nerezza, in her black gown, a bloodred ruby at her throat. The birds, yellow eyes glinting, wings folding in.

And someone – something – crouched on the floor. Its skin rawly red and scorched black, peeling in sheets and flaps to reveal ... something else beneath. Hands and feet like claws, hair burned away to a scalp where glistening nubs rose. Eyes, yellow like the birds, slitted like a snake, that stared back in abject horror.

It moved when he moved. It rose on clawed feet when he rose.

'What am I?'

'Between, for now.' Nerezza flicked a finger at a flap of his skin. When it dropped away, fell to the floor, birds swooped down to fight over it.

'I ... I'm a monster.'

'A demi-demon, and in my service. Remember the pain, my pet. Remember who restored your sight. Remember your oath.'

'I'm a man.'

'You're mine, and will be for eternity or until I end you.' She walked to a door he hadn't seen, opened it. 'You'll know when I have use for you.'

He tried to run to the door, stumbled and fell. Once again he tried to crawl, but there was no door, no way out, only the stone, polished like glass. Polished like mirrors that showed him his own image everywhere he looked.

Malmon crawled into a corner, hunched and hunkered there with all he'd become staring back at him.

He began to laugh and laugh, until the chamber echoed with the sound. And the sound was madness

CHAPTER FOURTEEN

Sawyer slept deep. Dreams joined him, but quietly, soothingly. Voices – Annika's soft singing lulled him. Sasha's joined it on a murmur that offered peace – then Riley's a kind of determined cheer. Bran came into the dream, and Doyle, with a briskness that added hope.

Once he saw his grandfather, sat with him by a campfire. In its flames his grandfather's face was young, as young as his own, as they spoke of legacies and stars and gods, as the moon floated white overhead.

And he floated, as if inside a clear bubble. Gently, gently, over seas, over lands, over worlds. Over an island clear as glass with a castle on a hill, and a stone circle.

So beautiful.

Then the bubble popped, and he woke.

Annika sat beside him on the bed, holding his hand, so hers was the first face he saw.

And his first thought was, she was safe. He'd gotten her back.

'Hush, don't try to speak yet. Bran made you sleep.' She brought his hand to her lips, pressed kisses to it, then to the wrist still raw. 'For healing. They hurt you. They hurt you.'

'Annika.'

'No, you should be quiet. Bran said to get him when you woke.'

'Wait. Just wait.' He started to sit up, despite her distress, and felt it. Oh boy, he felt the remnants of the torture.

'You have pain. Bran said to have you drink this if you woke with pain.' Annika grabbed a small bottle from the nightstand. 'It will help you sleep.'

'How long?' He had to clear his throat, and breathe through the aches. 'How long have I been out? Asleep,' he explained.

'You brought us back it was night, and there was another night, and this is the day after. Not the morning, but after the noon. Please drink, Sawyer.'

'I've slept long enough.'

'I'll get Bran.'

But he kept his grip firm on her hand. 'They hurt you, too.'

'Bran and Sasha helped, and I slept, too. Not so long, but I wasn't hurt like you. He put the knife in you. Here.' Gently, she touched his side. 'It's healing well. Bran said. And they struck you in the face, and...'

'Yeah.' Gingerly, he probed at his cheek, his jaw. 'They broke something in there. It's just a little sore now.'

'You came back for me.'

'Sure I did. I'd never leave you like that. I just had to– Don't cry. Come on, don't cry.'

'I knew you would come back for me.' The hours and hours of waiting for him to wake crashed down on her. 'I couldn't get out. I couldn't help. They kept hurting you, and hurting you. They had something that stopped my bracelets. Bran fixed them, but I couldn't break the glass and help you.

268

I wanted to cause their deaths – especially the man with the knives. But I couldn't.'

'We're here.' He stroked her hair. 'We're safe, and we're here. That's what counts. The compass.'

She got up quickly, took it from her dresser. 'It's here. It's safe, too. I'll get Bran.'

'How about this? I need some clothes because I'm completely naked here. Help me get dressed, and we'll go to Bran.'

'There's pain in your eyes.'

And there were shadows under hers.

'It's not so bad. Scout's honor – I promise,' he corrected. 'I need to move, Anni. I just need to move, and to eat something, and to find out what the hell happened.'

'Riley said you wouldn't sleep again if you woke.' On a sigh, Annika turned back to the dresser. 'I brought your clothes into my room. I want you to stay with me.'

'Good, that's what I want, too. Just grab me some pants and a shirt.'

She did as he asked, helped him dress.

'Sawyer?'

'Yeah.'

'You are a hero to me.'

'Anni? You're a hero to me. How about helping me downstairs so we can talk to the other heroes?'

It hurt, but nothing he figured a few aspirin wouldn't deal with. And some food. And a beer. As they came out of Annika's room, Riley came out of hers.

'I just– Hey! There he is.'

'He wouldn't take the medicine, just as you said.'

269

'He's okay, aren't you, cowboy?' Riley stepped closer, gently rubbed a hand over the few days' worth of beard. 'A little scruffy, but it looks good on you. You scared the shit out of us.'

'Hey, me, too.'

'Let's get you downstairs. I bet you could use some food.'

'I could eat. A lot.'

'Good sign.' Like Annika, Riley wrapped an arm around his waist, and together they helped him downstairs. 'Outside,' Riley prescribed. 'Fresh air, sunshine. I've got him, Annika. Why don't you get him a big cold glass of the sun tea.'

'Beer.'

'Not yet, pal. And some food. There's pasta from last night, and—'

'Yes, yes, I can fix the food, and the drink.'

'She's filled us in,' Riley said in a low voice the moment they stepped outside. 'But we'll want your end of it. I'm going to tell you, she beat her tail bloody trying to get out to you, and she's stuck with you since Bran put you under. She hasn't been out of the room either. She needs the sun and the water.'

'Okay.' More than a little rocky, he sat under the pergola. 'The pool's just a stopgap. She needs the sea. Bran can get her down to the water. I can't make it yet.'

'We'll take care of it.'

Riley stepped back, spotted Sasha painting on the terrace, signaled her. 'Sawyer's awake, he's down here. You want to get Bran?'

'We'll be right down.'

Then glancing toward the grove, Riley put two

270

fingers in her mouth, let out a long, loud whistle.

'Hey, a wolf whistle.'

Riley glanced back, smirked. 'Glad to see you've got your lame humor back. Okay, shit.' She walked to him, took his face in her hands, kissed him hard on the mouth. 'I'm going to help Anni. And get a beer.'

'I want a beer.'

'No alcohol without Dr. Sorcerer signing off.'

He'd have sulked over it, but as Riley strode away, Sasha dashed out. And as Riley had, kissed him.

'Maybe I should get tortured more often. It gets all the girls.'

'Your color's good. How's the pain?'

'It's there. Not bad, but there.'

'We'll take care of that. You're hungry.'

'I'm starved.'

'Let's see the knife wound.' Without ceremony, she lifted his shirt, gently probed as Doyle strode across the lawn. 'It's healing well. And the shoulder ... better. Your wrists, better yet. Stay with him,' she told Doyle. 'Bran's coming down, and I'm going to help put food together.'

With a nod, Doyle sat across from Sawyer, studied him.

'Aren't you going to kiss me? Everybody else has.'

'I'll pass on that. They beat the fuck out of you, brother, and sliced you good while they were at it. And a cattle prod, was it? From what Annika described.'

'Something like that. Malmon?'

'Not a sign or a sound. After some considerable

271

bitching by certain parties, Bran and Riley went up. You couldn't be left unconscious, so they won that battle. There's nothing left in the cave, and no survivors they could find. Malmon, according to Riley's sources, hasn't been back to the villa. His things are there right enough, but he hasn't been seen.'

'If I had a fucking beer, I'd drink to that.'

'Considering all, I'll get us both a beer.'

'Not for Sawyer, not as yet.' Bran, one of his kits in hand, walked out.

'Have a heart. I've been mostly dead all day.'

'Excellent *Princess Bride* usage.' Riley came out with a tray – the glass of sun tea, the pasta. 'There's more coming, but you can get started.'

'First, the pain – one to ten.'

Sawyer shrugged at Bran. 'Maybe four and a half.'

'That means a solid six,' Riley said. 'He's downplaying.'

'I agree.' Bran took a vial from the kit. 'For the pain,' he said. 'Not for sleep. Just to take the pain down a bit. Sasha will insist on dealing with it, and I'd as soon she didn't take on that much.'

'Fine.' Sawyer waited until Bran added a few drops to the glass, then downed the tea. 'I gotta eat.'

He shoved in two healthy bites, sat back, said, 'Whoa. For the pain?'

'It'll give you a bit of an energy boost as well.'

'I'll say. You need to get Annika to the water – seawater.'

'I'll see to it.'

Both Sasha and Annika came out with trays.

'We've got more pasta,' Sasha began. 'Bread, cheese, fruit, olives, peppers, and anything else Anni could think of.'

'Great. What are the rest of you going to eat?' Sawyer asked and grabbed a hunk of bread.

'Let's see about the pain.'

'It's barely there now,' he told Sasha.

'Then let's get it gone. I'm good at this now. Just relax and keep eating.'

'How about that beer?'

'Half a glass of wine to start,' Bran said. 'Then we'll see how we go. Are you up for a report?'

'I'm definitely up. Thanks, Anni, this is great.'

'I didn't set the table.'

'Next time. Here's my POV. When I went back in the water, they had her in a goddamn net. She was out, unconscious. Between us and the sharks, their numbers were down, but not enough. They hit me with something, some sort of tranq, I'd say. Same thing they used on Annika most likely. And the next thing I know, I'm hanging by my arms in that cave. Lots of equipment – thugs with guns, and this tank. They had Annika in a tank of water.

'Sit down, Sash. Really, I'm good.'

'You had some torn muscles in your shoulders, in addition to where you were shot. And burns on your chest.' But Sasha sat.

'Feels okay now. Then he walks in. Mr. Torture.'

'Yadin,' Riley said.

'Introduced himself, real polite. Then he got started.'

He skimmed over the worst of it – what was the point? – but gave them the overview.

'Yadin had it rigged so he could send electrical

273

current into the water. The son of a bitch kept zapping her.'

'And you,' Annika said.

'Depending on your scale, you could say he kept it light, until Malmon got there,' Sawyer continued. 'Something off about him, Malmon. I want to say he walked different – like his shoes were too tight. And he wore shades inside the cave, and a long-sleeved shirt. And, I know it sounds weird, but his fingers were too long.'

'His fingers,' Riley repeated.

'Yeah, I know, weird, and I was feeling a little rough by the time he came to join the party.'

'Sawyer is right. He wasn't like the other men. I felt he was not...' Annika struggled for the words. 'Complete? Not one thing, not the other.'

'Seventh daughter of a seventh daughter's instincts,' Riley pointed out, 'which march right alongside our resident seer's. We saw him sign a contract with Nerezza, in blood. I restate my vote for demon.'

'He seemed human enough,' Sawyer continued. 'But edgy, jittery somehow. You know that's not his style, Riley.'

'Nope, cool, calm superiority. The kind that slits your throat – or more likely pays to have it slit – without the slightest rise in blood pressure.'

'He's pissed, too, because he can't get the compass to work.'

'He struck Sawyer very hard, and the bindings you took off, Bran, cut into him. The other man talked to him, so he stopped.'

'Yeah, yeah, I guess I blanked there a minute. Malmon lost it. Yadin talked him down.'

274

'He had the man put the knife in Sawyer, but he told the man to hurt me more.'

'Increase the voltage. He said he'd fry her, and he meant it. He was past thinking of the profit he'd get from her.'

'That's not like him either. Probably bluffing.'

'I don't think so,' Sawyer told Riley. 'I could see Yadin hesitate. He didn't want the game over so fast, but he'd have done it. I gave him coordinates, since he was focused on getting the Fire Star.'

'What coordinates?' Doyle demanded.

'To this uninhabited island – South Pacific.'

'How did you happen to have those on you?' Riley wondered.

'It's where my grandfather took me when he was teaching me. It's where his dad took him. We camped there for a few nights. I dreamed about it,' he remembered. 'When I was out. Anyway, I told them Bran had hidden it there.'

'You kept your wits about you,' Bran commented.

'Wits were about all I had. So I told them part of the truth. How it wouldn't work until I passed it on, but I embellished that. How I had to take him on the first shift. It couldn't pass to him without that sort of ritual. I figured my only chance was to get him out of there, get him to travel with me so I could deal with him, get back for Annika. But he wanted a test run, so he picked a Red Shirt.'

'The man with the gun didn't have a red shirt. It was brown.'

Now Sawyer smiled. '*Star Trek*. We have to catch you up.'

'It means expendable,' Riley explained. 'The

275

crewman in the red shirt going on the mission isn't going to make it back.'

'Why doesn't he change his shirt?'

Now Sawyer laughed until the pain bloomed in his side, bringing on a hiss.

'You have pain.'

'It only hurts when I laugh.'

'Don't laugh.'

He reached for Annika's hand, squeezed. 'Felt good anyway. So he has Yadin unhook the chain I'm hanging by, and has Red Shirt put the gun in my ear, get me in a headlock. He gives me ninety seconds – I said I needed two minutes. I didn't, but I figured he'd cut that back. If I'm not back in ninety, he takes Anni out – hits her with enough voltage to give her brain damage. He has Yadin give her a couple good jolts, just to prove his point. Then he gave me the compass, and I fed in coordinates.'

'Is Red Shirt wondering what the hell he's doing on some island in the South Pacific?' Riley wondered.

Sawyer shook his head, picked up the measly half glass of wine. Drank it down in one gulp. 'No. I couldn't risk it. I couldn't have taken him out on a one-to-one, and the time... So I let him go.'

'Let him go?' Doyle repeated.

'I disconnected. I just let him go. He's gone.' The color the food had brought back to his face drained again. 'You swear never to use the compass to hurt anyone, but I did. It's one thing to kill in battle, but I just let him go.'

'He had a gun to your head,' Riley reminded him. 'And Annika's life was on the line.'

'I know it. I know that. But–'

'You're thinking with great power comes great responsibility.'

He nodded at Riley. 'Uncle Ben was right.'

'The rice guy?'

Sawyer laughed again until it became a wheeze. 'Jesus, Sash, you're as bad as Anni. Peter Parker's uncle Ben. Spider-Man. And it's true, the responsibility. I've never killed anyone before they came at us underwater the other day, and that was battle. This was...'

'The same. It's the same,' Doyle insisted. 'He had a weapon, as did you. You used what you had to save Annika, and yourself. That, brother, was your responsibility.'

'An' it harm none.' Bran spoke the words gravely. 'This is my sacred oath. I've never used my gift to harm another human being. Until this. And though this weighs on me as well, I know what was done was done to protect, to fight evil.'

'They are right. I don't like fighting, and killing is against all I believe, but I would be dead, and you as well. You were only gone seconds, it seemed,' Annika continued. 'I was so weak – and I prayed you wouldn't come back. I knew you would, in my heart, because you're Sawyer. And I knew they would kill us both. I could feel it. As soon as this Malmon had what he wanted, he would give us to Yadin to kill in a terrible way. And then you were there, inside the glass with me, under the water with me. I knew we would live because you had the courage and the will to do what had to be done. If you think this was wrong, then you're wrong. If anyone believes you failed to

277

honor your oath, they are wrong and stupid.'

'Damn skippy.' Because Annika's eyes were full of tears, Riley reached across the table for her hands. 'Damn skippy, Anni.'

'It weighs on us.' Sasha rose, poured another half glass of wine for Sawyer. 'On all of us. We killed men. Humans. And it weighs.'

'Dying weighs more,' Riley said.

'And more than that, than even that,' Sasha continued, 'would be to fail. We're the guardians – the stars are our power and our responsibility. No one's broken an oath, or broken faith. They watch us, the goddesses, the guardians. They watch the six who came from them, and they see we take our power, shoulder our responsibility, keep our vows and our faith. To take a life is grief, to lose our lives is failure. The dark follows that failure across all the worlds.'

'Was that you?' Riley asked after a beat of silence, 'Or *you?* You had that seer look in your eyes.'

'Some of both.' Sasha let out an audible breath. 'Wherever it's from, it's truth. And here's another. Sawyer, if I'm following what you've reported, what Annika told us, you traveled with a gun to your head – and this after being shot, stabbed, electrocuted, and tortured – you disconnected, which was hard for you, but absolutely necessary, then you went back for Annika. In the tank. Does that mean you had to use her as your ... beacon?'

'Yeah, that's as good a term as any. I had the cave coordinates, but not the exact place where she was. I had to zero in on her, get inside to get her out.'

'And fast,' Sasha continued. 'Then you traveled again, here, with her. That's three shifts inside what, ninety seconds?'

'About that.'

'And that sort of traveling drains you, even if you're feeling like a party. You'd lost God knows how much blood, you were hung up like a side of beef and beaten, and worse, while you had to watch them hurt Annika, which is more torture. But you did what you had to do, and got back, barely alive. Am I right about that part?' she asked Bran.

'It was close, closer than I'd like.'

'Exactly. So I don't want to hear any more bull-shit out of you about any of it.'

'Damn skippy,' Annika said. Then laid her head on the table and wept.

'Oh, come on. Don't, don't, don't do that.' Desperate, Sawyer stroked her hair, rubbed her back. When he tried to just haul her up and onto his lap, he found he didn't have the strength. 'You're killing me, Anni.'

'No, no, they are almost all happy tears.' She wrapped herself around him. 'Almost all. We're here, we're all here, talking. And I heard you laugh, even though it hurt you, I heard you laugh.'

She brushed kisses over his face, met his lips, and simply drowned herself in him.

'Want some privacy?' Riley wondered.

'If only,' Sawyer murmured. 'I don't think I could manage it.'

'There will be sex again.' Through tears, Annika smiled at him. 'When you're healed. I will be very gentle until you're strong again.'

He ignored Doyle's snort of laughter. 'Good to know. So okay, no bullshit.' He picked up his wine, studied it. 'Power honored, responsibility met. I'll get there. There was more to the need to rush, to do what I had to do. Malmon called Berger in. He told him to kill Sasha. He wanted Bran wounded, but Sasha dead. He wanted the rest taken alive, so he ordered Trake to bring a team down here to take care of that while Berger took Sasha out.'

'You worry Nerezza, *fáidh*.' Under the table, Bran took her hand. 'She can't force her will on you, can't pull your power away and into herself as she believed. You worried for all of us,' he said to Sawyer. 'But we'd prepared for exactly that.'

'Yeah, I figured Berger for toast, but still. The tank shook. Did the tank shake?' he asked Annika. 'The light – it exploded?'

'Yes. Just as you came for me. Malmon ran, but he couldn't have run fast enough to escape the light.'

'We were dealing with Trake and company when you were heading in,' Riley continued. 'We were ready for them. Bran set off the chain reaction up in the hills, and we had plenty more for them here. There ... was nothing left of them. Wounding with the newly magickalized – I'm going with that word – weaponry, it puts a world of hurt on them. But a kill shot, it just obliterates. Nothing left.'

'No bodies to dispose of. That's the cold truth here,' Doyle added when Sasha winced.

'You're right,' she said. 'I know you're right. Bran and Riley went up to the cave yesterday. We had to check, and after some heated debate, Riley

280

went, Doyle stayed. We couldn't take the chance of Bran going alone, or of leaving us under-protected here. So...'

'Nothing left,' Bran told him. 'The cave is just a cave. There was ... a smear of something on the air, something dark. But faint and fading.'

'We salted the ground, and Bran did a cleansing.' Riley shrugged. 'And that was that.'

'So we won that round. We have to go back to the search,' Sawyer said. 'We have to get moving on it before she figures out how she'll come at us next.'

Sasha picked up her wine again. 'No.'

'What do you mean, no?'

'We go as six or not at all. Until you're strong enough to dive, it's not at all.'

'Jesus, I can handle a little swimming. Another little boost from Bran's magick potion, I could do a triathlon.'

Saying nothing, Doyle leaned over, gave Sawyer a light punch on the shoulder. And Sawyer saw stars.

'Fuck!'

'You're on the DL, brother, until you can take a love tap without whining.'

'Love tap, my ass.'

'The stars have waited centuries,' Bran pointed out. 'They can wait a few more days. When she does come again, we need you.'

'I can tell you when having sex causes him no pain.'

'That's a good benchmark.' Kicking back, Riley gestured with her beer. 'And maybe you should be specific. Like what kind of sex.'

'And how long he lasts,' Doyle added, and

281

made Riley grin.

'They're messing with us, Annika. Kidding.'

'I'm absolutely serious.' Riley cocked her head at Doyle. 'You?'

'Deadly. Keep us updated, Gorgeous.'

'I will. And when he's healed, we'll find the Bay of Sighs. We know we must be close because I heard them again.'

'What? When?'

'When you were bringing me back. Didn't you hear them sigh, hear them sing?'

He cast his mind back. 'I thought it was you. I did hear something. Jesus, I did.'

'And I've got something,' Riley put in. 'Since you've been in your magickally induced coma, I've been able to spend more time on it. I've got some nibbles.'

'And now you tell us?' Doyle demanded.

'I got the nibbles right before Sleeping Beauty here woke up. I was coming out to report. There is a legend. I know a guy who knows a guy who knows. But the guy who knows is currently on a retreat, so I can't tap him for more data for a couple days. Meanwhile, I'm digging on my own. Like most legends, it has a lot of variations, but the one that strikes me connects the Bay of Sighs to the Island of Glass.'

'Interesting.' Bran leaned forward. 'What do you know?'

'Know, not much. Speculate, a lot more. In the version I'm leaning toward, at one time, long ago, the bay and the island were connected. And like the legends regarding the island, the bay moved, and could only be seen by a chosen few.'

Since she'd swapped research for lunch, Riley helped herself to some pasta.

'Then we've got a race of people who shared the island. A race that could live on land and in water, and did so peacefully. All's happy and joy until some dude – names vary, but most common is Odhran.'

'That's an Irish name,' Doyle said.

'Got that. So Odhran decided, hey, we can live on land or in the sea, why shouldn't we have everything? They've got that fancy castle on the hill. Maybe I want to have that. And we're better and stronger than they are.'

Bran nodded. 'A popular excuse for war.'

'Yeah, and they got one. First, they lured people into the bay, drowned them.'

'With the songs?'

'Not clear,' Riley told Annika, 'but possible. Then they burned, pillaged, on their way to storming the castle. But the queen ruling them wasn't afraid to fight back. Which she did. I've got variety again. Raining fire, earthquakes, her riding a winged horse and sweeping the ever-popular fiery sword, and so on. But the result's basically the same in my research. While the rebels scattered, tried to get back to the bay, the queen rounded them up. She gave them a choice. Death or banishment. Odhran chose death, and got it – according to most of my digging. So did a few others. But the bulk chose banishment. So she blew the bay out to sea. She would spare their lives, and some were innocents. But they would float and wander forever, cast away from their home. Or in some versions until one who came from them redeemed them. Redeemed, they could once again join with the island and live in peace.'

'Mermaids?' As he spoke, Sawyer ran a hand down Annika's hair.

'I have never heard this story,' she told them. 'It is not one we sing of in my world.'

'It's pretty damn obscure,' Riley said. 'And I've yet to find the source. But like Doyle said, the rebel leader's name's of Irish origin. Or English. In some it's spelled Odran, and that's the English variation.'

'There must be more.'

Riley gestured at Bran. 'I'm looking, but this is the first layer I've uncovered. It fits. I've been trying to translate varieties from Greek, Latin, and some old Irish. And I'll keep at it.'

'I can help with that.'

Intrigued, she shifted her gaze to Doyle. 'You read Greek, Latin, and old Irish?'

'Well enough.'

'Okay then. And when I can contact the guy who supposedly knows more, I'll tap him for it. But all in all, it feels like we're being pointed toward the Bay of Sighs.'

'The trick is to find it. Annika's heard it twice when we're traveling. I could—'

'Recover.' Sasha simply cut him off. 'No diving, no heavy lifting, no traveling until you're fully healed. It's five to one on that, Sawyer. No point in arguing.'

Because whatever Bran had given him was wearing off, and he felt as if he could sleep a week, he didn't.

'You should rest again.' Rising Annika took his hand.

'Don't argue there either. I can feel your pain coming back,' Sasha told him. 'Sleep's healing. Anni, do you have enough balm?'

'Yes, there's enough. I'll tend him.'

'I'll be ready tomorrow.' And though he meant to be, was determined to be, even the effort of getting to his feet left him light-headed.

By the time he'd climbed the stairs, with Annika's help, sweat popped out on his skin. When he passed out on the bed, even without the medicine, Annika gently undressed him, carefully spread the healing balm on his wounds.

Then she lay down beside him, covered his heart with her hand so she could feel the beat. And for the first time since they'd been taken, slept soundly.

CHAPTER FIFTEEN

When he could walk on his own, but couldn't have run fifty yards if his life depended on it, Sawyer accepted he wasn't ready to come off the bench. Since his right arm remained weak, he worked on improving his left-handed aim. But even target practice tired him out in under an hour.

The others divvied up his household chores, and though he knew he'd have done the same for any of them, it *wasn't* any of them.

He'd lived a largely healthy life, had never dealt

285

with serious illness. In fact, he couldn't remember even being under the weather for more than a day in his life – though he'd faked it a few times to cop another day off school.

His current weakness, and the fatigue that dropped down on him like a lead blanket after the most ordinary exercise, frustrated the hell out of him.

While he dangled his legs in the pool and sulked, Riley strolled over, pulled off her Chucks, and dropped down beside him.

'I'd probably sink and drown if I tried swimming from one end to the other.'

'Boo hoo. You should be dead,' she said flatly, and shoved a glass of sparkling pale orange at him. 'I mean that, pal. I couldn't stop the bleeding in your side, and you'd already left a wading pool of it on the ground. The shoulder was worse – I know because I've seen gunshot wounds, and it was bad. I know because I watched Sasha's face while she and Bran worked on it. He had to make her stop taking on some of the pain because she was nearly as white as you were. That's not even getting to your face, your eye socket, the torn muscles, the shock of being shocked, and all the rest.'

'I know all this.'

'Then know this.' She gave him a solid punch in his good arm. 'Bran and Sasha saved your life. Without them, nothing the rest of us could've done would've pulled you out. The life was just pouring out of you, Sawyer. I don't have to be an empath to feel it because I could see it. You saved Annika, and they saved you.'

Frowning, he punched her back. 'I'm being a bitch.'

'Yeah, and you got a pass for a day, nearly dying in a heroic manner and all that. Now it's time to suck it up.'

'Okay.' Oddly, the verbal slap knocked away the self-pity. But he continued to frown as he looked at the glass in his hand. 'What the hell is this, and where's my beer?'

'You're limited to one a day until.'

'I feel my bitch coming on again.'

'Just drink it, Sally. It's something Bran and Sasha made up. Healing and energy booster.'

'It doesn't look like what they gave me before.'

'New and improved. Take your medicine, cowboy.'

What the hell. He took a drink. 'It's good.' And drank again. 'It's really good.'

'I – with their consent – put a half jigger of tequila in it.'

'Best pal ever.' This time, he gave her a bump with his good shoulder. 'How goes the research?'

'Slow. I have to say Doyle's damn good at the translating, but he doesn't have the patience to dig or know when to stop and regroup. We've had some words on that.'

'What! You and Doyle argued? Observe my shocked face.'

She rolled her eyes at his comic expression. 'He started it.'

'That's what they all say.'

Idly, she kicked her feet, splashing up lazy drops of water. 'The thing is, this break – you being in recovery – it's good for all of us. We needed it.

287

Sasha and I had words about that. Nonargument-
ative, agreeable words. It's given Bran time to
resupply, and her a little time to paint. Physically,
Annika needed a break, too. They didn't just hurt
her, they took the shine off her.'

Rage, cold and keen, shot through his belly. 'I
know it. If they weren't dead...'

'Yeah, I'm with you. But the shine's coming
back – I swear nothing dulls Anni for long. Doyle
and I, we got off easy, but–'

'Wait. You got shot. I forgot. Jesus, Riley, you
got hit down there.'

She turned to show him the healing wound on
her arm – barely a scratch now. 'Bran's balm.
Only grazed me – though I'll tell you it hurt like
a mother. But figure this. Grazed my arm, hit
your shoulder.'

'They weren't trying to kill us. Brain's still
working.'

'Panic and debilitate,' she concurred. 'Capture
might have been the goal, but that didn't mean
they couldn't make us bleed some. Would've
ruined a good wet suit, too, but Bran fixed that as
well. He's handy. Couldn't fix yours because we
don't know what the hell they did with it. But I've
got one lined up for you when we go out again.'

'I repeat, best pal ever. Speaking of mothers,
what the hell's she doing, the mother of lies?'

'Well, we took her down hard in Corfu.'

'Kicked her bitch-goddess ass.'

'Every square inch.' Riley paused long enough
for a fist bump. 'Then she pulls in Malmon. That
was good strategy, gotta give it to her. Let him do
the dirty, sweaty work, and she bags the stars

288

along with a demon love slave.'

'And still.' He hefted his glass. 'Another swing and a miss.'

'Yeah, both times her plans go – I was going to say up in smoke, but let's be accurate. Up in light. The thing is, Malmon wasn't on his game.'

'It hurts to agree, since I'm currently sidelined thanks to that fucker, but no, he wasn't on his game. Want to know why I figure?'

Tipping down her sunglasses, she met his eyes. 'Yeah, then we'll see if that's what I figure.'

'She miscalculated. Whatever she did to him, whatever she was making him into, it made him stronger – I can attest. But it dimmed some of the canny lights. He wasn't smart, Rile, and he's goddamn smart.'

'Once again, we're in full accord. He should've had Anni on a transport out of here. He'd bagged himself a mermaid, Sawyer, and the Malmon you and I know and hate? He'd have cashed in on that pronto. Using her, risking damaging or killing her to hammer at you? Not smart. Get her to an undisclosed location to work with later, leave you to Yadin. That's what Malmon, being Malmon, would do.'

'He was all about the compass. Even the stars didn't seem as important.'

'You got away once before. With those cannies dimmed? I'm thinking he couldn't see past that. And ordering the hit on Sash? That's straight crazy dark god, not Malmon. Take us all, bag us all – have Berger do a head shot on Doyle to take him temporarily out of the game, and come in hard on the rest of us. Give Sasha to Yadin, make her his own personal prognosticator.'

In full agreement, he kicked his legs in rhythm with hers. 'And because he didn't play it cool and tight, he loses the two he had. I never expected him to give me back the compass, even with a gun to my head. That was a Hail Mary on my part, but it sucked him in.'

'I also figure if the light bombs hadn't obliterated him, Nerezza would have. He should be glad he's dead.'

'He's not.' Feet bare, hair bundled up, and deathly pale, Sasha walked toward them with a sketchbook.

'Hey, hey.' Sawyer shoved the glass at Riley, pushed up fast enough to make his own head spin. But he hurried to Sasha, took her arm. 'You should sit down.'

'Yes, I should. We should all sit down. Bran and Doyle went to the village for supplies. I wish they'd come back. If I'd seen... I wish they'd come back.'

'They won't be much longer.' On her feet now, Riley walked from sun to shade as Sawyer nudged Sasha into a chair under the pergola.

'Where's Annika?'

'She's— I think she's finishing the laundry. She loves doing laundry.'

'I'll get her.'

'No, sit.' Riley pointed at a chair. 'I'll get her. Water, alcohol, juice?' she asked Sasha.

'Water, just water. Thanks.'

'You said Malmon's not dead,' Sawyer began, 'but—'

'He's not. He's alive. What he is now lives.'

'I don't– Just get your bearings again. Let me go get that water for you.'

'No, let's just sit here a minute. It's overwhelming when it comes like that.'

'Headache? You need some aspirin – or, shit, that stuff Bran has for you.'

'No, no headache.' But she pulled pins out of her hair as if even the loose knot squeezed too tight. 'It's like opening a window, expecting a nice breeze, and having a tempest blow in. It just takes a minute to settle down again.'

'And Bran's not here to help you settle.'

'You are. You're steady, Sawyer. It's your compassion. You have so much of it.'

Annika raced out of the house well ahead of Riley. 'I can run to the village, very fast, and find Bran.'

'No, he'll be back soon.'

Riley set down a large bottle of water, opened it, then poured some into a glass. 'Hydrate, level off. We're all fine here, and so are Bran and Doyle. You'd know if they weren't.'

'Yes, you're right. I just panicked for a minute.' Slowly, she sipped water. 'I was painting. It felt so good, just so good to paint. Not to worry about anything for just a single day. I wanted to paint the hills, and the green, the way the light washes over the land. Not the sea this time. I prepped the canvas. I'd done some sketches before, and I set them out, organized my tools. I started to mix paints.'

She paused, looked down at the smear of sage green on her thumb.

'Then I turned away from the canvas, picked up my sketchbook. That wind,' she said to

Sawyer. 'It was blowing through me, so fast and fierce. I could barely catch my breath.

'I started to sketch.'

Setting the water aside, she opened the sketchbook to the first page she'd used.

'Malmon. In black tie,' Riley observed. 'And Nerezza. But that doesn't look like the room you saw them in before.'

'No, I think this is before. I think this is his house, in London. She went to him. And here.' Quickly, Sasha turned the page. 'He went to her, and it really began. This is a kind of progression. Flashes, there were flashes of them. I could barely keep up.'

She turned the next page to a series of sketches.

'His arms,' Annika noted. 'They have changed.'

'You see how the veins are so prominent. And they pulsed. And here.' With a fingertip, Sasha traced along the shoulder of one of the sketches.

'It looks like ... scales.' Riley leaned closer. 'A patch right there, of scales.'

'The light burns his eyes. The whites turned a pale, sickly yellow. And I know it's subtle, but can you see the change?'

'The shape of his eyes,' Sawyer confirmed. 'Longer.'

'He starts to wear dark glasses, all the time. Even in sleep. And every night he goes to her, and she puts more of this into him. She puts blood in wine, little by little, until she's putting wine in the blood. He drinks. He drinks,' she repeated as she turned the page. 'She rules him now. Some of the blood is hers, so she rules him now. My pet.'

Sawyer saw Bran come out, put his finger to his lips.

'He's her creature, not fully changed, but hers. Through him she'll have what she wants, what belongs to her. Perhaps she'll keep him when it's done. My pet. Until he no longer amuses her.'

Gently, Bran laid a hand on her shoulder. She breathed in, breathed out.

'Here he meets with the men. The torturer, the soldier, the assassin. He meets with others who will do what he says for the money he pays. He's no longer bored, but he feels different. His mind gets clouded. He gets so angry. He kills a prostitute and gloats. His nails. Clip, clip, clip, every night, every morning. Is he losing his hair? But he's so strong. And she's promised him more, more strength, more power. Life eternal. She's his god now.

'Now at the villa – he'll have a palace soon, but this will do. But his skin, it feels so tight on his bones, and the light sears his eyes. See his eyes.'

'Changed,' Riley said, glancing over as Doyle joined them. 'Reptilian.'

'He can see in the dark. He craves the dark. Together, they'll extinguish the light. All the men, working, guarding. Helicopters bring in what's needed, but he goes at night, only at night, and he runs. He's so fast, fast as a snake. But she rarely comes to him now, not enough. He craves her like the dark.

'She'll come now. Two enemies captured. She'll come now, give him what he wants. What he needs.'

She turned the page to the sketch of the cave,

of Sawyer bloodied and battered, hanging from chains. Of Annika trapped in the tank.

'He wants the compass, its power. He nearly had it once, and won't be denied a second time. The traveler must pay for denying him, for defying him. She wants the stars, his queen. With the compass, he'll have what they both desire. Kill them both, kill them all, but first, take what's his. Find what's hers. Oh, their pain thrills. Give them more.

'The light! The light! It burns beyond bearing. The heat scorches. He screams for her, but she doesn't come.'

'Jesus Christ.' Despite everything, when she turned to the next sketch, Sawyer stared at it with horrified pity. 'That's Malmon?'

'He's still between, but more beast than man. Trapped in the dark, the pain – the burning – terrible.'

'Mephisto demon. Lower demon,' Riley continued. 'Often enslaved to a ruler demon or dark god. A shunner of light. Mythologically speaking.'

'There's an actual name for this?'

'There's a name for everything,' she told Sawyer, 'if you dig deep enough.'

'She comes to him.' Again, Sasha turned a page. 'He weeps bloody tears. She could destroy him, such is her rage. And there's a madness in her, as in him. But she's still canny, and he'll be useful. She makes him beg, grovel, supplicate himself, but she gives him back his sight, and she takes him to her palace inside the mountain, to a chamber already prepared. It didn't matter if he'd failed or succeeded, this was always his fate.

The mother of lies promised riches, power, eternal youth. Instead he'll live as she wills, as long as she wills, and have only what she wills.'

She turned the page. There birds pecked at flaps of blackened skin while mirrored walls of stone showed the horror Malmon had become. He sat hunched in a corner, wearing a mad grin.

'They say there are some things you wouldn't wish on your worst enemy. Malmon's definitely high on the enemy list.' Riley blew out a long breath. 'But no, I wouldn't wish this, even on him.'

'She denied him a clean death, and that's a cruelty. But–' On a pause, Doyle studied the final sketch, coolly. 'This is his true self, isn't it? This is what he always was inside. She just brought it out, made it visible.'

'Yes. Yes,' Sasha repeated before anyone else could speak. 'She recognized the monster inside him. Now he'll become.' She picked up her glass, took a long drink. 'And she'll rule him. He's mad – she's driven him into madness and delusion, but he's stronger, faster, and more vicious. He's more dangerous now than before.'

She reached for Bran's hand. 'I'm so glad you're here.'

'You didn't have your quiet day of painting.'

'No. But the day's not over. His life is. All the wealth, the privilege, he traded it for her lies. No, not on even the worst of enemies, but he gave himself to her because the monster already inside him craved more.'

She took another drink, took another breath. 'How do we kill him?'

'Demon disposal.' Riley took one last look at

295

the sketch. 'Beheading, mythologically speaking again, is tried and true. Otherwise, for some it's fire, others water or salt or the right incantation. I can look into it. I'm pretty sure he's on his way to the mephisto, but I'll find out what I can.'

'I'll do the same.' Concern in his eyes, Bran kissed the top of Sasha's head. 'You should paint, Sasha. Something bright and beautiful.'

'I will. Annika, would you pose for me?'

'Pose?'

'After this?' She closed the sketchbook. 'Bran's exactly right. I'd like to paint something beautiful, something full of light and joy.'

'You'd paint me? Oh!' Annika crossed her hands over her heart. 'I have such a happy.'

'Ah.' With a shake of his head, rubbing the back of his neck, Sawyer said, 'That's actually slang for something else, that being a girl, you can't have.'

'I can't have happy?'

'A happy. It's...'

'Jesus, Sawyer, be direct. It's a hard-on.' Riley pointed to Sawyer's crotch; he batted her hand away. 'When a guy gets hard.'

'Oh! That is happy, isn't it? I should say I *am* happy. I would love to pose for you, Sasha.'

'Would you pose in the pool, in the water, a mermaid?'

'Yes!' Instantly, she reached for the hem of her dress.

'Wait, whoa. You don't just take off your clothes.'

Baffled, Annika lifted her hands at Sawyer. 'I don't go in the water in clothes, and I can't wear the suit for swimming in my true form.'

'Yeah, but.' He looked directly at Doyle. 'Go

296

find somewhere else to be.'

'I like it here.'

'Doyle and Bran have seen me without clothes.'

'What?'

'When we came back, I had no clothes. Doyle gave me his coat so I wouldn't be cold. You're too shy,' she said to Sawyer. Walking toward the pool, she pulled her dress off as she went, tossed it on a chair, then dived in.

'She's already art. And she's yours, brother.' On a last admiring glance, Doyle rose. 'I'll do more translating while you dig up demons,' he said to Riley.

And to Sawyer's relief, strolled inside.

Since searching and diving, even training seemed to be off the agenda, Sawyer took the day. It annoyed him to conk out over his own research, but he felt better after the hour's sleep.

But even after the rest, the compass told him nothing. Part of him worried, despite the reassurances, that using it as he'd used it had cost him the right to it.

Braced for that, he took his phone, walked outside. Annika sat – more lounged – on the steps of the pool, wet hair sleek and not quite covering her breasts. Her tail glistened, a thousand small, bright jewels. She turned her head, just a little, smiled at him.

'I'm supposed to stay still for a few minutes more. Sasha says I can't see until she's finished.'

But he could, and circled around to where Sasha stood at her easel. He saw she'd pinned up several quick sketches, different poses, expressions. And on the canvas she'd captured joy and beauty.

'It's great. It's … amazing.'

'So many tones and shades and hues.' Sasha mixed more paint on her palette, dabbed at the canvas with a thin brush. 'And the way they all catch the light.'

'You could come in the pool, and talk to me. Sasha says I can talk.'

'Maybe later. I need to make a call.'

'Will you paint Sawyer, Sasha?'

'She doesn't want to–'

'It's on my list.'

'What? Really?'

'I want to do a painting of each of us, and one of all of us together. I just have to … find it. Like this with Annika. I've done Bran's, from memory. At night, with the power on him, like the jewels in Annika's tail. Bright, brilliant, and marvelous. But I need to find it, and find the right time. Today was Anni's.'

'It's…' He really didn't have the words. 'You're going to love it,' he told Anni. 'I'm going to take a walk, make this call.'

He chose the grove for the quiet, the shade, the scents. He took out the compass again, considered simply traveling to his grandparents' home. But with his energy still on the low end, it wouldn't be smart. And more, he didn't want to worry his family.

He settled for the phone.

'*Dedushka.*' Even the sound of his grandfather's voice lifted him. '*Kak pozhivaesh?*'

He kept it casual initially, sliding from Russian

to English and back again, catching up on family news.

'*Zolotse.*' His grandfather's use of the affectionate term, and the gentle tone stopped Sawyer's rambling. '*Chto sluchilos?*'

What's wrong? Sawyer thought. Where do I start?

'*Dedushka*. I'm afraid I've... Let me tell you what happened.'

Bran walked into the grove. He looked for Sawyer, as Sasha had some mild concern. Apparently Sawyer had been gone nearly an hour.

He found him, sitting on the ground, back resting against a tree pregnant with lemons. And the compass in his hand.

'I hope you haven't taken any recent trips.'

'What? Oh, hey. And no, no. I've been right here. I just talked to my grandfather.'

Bran joined him on the ground, stretched out his legs. 'Is he well then, your grandfather?'

'Yeah. Since that scare a while back, he's stronger than ever.'

'It's good to speak with family. I spoke with my mother only yesterday.'

'Is she worried about you?'

For a moment, in the bright, hot Italian afternoon, Bran felt the cool, damp kiss of Ireland.

'She's my mother. Of course she has worries. She also has faith. And though I don't like the worrying of her, her faith gives me more of my own.'

'Yeah. I love my dad, you know? And my mom, my sibs, my grandmother. But *Dedushka*...'

299

'It's a special bond, isn't it? The compass was his, and he passed it to you. I love my father, and all the rest of my family. But it's my mother who taught me, who helped me learn to open myself to what I am.'

'So you get it.'

'I do, yes. Now you've told him what troubles you still.'

'Everything y'all said made sense, and it helped. A hell of a lot. But... You know your power's there all the time, right? You don't have to use it to feel it.'

'I know what's in me, yes.'

'Since we came back from the cave, I haven't felt the connection.'

A dragonfly winged by, gossamer in the dappled sunlight. Sawyer watched its flight, and how it zipped away. He knew what it was to fly.

'When I knew I had to tell my grandfather, I thought about going to him. And I told myself I needed to keep recharging the batteries, you know, and how I didn't want to worry them anyway. But under that was the fear I couldn't do it anyway. I couldn't travel again because I'd lost the right.'

'And what did your grandfather say to that?'

'Well, he listened when I told him what happened, about Malmon, the cave, Annika, all of it. And how I'd used this, this gift, to kill a man. And I thought that might have cost me the right to have it.'

'And?'

'Basically, he told me to stop being a pussy.'

On a half laugh, Sawyer shrugged, and easily, as

300

the weight of guilt no longer sat on his shoulders.

'It was longer than that, had pretty much everything y'all said to me, but with that "don't be a pussy" tagged on tight. Then he said he loved me, and he believed in me, believed I'd do what I'd been born to do. To get it the hell done and come home safe.'

'I look forward to meeting him one day.'

'Yeah, we'll have a post-quest party that rocks the house.'

Emotion shuddered through him, and leading it was gratitude. 'I feel it again. That connection. I know it's mine until it's time to pass it on. Had to stop being a pussy, stop moping over dropping some asshole into the void who'd have put a bullet in my brain.'

'Brilliant. I'd say that's earned you a beer.'

'A whole one?'

Testing, Bran laid a hand on Sawyer's wounded shoulder, then on his side. And pleased with what he felt, he nodded. 'It's a full pint for you.' Bran rose, held out a hand. 'Welcome back.'

'So we can dive tomorrow?' With barely a twinge, Sawyer let Bran pull him to his feet.

'Another day or two for that. We may as well let our digger dig.'

'A couple more days, our digger's going to go wolf on us.'

'Only from moonrise to moonset. It's this Bay of Sighs clearly enough. Let's give her, and Doyle, time to find it, and you and Annika a bit more time. And let's go have that pint.'

'I'd be a fool to argue.'

Annika no longer lounged in the pool. Sawyer

301

didn't see Sasha, but cut across toward the canvas still on her easel.

And just stared. Joy and beauty, magick and marvel. He didn't know how Sasha captured the gleam, the sparkle with only paint.

Didn't know how anyone could so clearly show the light in those sea-green eyes.

How could a painting so perfectly show sweetness and sex and strength?

'You like it.' With one of Riley's famed Bellinis in hand, Sasha wandered out, hooked her arm through Sawyer's.

'It's everything she is.'

'I'm going to do others. It's why I did so many sketches. I want her in the classic mermaid on the rock in the sea, and I want her doing cartwheels or flips on the lawn.'

Hearing how relaxed she sounded, seeing all the strain had vanished from her face, Sawyer understood Bran's reasons for waiting another day or two.

Riley had it right, too. They needed the break.

'I could paint her for years,' Sasha continued. 'And I likely will. But this one's for you.'

'For – for me?'

'Absolutely.' While she sipped her Bellini, Sasha studied her work with a critical eye. 'I need maybe another hour with it, just to punch it up, then it's yours. Just like she is.'

'But I can't take her, can I?'

'We're in a world of miracles and magicks. I'm going to believe in both.'

'This painting. It means a lot, more than I can tell you. I need to give you something for it. Not money,' he said when she started to pull away. 'I get that, and it'd be insulting between us. But when this is over, when we've done what we're meant to do, if you want that conversation with Monet, I'll take you.'

She gasped, bounced on her toes, grabbed him in a hug. 'Oh, my God! Sawyer, that would be– Oh, my God! I have to brush up, big-time, on my French.'

'With just one down and two to go, I figure there's time.'

'Riley will find the Bay of Sighs, then we'll have two, and one to go. I just... I haven't felt where we go from here. Have you?'

He shook his head. 'No hints from the compass yet.'

'It'll come, for both of us. And you need another day, at least, before we pick all this up again. So, tomorrow it's you.'

'It's me what?'

'I'm going to paint you tomorrow. I haven't figured out what I'm after with you yet.' She stepped back a pace, studied him with a keen and curious eye that made him feel ... goofy.

'But it's you,' she said firmly.

'It already feels weird.'

But he took a seat in the sun, and looked forward to having a beer with friends.

CHAPTER SIXTEEN

Sawyer knew he was well on the mend when Doyle ordered him into training – on the light side – in the morning. And he managed five pull-ups before his shoulder screamed like a woman getting a hard pinch on the ass. Maybe it scored the pride, a little, when Sasha did five, then gutted her way through a sixth.

'I'm not last.' Sliding to the ground, panting, Sasha wagged a fist in victory. 'I'm not last.'

'Hey, bum shoulder. Near-death experience.'

'I don't care. Today, this fine day, I'm not last. And you're on breakfast detail.'

Maybe he shouldn't have been so impatient to get back to it all.

But he could admit to relief when he didn't want to crawl back into bed after an hour's activity. And when he *did* crawl back into bed again, with Annika, he'd do something – at last – besides sleep.

So that did make it a very fine day.

Though it did feel weird, he posed for Sasha – mostly because she hounded him. He stood for an hour – another triumph – wearing his guns, left hand on the butt of one, compass held in the other.

At one point Riley wandered out.

'Did you find something?' he demanded.

'No – and you and Doyle can stuff it. I'm taking

a break. The guy who knows what we want to know should be available tomorrow.'

'Hope you get him before you wolf out.' Hip cocked now, the thumb of the hand holding the compass hooking in his pocket, Sawyer sent Riley a quick, insolent grin. 'Hey, you could bark in Morse code.'

Riley merely shot up her middle finger, studied the painting. 'Yeah, you're getting him, Sash, right down to the beady little eyes.'

'You need to do Rile here in wolf form, Sasha. An action shot. Like when she's scratching at fleas.'

'I don't have–' Riley hissed out a breath; Sasha just kept working.

'Do you believe in reincarnation?' she asked Riley.

'Absolutely. One go-round? What's the point?'

'I strongly believe the two of you were siblings in another life. And I do want to paint you in wolf form. And as you are now.'

'I don't think–'

'All sides of us,' Sasha interrupted, and chose another brush. 'Now that I've started, I know it's something I need to do. Do you need a break, Sawyer?'

'I'm good, unless you do.'

'I'd like to keep going – until you tell me you need a break. And you have to tell me. Painting helps me focus, and she's trying to get in.'

'What? Nerezza?' Riley squeezed Sasha's shoulder. 'I'll get Bran.'

'No, it's all right.' Calmly, Sasha worked on Sawyer's hair – he had a lot of it – sweeping in

305

sunstreaks. 'I'm all right, and he's busy. Annika's helping him mix medicines. I want Nerezza to try, and if I feel she's getting through, we'll get Bran.' Focused, Sasha continued to paint, switching brushes to detail the curve of Sawyer's fingers on the compass. 'I don't want to push back today, just block. I can't explain why–'

'You don't have to.' With her hand still on Sasha's shoulder, Riley exchanged a look with Sawyer. 'All you need to do is tell Sawyer when and if you need Bran, or anything else.'

'That's right.' Without realizing it, Sawyer took a firmer grip on his gun.

'It's like – you can tell Bran when you go back in, Riley – it's like she's playing with me, just trying to distract me. I know she's waiting, waiting for Malmon to fully become. There's more but ... it's as if she wants me to try to see.'

'Maybe misdirection?'

'I don't know, Riley. But I feel, I *know* she's trying to lure me, and I'm not falling for it. Just as I know this interlude we've had, this really lovely break from searching, from fighting, from bleeding, is nearly done.'

'Then let's enjoy it while it lasts.' Giving Sasha's shoulder a final squeeze, exchanging a last look with Sawyer, Riley went back inside to tell Bran everything.

He watched her while she painted him. Flicked a glance up once when he saw Bran come out on the terrace, obviously checking for himself if he was needed.

Shortly after, Doyle strolled out, angled a chair, and sat, gaze on Sasha's back. So Riley had made the rounds, Sawyer thought, and one way or another, Sasha was guarded.

He relaxed a little, let his mind drift a little. Wished Annika would come out. He wondered if, when they had the stars, when they found the Island of Glass and returned them – not if, but when – there would be time, just a few days, for him to be with her. Without war and vengeful gods, without responsibilities and risk.

It didn't seem like much to ask, those few days.

'Have you told her you love her? I feel it,' Sasha said. 'It's so strong, I can't not feel it. Have you told her?'

'What good would it do? It seems like it would only make her sad. I don't want her to go back with regrets.'

'I don't think a heart like Annika's ever regrets love. And I believe love makes its own miracles.'

'The moon's about to turn.' He could see the ghost of it behind the bold blue sky. 'After that, she gets two more. Some people get lifetimes, some get moments. I've got to tell myself it's what you do with what you get that counts.'

'I believe that, too. I've come to believe exactly that. Don't you regret what you didn't say, didn't do.'

Lowering her brush, studying the canvas, she stepped back. 'That's it for now. I can finish it without you.' To loosen them, she rolled her shoulders. 'And we can both use a break.'

Ready for that break, he walked over, stood beside her to see the work.

'Well, wow.'

'You like it?'

'Yeah. It's ... again, wow.'

She'd painted him with the hills rising at his back, everything sunbaked, brilliant, alive.

'How do you get the light to just ... pour like that?'

'Trick of the trade.'

He shook his head. 'Scope of the talent. I know it's here, because I know those hills, but the way you've painted the background, it could be anywhere with hills, mountains, sky.'

'That's what I wanted, because that's the scope of your gift. And you look out from the painting knowing it, sure in it. Riley helped with that.'

'Riley?'

'I couldn't get what I wanted from you until she did, and you got loose, poked at her, grinned with it. That's you, Sawyer. Hand on your gun, ready to fight when you must, compass in your hand, ready to travel where you're needed. But just as ready for a friend.'

'You made it glow – the compass.'

'It did glow.'

'No, it didn't. I'd have felt it.'

'It glowed for me.' She hesitated when, as he still held it, he looked down at it. 'It may be I just saw what it will do, or has done,' she told him.

But she knew better. It had glowed, soft, steady, when he'd thought of Annika.

He waited until after the evening meal, after the decision to wait one more full day before diving again. He wouldn't argue that, because with what he hoped to do, he might need that extra recovery day.

'With any luck when we do go out, I'll have a location, or at least a direction. We'll know where we want to be,' Riley concluded.

'Good enough. Now, Annika needs the sea.'

Bran nodded at Sawyer. 'I'll take her down later.'

'No, I'll take her.' As Doyle shook his head, Sawyer aimed a pointed look. 'I wouldn't say I'd take her if I wasn't sure I could, and it won't be here, where Nerezza may sniff us out. I've got a place she can have some freedom.'

'You're not a hundred percent, Sawyer,' Riley began.

'No, but I'm closer, and this is something I've been doing for a while now. I know what I can handle. I wouldn't take chances with Annika, with any of us.'

'The pool is very nice. I'm happy with it.'

'You need the sea. You'll be stronger for it. And I need to work muscles other than biceps. I need to tune up, and this is a way to do both. Can you trust me for this?'

'I do. I trust you for anything,' Annika said.

'We need to know where you are, and a time frame.' Bran glanced around the table. 'That's nonnegotiable.'

'Two hours. That gives Annika plenty of sea time, and me some recharge time if I need it. I don't feel like I will, but if I do, that's enough. And where?'

He blinked away, and seconds later, blinked back with a map.

'Show-off.' But Riley grinned.

'Just demonstrating I'm coming off the DL.

We'll be here.'

'But ... the South Pacific?' Sasha looked at Bran, worry in her eyes. 'It's so far.'

'It's one of my places – it's ... like driving home.'

'Can you get there?' Sasha asked Bran.

'If needed, yes.'

'And how's this? If I think or feel hard enough, will you be able to read me? If I can try to let you know we're there safe.'

'I can try.' Sasha nodded. 'I can try. Bran can help. It's just so far away.'

'It's one of my places,' Sawyer repeated, and slid a small duffle out from under the table.

'What's in there?' Riley demanded.

'Nothing much.' He held out a hand for Annika's. 'Ready?'

'It's nine. Curfew's eleven. Sharp,' Sasha added.

'Yes, Mom. Let's go.'

When they vanished, Doyle picked up his beer. 'So do you think he's going all the way to the South Pacific to bang her?'

'Not just, but it's a factor.'

Sasha poked Riley's shoulder. 'He needs to do this, needs to rebuild his confidence. He nearly died, and he's been weak and shaken. Anni needs the sea; he needs to give it to her.'

'The sex is just the bonus round,' Riley decided.

'They've two hours for the sea, for confidence building, for sex.' And to make the point, Bran flicked his wrist. An old-fashioned hourglass sat in the center of the table. 'It's on two hours. Last grain of sand falls through, I go.'

'I like it. I already set the alarm on my watch,' Riley added as she studied the glass. 'But this is much cooler.'

'He's taking his moments,' Sasha told him, then went still. 'I...' She reached for Bran's hand, drew from him. 'I feel them. I feel them. They're safe.'

Sawyer brought them right to the verge of land where the surf rolled, smooth and gentle under star-struck skies. It felt as if he'd taken a good, solid jog – and that worked for him.

'Oh, Sawyer.' In absolute delight, she spun, then stood, one foot in sea, one on shore.

'Great spot, huh?'

'It's wonderful. I've been here before.'

'Really?'

'Yes, with my family. Many times.'

'How do you know?'

'I know the water – the sea – like you know a road. It's the best I can explain. This place, these waters, we come on...' Annoyed with herself she shook back her hair. 'I can't remember the word. A journey to a special place. A holy place.'

'Pilgrimage?'

'Yes! Pilgrimage, pilgrimage,' she repeated to fix the word in her mind. 'We believe Annika – I was named for her. She was holy and powerful, and swam all the seas to spread kindness and love.'

He brought her hand to his lips. 'Then you're well named.'

'It's an honor to be named after one so beloved. It's said she was nearly captured, and badly injured by seamen who hunted these waters. But one found her, helped her, tended her until she was well again. He saved her, and she saved him. He was lost, you understand? And she helped

311

him find his way home. She gave him a gift so he would never lose his way again, on land or sea.'

Sawyer set his duffle down on the beach. 'That's pretty similar to the story passed down in my family, about the compass. But that was in the North Sea, so...'

He looked down at the compass, still in his hand. 'Unless it wasn't. The sailor and the mermaid, saving each other. The gift of direction. That's a lot of parallels. Maybe it is the same, but the locations in your version or mine changed in the telling over the years. You're Annika.'

'Yes, I'm Annika.'

'I'm Sawyer Alexei King – Alexei was the name of the sailor who was given the compass. So I'm named for him. Parallels, or maybe just fate.'

'This sacred place is where your grandfather brought you?'

'Yeah, we camped right here, on the beach.'

'So, we've both been here before. This place is important to us both. That's also parallel?'

'In my book, yeah. Go on in. It's a great night for a swim.'

'Swim with me.' And in her carefree way, she pulled off her dress, tossed it aside.

She raced into the water, dived into the roll of surf. Her tail flipped up, fluid as the water itself, then slid under the indigo sea.

Seconds later, she rose up, just to her shoulders, her smile brilliant. 'Swim with me!'

'Be right there.'

He needed to set things up first, and did so quickly as she slipped under the water again. Then he stripped down, and as she had, dived into the surf. He swam out beyond the breakers, pleased his shoulder didn't twinge, his side didn't ache with the movement.

Then he let himself float in the cool with the white moon sailing above and stars like scattered diamonds. And he realized as everything in him eased, he'd needed this as much as she had.

Like Sasha had needed to paint, he'd needed something bright and beautiful.

And the bright and the beautiful arrowed up, head back, hair streaming. She seemed to bump the moon before she folded herself and dived in again. Her tail wound around his waist. When he started to laugh, he found himself propelled up, toward the sky. And he heard her laugh as he managed to tuck in, hit the water again in a ferocious cannonball.

'You make such a big splash.'

'I'll say. Do it again.'

'It was fun?'

'Completely.'

This time, prepared, he pulled off a jackknife. His entry would never match hers, but he figured he rated a seven-point-five.

They played, diving, leaping, splashing, gliding. Then floated.

'Does this hurt your arm, your side?'

'No. Almost a hundred percent all around now.'

'You're strong.'

'Getting there.'

She turned in the water, put her arms around him. 'You're strong,' she repeated. 'Sasha and Bran are strong healers. So you can be well again. I was afraid. In the cave, even after.'

'Me, too. But here we are.'

'Yes.' She brought her lips to his. 'Will you touch me? I miss having you touch me when you want me.'

'I always want you.' He ran his hands over the sleek hair that fell past her waist, and under it to skin, over the strange and marvelous transition from skin to scale. Both smooth, both beautiful.

Automatically, he kicked his legs to keep them above water, then her tail curved around him and kept them both afloat.

'I wanted you the first time I saw you.'

She stroked his cheek. 'This is truth?'

'Absolute truth. You were just a drawing in Sasha's book, but I wanted you.' He found her lips again. 'And when I saw you on the beach in Corfu, in the moonlight, in the white dress, I wanted you.'

'But you were only my friend.'

'I am your friend, but it wasn't easy to stay only your friend.'

Her heart sighed, her body shivered when he cupped her breasts. 'Why did you?'

'I thought it was the right thing for you. You had so much to learn. I didn't want to confuse you.'

'I'm not confused.'

She rose higher in the water, offered her breasts to his lips. When he took them, she let her head fall back. Her hair flowed over the water – a black silk pool over the dark sea.

Strong, she thought again, and how she'd needed those strong hands on her. His mouth tasting her, feasting now in a way that showed her he desired.

The thrill poured into her, had her streaming up with him, to circle and spin on the surface.

She clung tight, pressed his head to her, spilled down again on a sighing moan. There she circled, circled slowly so the water flowed around them while their lips met, their tongues met, in a kiss gone suddenly urgent.

Her hands ran over him, her fingers tracing the healing wounds. 'Does this hurt?'

'Nothing hurts.' But his blood pounded everywhere. 'We need to go in to shore. I want to cover you. I want to fill you. God, I have to have you.'

'Would you have me here?'

'Yes. Yes.' Half mad for her, he ravaged her mouth. 'Closer in. I need to be able to stand.'

'No, here.' She took his face in her hands to draw him back. She read the desire, the need, a mirror of her own. But...

'Would you want me, like this? Would you have me in my true form?'

'I want you, Anni. It's you.'

'I can open for you.'

'Open for me.' Over his head, out of his mind, he pulled her back to him. 'Take me in.'

It was a gift, a truth. She looked into his eyes as she opened. Looked into his eyes as she took him in. And then the meaning of the moment, of the gift, was so radiant, she let her eyes close as the light pulsed against her lids.

It ripped through him, that stunning, sumptuous sensation of sliding into her. Of feeling her close around him, tight, for a moment, tight like a fist.

She trembled against him, and still they floated,

lovers cradled in the sea.

He moved in her, slowly, slowly, aware of the wonder of her belonging to him – absolutely – the magic of that beat of time. A time not to be rushed. Buoyed by her, he brushed kisses over her cheeks, her eyelids, her lips, all the while stroking, stroking, matching his rhythm to the easy dance of the sea that held them.

Love swept through him, a warm breeze scented with her.

Trapped in her own bliss, she rose up again, circled with him. And down, taking him under, her mouth fixed on his to give him her breath with the kiss.

Covered by the dark sea, he moved in her, felt her peak, drew her breath into him to give her more. And knew, when love all but shattered him, if he could find the miracle he would have stayed with her, would have made her world his own.

Then she took him up, into the air, into the light of moon and stars, into the sounds of water rolling to shore and back. And there, caught between worlds, she once more tightened around him. Said his name against his lips.

And there, did shatter him.

She held him close, her head on his shoulder, the marvelous symmetry of her body pressed to his.

'You're not disappointed?' she murmured.

'Annika, I'm... I don't have the words, but I'm everything that's the opposite of disappointed.'

'There is more to do with legs.'

'Annika.' Once again undone, he brushed his lips over her hair. 'You're a fantasy come true. More beautiful, more miraculous than anyone

I've ever known.'

'You're the same to me. The same.'

Rolling onto her back, she smiled up at him all the way to shore.

When she stood with him in the shallows, she laid a hand on her heart. 'You brought a blanket, and candles and wine, even flowers. It's so pretty.'

'You'll make it prettier.' Now he tugged her to the beach. 'Are you cold?'

'No, are you?'

'I feel pretty close to perfect.' After fishing a lighter out of the duffle, he lit the little candles, and used his multitool to open the wine.

'We have time?'

'We've got some time left.' He pulled her down to the blanket, poured the wine. 'You-and-me time.'

'I like you-and-me time, very much. But I have to use it to tell you something. I didn't give you the truth.'

'About what?'

She dropped her gaze. 'You believe I saw you, as you saw me, for the first time on the beach in Corfu. But it's not the truth.'

'No? What is?'

'When I was training for the quest, the sea witch took me to another island, and I saw you there, on the beach, under the moon like we are now. You were alone, but you didn't look lonely.'

Intrigued, he tipped her face back so their eyes met. 'What island?'

'I was told to remember what the land people called it. Isle au Haut.'

'Maine? I haven't been there in ... that had to be

at least five years ago. How long did you train?'

'Until I was chosen, then longer, then until I knew, because I was chosen, to come to you.'

'Did you see the others before?'

'Only you. The sea witch said only you, and you would be enough to tell me when and where I should come to begin. You were enough. Are you angry I didn't give you the truth?'

'No.' To prove it, he threaded his fingers with hers. 'I'm not angry.'

'I wanted you then, but it wasn't time, and I had to wait.'

And he'd thought the weeks he'd waited had been endless. 'Five years. That's a chunk of waiting time.'

'Not when I have this.'

She snuggled against him, her head on his shoulder, her gaze – as his – on the sea. He'd meant to give her that sea, and some romance, some time out of time in a place that mattered to him.

Without knowing it mattered as much to her.

He hadn't intended to give more, ask more. But it felt right, there in that place that mattered to both of them, in this time belonging only to them, that he give her more. With no regrets.

'I didn't give you the whole truth either.'

'What isn't the whole truth?'

'I want you, but that's not all. I'm your friend, but that's not all.' He screwed the stem of his glass into the sand so he could take her hands, bring one, then the other to his lips. 'I'm in love with you.'

Those eyes, those eyes that mesmerized him, went wide. Her breath caught, then released on what sounded perilously close to a sob. 'You love me... Do you mean the way you love Sasha and Riley?'

'No. I love them, like family. Like sisters. But I'm in love with you. It means–'

'I know. I know.' Her eyes glinted with joy, with tears. 'I know,' she said again. 'I love, but you are the only one for me to be in love. I couldn't tell you.' She threw her arms around him, pressed her cheek to his. 'It's like the first kiss. I couldn't tell you unless you told me. Unless you were with me.'

'I am with you.' He shifted, took her lips. 'In love with you, Annika. I know we can't–'

'No, no. Please. Don't say can't with love. We have love. You're my love, my only. I swam through the Canal d'Amour, and you came to me.'

'The canal. In Corfu?'

'I loved you when I saw you on the beach before, and I waited. And when you pulled me to you, to begin, I swam through the canal. It's said you do this, and will meet your one true love. And I did, and you came for me. But I couldn't tell you.'

Her fingers traced over his cheeks, his jaw, his mouth. 'I knew your face, and your smile, but not your name. Until that night. And still I couldn't tell you. Not when you fought beside me, or kissed me, or mated with me, or saved me from death. But I can give the words back to you. I'm in love with you.'

She spilled her wine, but it hardly mattered, as she flung herself at him, tumbled them both back on the blanket. The kiss went from gentle to deep, from tender to strong.

'I wanted to give you a gift, in the sea.'

'You did.'

'But you've given me a gift.' In reverence, in joy, she laid her hand on his heart. 'There's no more precious gift than love. I'll keep yours safe, always. Can you be with me again? Is there time? I want to celebrate the gift.'

'We'll make time. We'll make our own time.'

'They're late.' Restless, Bran pushed up to pace under the pergola where they'd all gathered in a kind of vigil.

'They're safe,' Sasha assured him. 'Give them a little longer. They're safe. They're happy. We all have to face what's coming soon enough.'

'If the man can't get it done in two hours–'

'Put a sock in it,' Riley advised Doyle. 'Not everybody just wants to knock one out and be done.'

'Two hours was the deal,' he insisted, and Bran nodded when Doyle pointed to the hourglass.

'Exactly.'

'It's barely ten minutes more. And they're safe. There's no need to– They're coming.'

At Sasha's words, Doyle got to his feet, reached for his sword. 'No, not her. Them. Sawyer and Annika. So everyone relax.' Even as Sasha spoke, they were there.

'I could've cheated,' Sawyer said immediately, and his grin could've lit the entire island. 'And done a time shift.'

'He wanted to, but I said it was a kind of lie, and we had a night of truths.'

'Yeah, we did.' Still grinning, he hugged Annika

320

close to his side. 'Are we grounded?'

'Time matters,' Bran began.

'Don't have angry.' Annika spun over to hug Bran. 'I'm too happy for angry. Sawyer loves me.'

'There's a news flash,' Riley commented.

Still hugging Bran, Annika frowned at Riley. 'I know this voice is ... sarcastical.'

'Just sarcastic,' Bran corrected.

'Sarcastic. You know he loved me?'

'If you just figured it out tonight, you're the only one here who didn't. But yay – sincerely. Now, since the kids are back, I'm going to get some sleep.' Riley looked up at the moon. 'I won't get any tomorrow night.'

'Sawyer needs sleep, too. We had much sex and he should rest now. He's ready to dive again,' she told Doyle. 'But because of the sex, it's good to wait one more day.'

Riley rolled her eyes, kept walking. Doyle rose.

'I'm going to take a last patrol. Get that rest, brother. Another day for the dive, but you're in for full training tomorrow.'

'Right. Well, we'll go up, get that rest.'

Sasha looked after them with a sentimental smile. 'That's why their happiness kept ringing like bells.' She rose, took Bran's hand. 'No point in being annoyed with them. All's well – right now much, much more than well. And we should get some rest, too.'

'So we will. After much sex.'

To amuse her, he floated them both up to the terrace, and into bed.

CHAPTER SEVENTEEN

In the chamber inside the palace inside the mountain, what had been Malmon ran up the wall, across the ceiling, down the wall, over the floor – a monstrous hamster on a wheel.

He ran for hours, occasionally snagging one of the birds in a clawed hand, consuming it. Often more for amusement than hunger.

More rarely than that, as he ran, chortling, something would flash inside his mad mind. Images of colorful rooms, plush beds, of a man with golden hair in a dark suit staring back at him in horror, as if through a fogged glass.

The flashes made him scream, and the screams echoed off the polished stone.

Whenever she came, his queen, his goddess, his world, he would drop to the bulbous knobs of his knees. Tears of fear and joy and crazed love filled his slitted eyes when she stroked his head. He would call out to her in a guttural grunt when she left him again.

Then he would go back to the wheel.

On the day she came to him, took him by the hand, led him out of the chamber, he trembled. His small, spiked tail twitched.

She guided him through a maze of stone hazed with smoke from sputtering torches. Bats and birds perched among the flames, eyes glinting, watching. He saw a creature with wings and three heads shackled, saw the bones and blood scattered around it.

Then they entered a large chamber, alight with candle-glow, glinting with gold and silver and jewels. Like his, the walls were mirrored and reflected the throne on a gilded floor that rose on three silver steps.

She released him, ascended, sat. Then gestured with long fingers ringed with rubies. 'Pour us wine, my pet.' When he neither moved nor spoke, she inclined her head. 'Don't you remember how?'

Words grunted out of him. 'Remembering hurts.'

'I wish for you to pour the wine. Do you not want to give me whatever I wish?'

'Yes! All you wish. All!'

'Then give me what I wish.'

His hands shook. The man with golden hair flashed again, and the pain spiked in his head. But he picked up the glass bottle, poured the red liquid into a goblet studded with the bloodred rubies she favored.

The claws of his feet clacked against the silver steps as he carried it to her.

'And for you.'

'For me?'

'We'll have wine together, my pet. Pour the wine, and sit.' She gestured to the steps at her feet.

Quaking – such joy, such fear! – he did as she bid. He wanted to lap at the wine in the goblet, but remembered, painfully, drank with his long sharp teeth clicking against the silver.

'And now, Andre–'

Hearing the name had the pain erupting inside

323

him. He cried out, spilled wine, red on silver.

'You needed to forget,' Nerezza continued, 'so you could become. Now you are become, and must remember. Remembering will be useful.'

'It hurts!'

'Do you love me?'

'I love. You are my worship.'

'Then you will bear the pain for me. There is a man's mind inside you still, and I will have need of it. I will have need of you ... Andre. You failed me once, but I show mercy. You sit at my hand and drink wine. You live, and with speed and strength no human can match. How will you repay my mercy?'

'As you command me.'

'Yes. As I command you.' She smiled, sipped wine. 'Do you remember the guardians? The six?'

His breath burned his throat; his clawed hand dented the silver goblet. 'Enemies.'

'Which of them would you choose to kill first?'

'Sawyer King! Sawyer King! Sawyer King!'

'Ah, yes, he who outwitted you. I will allow you to take that life. But not first. I need the death of the seer. As she dies, I can drain her. She's powerful, and that power is ... young. It will feed me, and she will no longer guide the others.'

'I will kill her for you, my queen.'

'Perhaps.' She picked up the Globe of All. Frustrated mists swirled inside, hiding much from her. 'If she dies by your hand, you may take the one you want, do what you want. You must prepare now, Andre, for the battle.'

And if he failed, she thought, even if he died in the attempt, there would still be blood.

Setting aside the globe, she picked up her mirror. Saw the white streak through her beautiful black hair, the signs of age on her beautiful face.

They had caused this. The guardians had marred the perfection of her beauty.

But when she drank the seer's blood, she drank the power. With it, she would restore her endless youth.

As he felt the connection again, strongly, Sawyer spread out his maps, laid down his compass. When it glowed, he expelled a breath – relief and gratitude – watched it glide over the maps. It settled on the map of Capri, then lay still.

'Yeah, yeah, I got that part. But *where?*' Scowling, he sat back. 'Why does everything have to be so damn cryptic? Just once, why not give a clear, exact, no-bullshit answer?'

He continued to scowl when Riley sat across from him under the pergola. 'No luck?'

He shook his head. 'You?'

'I've broken my never-nag rule and left yet another urgent voice mail, sent another urgent email to this Dr. White – Jonas White – my source claims is the expert on the Bay of Sighs. The retreat ended this morning, so he should be connected to the damn world by now, but nothing.'

Like Sawyer, she stared at the compass. 'Does that do any good?' she wondered. 'Staring at it?'

'No.'

'Figured. Like it's not doing any good, right now, for me to keep trying to dig up more on this mythical bay. I hit bottom, and have to suck it up and wait. I hate sucking it up.'

'At least we'll dive tomorrow. And maybe that's the way it has to be. Just keep looking. Suck it up.' He looked at her now. 'Because it's not showing me where this bay is, and it's sure as hell not giving any handy hints of where we'd go next – when we do find it. And that's going to be important.'

'Vital, once we find the Water Star, so it's hard to hold that no-nag rule where Sasha's concerned.'

'Nerezza will know when we find it, and come hard.'

'You've got to figure.' Thinking it through yet again, Riley twirled her sunglasses by the earpiece. 'First order, when we do, is getting it to safety. I guess Bran will hide it where we have the first. Then we're going to have to book or be ready to kick her ass here.'

'We'll be ready. But it doesn't feel like here.'

Intrigued, Riley propped her chin on her fist. 'No, it doesn't. I keep thinking that. It doesn't feel as if we'd have a big, final showdown with the bitch god in a lemon grove outside a nice house in Capri. A showdown, sure, but the big one?'

'Water Star, so maybe the big one comes when we're in or on the water.'

'Yeah, I've played with that one, too. And with the fact that we've gotten pretty relaxed around here the last couple days, so it just doesn't feel like Fight Club. I guess it doesn't matter when or where, as long as we're ready.' Riley glanced up. 'Bran's in his magick shop doing what he does.'

'Where's everybody else?'

'You mean Annika, so you should say Annika. I

think she's up working with Bran so Sasha has time to paint. Because we're all hoping she'll paint something we need to know. And Doyle is in the kitchen cleaning his weapons.

'Anyway, the next – if we leap forward – is ice. So maybe Iceland or Greenland or the fricking Arctic. We may look back on the sun and heat fondly before much longer.'

'It's a big leap until we find the Water Star.' He noted she stared at her phone, as he'd stared at the compass. 'Let's go shoot something.'

'What?'

'Target practice. Sitting here trying to will the compass to move or your phone to ring? I'm getting jumpy.'

'Neither of us needs practice there, and we shouldn't waste the ammo. Knife-throwing contest.'

'You're on.'

He took the compass; she took her phone, and together they killed an hour and a few targets.

'Tiebreaker,' Riley said, but he shook his head.

'Let's leave it as a tie. I'm dinner chef tonight, and I should get started.'

'It's early.'

'It's the first night of your three, right? You need to eat before sundown. I'm going for beef manicotti. I figure you could use the red meat.'

'Yeah. Appreciate it.' She pulled the phone out of her pocket as they walked back. 'Watch this White call after sundown, when I can't talk to him.'

'Told you. Bark in Morse code.'

She elbow-punched him, then split off to head

up to her room. She wouldn't sleep that night, so a nap wouldn't hurt.

Later, they ate a quiet meal, each of them preoccupied. Since the next day's agenda was already set, it came down to waiting.

'That should hold me till morning.'

'You still have time,' Sasha said when Riley rose.

'Yeah, and I'm going to try to contact this White guy again. Push some other buttons that may get through to him. The harder it is to reach him, the more I think he's got some answers. If I crap out on that, I'll just see everybody in the morning.'

'Stay out of the neighbor's chicken coop,' Sawyer advised, and earned a narrow stare.

'I'll take her turn,' Annika said when Riley went inside.

'Turn?' Distracted, Sasha rubbed a small ache at her temple. 'Oh. Oh, the chart. It's Riley and Doyle on cleanup.'

'I don't mind. Maybe she'll find the Dr. White, and learn what we need. And after we clean up, if there's time, I can take her some of the gelato that comes in the box.'

'Right.' With some reluctance, Doyle rose when Annika did. He'd solved his cooking duties – he bought pizza – but had yet to figure a way out of cleanup when his turn came around.

'It's nice to make things clean again,' Annika said after they'd carted dishes inside.

'It's nice to have them clean.'

'You cleaned your guns today, and polished your sword, even your knives.' Content enough, she went to work at the sink. 'This isn't so different.'

And she liked filling the big sink with water and

the suds, liked the smell of the suds when she scrubbed the pots Sawyer had used. 'The meal was very good.'

'Yeah, the man can cook.' Doyle clattered dishes into the dishwasher. Since he knew what it was to try cleaning a pot or plate in a fast stream, he figured he shouldn't complain.

'I can cook a little now. It's fun. You've lived so long, but don't cook.'

'I can get by.' He pulled out a dishcloth, started drying the pots. 'I learned to cook over a fire, on hunting trips.'

'You've seen the wonders come. Riley let me look at some of her books. Once land people walked or rode horses. Then they learned to make cars, and motorcycles like yours. And there was no phone like Riley so enjoys, or the movies Sawyer likes to watch.'

'Things change. People not as much.'

'But things can't change themselves. People can. Sasha has changed so much in hardly one turn of the moon. She's stronger and she's learned to fight. And she can do six pull-ups where she could not do one.'

'You've got a point. And I'm betting she'll get up to ten before we're done with this.'

'And we've all seen wonders, of dark and light.'

For a while they worked in silence.

'I have a hard question,' Annika began. 'I want to ask when it's just you.'

'All right.'

'You've lived a long time. You've had people who...' She touched a hand to her heart. 'Matter, who mean much.'

329

'After a while, you try not to let that happen.'

'But it does. We matter to you, not just as guardians, as warriors. We matter to you.'

He looked at her, the stunning mermaid, thought of the others, one by one. 'You matter, yes.'

'How do you say good-bye?'

He set down the cloth because he understood she needed a real answer. 'I've never found an easy way. If it's easy, they didn't matter.'

'Is there a way to make it easy for the one you leave?'

'Convince him he doesn't matter. But that's not going to work for you, Gorgeous. Not going to work with Sawyer.'

'No, I couldn't pretend that. It would make what we have nothing.'

'He'd never believe you anyway. And he's never going to forget you.'

'I think how it would be best if he did, then I know if he could, I would just fade away. So, I have to hold on to the wonder.'

'If anyone can, it's you.'

'You're my very good friend.' She turned, hugged him. 'I'll be sad to say good-bye to you. But I have two turns of the moon before... Oh, it's nearly sunset. I have no time to take Riley the gelato. There are still dishes to put away. Cookies.'

Inspired, she pulled a bag of fancy cookies from the pantry. 'I'll finish if you could take these to her. She has enough time for a cookie. And they could be in her room in the morning when she's hungry and tired.'

'I don't think she wants–'

'Please.' Smiling, Annika held out the bag.

Doyle thought there wasn't a man alive who could say no to that smile. 'Fine.'

He carried them upstairs. At least the chore got him out of tubbing up leftovers or washing off counters – all on the duty list.

He heard Riley's voice, caught the quick interest in it.

'Yeah, if you could do that, even better.'

He stepped into her room – one where books were piled everywhere, and where she'd put a nightstand into service as a small desk, which she used now to scribble notes.

Spotting Doyle, she twirled a finger in the air, jabbed it, in a sign he took to mean she was wrapping things up, to wait.

'Yeah, agreed, Atlantis is a whole different kettle. I'm happy to do that, and will first thing in the morning. Uh-huh, right. I just need a little time to put it all together for you first.'

Doyle opened the bag of cookies – it was right there – pulled one out. She kept talking while he ate, while he wandered her room, looking at the books, the maps stuck to the walls, the notes only organized by her eye.

They'd had a few words on her lack of system, but she could, indeed, put her hand on any and everything she wanted in seconds, so he'd lost that round.

The room smelled of her soap – just a faintest hint of vanilla – and the flowers Annika insisted on putting in every bedroom. Including his own.

He ate another cookie, bent over a new translation she must have worked on by herself, lost track a bit until her voice cut through his thoughts again.

'I'm grateful, Doctor. This is a big help. I will absolutely do that. Thanks. Yeah, thanks. Bye.'

She clicked off the phone, did a little dance in place. Her dark gold eyes read smug. For some strange reason, he liked them smug.

'You've had good news.'

'Bet your fine ass. He forgot to turn his phone back on, never turned on his computer. White – my source. And he gave me–'

The phone slipped out of her hand, bounced on the bed as she gasped. 'Oh, fuck it, fuck it, I waited too long. Get out, get out, get out!'

She dropped straight to the floor, began to fight with her bootlaces.

And Doyle realized he hadn't paid attention either. The sun was setting in a fiery red ball.

Her breath came fast and harsh, and her fingers fumbled over the double knots in her laces.

He started to back out, then tossing the bag of cookies aside, crouched down. 'I've got these. I've got them.'

'Get out! Oh, shit.'

She grabbed the bottom of her tank, yanked it over her head.

'I've got it.' He dragged off her boots, the socks, and when she threw her head back, when he saw the change glint in her eyes, gritted his teeth, pulled her belt open.

'Hold on.'

'I can't.'

She moaned, and he heard bones begin to

creak, shift.

'Riley.' Sasha stopped in the doorway.

'I've got it, I've got it. Don't fucking bite me.' While her spine arched, Doyle flipped open the button of her cargo shorts, yanked them and the panties beneath down her legs. Then hooked his fingers in the sports bra she wore, and dragged it over her head and clear.

Naked, she twisted away, rose on all fours.

Her shoulders bunched, and the muscles bulged. Her hands curled, with nails lengthening, going sharp, as skin became pelt.

Again, she threw back her head, and somehow caught between wolf and woman, howled. And the woman was gone.

The wolf growled low, then ran for the terrace doors. In one spring she landed on the stone rail, in another she leaped into the night. 'Oh, my God. Riley.'

Sasha dashed to the terrace, ran out a step behind Doyle. And saw the wolf land neatly, impossibly on the lawn on the other side of the pool. With one glance toward them, she turned and loped into the grove.

'I didn't know she could... It seems an impossible jump.'

Magnificent – he couldn't block the reaction – fierce and magnificent. 'Apparently not for her.'

'She needs to run,' Sasha remembered. 'She told us she needs to run right after the change. All that energy. Why were you...' She glanced at the scattered clothes, cleared her throat. 'Not my business.'

'And not like that. Annika asked me to bring

her up some bloody cookies, and she was on that bloody phone of hers. With the guy she's been after. She wasn't paying attention, and neither was I. She was excited, whatever he told her got her juices running, and she started the change while she was still dressed.'

'You helped her.'

'She couldn't get her damn boots off, then...'

Sasha laid a hand on his arm. 'You helped her. Even if she's embarrassed by that, and snarls – ha – a little tomorrow, she's grateful for the help.'

On a sigh, she turned back into the room. 'I'll pick up her things so she doesn't...'

Doyle turned to her when she trailed off, saw the sight come into her eyes. More magnificence, he thought. He'd never known three women more compelling.

'They're coming. She sends him, transformed as one of us has transformed. For me, for my blood, for my blood to feed her.'

'She can forget it.' Firmly, Doyle took her shoulders. 'Get Bran, get your bow. I'll tell the others.'

'While we're five, and weaker, she watches.'

'Let her watch. Go!'

He unclipped Riley's holster from her belt, clipped it to his own, and called the others to arm as he ran down the steps for his sword.

Inside, Sawyer grabbed more clips, shoved them in his pocket. He could admit, at least to himself, he wanted nothing more than one clear shot at Malmon. He shoved a spare knife in his boot and hurried out to join the others.

'In the grove?'

'No time.'

Bran pointed to where Sasha's gaze was locked. It resembled a cloud, dark and boiling, spewing out of the sky and filled with storms.

'Riley.' Quickly Annika took his hand. 'She–'

'Sun's down, moon's up. Let's make sure they can't get to her, wherever she is. We've got this.' He gave her hand a squeeze, released it. Drew both guns.

He took out the leaders, one shot, and the light flared, flamed them. 'On your six!' Doyle shouted, and Sawyer whirled. A second cloud rolled over the west.

'Sasha and I have the west.' Though he'd armed himself, Bran left the gun holstered. Lightning bolted from his extended hands. 'Sawyer and Annika the east. Doyle–'

'Some of each.'

Sawyer emptied both clips, dodged a razor swipe of claws as he reloaded. However much he trusted Annika's skill, he kept her in sight, ready to defend, protect while she shot charges, flipped to kick, spun to shower the light through the dark.

But he saw nothing of Malmon.

'Come on, fucker,' he muttered, ignoring the backwash of blood and ash splattering from Doyle's whirling sword. 'Show yourself.'

Something rushed past him; he caught the dark blur, felt the sudden shock of pain from claws raking his arm.

He turned, tried to follow the blur, hold it in his sights, but it moved like Bran's lightning, and erratically at that.

But his heart bounded to his throat as he realized that blur was a zigzagging arrow aimed at Sasha.

She released a bolt, struck her target, drew another.

'Sasha! Move, move.'

She hesitated only a second at Sawyer's shout, retreated two quick steps to the side. He saw the blood bloom on her arm, heard her quick cry of pain.

Because his gun was useless – she was too close – Sawyer ran toward her even as Bran yanked her behind him. Sawyer moved to block her from attack, but the attack changed directions so fast Doyle's sword cleaved down, met only air.

Now blood seeped from Sasha's leg.

'Take her in, get her inside.' Sawyer laid down suppressing fire. 'We'll hold them off.'

'No, there's too many.' Shaking off Bran's hold, Sasha fired another bolt.

Sawyer saw the blur, the leap of it. Fired. Missed. He saw Bran once again yank Sasha behind him, knew in that instant Bran would go down.

The wolf all but flew out of the dark, its howl fierce and as deadly as its fangs. Another instant, the blur took form, hideous form, raw red skin, bumpy with scales, wild yellow eyes in a long narrow face crowned with nubs.

The wolf sank those fangs into the demon's shoulder – Malmon's shoulder – and its scream shattered the air. The demon struck out, its face contorted with rage and pain. The blow sent the wolf tumbling through the air. When it struck the ground, it lay still.

'Keep them off her.' On a one-handed hand-

336

spring, Doyle flipped to the wolf, sweeping his sword out to destroy the birds that swooped low to attack the fallen.

In seconds the five circled the wolf, forming a wall of defense. Sawyer caught one last glance of Malmon, took aim, but the dark swallowed the demon and the birds.

And the night went still with the silent moon gliding overhead.

'Riley.' Sasha fell to her knees. 'Oh, God, Riley. Bran.'

'Let me see her, let me see. You're bleeding, *a ghrá.*'

'Riley. How bad is Riley?'

Blood ran down her arm, onto fur as Sasha laid her hands on her friend. 'She's alive. I feel her heart.'

'Stunned, at least. We'll get her inside.'

'I have her.' Sheathing his sword, Doyle crouched, lifted the unconscious wolf.

With a nod, Bran lifted Sasha. 'You're losing blood, as is Sawyer. Annika.'

'I'm not hurt. I'll get what you need.'

'I'm all right. Riley first.'

'You're not all right, no, but you will be. Lay Riley on the table, Doyle, and get towels.'

'Let me check for breaks.' After he laid Riley down, Doyle ran his hands over her, checked legs, worked over her body. 'A couple of ribs, it feels like, but Christ, they're knitting. I can feel the breaks fusing. Heals fast as a wolf. I feel a little...'

'Yeah, me, too.' When his legs buckled, Sawyer simply sat on the floor. 'There's a burning, and a weakness.'

337

'Poison, no doubt. Get the towels, Doyle, and water. Annika,' Bran said as she rushed in. 'Help me here. I need to clean out the wounds, but we'll want the potion, six drops for each. You'll do that now, and quickly.'

He chose another bottle out of the kit as Annika measured the potion. 'It will hurt,' he murmured to Sasha. 'I'm sorry for it. Look at me, open for me.'

She gasped as the liquid met the gash, then simply closed her eyes. 'It's better.'

'Almost. And I've your leg to do as well. A few moments, just a few more. Sawyer, go ahead and drink that. There now, there, *fáidh*, they're clean, and purified. The balm will soothe.'

'Sawyer first.'

'I've got him, finish her.' Doyle took the bottle, crouched by Sawyer. 'Ready?'

'Go for it. Shit, shit, fucking shit.'

Annika pressed a kiss to his head as the burning seared the gashes on his arm, and he felt Sasha – partner in pain – take his hand.

'He would have done worse, much worse, if you hadn't warned me.'

'I couldn't get a clear shot. He's too fast, and then you were too close.'

'He wanted my throat. I had an instant to feel that from him, but you'd shouted and he missed the mark. You saved my life, then Riley saved Bran's, which is the same to me. Please, Bran, please, see to Riley. She fell so hard.'

'Just another moment. Annika, you'll treat Sawyer with the balm.'

'Yes, I know how. The wound is clean. It's deep,

but it's clean.'

'Yeah, it is, I can feel it. And I can stand.' Steady again, Sawyer got to his feet. 'You must have something in the magick box for Riley.'

'Nothing broken.' Once again Doyle ran his hands over her. 'The ribs are healed already.'

As he spoke, the wolf's eyes opened, tawny and clear, met his. The low growl had him lifting his hands, holding them palms out. 'Take it easy.'

'You were hurt,' Sasha said as Riley shifted and jumped nimbly to the floor. 'Will you tell me if you have pain? Let me in?'

Their eyes met, and Sasha's lips curved. 'He wasn't copping a feel. Will you take some medicine? But the fast can't mean... All right. At sunrise. Go rest awhile.'

The wolf gave Doyle one last, long stare, then stalked out of the kitchen.

'You were talking to a wolf. I mean, sure it's Riley, but—'

Grinning, Sawyer shook his head. 'A wolf. Like Dr. Dolittle.'

'She's got some pain, not severe, and she'll sleep awhile. It's rare for her to sleep when in wolf form, but it will help the healing. It's not really talking,' Sasha explained. 'It's more she can let me read her feelings, and they more or less translate into words. She understands us perfectly well, and I can get the gist of what she wants me to know.'

With a sigh, she looked down at the blood on the floor. 'We need to clean this up.'

'I will clean it. I wasn't hurt. You should rest, and you, Sawyer. It helps you heal, too. Is that right, Bran?'

'It is, and they will. We'll talk about all this in the morning.'

'There's a question I'd have liked to ask before she walked out on us.' Doyle glanced at the door-way. 'That was Malmon, I take it.'

'It was,' Sasha told him. 'But not Malmon any longer.'

'So man into demon. And a demon who was just bitten by a werewolf – or lycan, as she prefers. Will the demon be turned by the bite?'

'Good question,' Sawyer said. 'And would that be good or bad news for our side?'

CHAPTER EIGHTEEN

Because she wanted to surprise everyone, Annika slid out of bed very early. Quietly, she pulled on one of her dresses – one with all the favorite colors swirled over it, like a rainbow storm. With a glance back at Sawyer, she slipped from the room while he slept. As she went downstairs, she braided her hair. She wanted it out of the way for the work she would do.

She'd watched the cooking many times, and had been allowed to help. But today she would cook breakfast by herself while the others rested. Doyle had said the night before that because of battle and blood and the diving they would do that day, they could take a day off from the calisthenics.

Annika liked the calisthenics, but she suspected she was the only one who did.

340

She sang to herself as she chose pans and pots, and what she needed from the big silver box that kept things cold. The night had been full of fear and blood, but she had a good, strong feeling about the day to come.

If she could make a good breakfast, with no mistakes, the day would be bright. Pouring herself juice, she shook her head at the machine that made coffee. Everyone liked coffee, but she didn't. She'd rather do calisthenics.

She drank the juice, so cool and fresh, then took a deep breath, hugged herself. Now she would make the bacon.

As the sun peeked through the eastern windows, she had a platter of bacon in the oven on the low, the way Sasha showed her, and a nice pile of the bread of France – French toast, she corrected herself – as Sawyer had showed her.

She would make the scrambled eggs and the potatoes that Bran made on his turn. Riley would be very hungry after her fast. And when everything was cooked, and in the warm, she would set the table.

She heard someone coming, too soon for her to finish as she'd hoped. But smiled when she saw Riley.

'Good morning! I can make you coffee.'

'Okay. I smell bacon.'

'I made bacon.' Delighted, Annika opened the oven, remembered the big mitts that kept hands protected from burns, and pulled out the platter.

'I'll say you did.' Riley took a handful at once. 'Enough for an army.'

'I made too much?'

'I feel like an army,' Riley said with her mouth full. 'French toast?' Without waiting, Riley grabbed a piece, stuffed it in.

'Is it good?'

'It's great. I'm starving. Where's Sasha?'

'Sleeping. Everyone's sleeping but you and me.'

Riley ate more bacon. 'You're cooking solo?'

'By myself? Yes, a surprise. Sawyer and Sasha and you were hurt, and Doyle said no calisthenics.'

'Yay.'

'Do you have pain?'

'No, all good.' Still eating, Riley turned to the coffeemaker.

'I'll make it! You can sit. I like to make coffee, but I don't like to drink it.' She made a big mug, set it down, then hugged Riley. 'You saved Bran and Sasha. I think you saved us all because when you came, the evil things went away.'

'I ran too far. I should've stayed closer. If I'd been back sooner—'

'I think you were here when needed. The demon Malmon hurt you, but you hurt him more, I think.'

'He clocked me a good one. He's Hulk Smash strong.'

'I don't understand.'

'Seriously strong. The coffee's good, Anni. I think you've just graduated to regular kitchen rotation.'

A beaming smile followed a quick gasp of joy. 'Do you really think?'

'Don't know why it would thrill you, but yeah, I definitely think. Hey, Sash, looks like Anni

342

leapfrogged into your slot today.'

'Oh, Riley, you're all right.'

'I am now,' she said and ate more bacon.

'Annika, you ... you made all this?'

'Riley says it's good. I can be on rotation. Will you put me on the chart for cooking?'

'I will, and thank you for stepping in for me.'

'You feel good?'

'I'm fine. We're all fine. Since you're breakfast chef, I'll set the table.'

'I can do it.'

'Let me help.' Sasha ran a hand down Annika's arm. 'After coffee.'

It pleased her so much she wanted to dance to see everyone eat her food. To have Sawyer kiss her as he reached over for more.

She'd made a meal for her family, and of all she'd learned it seemed the best.

'First question.' Doyle looked at Riley. 'Will he turn? Malmon.'

Riley scooped up eggs. 'That's something I've been thinking about most of the night. I've never bitten anyone – human or demon. Big-time violation, though that's for humans, and he's not. Not anymore. And the answer is, I don't know. New territory. I'm going to consult some experts on it, but it may be completely new territory.'

'If he does, when?' Sawyer asked.

'Not this moon. If he were human, he'd be pretty sick for this round. Chills, fever, and when the moon began to wane, he'd be fine again. Until the next moon.'

'But he's not human,' Doyle pointed out.

'Got that, and I'm going to consult, but I don't see any way for him to turn, if he turns, straight off. In any case, the first change is hard, especially for someone infected and not prepared and trained. The thing is, I don't know if a lycan bite infects a demon. I'm not sure anyone knows.'

'It may be wait and see then.' Considering, Bran drank more coffee. 'I wasn't as prepared as I should have been. I couldn't see him, not clearly, and that I need to work on.'

'But you could,' Doyle said.

'I could see him.' Still eating, Riley nodded. 'Ugly son of a bitch, which is nice and ironic as previously he considered himself God's gift. With apologies to God,' she added, and ate more. 'I could see him, and see he'd homed in on Sasha. He'd have gone through Bran to get to her, but getting to her was the goal.'

'She wanted me dead – and wanted my blood. She'll have some of it.'

'I didn't stay close enough. I was distracted, and the change started before I'd taken care of things. Thanks for helping me with that.'

Doyle shrugged. 'Never a problem to get a woman out of her clothes.'

'Cute. But it... Changing in front of anyone is... It's a private thing, and I reacted to how it went down. So I wasn't as close as I should have been. If I had been, she might not have the blood.'

'If you hadn't come when you did, she'd have Bran's blood, too, and I might be dead. So let's table any timing issue.'

'If the Malmon demon is also lycan from the bite, will he be stronger than Hulk Smash?'

'Hulk Smash.' Despite the possibility, Sawyer grinned. 'Where did you get...' He shifted his gaze from Annika to Riley, nodded. Gave her a thumbs-up as he ate more French toast.

'Maybe, but not until the first change, and the first change will hit him hard – if he's infected. Let me make some calls and– Shit! Calls. My brain got scrambled. White. Dr. White.'

'Doyle said you connected. Get anything useful?' Sawyer asked.

'Yeah, I did – and he's sending more. Let me get my notes.'

'In my room.'

She paused, half out of her chair, to stare at Doyle. 'What?'

'I took them to my room last night, to try to decipher them.'

'You can't go riffling through my things.'

'They were right there by the phone. You started to say something – looked like you'd struck some gold – then the sun went down.'

'My room, my notes. And you couldn't decipher them because I have my own code due to people who try to jump claims.'

Deliberately, he met her outrage with dismissal. 'It's half-assed shorthand, Morse, and I'm pretty sure some Navajo. I'd've broken it in a few more hours.'

'My ass,' she said and stalked off.

'It's a good code,' Doyle said when she was out of earshot. 'I'm surprised she can read it herself.'

'I'm going to get my maps.' Sawyer pushed up. 'If she's got a direction, maybe I can verify, or pin it down. Maybe this is enough.'

'Just Capri,' Sasha told him. 'Because it's here. I'm absolutely sure. I need...' She, too, got to her feet. 'I need to paint. Don't wait for me.'

'That is it?'

'I don't know,' she said to Bran, 'but I will. It's today. I know that. It's today, and I have to... Don't wait for me.'

'Should you go with her?' Sawyer asked.

'No, let her begin without distractions.'

'Where the hell is Sasha going?' Riley demanded. 'I think I have big news here.'

'As she does.'

'Vision time,' Sawyer said. 'We're supposed to go on this without her.'

'Fine. Okay, it started falling into place about halfway through the conversation with White. He's smart, but boy does he ramble, and he takes winding paths. Anyway.' She set down her notes. 'He's a proponent of the Bay of Sighs – slash – Island of Glass connection. He's eliminated Atlantis from the mix – that took a while for him to wade through. He thinks he's dated the rebellion and the disconnect to about three thousand years ago, and during that time, while the island goes where and how it chooses, shows itself to those it chooses, the bay's been adrift. Powerless, rudderless, you could say. And those imprisoned in its waters – his words – sigh and sing in the hopes of calling to a redeemer.'

She flipped a page over. 'And catch this. The redeemer, like they once were, is of the land, of the sea, seeks and is sought, and will come, defy the witches and monsters, will redeem them, help them redeem themselves when a star, a queen star, falls from the sky into the bay.'

'We've been looking for the bloody bay,' Doyle began.

'There's more, and here's where I got it. The star, blue as the bay, the bay, blue as the star, are one until the redeemer lifts it from the hand of the queen of the sea who holds it safe for the queen of all.'

Riley looked up expectantly. 'Don't you get it?'

'We're supposed to find the queen of the sea now?' Doyle demanded. 'Would that be Salacia, as we're into the Romans here?'

'Yeah, it would be, and I've got a pretty good idea where to find her. Wife of Neptune. Look, Tiberius retired here, right, and built his palaces, his villas – and commissioned a lot of statues. Some of which have been found in the one place we figured was off the list.'

'The Blue Grotto,' Sawyer declared as his compass glowed and began to move over the map.

'The Blue Grotto, once feared by locals because they believed witches and monsters lived there. Once used by Tiberius, who placed statues in the cave. Some have been found, and it's believed there could be more – deeper.'

'It's a tourist attraction,' Doyle pointed out.

'Now it is. He's got more theories and papers – but White, he's going in the wrong direction. He's focusing right now on Florida. I mean, seriously? Blue as the star.'

She shifted to Annika. 'And what do we have here? Why, we have a guardian who is of the land and of the sea. You're up, Anni.'

'But I don't know where to find the queen and

her hand. I've been in the waters there, but never heard the sighs or the songs before this.'

'It wasn't time,' Bran said simply. 'We weren't together, and it's clear this quest demands that. Sawyer's compass agrees. The Blue Grotto. Now we work our way to diving for the star in a place where they sell tickets to tourists.'

'Not at night, they don't,' Riley pointed out. 'It's closed at night, and diving's not permitted – though I betcha it happens. The problem with that is I have two more nights before I can strap on a tank.'

'Bubble helmet. I saw it on YouTube,' Sawyer told her. 'Scuba-diving dog. Cat, too. Awesome.'

'Not going to happen.'

'Since it would take longer to outfit you when you go furry than to wait, it doesn't work here. But it could – just saying.'

'Theories from some friend of a friend and the compass aside,' Doyle began, 'we need to go there, or the vicinity, and see.'

'A theory that slides in like a key in a lock, and the compass makes the location a bull's-eye. But,' Riley continued, 'since we need to wait if we try the night dive, it wouldn't hurt to head there. With the Fire Star, it was Sasha. It called her, we can say, pulled her.'

'Nearly drowned her,' Sawyer pointed out. 'So when we do this, the rest of us watch Annika.'

'I can't drown in the water as you can't drown in air.'

'There are other ways to come to harm,' Bran reminded her. 'If the Water Star is for you, and everything indicates it is, we're with you.'

'It's an honor,' Annika said slowly, 'to be chosen. I don't want to disappoint, to fail you, or my duty. If I'm meant to find the star. Will you trust me to try?'

'No question there,' Sawyer assured her. 'But that doesn't mean we don't protect each other.'

'I understand. The ... all for one, one for all.'

'You got it.'

'But if it's for me, I don't want to wear the tanks, the suit. If it can be at night, and no one will see, I want to be free in the water.'

'I'm going to vote that's probably the way it's supposed to be. Especially if you feel strongly about it. And it's part of the trust,' Riley added. 'Right?'

'No bubble helmet for Riley, no tanks for you.' Sawyer glanced at Bran, Doyle. 'Any objections?'

'I think not, and don't believe Sasha would have any.' As he spoke, Bran glanced up toward the terrace.

'You're trying not to worry about her, but you are. Go check,' Sawyer suggested. 'Then we'll all stop worrying about her.'

'She's learned control and focus so quickly, accepted as a gift what was, all of her life, a burden to her. It goes to trust, but...' As he couldn't settle, Bran got to his feet. 'I'll just have a look.'

'If she must paint,' Annika said as Bran walked into the villa, 'it will be something we need.'

'Odds are.' Thoughtfully, Sawyer picked up the compass, felt it vibrate softly in his hand. 'And I've got something we could use, if it works for everybody.'

'We could gear up here,' Riley said. 'And you

349

could just zap us to the grotto after the moon. No boat needed.'

'That – and with that no patrols wondering what a dive boat's doing in that vicinity at night. But I'm more thinking why wait?'

'Because I'm not scuba diving in wolf form, cowboy, awesome or not.'

Sawyer simply turned the compass, revealed the watch.

'Well, shit.' On a half laugh, Riley shook her head. 'I didn't think of that.'

'Forward or back, either way, we wouldn't have to wait to go.'

'Back. I did think of it.' Doyle shifted to give the watch a closer study. 'And back far enough there'd be no patrols. When did all the tours and tickets and regulations start? You'd know,' he said to Riley.

Since it was a simple matter for her to flip through the encyclopedia in her mind, Riley shrugged. 'A couple of Germans – writer and pal – visited the cave in the 1820s, guided by local fishermen. The writer wrote a book about it, and the statuary they saw. By the 1830s, it was a tourist destination. Back,' she murmured, and her archaeologist heart glowed in her eyes. 'We could go back to the time of Tiberius, even Augustus, and ... that's not what this is about.'

She propped her elbows on the table, nested her chin in her fists. 'But man, it's cool to think about.'

'So to be safe, before 1820?'

'Yeah. And you'd probably want to avoid the French occupation, the back and forthing there, early 1800s.'

'Believe me,' Doyle confirmed. 'You do.'

'You can do this?' Annika asked. 'Do the travel to a different place, a different time, at once?'

'Yeah. It's a wilder ride, but I've done it.'

'I won't mind the wild.'

He grinned at her, and unable to resist, kissed her hand. 'You'll get it. Riley should pick the when. I'll get the coordinates for where. Once Bran and Sasha are on board, we can start prepping for the trip. One thing.' Sawyer looked at Riley. 'If we can do this before sundown in the now – there and back, it won't matter to you. If we can't get back until after sundown, what happens to – with you?'

'Never done it, but I'm going to say the change will hit me like a mother. I can handle it. But there and back before the moon? Better.'

'Nerezza will be on us,' Doyle said. 'Either in the cave when we find it, or when we come back.'

'The shift – time and place?' Sawyer lifted a shoulder. 'I'm not saying don't be ready, but I think it might be enough to at least confuse her. But yeah, once we have it, she'll hit. So, battle plan.'

Annika also considered it an honor to be part of the council of war. 'We must protect Bran, so he can make the star safe if I find it. But ... the compass doesn't say where to go when we have it safe.'

'Not yet.'

'It's a lot to take on faith.'

'Got a better option, Mr. Bright Side?' Riley asked Doyle.

'We go anywhere. Get the star, secure the star,

then go anywhere until we know. I've looked for centuries, and never got close, to the star or Nerezza, until the day in the cave on Corfu. If we're booking odds, they're long for us to find all three in a matter of months. And then find the Island of Glass?'

'We're six.' Sawyer took Annika's hand in a firm grip. 'We have two months more, and that's it. I don't believe, not for a second, we won't find them before that.'

'If I must go back to the sea before ... I can still help. I will help.'

'We're not even going there,' Sawyer began, pausing only when Bran came out. 'Everything okay?'

'It is. She's ... amazing. I didn't disturb her – doubt I could have.'

'What's she painting?' Riley wanted to know.

'Beauty, and I believe the place to send the Water Star. I believe the place we're to go once we have it.'

'Where? If we can pin it down, I can start working on a house or villa, or a bunch of pup tents.'

Bran merely smiled at Riley. 'If I'm reading the painting correctly, that won't be necessary. As it's my house in Ireland she paints – to my eye. The house I built at the end of a path, the painting she created before any of us met. The one I bought before I knew her.'

'Another island.' Riley sat back. 'So that fits. Coast?'

'West. It's in Clare, where Doyle is from. I think it's a fine fit, yes.'

'We'd stay at your house. Oh, I would like that

very much. It must be beautiful.'

'For me, it is,' he told Annika. 'And there's room enough for all of us. I wondered when I had it done why I wanted such a large place, but I saw it in my head, felt it should be just so, and that's what I did. Problem?' he said to Doyle.

'I haven't been back to Ireland in some time, and to Clare in longer yet. I should've known this would be a part of it. Well, you can fill Bran in on what we've worked out.'

When he rose, walked away, Annika looked after him. 'It hurts his heart.'

'Going back to where he started, to where he lived when he just lived. That's a price to pay.' Riley rose. 'I'll go piss him off about something, get his mind off it. Clare,' she said to Bran. 'Your family's from Sligo, but you built a house in Clare.'

'It called to me, the path, and what was at the end of it. The ruins of an old manor on the cliffs above the thrashing sea. Different from the rolling hills of my birth, but it called to me.'

'I guess this is why. I'm going to piss Doyle off, then pack. Might as well be ready to go.'

By noon Sawyer sat on the terrace watching Sasha. No one wanted her left alone for long, and he'd opted to sit there for an hour while Bran worked.

He'd set up a table, cleaned his guns. After that he laid out his map of Ireland, and watched his compass glide unerringly to the coast of County Clare.

He told himself not to worry about Annika, and not to think about time other than whatever year,

353

month, night Riley chose. But his mind circled around all of that, until he really focused in on Sasha's painting.

He didn't know a lot about art, other than what appealed to him or didn't. And knew nothing at all about the creating of it, except for what he'd watched Sasha do when she sketched or painted.

What lived on the canvas now struck him as ridiculously beautiful. Almost impossibly. The light – how did she create that luminous, inside-a-seashell sort of light? – just bloomed over a stately (that was the word that kept coming back to him) stone manor. All tall, arched, leaded-glass windows. It held two towers, round and peaked, and what he supposed were terraces built to resemble battlements.

Flowers and shrubs spread at its feet like color-ful skirts, and trees, summer green, spread their shade, dappling the spread of grass, greener than emeralds.

And all of it rose above cliffs, dramatic, stormy gray, and the thundering sea that crashed below.

He could see Bran there, perfectly. The magician in his cliffside castle. For himself, when he settled, he'd look for a cottage-type place, on the beach somewhere – anywhere – with blue water and the sway of palms. But he could see the heart-clutch-ing appeal of Bran's home on the cliffs.

When Sasha stepped back, he started to speak. But one look at her eyes had him holding his silence.

She picked up the painting, set it on the work-table, then propped her sketch pad on the easel.

So there was more.

After opening a box, she picked up colored chalk, and began to sweep and guide it over the page.

He watched Annika come to life, but as he'd never seen her. Rising up in the water, or so it seemed to him, her face toward the surface, and transported. Her hair swirling through the impossible blue.

For a moment Sawyer thought it was like watching a photograph develop, so quick and sure were Sasha's strokes.

Annika's arms lifted high above her head, wrists touching, hands cupped. And with Sasha's chalks, with her gift, the star appeared in Annika's hands, brilliant and blue.

'In the water and of it,' Sasha said. 'From the goddess's hands into the guardian's. And she is in the water and of it. Luna's star, star of water, gifted with grace, with joy, with love, now held by the daughter.'

Slowly, Sasha set the chalks down, turned to Sawyer. 'But the night comes, brutal and bloody, and must be faced. The risk will be yours, traveler. And the choice to take it.'

'What risk?'

'Your life, to save all else. Will you embrace the goddess of dark, take her to the light, leave her lost? She will find her way again, but will you risk to spare the blood of friends? To make the time to heal again?'

'Pull her into a shift? Is it possible?'

'Only you can know. You are the traveler. She is the daughter,' Sasha said, gesturing to the portrait. 'You must both choose. So do we all.'

Sasha's eyes closed; she breathed out a sigh. 'Sawyer?'

'Yeah, hey, welcome home. You need to sit down.'

'No, I'm fine.' She waved him off. 'Really, even a little buzzed. I know what I said to you, but–'

'Let's just let that simmer. Annika finds the star, the Water Star.'

'I know she can.' As she studied her own work, Sasha picked up a rag to wipe chalk from her hands. 'And I know there will be voices all around her, and weeping with the sighs and songs. It's all I know.'

Now she turned to her worktable, and the painting.

'This is where we need to go, and the star of ice waits for us. It's Bran's home, isn't it?'

'Yeah, he recognized it when you were working on it earlier.'

'Bran's,' she repeated. 'And more. Could you ask the others to come up? They should see.'

'Yeah, I'll get them. Here.' He offered her a bottle of water. 'You've been at this for a good four hours straight.'

'It needs a little more work, but– It's enough for now.'

Bran came first, slid an arm around her as he studied the portrait of Annika.

'Does it illuminate her, or does she illuminate it?'

'I think it's both. I felt I needed to rush, that time is running out. I didn't capture the glow – of her, of the star. It would bring tears, that glow.'

She turned her face into his shoulder. 'Bran, are

356

you sure you can't help them? Sure there's nothing you can do to allow her to stay with him?'

'Even if it wasn't beyond my powers, and I believe it is, the spell wasn't done to harm. She was given the gift of legs, and for a purpose. And she took an oath, of her own free will. I can't circumvent that.'

'It breaks my heart.' She held close a moment, made herself step back. 'You're going home.'

'We are. It's yours, *fáidh,* if you'll have it. Would you live there with me, and me with you in your mountains in America? And my flats in Dublin and New York. Any and all.'

'I'd live with you anywhere. Any and all, Bran.' She held him again as she looked at the painting. 'It's beautiful and powerful. It's so yours. Do you know why you built a home just there?'

'Only that when I walked that path the first time, came to the cliffs and the ruins there, I knew it was for me. It needed a home, and I needed to be there.'

Annika stepped out, gave a gasp. 'You've drawn me. I found the star. I hold it. I will find it.'

'You can, and I believe you will.'

Doyle came out, just ahead of Riley. Sasha felt her heart wring out tears of sympathy.

'Got yourself a star, Anni. And I'm betting that portrait's reality before today's over.' Buoyed, Riley shifted over to where Doyle stood, staring down at the painting.

'Some digs, Bran. I think we could rough it there on the last and final leg of this quest. How many bedrooms?' she asked.

'Ten, though two are only put into use for that

357

when my family comes in a herd.'

'Is there one in either of those towers?'

'Yes.'

'Dibs on it.'

'This is yours?' Doyle spoke, but never took his gaze from the painting. 'This house, on these cliffs, with the woods thick at its back? And to the north, just on the verge of the woods, is a well.'

'There's an old well, and I was told the woods came in closer at one time. How do... Ah.' It struck him. 'You know this land, these cliffs.'

'This sea, the woods. I know it. It's my home. Or was. My grandfather helped his father build it, or the first of it. A fine stone house. And my father helped his father add rooms to the south side, as my father was one of ten children and all of them lived. That was McCleary blood, they said. Strong and healthy. And I helped my father repair the old stable his grandfather had first built. And the sheep grazed on the rocky hills, and we hunted deer and rabbit in those woods.

'And my brother died in my arms less than a day's hard ride from where we were born. Now they'd have me go back, these gods.'

'I'm so sorry, Doyle—' Sasha began, but Riley shook her head.

'Who came before us, how they lived, what they built? It matters. We honor them by going back, by walking where they walked, living where they lived. They're never gone if they matter, if they're honored.'

Doyle looked at her for a long moment. 'It's the one place on this world I never wanted to walk again.'

'Gods are bastards.'

'They are, yes. They are.'

'But Bran built a house where yours once stood. That's not happenstance. We've got to go with it, learn why.'

'There's no question of not going. And this is where you'll put the star, as you put the other in the painting of the woods?'

'Yes.'

'Then we'd best go find it.'

CHAPTER NINETEEN

Though it ate more daylight, they opted to pack. They might have to travel quickly. Sawyer took Annika's hand as she cheerfully folded dresses into her colorful bag.

'I need a few minutes.'

'Oh, Sawyer, I don't think we have time for sex.'

'Not for that – though I really appreciate your mind just goes there. I need to ask you something.'

'You can ask anything of me.'

'I need you to tell me if – and I know it's a big if – but if when we've done all we've been asked to do, done the duty we've been given, and if after that your elders and sea witch, and whoever's in charge of the big picture, if they'd let you stay, let you stay on land, with me ... would you?'

Seriously, with hints of sorrow, those mermaid eyes met his. 'I would stay anywhere with you.

You are my only, my own Sawyer, my love. But it can't be. The legs are only borrowed. They're mine until the quest is done, or because I had to tell you what I am, in three turns of the moon. Two now. They don't wish me grief, or wish you grief, but it is beyond them to give me this.'

'Maybe Bran–'

'I asked.' For a moment, her gaze dropped to the ground. 'I know I shouldn't have, but after I knew you loved me, I asked. It is beyond him. He promised to do offerings, but he can't break a spell done for the good, for the light. Even for love, for you, I can't break my oath.'

'Okay. Okay.' He pressed his lips to her forehead. 'Maybe I can do a Tom Hanks.'

'What is it to do a tomhanks?'

'No, it's a name. Tom, first name, Hanks, last name. An actor. He did this movie where he fell for a mermaid.'

'Oh. I would like to see this.'

'Yeah, we'll get to it. Anyway, she fell for him, too.'

'Yes, so it's a good story.'

'But there were bad people.'

'Evil gods?'

'No, but bad people, and they would've hurt her, or worse. She couldn't stay with him, so in the end, he jumped in the water after her. And she did something so he could stay with her. So he could live in the water with her.'

Gently, Annika kissed his cheeks, skimmed her fingers back into his hair. 'It would be a pretty story. There is nothing I could do to make you live under the water. You are of the land.'

'Maybe the sea witch–'

'That you would think to do this for me makes my heart full of joy and tears. But she has no power to change you.' Because the tears threatened, she started to turn away. 'We should pack now.'

'Okay, but I've got one more. Don't cry, Anni, just listen to this one more possibility. The island where I took you. It's kind of got a magick of its own, right?'

How she wished they wouldn't talk of possibilities that could never be. 'Yes. The water around it is sacred, and the land is important.'

'Right. And it's not in the shipping lanes. We're both connected to it. I could live there. I'm handy, so I could build a little house – I'm all about living on the beach. And you could live in the water there. We could be together. I could swim with you, and sit on the beach while you sat on the rocks. Talk to you, see you, touch you.'

Inside her breast her heart trembled and shook. 'Your family.'

'Hey, I've got the compass. I can see them, bring them to see us – same with yours if they want. But the bottom line?' Eyes on hers, he skimmed his hands down her arms, up again. 'Bottom line, Annika, you're my only, too. I don't want to live in a world where you're not. And I'm not going to believe that we found each other, we've fought together, and done all we've been asked to do only to never be together. I'm not going to accept that. Would you stay with me – you in the water, me on the land?'

'I can't give you young.'

'Annika, just give me you.'

'I have. I will. Yes, I will stay with you. I don't want to live in a world where you're not.' She threw her arms around him. 'I will be yours, and you will be mine.'

Closing his eyes, he held on. 'And that's enough for anybody.'

'I love you with all I am.'

When he kissed her, they both forgot about packing and everything else until Sasha rapped sharply on the doorjamb.

'Sorry, but we've got to get everything downstairs and go over all the steps. It's nearly four.'

'Sawyer is going to build a house on the island, and live there, and I can live in the water, so we can be together.'

'Love finds a way.' Touched, Sasha moved in to hug them both. 'A good and loving way. And don't think moving to some deserted island in the South Seas will stop us from visiting.'

'Counting on it,' Sawyer told her.

'But now, get moving. We're getting antsy.'

'Five minutes.'

It took a little longer, but they hauled everything down, steered Doyle's motorcycle in from the side room.

'At least I'll be able to ride this again once we're in Ireland.'

'I like riding the motorcycle.'

'Anytime, Gorgeous.'

'Until that happy day, we've got three hours and...' Riley checked her watch. 'Thirty-two minutes until sunset. If we're going to do this, we'd better do it.'

'One more thing. Sasha's last vision.'

'Sawyer, no.' Alarmed, Annika clutched at him. 'She is a god.'

'And Bran and Sasha took her down pretty hard in Corfu. This time it looks like it's my turn. My risk, my choice – that's what Sasha said, that's what we explained to everybody. I'm making the choice, and I have to believe I can do it, buy us that time. But I'm going to need help.'

'Whatever you need, brother,' Doyle told him, 'you've got.'

'The timing has to be close to perfect, and I need to get close enough to her to connect.'

'She could rip you to pieces.' At Riley's words Annika turned her face into Sawyer's shoulder. 'Sorry, really, but we've got to be straight. Maybe we wait, take more time to plan it out.'

'It's now. I'm sorry, too.' Sasha reached out to stroke Annika's hair. 'But it's now. For the star, for the battle, for the risk.'

'She could rip me to pieces, but I'm banking she won't, especially if Bran softens her up a bit.'

'And that I will, my word on it.'

'I get close enough, when she's softened up some, I pull her into a shift, and when we're clear, I disconnect. It can work.'

'You'll be alone,' Annika stated.

'No.' He used her hand to tap his own heart. 'Okay, everybody gear up – except for you.' He tipped Annika's face, kissed her.

They strapped on the equipment Riley and Doyle had carted up from the boathouse – the hard way. And though it still made him wince, he waited while Annika tossed her pink dress aside.

'There may be a little jolt. I've never gone from solid ground to underwater.'

'And in 1742,' Riley added.

'Time's set, just remember it's a wilder tide than just a location shift. And when' – he deliberately didn't say if – 'Anni has the star, the trip back's going to be just as wild. Stay close, stay together. The tighter we are, the easier it'll be. Be ready.'

He put on his mask, adjusted it, slipped in his mouthpiece. With the underwater pistol on one hip, the diving knife in his belt, he took Annika's hand.

With another look at his friends, Sawyer nodded. Closed his eyes. And activated both compass and watch simultaneously.

It had a kick, bigger than he'd expected. Then again, he'd only traveled simultaneously with one companion before this.

The air whistled, rushing by him, through him, around him as he gripped Annika's hand, as he kept the connection with the others gripped tight in his mind.

The world turned, or so it seemed, revolving faster, faster, as years whizzed by like the air.

For a moment he thought he heard the song, and the sighs that blended with it. Then water swallowed him, swirled over him, slapped at him.

And dark fell deep.

Night, he thought, and a moonless night at that. Riley hadn't taken any chances. And he hadn't considered the lack of light in the cave.

He felt Annika's hand still in his, and the brush of her tail against his legs. But the others...

A light glowed, suspended above Bran's palm.

364

When Bran waved a hand over it, the glow increased.

Relieved, Sawyer slowed his breathing, tried to orient himself.

Without sun or moon, with no light to reflect, the cave would be dark as a tomb, not that pretty, almost unearthly blue he'd seen in all the pictures.

But he could see Annika smile as she swam around them, as she nudged them all closer together.

And she tapped her ear.

Sawyer started to shake his head, but he did hear it. Faintly, a chorus of sighs, as if the water itself breathed them.

Still smiling, her eyes brilliant and beautiful, she gestured down. With a twist of her body, a liquid swirl of her tail, she swam straight down, and into the dark.

Stunned, he went with instinct, kicked hard after her. But in seconds, even with Bran's light, he couldn't see her.

She went deep, and oh, it was heaven to take the depths again. The sighs echoed around her now, and now she understood words hid in them.

We wait. We wait.

And in the songs lived pleas.

Forgive us. Redeem us. Free us. Embrace us.

The deeper she dived, the deeper her eyes. The dark of depths posed no obstacle. She could see the rocks, the statues made by men, and more as she swam, the shapes and shadows of those banished, those who waited, those who pleaded.

With sigh and song.

And she felt them, the brush of fingers as she

365

moved through them. While their sorrows weighed on her, she could only follow the sighs and the faith.

The goddess waited. White in the dark sea, her face lovely and regal, her gown flowing down. She held one hand to her skirts, and the other lifted at her side. But there was nothing in that curved palm.

Help us. See us. Restore us.

I see you, Annika thought. I see you. I hear you.

She laid her hand in the hand of the goddess, looked into those stone eyes. A statue, she thought. And it wasn't stone and carvings that held the star.

In the water, of the water.

As she said it in her head, all that surrounded her sighed it.

In the water, of the water. As was she.

Annika spread her arms, accepted, embraced. And began to spin.

I am of the water. I am the chosen from my world. I am the guardian. I am the redeemer. I am one who seeks. I am of the water.

She repeated it over and over in her head, spun faster and faster. She felt movement above her – Sawyer, her friends.

Of the water, to bring light to the dark. Redeemer, the Water Star waits. We wait.

I am of the water. The star is of the water. The goddess is of the water. From her hand to my hand.

As she spun, faster, faster, the water brightened, the light began to glow. Soft, soft, blue. Brighter, deeper, bluer.

As she had been born to, she lifted her arms, cupped her hands together. Above them, the water spun, glittered, warmed.

Above them, the star burst bright.

She laughed, pure joy, and around her the sighs filled with tears that echoed the joy.

Arms high, she began to rise, and the songs rang, rejoicing.

He watched her, heart thudding, the image from the portrait, but more brilliant, more stunning. With the star, blazing blue in the vee of her hands.

When she reached them, she seemed to fly, a glorious bird, higher, higher. And then spilling over, came back to them.

Back to him.

She held the star out to him, like an offering.

Gently, Sawyer closed her hands around it.

He slid an arm around her waist, looked to each of his friends. Together, guided by the blue, they surfaced in the cave.

He tore away his mouthpiece. 'Anni.'

And crushed his lips to hers.

'You vanished, you scared me. You're beautiful. You're everything.'

'I had to go deep. Didn't you hear the songs?'

'They tore at my heart,' Sasha said.

'You should take it.' Annika held the star out to Bran.

'When we get back. You're made of magick, Annika. And we should go back, finish this.'

'Couldn't we just take ten? I just want to swim out, see–'

Doyle grabbed Riley's arm before she could. 'Now.'

367

'Now,' Sawyer agreed. 'Hold on to your hats.'

It took seconds in a whirling kick that seemed to punch them out of the water and onto the floor of the villa.

'Holy shit, Sawyer.'

A little wide-eyed himself, he grinned at Riley. 'What a rush! Rock-in-a-slingshot time. It must've been the star. Swear to God it wasn't me.'

'It's so beautiful.' Annika looked down at it, glinting, glimmering, madly blue in her hand.

Sawyer looked down as well, not only at the star, but at Annika who sat, tail curled under her, on the floor.

'You may want to, you know, change. And–' He grabbed her dress. 'Put this on.'

'Oh, yes, I forgot. It lives. It breathes.' She offered it up to Sawyer.

And it pulsed, without mass, but warm and real in his hands. 'Whoa, I'll say. Over to you.'

As Bran took it, Annika rose on her legs, shimmied into her dress. As Bran had with the Fire Star, he shielded it in a clear globe. 'To protect, to respect, to shield, to hold.'

'We should do it quickly. She knows.'

With a nod at Sasha, Bran crossed to the painting. The rest gathered around him, washed in that blue light. 'As before, we each lay a hand on the globe, all say the words. To protect this bright water, this pure light, I send it safe where no eye can see, no hand can touch, no darkness shadow.'

Power shimmered, swirled. The encased star pulsed its light, and that light spread over the house on the cliffs, turned the soft sky into brilliance. Then slipped into the painting. With a final flash of blue, it was gone.

'It's quiet now,' Annika murmured. 'And safe from her.'

'It will be safer – and stronger I think.' Bran held out a hand. The painting vanished. 'Stronger now that two are together.'

'She's fury.' Beside Bran, Sasha shuddered. 'All fury and madness. She'll rain fire, burn us to ash.'

'We should just go – you know – zip right to Ireland.' Glancing around, Riley shoved her wet hair back. 'I'm always up for a fight, but this might be the time to retreat and regroup.'

'She'll follow, and the fire rains there. It's fire – I can feel the burn. It's cold.'

'If it's here or there, I want to take the shot.' In fact, Sawyer craved it. 'I can buy us time, turn her around so she'll have to find us again rather than just follow our trail. Either way, we need to suit up.'

Sawyer unstrapped the underwater gun. 'And fight some fire with fire.'

'Fire with fire,' Bran agreed, but added a sharp smile, 'and given all, I think, with water.'

'So we're going to get hot and wet – sexual innuendo absolutely intended because, why not. Scuba gear under the pergola. I'll have it picked up there.' Riley shrugged. 'They already figure I'm way over-eccentric.'

Annika followed Sawyer to his old room where he'd left a change of clothes, his boots. His weapons. 'She's a god, Sawyer. She may not let you go.'

'I'm not going to give her a choice.'

'But she–'

'Listen.' He paused to take her shoulders, look into her eyes. 'You need to trust me on this, like I trusted you in the cave. Okay, I had a minute of panic when you went down, when I couldn't see you.'

And it had taken Doyle and Bran together to hold him back.

'But I pulled it together. Because I knew you were doing what you were meant to do, had to do. And would do. I need you to trust me, to believe in me. I need that or I can't do it.'

'If I believe, it helps you?'

'All the difference in the world.'

'Then I believe.' She cupped his face, laid her lips on his, poured all she was into that one moment. 'You have all my faith.'

'Then I can't lose.'

He changed quickly, joined the others.

'You'll be in the firestorm, and in the deluge,' Bran told them. 'I'll do what I can to send it up, away from you, but it's going to be rough.'

'I like it rough.' Doyle drew his sword, sent Riley a glance. 'Sexual innuendo intended.'

'Good one.' She drew her gun, gripped her knife.

'Keep her minions off me when you can.' Sawyer looked up, realized he didn't need Sasha to tell him they were coming. Overhead, the sky already thrashed. 'If she's with them, and the seer says yeah, I need to get close enough to pull her in. I may need a toss-up,' he said to Bran.

'You'll have it.'

The sky cracked open, shaking the world. And the bitter, flaming dark poured out.

'All my faith,' Annika told him.

Then they charged.

He dodged fire that speared out of the sky, lanced into the ground to sizzle. Whatever protection Bran had wound around the villa had that fire bouncing off – like striking a force field. And some of those fiery balls and lances ricocheted into the sharp wings of diving birds.

Yeah, a little of your own medicine, he thought, and took out a swarm with bullets.

Hot, spinning sparks spewed up, and he learned they had a nasty bite.

He fired, fired, slapped in fresh clips, fired. The world was fire and smoke, the blast of bullets, the slice of blade, the whoosh of bolts. And the lightning.

Then came the flood.

He'd been warned, Sawyer reminded himself as the force of Bran's storm whipped over him. Wind and madly driving rain, lightning jagging through the dark.

He saw Annika's bracelets flash, laid down a stream of shots over her head to destroy what came at her.

Spears of fire drowned in the rain, and the cool, clean wet soothed his burns. He caught the blur, thought Malmon. Fast, but not as fast as he'd been. Still healing, Sawyer thought as he took aim.

But the ground heaved up, knocked him back into a crawling fog that hissed and bit. He flipped up, for the first time really grateful for the dawn training. He nearly lost Malmon in the haze as that blur arrowed toward Sasha.

He gave a shout of warning, spun to shoot. But Bran's lightning glanced off that blur, sent it spinning away. He caught a glimpse of Riley charging Doyle, and Doyle catching her foot in his hand, heaving up so she flipped high, firing at a circle of birds.

He wondered when the hell they'd worked that one out, then had no time to think.

She broke out of the dark, shocking the air so he felt the charge of it lift the hair on his arms, the back of his neck. Once again she rode the three-headed beast, but now wore some sort of armor, black as the night.

She heaved thunderbolts, flooded the rain with liquid fire that burned a vicious orange as it fought to slide through the storm.

Focused on Bran, he noted, as the rest rushed to circle around him. Take out our magick, then scorch the rest. The Cerberus screamed in triumph, tongues flicking more fire, eyes as crazed as its rider's. The world quaked as power clashed with power, and Sawyer braced his legs against it, took aim.

His bullets struck each head, had them whipping back in shock as those triumphant screams went to shrieks of pain.

'It's now,' he shouted. 'Right now! Send me up!'

Shooting his weapons home, he gripped the compass.

He flew, grateful now he'd had the experience with Bran once before or he might have fumbled. With Nerezza fighting to control her beast, with her rage focused on the five, Sawyer put everything he had into the moment.

His hand gripped her flying hair, and with the

shock of it rocketing up his arm, he shifted.

Like a tornado, the dark funneled around him, full of sound, burning with her fury. The stinging whip of her power lashed his arm, his face, his body. But he held on.

Then her eyes met his, and her madness smiled.

'Inside,' Bran ordered. 'Inside now. Be ready. Injuries?'

'Burns, cuts, crap. And more crap,' Riley managed. 'The sun's going down.'

To solve the problem, and because she limped as she ran, Doyle simply scooped her up, carried her like a football into the villa.

'We'll deal with injuries in Ireland. Let me help you.' Sasha dropped down to drag off Riley's boots.

'Look, I'm not a priss, but how about averting your– Damn it, no time.'

She tossed modesty away with her shirt.

Doyle unhooked her belt. 'You can't run.'

'I know it, I know it. Sawyer–'

'He'll come back to us. We have to believe.' Sasha gripped Riley's hand even as it began to change. 'We all have to believe.'

Riley's only answer was a howl as she rolled to her hands and knees, gave herself over to the moon.

'Can you see him?' Annika knelt down, wrapped her arms around the wolf, pressed her face into the warm fur to comfort them both. 'Sasha, can you feel him? Please. Please.'

'No, but I don't when he's traveling. He's

373

strong, Anni, and smart. He pulled her away.'

'She never saw him coming,' Doyle added. 'He took her by surprise. The kid's got balls of steel. He'll come through. He'll come back.'

'We're going to live on the island.' As she spoke it, like a prayer, tears streamed down her cheeks. 'He's going to build a house, and I'll stay in the sea. We'll swim together.'

'I know.' Because she felt Annika's fight not to despair, Sasha knelt beside her, took her and the wolf into an embrace. 'It's lovely. We'll all come see you, swim with you.'

'He'll come back to me.' Annika drew in a breath, raised her head. 'Just as he did before. He'll come back to me.'

When he did, he fell at her feet.

'Sawyer, Sawyer.' She dropped onto him, covering his face with kisses. 'You're hurt.'

'Not that bad.' He kissed her back, and hissed as he managed to get to his knees. 'Pretty bad,' he admitted. 'The disconnect was tricky. She's got a hell of a grip. I don't know where I dumped her, or how long we have until she figures it out, but we should get the hell of out Dodge.'

'You're weak, brother.'

'Not that fucking weak,' he shot back at Doyle, but accepted the hand to help him to his feet.

'I believed in you.' Annika took his bloody hand, pressed it to her cheek.

'I could feel it. Keep it up.'

'You have the coordinates.'

He nodded at Bran, tapped his temple. 'Set. I could probably use a boost.'

'You'll have it.'

374

'Don't forget my bike,' Doyle told him.

'Got you covered.' He glanced at Riley. 'First time I've ever traveled with a werewolf.' And grinned at her low growl. 'Okay, gang, second star to the right and straight on till morning.'

'I love you, Sawyer King.'

'Keep that up, too.' He pressed his lips to Annika's, mentally pulled his battle-scarred friends in close.

With Annika's arms around him, he took them traveling to where two stars shined quiet, and the third waited to light again.

The mother of lies tumbled through time and space. A storm of wind and sound whirled around her. Worlds rushed by, grazing her flesh with their edges as she fell.

As she bled – bled! – power seeped out of her, drop by drop. She gripped the reins of her fury in hands that burned and burned, gathered all she was, all she had.

Weak, weaker, fading.

She dropped through the world like a comet of ice, and the earth quaked when she fell onto the floor of the cave, by the silver steps she'd created.

She tasted her own blood in her mouth, swallowed it, but had no strength to rise. So she lay, wrapped in pain.

Dimly she heard the click of claws on stone.

'My queen, my god, my love.'

Scaled hands lifted her head, stroked her, while the beast she'd created from man made guttural croons.

'I will kill them all for you,' it promised. 'I will

help you heal, grow strong. Drink.' It held a goblet to her lips. 'Drink, and rest and heal.'

She drank, but the few drops of the seer's blood barely touched the pain, barely cleared a single layer of mist from her mind.

But she saw now, reflected over and over on the polished stones of the chamber, the beast who cradled her. Saw her garments tattered, torn, singed. Saw a second white streak snaking through her hair.

And the lines carved deep around her mouth.

In her eyes, where lines, more lines, fanned, a vengeful madness bloomed.

It lifted her.

'You will sleep. I will feed you, and tend you, and bathe your wounds. You will heal again, my queen, and I will avenge you.'

Something stirred inside the pain, the fury, that might have been gratitude. Then as it carried her to her bedchamber, she slept, and dropped into bloody dreams.

The publishers hope that this book has given you enjoyable reading. Large Print Books are especially designed to be as easy to see and hold as possible. If you wish a complete list of our books please ask at your local library or write directly to:

Magna Large Print Books
Magna House, Long Preston,
Skipton, North Yorkshire.
BD23 4ND